A FARRAGO OF FOXES

In history books, Earl Godwin of Wessex and his sons are dismissed as murderers, oath-breakers, renegades and usurpers. Is this the result of Norman post-Conquest propaganda? The *Anglo-Saxon Chronicles* show this to be more than a possibility. Based on the facts in the *Chronicles*, this is the story of the Earl's lone campaign to keep England for the English, in the face of the apathy and jealousy of his countrymen, the hatred of King Edward the Confessor, and the soft intrigues of the Norman Court favourite, Robert of Jumièges.

COLIN LESLIE

◆

A FARRAGO OF FOXES

Complete and Unabridged

LINFORD
Leicester

First published in Great Britain in 1976 by
Robert Hale Limited
London

First Linford Edition
published 2004
by arrangement with
Robert Hale Limited
London

British Library CIP Data

Leslie, Colin
  A farrago of foxes.—Large print ed.—
Linford mystery library
  1. Detective and mystery stories
  2. Large type books
  I. Title
  823.9'14 [F]

  ISBN 1–84395–463–X

Published by
F. A. Thorpe (Publishing)
Anstey, Leicestershire

Set by Words & Graphics Ltd.
Anstey, Leicestershire
Printed and bound in Great Britain by
T. J. International Ltd., Padstow, Cornwall

This book is printed on acid-free paper

Prelude

It was perhaps suitable that Canute should die in November, a month of grey skies and drizzle that dripped, like tears, from the branches of the leafless trees and off the eaves of the thatched roofs. The air was damp and the wind had a cutting edge: even at mid-day one could feel the chill of approaching winter and sense the cold, wet drudgery of the months ahead.

Canute the Dane, whose strength and wisdom had given the English almost twenty years of comparative peace. Comparative, that is, to the chaos and anarchy they had suffered during the time of his predecessor, Ethelred. And when they heard of his death, those who could remember back to those times glanced at each other with troubled eyes and pulled their cloaks tighter around themselves.

He had lived the life of an autocrat: men came and went at his command, but death caught him unawares, and he had omitted to recommend an heir to his Counsellors. Therefore, his passing left a political vacuum, the sort of void which could cause claimants to come scurrying forward like dry leaves before a breeze. And there was no shortage of claimants: there was Edward the Exile, son of Edmund Ironside who had ruled England before Ethelred; there were Edward and Alfred, sons of Ethelred and Emma of Normandy; there was Canute's own son, Harthacanute.

These four were abroad at the time of Canute's death, but in England there was Harold, called the Harefoot. He, too, was a son of Canute, but there was some doubt as to the identity of his mother. Nevertheless, he was in the right place at the right time, and at the meeting of the Great Council at Oxford, shortly after Canute's burial at Winchester, it was decided that he should be the Regent of the country on behalf of himself and Harthacanute. The latter had the good sense to stay out of the country while his half-brother was alive.

The decision taken by the Great

Council was anything but unanimous: the arguments went on for several days, and the Council split into two factions — those of the North and Midlands who wished for a Danish succession, and those of the South, led by earl Godwin of Wessex, who wanted the return of the Royal House of Wessex, the line of Alfred the Great. In the end, the southerners gave way to expediency and an atmosphere of brooding disquiet settled over the country. There was a feeling in the air that nothing was settled — that bloodshed was in the offing.

There was not long to wait: in the early summer of the following year there landed at Dover no less a person than Alfred the Atheling, son of Ethelred and scion of the Royal House of Wessex, together with a small contingent of Norman footsoldiers as befitted his rank. A charming young man with fair hair and blue eyes and a ready smile, he made a fine impression on all those who saw him. With disarming naïvete, he let it be known that he was on his way to visit his mother who lived in Winchester. Nothing more than that.

Happy to be back in his native land, which he had last seen as a five-year-old, and at the head of his escort, he set off along the North Downs trackway. The weather was warm and progress was slow: the news of his coming preceded him, and the simple folk who gathered to see him pass looked on him with awe. So this was the descendant of the fabled Alfred — the lad with the blood of Cerdic in his veins. They looked at each other and sighed. Perhaps . . . if only . . . But it was none of their business — they were voiceless in the affairs of the realm, but they knew through bitter experience that if anything went amiss they would be the first to suffer.

From the west, there came a party of about twenty horsemen, lightly armed and armoured. They eased their pace as they came to the steep hill which led down to the town of Guildford, splashed across the ford and made their way to the gate of the timber castle. The townsfolk looked up curiously from their work:

4

'Godwin's men,' said the knowledgeable. 'Come to take the young Atheling to Winchester.'

Probably they stopped their work later on to watch Alfred and his retinue come down the slope from the east, tired and dusty, looking forward to a meal and a night's rest, but above all a drink — a long drink to wash the chalky dust from their throats.

Twelve hours later, they were all dead, except for the Atheling. The Norman footsoldiers were driven like sheep half-way up the hill to the west and there slaughtered. In all the noise, the confusion and the horror, none of the townsfolk were quite certain who was responsible for the killings. Some said that Godwin's men had left early in the morning, before the massacre began. Others thought that the original twenty horsemen had been joined during the night by many more. Whatever the truth, it was none of their business and they knew enough to keep their mouths shut and their eyes on the ground.

As for Alfred the Atheling, he survived

for a few days longer, but his end was predictable from the moment he set foot on English soil. A victim of power politics the like of which, in his carefree state of youth, he never knew existed — an impediment no weightier than a pebble, to be tossed into a dark, deep pool and forgotten as soon as the ripples died away.

But the ripples persisted. There was one man who would never forget . . .

1

Edwardius Rex Anglorum . . .

Godwin knew the Latin words by heart: they were on the king's seal, and on the coins he carried in the purse at his belt.

He knew the man by heart, too . . . Edward, son of Ethelred and Emma, brother of the ill-starred Alfred the Atheling, descendant of Cerdic. Edward, whose snow-white hair and beard gave him the appearance of an old man but whose smooth pink cheeks were those of a country maiden; whose long, thin, tapering fingers were those of a saint.

Listening to the king's high-pitched monotone as he rambled on, flitting bird-like from point to point, Godwin folded his arms across his chest and allowed his mind to wander. He thought of a ride from London to Winchester in the king's company seven years ago and remembered the spiteful smile of triumph on Edward's face as his mother's hall was ransacked for gold and silver, the rings snatched from her fingers and the jewelled clasps and brooches torn from her clothes.

'It is justice,' Edward had said, his voice shrill with malice. 'When I was a child she gave me nothing. Now that I am king she shall give me everything.'

Years before that, the Lady Emma had spoken to Godwin of her son: 'A difficult brat — he would never join in the games of the others . . . always to be found in some dark place, watching through those pale blue eyes for the chance to take what he wanted by stealth . . . '

Even now, the king was sitting in the shadows, shielding his eyes from the March sunlight which lanced through the window opening. He had not changed, thought Godwin. A just and simple request, but he could not grant it without an argument for fear of being thought weak. But because he knew he would get his way in the end, Godwin stifled his impatience and played the king's game.

Sweyn, his eldest son, and once earl of

Hereford, had been exiled over two years before as the result of some trifling bother over a woman. It had been nothing more than a young man's escapade, but the fact that the lady concerned had been the abbess of Leominster had outraged Edward. And it seemed that he was still outraged — certainly more than the abbess had been.

'My lord,' said Godwin, mildly, 'we must not forget that the lady was not raped, but seduced. Seduction is not a crime — not even against a lady of the Church — and two years in exile is a harsh sentence for a breach of good behaviour.'

The argument droned on until, with a sudden petulant gesture, Edward grew tired of the game and gave way.

'So be it, earl Godwin. Sweyn may return to this country — and let us hope that he has learned his lesson.'

Godwin made himself humbly grateful, but the matter was not yet finished.

'My lord,' he said. 'You will remember that his old earldom of Hereford was divided between my second son, Harold, and my nephew, Beorn. So that Sweyn may regain his old rank, I had in mind to surrender a part of my own earldom of Wessex. God knows I should be glad enough to slip some of the load from my shoulders.'

'Create a new earldom?' The pale blue eyes became suddenly alert and gazed for a moment into Godwin's. Then the hand went to the forehead again, and the pink lips pouted in thought. Godwin must think him a fool . . . A new earldom for Sweyn meant still more power in the Councils for the Godwin family. Would the man never be satisfied?

He gave a sudden shrill giggle and wiped his mouth on his sleeve, pleased at his own astuteness.

'Lord earl, there can be no new earldom for Sweyn. He may return to Hereford, if he must, provided that Harold and Beorn are willing to surrender their holdings.'

Godwin was surprised: he had expected an argument, perhaps even a half-hearted refusal which would leave grounds for further negotiation. But this counter-proposal had a ring of finality which was hard to swallow. His tone, hitherto mild and conciliatory, became almost aggressive.

'But why should Harold and Beorn be deprived of their rank? What crime have they committed?'

'They will not be deprived,' said Edward smugly, 'they will surrender their earldoms as a mark of respect and affection for their kinsman.' He looked Godwin in the eye, smiling slightly.

The expression on the king's face — the upward tilt of the chin and the twist of the lips — told Godwin that there was nothing to be gained by further argument. That . . . and the fact that his grasp on his own temper was becoming tenuous. He rose to his feet, growled his respects and left the chamber. Beyond the doorway, in the small ante-room was Robert of Jumièges, bishop of London. Godwin realised in a flash the reason for the stiffening in the king's attitude towards him; and the certainty that the man of God had been eavesdropping caused his irritation to turn to anger. As though the bishop did not exist, he

11

stalked past him towards the great hall.

In spite of himself, Robert drew aside as the earl passed, unwillingly compelled to show respect, not by the physical bulk of the man or the anger which flashed from the clear blue eyes, but by the almost solid aura of determination which emanated from him like heat from a fire. The small, pugnacious nose and the aggressive chin, emphasised by a straw-coloured beard, trimmed short and combed to perfection, were part of the aura, but the clothes cut from the finest Flemish cloth and the bejewelled gold pendant and clasps hinted at another side to his character which Robert did not know.

Edward was leaning back in his chair, laughing silently when Robert reached his side.

'You heard that, Robert?'

'Most of it, Sire.' Robert's dark Norman features were unsmiling. He was an ambitious man, not given to laughter, and he had a mind which enabled him to see far into the future, and the cunning to take advantage of his intelligence. He feared no man, and respected only one; and his influence over the king was strengthened by Edward's regard for him and by their common hatred of Godwin.

'You heard him try to extend his family's power with a new earldom?'

'You did well to refuse him, Sire. That family has too much power already — they rule all England south of the Thames, and more besides.'

'I know it, Robert. We must keep them in check.'

'It would be better,' said Robert weightily, 'to destroy their power and share out their honours among men more loyal to yourself.'

Edward looked up sharply. 'I am a man of peace. I will not have bloodshed.'

'It can be done without bloodshed,' Robert said, quietly. 'We must wait for a favourable opportunity. Or the chance to create one.'

The king glanced at him dubiously: Robert gave the slightest of smiles and went on: 'To allow such wealth and power in the hands of one man is folly. Your cousin, Duke William of Normandy, grants meagre honours so that no one man has the power to oppose him.'

'Yet Normandy is a cauldron of civil war,' said Edward. 'It does not say much for his policies.'

A shadow of annoyance clouded Robert's face for a moment. 'Normandy,' he said, 'is a piece of red hot metal on an anvil: Duke William uses the hammer with strength and skill, and in a few years, when the metal has cooled, you will see a well-wrought State.'

Edward nodded thoughtfully. He loved bishop Robert as a brother and had complete trust in his political skills. Priestly by nature and inclination, he was content to leave such things in his adviser's hands.

Meanwhile, Godwin stood in the great hall of the king's palace, feeling like a stranger in a foreign country, searching in vain for the sight of a familiar face — or even an English one. The servants busy about the place chattered among themselves in their foreign tongue, and not one of them appeared to notice him, let alone recognise him for who he was.

The richest and most powerful magnate in the country, earl Godwin of Wessex was not of noble birth. From his father, a minor Sussex thane, he had inherited no more than an ability to think clearly and rapidly, while his mother had granted him the gift of charm, and the ability to express his thoughts to their best advantage. When his father, widowed and facing ruin through the depredations of marauding Danes during the later years of Ethelred's reign, had decided in desperation to cut his losses and turn pirate, Godwin had gone with him because the alternative, the life of a monk, did not appeal to him. But it had not taken him long to see that whereas piracy offered a limited future, to be on the winning side in a war of conquest opened unlimited horizons.

Although he was English to the marrow, and had the native love of his country, to make the decision caused him no heart-searching, and afterwards there had been no feeling of guilt: England under Ethelred was dying of apathy and lethargy in high places. Treachery was rife, but whereas his fellow traitors were mostly birds of passage, flying from one side to the other on the prevailing wind, young Godwin's clear mind could see that there was only one possible outcome to the struggle between Ethelred and Canute. It was the quality of Godwin's brain, plus his undoubted charm, which had commended him to the shrewd and level-headed Canute.

The long struggle to the top had not been easy: that he had been lucky was undeniable, but he had had the perspicacity to take his chances, and the wit to create the chance where none was offered. His enemies — and he had many in high places — said that his path to success was strewn with rotting corpses, but the number of his enemies was as nothing to the number of his friends, for despite his great wealth he had never lost his easy manner with the common folk, and his people of Wessex loved and respected him as a father. But those who knew him well stood in awe of his temper.

It was his temper that got the better of him as he stood in the great hall, ignored by the servants as though he were a person of no account. He seized the arm of a man who passed close by and swung him round so that the man nearly lost his balance and all but dropped the tray of sweepings that he carried.

'My daughter,' said Godwin, imperiously.

The man looked at him, his eyes full of alarm and incomprehension.

'The lady Edith — the king's wife . . . ' his voice echoed round the hall like a clap of thunder.

The man shook himself free and scurried off. Godwin paced angrily, his head thrust forward.

Presently, Edith appeared; by her side was a monk who stared almost impertinently at Godwin before bowing slightly and turning away. Godwin followed his daughter up a concealed flight of wooden stairs.

'Who was that fellow?' he asked.

'My chaplain,' said Edith, over her shoulder.

Godwin thought him too handsome and too much of a man to be a monk. He said: 'You should have picked an Englishman.'

'I had not the choice . . . ' they had entered Edith's bower, ' . . . he was found for me by bishop Robert. What do you think of my room?'

Godwin glanced around. The bower was richly furnished with tapestries and wall hangings; there were cushions on the chairs and couch, and animal furs and an eastern rug on the floor.

'No better than you deserve as the king's lady,' he said, grudgingly.

Edith smiled and sat down with elegant grace upon the couch. She could read on his face the signs of his irritability. Godwin sank into one of the cushioned chairs and looked at his daughter with self-gratification: she was a fine woman, handsome of face with well-defined features and wide-spaced green eyes which met his own with sympathy and frankness. He noted approvingly that she had inherited his own passion for personal neatness and that her auburn hair was immaculately combed and plaited. He also noted that she had acquired her mother's aptitude for putting a man at his ease. Already he was relaxing in mind and body.

'Was Edward not amenable?' she asked, gently.

He passed his hand across his brow. 'He and I are like two dogs together — wary, distrustful with hackles raised. I wish it could be otherwise.'

Edith looked away for a moment. It was the sadness of her life that her father and her husband could not be friends, for she loved them both.

'Tell me,' she said at last, 'what it was all about.'

He told her what had passed between himself and the king and noticed that at the mention of Sweyn's name the ghost of a frown flitted across her face. When he had finished, she asked what Harold and Beorn were likely to do.

'Beorn can be persuaded. He is an easy-going fellow and he has estates in Denmark. But Harold . . . He is not his brother's best friend.'

Edith picked up the tapestry frame she had been working on and turned it this way and that. Her green eyes were thoughtful.

'Edward has a liking for Harold. Might not a new earldom be created for him?'

Godwin slapped his knee. 'I wish,' he said, smiling, 'that I had consulted you first. Or better still, perhaps you should plead my cause for me.'

Edith caressed the stitches of her tapestry with the tips of her fingers. She wished he had not said that. But Godwin was leaning forward earnestly in his chair.

'Edith . . . Edward will listen to you without pre-judging the case. A new earldom for Harold . . . do this thing for me and for your brother.'

She sighed and put the frame down beside her.

'Father, it would please me to serve you, but I have no influence with Edward in matters of State. Bishop Robert advises him on these things.'

'Bishop Robert . . . Have you never tried?'

'No, but I am certain Edward would not permit it.'

Godwin chuckled. 'What's this? Show me a woman who cannot influence her husband, and I will show you a dog that

20

cannot bark. Why, even the plainest and most stupid of women can get her way once she knows how to set about it. And you are neither plain nor stupid.'

There was a pink flush on Edith's cheeks. 'I do not have the advantages of your plain and stupid woman. You see . . . I do not share Edward's bed. On the evening of our wedding day, we both made vows of chastity before God.'

There was a shocked silence. Godwin leaned forward in his chair, his face tense. 'Vows of chastity . . . By God, Edith, what sort of a man is he? Does he not realise that he has a duty to his people to produce an heir?'

'He is a man of God, father. He would have preferred to be a monk rather than king. And he says that God will provide an heir for England.'

Godwin stifled an angry retort. Edith must have been hurt enough already — and it was not her fault. But the rumours were true: there would be no line of Succession. And no grandson of his would ever be King of all England.

And there was poor Edith . . .

'My God,' he said, mournfully, 'what sort of a marriage did I make for you? How will you ever forgive me?'

Edith smiled. 'But, father, there is nothing to forgive. Edward is thoughtful and kind, and there is love and respect between us. There are many who would say we are fortunate.'

Glumly, Godwin admitted that this might be so. Edith laughed her gayest laugh and changed the subject by asking after her mother and affairs at Winchester. Godwin answered as cheerfully as he could, but his mind was on other things.

Presently he rose to go, kissed his daughter fondly and made his way down the steps to the great hall. He noticed that the handsome monk was standing at the far end, and that he turned his back as Godwin strode to the entrance door.

There was nothing to be gained by staying longer. He gathered his escort of housecarls and set off across London Bridge towards the south. It had been a severe winter, with an iron frost gripping the ground until the middle of March, and now that the warmth had at last returned to the sun and with the help of recent rain, the top few inches of the road had turned to mud. And where there was no mud there was water, disguising the depth of the potholes and hiding the wagon ruts. The housecarls cursed and wiped mud-spattered faces and thought gloomily of the state of the legs and underbellies of their horses. The little column lengthened, and the pace grew slower.

At the head of the column was Godwin, oblivious of mud, time and place. Beside him rode Brand, who had served him for twenty years and knew him as a brother. He sensed Godwin's mood and rode in silence, occasionally glancing at the sun which, with the blue sky to itself, was sliding down towards the west.

Now that the shock of Edith's revelation was absorbed, Godwin's thoughts were on his most immediate problem: should he, or should he not send for Sweyn before a new earldom had been found for Harold? With the king in his present mood, it seemed plain that a bargain would have to be struck with Edward — a favour for a favour. Months might pass in waiting for the right opportunity, and if, in the meantime, Sweyn returned to find the way to his earldom resolutely barred by Harold, there would be trouble. And a fight in the family, however bloodless, was the last thing that Godwin wanted.

Then there was the line of Succession. Edward was not such a fool that he could not foresee the dangerous situation that would arise if there was no natural heir to succeed him on his death. Neither was he so strong in will that he could deny himself one of the pleasures of marriage to ensure that the Crown would not one day rest on the head of a man with Godwin blood in his veins. Edith was attractive enough to make any man forget his prejudices.

In a flash, the answer to the conundrum occurred to him, and he laughed aloud. Brand looked across at him, sharply.

'The man is impotent,' said Godwin, still laughing.

'What man?' Brand was puzzled by his lord's change of mood. Godwin drew his horse close to Brand's so that they could talk unheard.

'The king, Brand . . . ' he knew that he could trust Brand with any secret, and he told him of what Edith had said to him that morning. Brand listened, his smile growing broader.

'A likely tale,' he said at last. 'I doubt that my wife would have believed that story from me.' He laughed loudly at the thought.

Godwin grew serious. 'You see what this means, Brand? Not now, but in six weeks or six years . . . whenever the poor fool drops dead?'

Brand nodded. 'Do I not . . . ' He could remember the time of Ethelred and Edmund and — not so long ago — the years of Harefoot and Harthacanute. He would never forget the sight of blazing crops and the stench of burning homesteads. 'A fine thing,' he said, 'to look forward to in our old age.'

'It need not happen,' said Godwin, 'if we guard against it.'

Brand sighed. He had no head for politics. He looked to the west, where the sun hovered low in a blaze of yellow, and felt his cloak clammy about his shoulders.

'We shall have a hard frost soon, Godwin, and the road over the Hog's Back will be encrusted with ice. I doubt that we shall reach Farnham tonight.' Although it had never been mentioned between them, he knew the earl's aversion to lodging the night at his hall in Guildford. And he could guess the reason for it.

Godwin said: 'There will be hot food and a fire at Guildford.'

Brand sighed his relief. 'It will be nice to be among the English again.'

Godwin looked sharply at him. 'You noticed it too, Brand? All the foreigners at the palace?'

'Noticed it . . . ? If I closed my eyes, I could imagine I was in Normandy instead of London.'

Godwin said nothing, but his mouth turned down at the corners. It seemed that there were three problems . . . and all of them were urgent.

2

Like other men who have the ambition, the verve and the luck to rise above their normal station in life, Godwin had the ability to submerge his conscience in self-justification. He was able to reason with himself that it had been necessary to do *this* — which was bad — in order to avoid *that* — which would have been worse. It was a measure of his stature among his contemporaries that, more often than not, he was able to convince them as well as himself.

Nevertheless he had not visited his hall at Guildford for nearly thirteen years — not since the night that Alfred the Atheling had been taken, and as soon as he entered the doorway the memory of that night stirred in his mind and added to his depression. He ate his meal moodily, taking little part in the conversation, eyeing the top of the oak table in front of him: scarred and marked by knife cuts, stained by meat juice and wine, it was probably the same table and more likely than not he was sitting in the same chair.

It had been a festive occasion that night, thirteen years ago: he had been relaxed, laughing easily, enjoying the facile talk which flowed along the table. His memory told him that he had been carefree, but it was hard to understand why, since his position at that time was anything but secure. King Harold Harefoot knew that he was a supporter of the Royal House of Wessex; he had only enemies at court, and he was clinging to his earldom by his fingertips.

Godwin could remember that night in minute detail. The drinking had gone on into the small hours: there had been songs and counter-songs, voices had been raised to shouting level, speech became drink-thickened, Godwin, who prided himself that he could drink any man under the table, was sober enough to notice that Alfred, sitting beside him in the place of honour, was flushed but coherent. But that Sweyn, on the far side of the Atheling had collapsed so that his head rested on the table. The sight annoyed Godwin, and he made a mental note to tell Sweyn that if he could not hold his liquor he would have to learn to take longer drinking less. But his chief thought was that it would be a fine thing if one day young Alfred were to be crowned king. A fine thing for England and for Godwin.

And then suddenly the great outer door had burst open and armed men had poured into the hall like flood water from a breached dam. The light from the candles and the great fire reflected redly on their drawn swords.

The hubbub of revelry ceased abruptly: everyone stared towards the door. A tall man in full armour pushed himself to the front and took off his helmet. He gazed along the length of the top table and gave a toothy grin, full of menace.

'Alfred Atheling,' he said slowly, 'and Godwin of Wessex. Two birds with one stone.'

The silence became oppressive. Godwin, his brain like ice, watched

Harefoot as he stood grinning and shifting his weight from one foot to the other.

'Well, Godwin? Is it a fight . . . or do we talk?'

Fight or talk . . . Godwin winced as he recalled the words. Not that he blamed himself for what he had or had not done. To fight would have been suicidal and pointless. And so in the privacy of a sleeping chamber lit by six candles, they had talked in an endless circle.

Harefoot had said: 'I have fifty armed men against your score of drunks. Give me the Atheling.'

'My lord,' said Godwin, 'I am to take him to his mother at Winchester.'

Harefoot spat on the floor. 'That old sow . . . I am giving you a choice Godwin. You can either be dead and a hero for a few weeks, or you can remain alive as my friend. Whatever you decide, I shall take the Atheling.'

Godwin argued with all the skill he possessed. Alfred, he said, was on a visit to his mother. Nothing more than that. He had no interest in the crown of

England. And to add weight to his plea he offered Sweyn as hostage until Alfred had left the country.

But Harefoot scoffed contemptuously. 'What good is your son to me? It is the Atheling I want.'

And so it went on. Harefoot was implacable, and to Godwin it was like beating his fists against a stone wall.

At length, Harefoot said: 'Godwin, I had thought to deprive you of your earldom, but I see you are a better man than I took you for. Give me the Atheling, and you shall keep Wessex for as long as I live.'

Godwin looked at the man who seemed to tower over him. He was tired and his head was aching. Harefoot bared his teeth in a smile: 'Come on, man. I am offering you a friendship which could be rewarding for both of us.'

'What will you do with him?' It was a pointless question because he already knew the answer. But it was not the truth that he wanted to hear.

Harefoot regarded him quizzically for a moment. 'He will not be harmed,' he said, 'providing he does what is asked of him.'

'I have your word on that?'

Harefoot chuckled at the back of his throat. 'You have my word — for what it is worth.'

They re-entered the hall where the fire had almost burned out and Harefoot's men stood around the walls with drawn swords. The chilled silence was broken by Harefoot directing that Godwin and his men might leave with their weapons and horses, and in the sudden commotion of exhaled fear and men rising to their feet, Godwin, glancing around for Sweyn, met the gaze of Alfred for a fleeting moment which seemed to last a lifetime.

★   ★   ★

Godwin became aware that his steward was speaking to him. 'My lord, it is late and I see you are tired. There is a couch made up for you in a private room.'

He looked in the direction the steward was pointing and saw it was the same room in which he had argued with

Harefoot all those years ago. He felt a sudden chill run like a mouse down his backbone and remembered that the steward had only been six years at Guildford.

'Thank you,' he said, 'but I shall lie by the fire with my men.'

He took his cloak and stepped down into the floor of the hall. The housecarls made a space for him and found him straw. One of them made a joke about the need to snore quietly now that the earl was among them, and Godwin joined in the laughter and made a coarse joke of his own to put them at their ease, for they were young and of them all, only Brand had been with him thirteen years before.

He was glad of their presence, and soon the chill wore off and he was able to think of more pressing things.

At first light next morning, he sought out Brand and took him to one side.

'Would you fancy a trip to Denmark, old friend?'

Brand laughed. 'There is never a dull moment with you, Godwin. When shall I start?'

'This morning. Ride from here to Bosham, where you will find Ulf Thurkilson who is a good ship-master and knows the Danish waters like the back of his hand. Tell him to take my fastest ship . . . and if the wind stays in the south-west you will be there before your wife misses you.'

Brand grinned. In spite of his forty years he was young in heart and restless in spirit. 'And what shall I do in Denmark?'

'Find Sweyn and bring him back to England.'

'Denmark,' said Brand, rubbing his chin, 'is a big place, and there may be people who have not heard of Sweyn Godwinson.'

Godwin laughed. 'Find the place where the ale is strongest and the women are easiest. You, of all people, should be able to do that blindfold.' He fumbled at the belt under his tunic and handed Brand two small leather bags. Brand felt the weight of the bags and whistled quietly.

'He will have debts,' said Godwin. 'Pay them off. And Brand . . . ' he nodded towards the group of housecarls ' . . . take one of the youngsters with you for company.'

When Brand and his companion had taken the road which led southwards through the Forest to Bosham, Godwin felt as though a weight had been taken from his shoulders. The decision had been made but it would be at least a month before Sweyn returned, and it seemed plenty of time to find a solution to the problem of the earldom. Light-hearted, he set off westwards along the ridge of the Hog's Back, talking and laughing with his house-carls.

It was early afternoon when they arrived at his hall in Winchester. Grooms led the tired horses away while Godwin shared with his men a meal of cold fowl and ale. Afterwards, he felt weary and the early morning elation had given way to pangs of doubt.

His wife was sitting by the window in her bower, busy with embroidery. She returned his kiss and watched, smiling, as he sprawled upon the couch.

He let out a great sigh. 'It is good to be home, Gytha.'

Gytha had been married to Godwin for thirty years and, although she had borne him nine children, she had managed to retain much of the lithe grace of her earlier years and the raven-dark hair which framed her face was carefully dressed to hide the flecks of grey around the temples. She was all things to him and knew him better than he knew himself, and she could see from his manner that his visit to Westminster had not been as fruitful as he would have wished. She asked for news of Edith and listened silently while he spoke of what their daughter had told him.

'She is wasted on the man,' he said angrily. 'I should have married her to Leofric's son. Imagine the power that would have sprung from a union of the Houses of Wessex and Mercia.'

Gytha smiled. 'It matters more to me that she is happy.'

'She says she is. I cannot see how.'

'She would not have said it unless it

was so,' said Gytha contentedly, 'not even to please you.'

There was a silence while Godwin watched his wife's nimble fingers work a silken design upon the dark red velvet. Gytha, knowing there was more to come, stitched away quietly. She did not have long to wait.

'I have sent Brand to fetch Sweyn from Denmark,' he said, as though it was of no account.

Gytha laid her embroidery on her lap and gazed out of the window. She loved all her children equally, but she found it easier to love Sweyn from a distance. Her husband would chide Harold for his preoccupation with sport and tease Tostig for his vanity, but to the faults of his first-born son he seemed completely blind. Gytha understood, and was sad for Godwin.

She listened while he spoke of the king's refusal to create a new earldom for Sweyn and of his half-formed plans for Harold and Beorn.

'Tell me,' he said at last, 'did I do right to send for Sweyn so soon?'

Gytha saw that he had the look of a perplexed child and she smiled kindly at him. 'It will depend on Sweyn. If he can be persuaded to be humble and patient . . . '

'He is too like me to be either.'

'If he were like you there would be no problem.'

There was a pause before Godwin said: 'He needs a good wife. I must see what can be done.'

Gytha said nothing.

Godwin rubbed his face with the palms of his hands. 'Problems . . . problems,' he said wearily, 'the world is full of problems. Solve one and you create two more. I am beginning to wish I was just a country thane with nothing more than a few acres to worry about.'

'Do you think you would be happy with that?'

'For a while, perhaps.'

Gytha laughed. 'For an hour or two, I think. Then you would set about acquiring more acres and more responsibility.' She became serious: 'My lord, you are over-tired. Your eyes show the strain of too many worries. Rest for a few days and concern yourself with trivial things.'

'I wish to God I could,' he said. He lay back on the couch and closed his eyes, listening to the scratch of Gytha's needle and the hiss of the drawn silk.

Presently he said: 'Is Harold still with us?'

'I dare say you will find him at the kennels,' said Gytha. 'His favourite dog is sick.'

Godwin got to his feet and kissed his wife, then left the room. Gytha watched him go before laying her work aside and then gazed out of the window to rest her eyes and think.

Godwin made his way to the kennels and found Harold on his knees beside a great wolfhound which lay on its side in the sun. He was a big man, the width of his shoulders in proportion to his height, his limbs well muscled. His fair hair was cut short and his flowing yellow moustache was carefully combed. He stood up and greeted his father absently.

'Grendel is ill,' he said. 'I have never known him refuse fresh meat before.' He stooped and dangled a piece of raw deermeat close to the dog's muzzle. The animal rolled its eyes but did not stir.

Godwin looked down at the dog. 'He is old,' he said. 'Let him rest.'

Harold's blue eyes were clouded. 'He was born the summer before Canute died.' He smiled sadly. 'We passed our puppyhood together.'

'There will be other dogs,' said Godwin.

'Never another Grendel,' said Harold.

From an enclosure beyond the kennels, there came excited shouting and the clatter of wood on wood. Godwin moved across to see what caused the commotion and saw two of his younger sons, Gyrth and Leofwin, each with helm, buckler and wooden practice sword, hacking and parrying as though there was hatred between them. Close by stood the auburn-haired Tostig, elegantly dressed as if for court. As Godwin watched, Gyrth, delivering a blow, slipped on damp grass and fell to the ground. Leofwin gave a shout of triumph and looked at Tostig.

'You are beaten, Gyrth,' said Tostig.

'It was a slip,' Gyrth protested from the ground.

From beside Godwin, Harold called: 'You were off-balance when you aimed your cut — you must learn to use your feet.'

The three turned and came across to greet their father. Smiling, the earl chaffed the two youngsters about their prowess as fighting men.

To Tostig, he said: 'And how goes it with my handsome peacock?'

'Well enough, father.' Tostig drew his green cloak tighter around him.

'Lovesick for Judith, I suppose?'

Tostig flushed but said nothing.

Presently, Godwin left them. He had meant to speak of what was on his mind to Harold, but he could see that the time was not ripe.

Harold went back to Grendel, and when he could not coax the dog to its feet he picked him up and carried him to the kennel building where he laid him on a litter of clean straw. He stayed beside him, stroking his head and flanks until the dog died shortly before dawn the next morning.

Now that there was nothing to keep him in Winchester, Harold had intended to return to Hereford, but Godwin, anxious to settle the matter of Sweyn's earldom, persuaded him that they should ride together to Bosham, knowing that Harold had a fondness for the place. So early the next day they set out with six housecarls as companions.

Time was not important, and several times they halted at the villages and homesteads on their path so that the earl could speak to his people. He also made a point of passing the time of day with lonely shepherds and swineherds, speaking to them in their own jargon and in a way that put them at their ease.

He said nothing of the matter which was uppermost in his mind until the late afternoon, when he told Harold that Sweyn would be home by midsummer. Harold listened in silence, but his eyes narrowed, and when the earl asked him if he would willingly return his estates to his brother he thought for a long time before replying.

'Father, Sweyn shall have my share of

his earldom willingly enough . . . on one condition.'

'Which is . . . ?'

'That you recognise my marriage and take my Edith into our family.'

Godwin looked into his son's eyes. 'My son, for your own good I will not do that.'

'But why not? She is my chosen wife and comes from good stock. Mother would not be unwilling to receive her.'

Godwin smiled sadly and explained that marriage was the surest way for a man of rank to extend his power and wealth, and that the time would undoubtedly come when Harold would have need of his eligibility for such a marriage.

Harold had heard the lecture before, but he heard his father out.

'Tell me . . . was your marriage to mother one of convenience?'

Godwin threw back his head and laughed. 'Indeed it was. I was in high favour with Canute and I sought a way to secure my position. I made up my mind to marry Canute's cousin even before I had seen her — the shrewdest thing I ever did. I have the best of both worlds.' He looked swiftly at his son. 'Never marry for love alone, Harold. Love is like a candle flame — apt to be snuffed out by a draught.'

'Tostig will marry Judith for love,' said Harold.

Godwin smiled. 'But I think he is not unaware that her father, Baldwin of Bruges, is rich. I think there is a streak of shrewdness in Tostig.'

'Or perhaps he has your luck.'

Godwin sensed Harold's dejection, and he spoke kindly: 'Believe me, my son, I bear no ill-will against you or your Edith, but if I recognised your marriage you would live to regret the day.'

Harold did not answer. Nothing, he decided, would ever part him from Edith.

The sun sank behind a sheet of cloud and the wind became sharp. In time, they came to Bosham.

The following day, Godwin was busy with affairs of the Bosham estate, and Harold passed the time at ease, revisiting old haunts and talking with the fishermen, many of whom had known him when he was a small and inquisitive boy.

At midday he swam in the estuary, afterwards drying himself by running along the water's edge, naked to the wind. The fishermen laughed at this and threatened to call out their womenfolk, and Harold laughed back, pink and glowing with a fresh warmth.

There was no formality to the meal in the hall that evening: the top table lay bare while Godwin and Harold sat with their men and the Bosham retainers. The talk turned to past battles and Godwin, who was by choice a seaman, listened to Harold as he spoke of his clashes with the Welsh cattle-thieves and explained his theory of waging war by surprising his enemies by his speed of movement. The housecarls asked searching questions, thinking to show up weaknesses in the plan, and the earl was impressed by his son's ready and well-reasoned answers.

Later, as he lay on his couch in the dark, he thought deeply, and after a while it seemed to him that he had found the bait which might lure Harold from his share of Sweyn's earldom.

The next morning they rode to Chichester, then turned northwards over the Downs until they came to a village not far from the edge of the Forest. Here, Godwin instructed his housecarls to wait, and together with Harold he followed a track which led into the Forest. The track was narrow and they rode one behind the other, Harold looking about him, his right hand close to the hilt of his sword, thinking of the possibility of ambush by a band of outlaws.

Soon, they came to a clearing with a rough homestead, outside which a man was cleaving the shoots of stunted hazels to make hurdles. He stopped his work to watch their approach, and Godwin called to him: 'I would speak with Edric Cuthbertson.'

The man threw down his cleaver. 'Wait here, earl Godwin,' he said, and disappeared among the trees.

'He knows you,' said Harold wonderingly.

Godwin smiled. 'I have been here often enough.'

They tethered their horses and sat

down, resting against the bole of a beech tree.

'Who is Edric Cuthbertson?' said Harold.

'He was a Sussex thane who crossed Harthacanute in some trivial matter and lost his estate. Now he is his own king and runs his domain as he sees fit. Which is well, because he is a good man.'

The earl lay relaxed, his eyes closed. Harold sat as though on a thorn bush, his eyes peering into the dense Forest with its carpet of brown leaves. Presently a man appeared soundlessly beside them: he had an imperious manner, but he gave Godwin a friendly greeting and nodded to Harold when Godwin made him known.

They spoke briefly of the hard winter and local affairs before Godwin broached the matter on which he had come.

'The Forest men in the east are causing trouble, Edric. I have had complaints of cattle stolen and stores of grain plundered. Even that men have been killed and their womenfolk have been carried off. Can you say who is at the bottom of this?'

Edric nodded. 'A man called Finn — a newcomer to the Forest. They say he fled from London where he had killed a man in a quarrel over a woman. He has gathered about him a band of hotheads and murderers and assumes the right to take what he needs by force instead of by bargaining. If he is not checked, life will become difficult for all the Forest dwellers.'

'How should he be dealt with?'

'How does one deal with a mad dog? And it should be done quickly because this dog is infecting others, and the larger the pack the bolder they will become.'

Godwin whistled through his teeth. 'We shall do what we can,' he said.

As they rode back to where the housecarls waited, Harold forced his horse alongside his father's.

'Why do you deal with this man Edric? He is an outlaw.'

'He makes no trouble,' said Godwin, smiling, 'and we can be of use to each other. Besides, he is English, and his people are English, and there may come a time when every Englishman in Wessex who can wield a sword will be worth his weight in gold.'

Harold would have known more, but Godwin cut him short. 'This man Finn, Harold. Should I send a force of men into the Forest?'

Harold laughed, glad to be set a problem which he could solve with authority. 'That is the one thing you should not do. They could search for weeks in the Forest and not see a single outlaw. Or they might be slaughtered one by one and never see their enemies.'

He was silent for a moment, marshalling his thoughts. Godwin waited, congratulating himself on his wilyness.

'Treat them as you would a pack of wolves,' said Harold. 'Dangle a bait in the jaws of a trap set on ground of your own choice. Then spring the trap while they are at the bait.'

'Easy enough for a young man,' grumbled Godwin. 'I am too old for strenuous pastimes. Harold, could you do this for me?'

'Give me a hundred housecarls and a month of time . . . ' Harold was excited at the thought, his eyes sparkling.

'You can have as many housecarls as you can raise and as much time as you like,' said Godwin. 'And ships . . . you will need warships and crews. Only last month, Winchelsea was attacked by pirates.'

The smile faded from Harold's face and he gazed at his father, half angry, half amused.

'And it was I who presumed to teach you about traps and bait . . . ' His laughter echoed off the trees.

'Fair exchange,' said Godwin, 'is no robbery. Kent and East Sussex for Herefordshire — is it a bargain?'

'Why only East Sussex?' said Harold.

'Because I would keep Bosham for myself. Your mother likes it in the summer.'

'Then you shall keep it as my tenant. Kent and all Sussex, or you shall catch your outlaws yourself.'

Laughing, they clasped hands on it.

Harold grew serious. 'Will the king approve a new earldom? I have heard that he is easily swayed by bishop Robert who, men say, is ill-disposed towards us.'

'We shall see about that,' said Godwin.

3

Godwin was relieved and a little surprised at his son's ready acceptance of his plan, for he knew from experience that Harold had more than his share of stubbornness. Now that he had only Edward to persuade he was already savouring the sweet fragrance of success, for under the right circumstances the king was as pliable as a willow sapling.

He tried to put the matter from his mind and spent a week or two hawking on the Downs and hunting in the forest that lay to the south of Winchester. But at times he was seized by a fierce impatience and would have ridden forthwith to Westminster to force the issue had not Gytha dissuaded him.

It was at times like this, when his impulsiveness overcame his good sense, that Gytha's soothing influence was invaluable. She spoke to him as she would to an impatient small boy, telling him to wait until Edward should send to him for advice or a favour. She suggested that to pass the time he should take the lovelorn Tostig on a visit to the estates at Dorchester.

Godwin saw the sense of this, and in due time they set off westwards. It was not long before Godwin realised that since he had last journeyed with him less than a year ago, a change had come over Tostig. No longer was he the dashing young blade, ready to turn a somersault at the flicker of a maiden's eyelash: instead, he was attentive and serious-minded, eager to learn the finer points of government.

More lightly built than either Sweyn or Harold, he had the colouring and delicate good looks of his sister, Edith, and he showed that he had the agile mind of his father. Yet Godwin would have been more pleased had he laughed more readily. At times he was sullen to the point of surliness.

One morning, Godwin spoke to his son concerning Sweyn's return and of the new earldom he planned for Harold.

Tostig listened in silence and then said: 'Father, what earldom shall I have and when?'

Godwin laughed a little. 'My son, it is too soon to speak of that. In time there will be an opportunity.'

'But if I am to marry Judith I cannot go to her empty handed.'

'I shall see to it that you two do not starve,' said Godwin. 'But an earldom . . . you must make friends with your brother-in-law, the king, for that.'

Tostig was silent. Glancing at him, Godwin recognised from a certain way that he held his head and the slight downward curve of his mouth that there was something of Sweyn in Tostig.

When, after the best part of ten days, they returned to Winchester, Gytha said to Godwin, 'Did you not meet my messenger?'

'We came back an unaccustomed way,' said Godwin. 'What message did he carry?'

'There was a courier from the king: there will be a meeting of the Council at Oxford on the first Wednesday in June.'

Godwin's eyes lit up, and Gytha laughed at his eagerness. 'Did I not tell you to be patient?' she said.

She could answer none of Godwin's questions, so he went immediately to see the bishop of Winchester at his palace by the old Minster.

Bishop Stigand, a thin man with a wrinkled face and hard, shrewd eyes, had been Godwin's chaplain not many years before, and owed his present rank to the earl. He was a crafty man who kept his ear to the ground in both Church and temporal matters.

'I hear,' he said, answering Godwin's query, 'that the Emperor Henry has asked Edward for help in some venture against Baldwin of Bruges.'

Godwin was taken aback. 'How can I go against Baldwin now that it is agreed between us that Tostig will marry his daughter?'

Stigand smiled a grey smile. 'My lord, the Emperor wields enough power through the Pope to frighten our king — and Edward listens to those who would be glad to see you humbled. This is a time when you should sway with the wind.'

Godwin said nothing for a while, chewing his lower lip. Stigand watched him, as though reading his mind.

'And Baldwin,' said Godwin at last. 'Will he call off the marriage?'

Stigand gave a wheezy chuckle which ended in a dry cough. 'My lord, there are ways of going against a man: one can be zealous — or can only seem to be zealous. I shall send a messenger to Baldwin to make sure of his understanding.'

Godwin returned to his hall well content that his luck was holding.

Edward took up residence in his hall at Oxford several days before the meeting of the Council, and waited for the earls of Mercia and Northumbria whom he had requested also to arrive early. He greeted them as brothers and took them to a private room where he spoke to them of the business of the forthcoming Council, for he was keen to have their backing since at one stroke he could ingratiate himself with the Emperor Henry and seriously embarrass earl Godwin.

He spoke eloquently in his high-pitched voice of the power of the Emperor Henry and of the advisability of falling in with his wishes, and during this discourse Siward of Northumbria leaned back in his chair, staring at the ceiling and tugging at his beard. He was a Dane, a burly man with a face as scarred and rugged as the cliffs on his coastline, and a great leader of men in battle. His life was mainly concerned in dealing with the unruly men of his earldom and keeping his northern neighbours, the Scots, on their own side of the border. He knew little of politics and religious intrigue and cared less.

When Edward had finished speaking, he said: 'I take it, my lord king, that your wish is to do as the Emperor asks?'

'Do you not agree that we should, earl Siward?'

Siward shrugged: it seemed that he had travelled a long way for next to nothing. 'If you think it wise, my lord.'

Edward turned to the earl of Mercia. Leofric was a tall man, white-haired and stiff in the joints. His frosty blue eyes and the length of his thin nose combined to give his face an expression of permanent disdain. 'My lord king,' he said primly, 'I hold no brief for Baldwin of Bruges, but if we aid the Emperor, where is the advantage to ourselves?'

'The Pope is the Emperor's man . . . ' Edward gesticulated with his hands. 'Besides,' he added quietly, 'Godwin will surely be against it.'

Leofric looked at the king from beneath his eyebrows and allowed himself the slightest of smiles. He had more than one score to settle with Godwin.

'In that case,' he said, 'I am for it.'

'And Alfgar . . . ?'

'My son,' said Leofric stiffly, 'will do as I do.'

Edward smiled and rubbed his long, delicate hands together. He, too, was content.

Meanwhile, Godwin also had made an early start, but he had avoided Oxford and lodged himself in Witney, where he waited for Harold and Beorn as they came from the west. When they arrived, he told them of what Stigand had said, and told them of his plan to turn the situation to his own advantage.

He also spoke to Beorn about the return of Sweyn and, as he had expected, his nephew was willing to give up his part of the earldom in return for certain favours. They clasped hands on their bargain, and both were happy.

When they all gathered in the Council chamber, the king, at the head of the table, had before him a parchment bearing the seal of the Emperor Henry. The message was written in Latin, but Edward spoke a translation of it.

'Because of an act of unwarranted aggression by Baldwin, Count of Flanders, the Emperor Henry is mounting a punitive expedition with a great force of men. He asks that we use our ships to blockade the harbours of Baldwin's domain so that he cannot make his escape by sea.'

On hearing this, Godwin glanced at Harold with relief in his eyes. Edward noticed the look and, mistaking it for a sign of dismay, smiled to himself. He laid the parchment aside and discoursed at length as he had done previously to

Leofric and Siward.

When he had finished, he looked down the table and said: 'What are your thoughts on this, earl Harold?'

Harold looked at the king in surprise: Edward's usual custom was to seek first the views of the senior earls, but by reversing the procedure he hoped to cut the ground from beneath Godwin's feet.

For a moment, it seemed that Harold was speechless, and Edward's voice became almost mocking. 'Surely, earl Harold, you have some views on this matter?'

Harold felt the blood surging to his cheeks. 'My lord, I have always looked on Baldwin as a friend, yet it seems that he has angered the Emperor of the Holy Roman States. I would hear other views on the subject before I cast my vote.'

When, at last, the question came to the earl of Wessex, there were three in favour of aiding the Emperor and two uncommitted. Edward leaned forward, his arms folded on the table, expecting an attempt by Godwin to sway the Council in defence of his friend Baldwin. But

Godwin was silent for a while, and when he did speak it was in a subdued tone.

'My lords,' he said. 'You will know that over the years I have been on friendly terms with the Count of Flanders. You may also know that a marriage was arranged between his daughter Judith and Tostig, my son. But recently I have come to learn that the pirates who plunder along the shores of Wessex and East Anglia use Baldwin's harbours as their bases. And this with his full knowledge. Therefore, my lords, it seems to me that the time has come to teach Baldwin that he cannot with impunity tweak the nose of the Emperor Henry or prey upon those who hold him as a friend.'

There was a long silence. Edward leaned back in his chair feeling as though he had been cheated: he had expected a battle of words and wits culminating, perhaps, in Godwin's refusal to accept the ruling of the Council. Which would have suited Edward's plans admirably. As it was . . .

'It seems that we are unanimous . . . ?' Edward looked questioningly round the table.

Godwin caught his eye. 'Lord king . . . there is another matter ripe for discussion.'

Edward frowned. His disappointment seemed to have tired him. 'Will it take long?'

'No, my lord. A few minutes of discussion . . . it concerns the piracy I mentioned . . . '

Edward relaxed into his chair and listened with half an ear to Godwin and Alfgar as they discussed the problems of defending their shores.

Leofric also listened, his cold eyes darting between Godwin and his son, ready to go to Alfgar's rescue should the boy seem to become too enmeshed in Godwin's web.

Leofric had never liked Godwin: the man was a brash adventurer, a silver-tongued intriguer, who had risen from nothing to become one of the wealthiest and most powerful men in the country. In Leofric's eyes it was a dreadful thing that an upstart nobody could achieve such a position.

Now the talk had turned to the

problem of outlaws and Siward had joined in and was telling Harold of his method of dealing with them. Soon, the king was interested, leaning forward, his eyes roving from speaker to speaker.

Leofric bestirred himself. It had suddenly occurred to him that Godwin had started this discussion with some objective in mind. He was not one to seek advice from Alfgar or Siward, therefore . . .

The king was saying: 'But, earl Godwin, if the matter is so pressing you should form a fleet of ships and a force of men whose job it would be to guard against these pillagings.'

Godwin made a deprecatory gesture. 'My lord, I have neither the time nor the energy for such a task. Harold, here, has said that he would do it.'

Edward looked appraisingly at Harold, who said: 'A small force of mounted men, lightly-armed for speed, and perhaps six ships at three different harbours. It should be enough.'

The king smiled. 'I wish you good luck, earl Harold.'

In a flash, Leofric saw Godwin's aim, and spoke up, thinking to warn the king. 'Earl Godwin, this task will keep earl Harold from Hereford for many months. Are you seeking to create a new earldom for him?'

Godwin gazed at him thoughtfully, as though the idea had never entered his head. 'My lord,' he said to the king, 'earl Leofric has made a good point. Perhaps we could discuss it later.'

Edward nodded. 'I shall think on it,' he said.

Leofric, who would gladly have bitten off his tongue had it not been too late, cursed himself for a fool and Godwin for a rogue.

The king rose to his feet. 'My lords, we have agreed to aid the Emperor. Let all ships possible be gathered at Sandwich without delay.'

Later, Godwin spoke privately to Harold and Beorn.

'We are lucky,' he said. 'I had thought we should be asked to lead our housecarls to Henry's aid. This business of ships is neither here nor there.'

Harold said: 'It was well done. I think I shall get my new earldom.'

'We shall put on a show at Sandwich that will clinch the matter. Shall you two ride back to Hereford?'

'No,' said Beorn, 'I have no wish to see Hereford again. We shall ride with you to the ships at Bosham.'

After all the earls had gone their separate ways, Edward rested in Oxford for three days before starting back for Westminster. During this time, bishop Robert, who had stayed in London, sent for Ralf, chaplain to the lady Edith.

Ralf had been a monk at the abbey of Jumièges when Robert had been abbot, and he had a reputation as a ram and a seducer of women. When Robert had been summoned to London and had seen the lie of the land between the king and the family of Godwin, he had sent for Ralf and given him certain instructions concerning the lady Edith.

When Ralf came before him, Robert said: 'You have had a clear field for the best part of a week, brother Ralf. Does the matter progress?'

Ralf did not answer, but stared at the floor and shifted his feet. Robert looked at him sternly and said: 'What is this? Has our prize stallion failed? Has he lost his powers of persuasion. Come on, man . . . speak up.'

Ralf looked up and said, 'Lord bishop, the lady Edith is not as other women: she laughs at my flattery and chides me for my lust. She makes me ashamed of myself.'

Robert regarded him thoughtfully for some moments. Then he said: 'You fool! I believe you are in love with her.'

'My lord, that is so and I cannot help it.'

'But surely that should make your task easier?'

Ralf looked pityingly at the bishop. 'It makes it impossible,' he said.

Robert was angry at Ralf's failure. He had set great store by his plan against Godwin's daughter. 'You have failed me, Ralf,' he said. 'Go back to Normandy. There is a ship at the wharf below this place which will sail at first light tomorrow. Go aboard her now and send the shipmaster to me.'

Robert knew the ship master as a man who, for a silver coin or two, would arrange for Ralf's journey to end in the dark waters of the Channel.

When the king arrived back in Westminster from Oxford, bishop Robert hastened to his side to find out what had happened. His surprise at Godwin's acceptance of the action against Baldwin turned to annoyance when he learned that a new earldom for Harold had been suggested.

'You did not agree to it?' he said, sharply.

'Nor did I refuse it. It seems a sensible measure, and the added power to the Godwins can be balanced by a new earldom for Siward's son.'

Robert frowned darkly: every favour to the Godwin family made his ultimate goal harder to achieve.

'Sire,' he said, 'it seems to me that history has repeated itself: to gain a new earldom for his family he has sold his friend, Baldwin, in the same way that he sold your brother to secure his hold on Wessex.'

'That may be so,' said Edward slowly. 'But if I grant this earldom it will not be for Godwin's sake. I have a regard for Harold: he has a straight eye — I think he is a man of honour.'

'He is a Godwin,' said Robert with venom.

Edward looked sharply at him. He thought to remind the bishop that his wife was also a Godwin.

'The lady Edith,' he said pointedly, 'tells me that her chaplain is nowhere to be found.'

Robert ignored the rebuke. He thought that he might salvage something from the wreckage of Ralf's failure.

'I had to send him away, Sire. There was talk . . . '

'Talk? What sort of talk?' Edward's voice was tense.

'Sire, it was just servants' talk . . . there can have been nothing in it. Nevertheless, I thought it best that brother Ralf should go.'

Edward's face went white, and he stared for a long time at Robert, then stood up and paced the floor with quick strides.

'And what of these servants who spread the gossip?'

'They, too, have been sent away,' said Robert smoothly.

As Edward continued to pace, his colour changed from white to burning red. He turned on Robert, his fists clenched.

'By all the Saints,' he shouted, 'let it be known that I will have the tongue out of any man or woman who spreads idle gossip about the court.'

Robert had never seen the king in such a rage so well controlled before. He bowed and withdrew.

Edward sat down. When the rage had left him, his hands trembled and his head ached; and as he sat and thought, the tears welled over his eyelids and trickled down his cheeks.

4

It was about midsummer when the ships began to nose their way into the harbour at Sandwich. Godwin's ships, borne on the south-west wind, from Bosham, Pevensey and other south coast harbours, were the first to arrive, led by the earl himself in a fine longship with fifty oarsmen. The tall prow was surmounted by a magnificent dragon's head and there was rich carving along the bulwarks below the prow, while the huge sail bore the emblem of the Dragon of Wessex worked in gold thread, and from the masthead fluttered a pennant with the same device. Harold, Tostig and Beorn were each in command of smaller warships with thirty oars apiece, and behind them were ten other ships of war, for Godwin wished it to seem that he was whole-hearted in his loyalty to the king.

Edward arrived with a contingent of ten warships from London, none of them as large as Godwin's own ship or as well-found as his other warships. Alfgar came with a dozen longships, and from Northumbria Siward sent six under the command of his nephew, Gospatric.

When they had all arrived, the king was delighted with the array and sent a messenger to the Emperor Henry, telling him of the size of the fleet and saying that he, himself, was taking command. For he was very keen to impress the Emperor with his friendship.

Next, with some of his housecarls, he paraded the foreshore, making himself known to the sailors and telling them what was afoot, stressing that the enterprise had the Papal blessing.

It was unfortunate that the next day the wind fell light and backed to the south-east, blowing from the direction of Flanders. The sailors laughed and said, 'So much for the Pope's blessing,' for with the wind against them they could do nothing.

Edward was not used to the command of seamen, nor did he understand the vagaries of wind and tide, and he gave many orders which could not be carried out, then followed them with counter-orders, so that men became bewildered and knew not what to do for the best.

The truth was that there were too many ships, and even if the weather had been favourable not all the seamen could have been kept busy. Godwin, Alfgar and Gospatric went together to the king and suggested that half the ships should be sent home, but he would not hear of it and, when they tried to argue the point, grew pettish and sent them away, for he feared the Emperor might learn of it. Alfgar and Gospatric shrugged their shoulders and rolled their eyes to Heaven, but Godwin was worried because he could foresee trouble which might prejudice his chance when he came to press the matter of Harold's new earldom.

Meanwhile Harold, wishing to keep the men out of mischief, arranged a series of wrestling contests in which each ship found a champion, who then fought the champions of other ships until only one man remained unbeaten. It was suggested that this man should try his skill against

Harold himself. Watched by the whole fleet, the two men fought together on the sand until the earl gained the upper hand.

Tostig, who was lithe and strong and considered himself no mean wrestler, had watched the contest and thought he saw a flaw in his brother's defence: he therefore challenged him to a bout. Amid much noise and excitement, they wrestled to and fro, but the earl's weight and strength were too much for Tostig, and he was soon beaten. Tostig was angry, because he thought his brother had humiliated him in front of a large crowd.

Among the onlookers was a wizened old seaman who had travelled over many seas, including the Mediterranean, where he had watched the Greeks wrestle. He pushed his way through the crowd to where Tostig was sullenly dressing and said to him: 'You need not have lost that match.'

Tostig looked at him, noting the weather-beaten face and the watchful eyes. 'Should I not? How so?'

'You were trying to meet force with force,' said the old man, and went on to

73

describe how a wrestler could very often defeat a man heavier and stronger than himself by cunning avoidance of a trial of strength.

Tostig listened carefully, and then said: 'By God, old man, if I beat him you shall have my golden armband.' Straight away, he challenged Harold to another match.

Harold laughed ruefully and said he was tired, but Tostig insisted, and soon they were at it hammer and tongs.

Tostig was careful to carry out the old man's instructions, and after a time, by means of clever footwork and a sharp push, he had Harold on his back on the sand. Tostig threw himself on top of his brother and grasped him by the throat. The crowd pressed round roaring their excitement.

Harold struggled to loosen his brother's grip, and at length managed to gasp, 'For God's sake, Tostig . . . this is only in fun.'

'Is it?' said Tostig through clenched teeth, and tightened his grip.

Harold saw a madness in his brother's eyes, and using every ounce of his strength, broke the grip and flung Tostig from him.

He got to his feet and massaged his throat, eyeing his brother askance. The crowd grew silent.

'I am sorry, brother . . . I should not have done that,' said Tostig.

Harold said nothing, but watched his brother push his way through the crowd.

The old seaman was waiting by Tostig's clothes.

'You had him beaten . . . you should have gone for his shoulders, not his throat. What came over you?'

Tostig did not answer, but thrust the gold armband into the old man's hand and walked off, carrying his clothes.

The weather remained perverse: when the wind veered at last to the west, it blew a gale and the open sea beyond the harbour boiled and swirled, flinging white spume high into the air, while the rain came down as silver rods from the low scudding cloud. Then there came a flat calm before the wind went round to the east again.

Food became short: there were daily

fights between the seamen and the townsfolk, and from inland there came complaints of stolen livestock. When Edward heard these things, he retired to a private room in his hall and would see nobody except for his chaplain, in front of whom he wept tears of vexation, and wondered what wrong he had done that God should punish him in this manner.

When Alfgar and Godwin were at last able to gain audience with him, he was vague and apart from the world, and they could obtain no decisions from him. As they left, Godwin said to Alfgar: 'He is not himself: we must make the necessary decisions ourselves.'

While they were with the king, two longships entered the harbour, and to those who watched it was obvious that they had been at sea for many days: their sails were ripped and tattered, the prows stained with salt and the oarsmen rowed raggedly, as if exhausted.

When Godwin returned to his tent, he did not at first recognise the unkempt individual who waited for him, but when at last he saw it was Brand, his heart leaped and he asked for news of Sweyn.

'He is here,' said Brand. 'He said he would join us as soon as he has cleaned himself a little.'

Godwin laughed joyously. 'He should have come as he was. How is he?'

'Well,' said Brand, brusquely.

'I did not mean in health. Has he changed in his ways?'

Brand looked into Godwin's eyes. 'If he has, it is for the worse.'

Godwin's eyes showed clearly his disappointment. Brand reached out to put his hand on his shoulder. 'My lord,' he said gently, 'that was why I came to you in this filthy state — to forewarn you.'

Godwin raised his head, smiling at the thought that, come hell or high water, his favourite son was home. 'Brand,' he said, 'you are a good friend — the best I ever had. And I am forgetting my hospitality.' He sent for food and water, and while Brand washed his hair and beard clear of the salt, and then ate and drank, he told the earl of the swift voyage out to Denmark and the search for Sweyn.

'We found him none too soon, hungry

and penniless. The Danes would have thrown him out had he not owed so much money. And there was his ship . . . '

'A ship?' said Godwin. 'Had he a ship?'

'If you can call it that. It was a fine ship once, but now . . . And there is a crew of forty — gallows-fodder, every one of them. The dregs of every midden in Europe.'

'You should have paid them off,' said Godwin.

Brand waved a half-eaten leg of mutton. 'What with?' he demanded. 'I had nothing left of the gold, and that mob of carrion crows wanted double what you gave me.'

'So?' said Godwin.

'So when the time came to leave, there they were behind us with Sweyn at the tiller. They would not let him come with us in case we managed to give them the slip, I suppose. We left Denmark with a brisk north-easter up our backsides: then there was half a day's calm. And then a howling gale right in our teeth . . . I tell you, Godwin, I don't frighten easily, but I said my prayers more times during the first hour of that storm than in all my years before. And on the crest of every wave I looked back, thinking to see them go under, but there they were, soft timber, rotten mast and all. It was a miracle.'

'Sweyn was always a good shipmaster,' said Godwin with pride in his voice. He looked towards the tent flap. 'Where is the boy? He's had time enough to walk from here to Winchester and back.'

Brand drank the last of his ale, then together they left the tent, walking in the direction of Sweyn's ship, Godwin searching among the crowds of idling seamen for the first sight of his son. Presently, Brand said: 'See the ship there? And look at the crew . . . '

Godwin saw the men, filthy and unkempt, stretched out asleep on the sand. He walked to the nearest of them and nudged him on the shoulder with his foot. The fellow opened his eyes and sat up, his hand moving swiftly to the knife at his belt. Brand stepped forward and made to kick him in the face, but Godwin stayed him.

'You there . . . where is your shipmaster, Sweyn?'

The man stared uncomprehendingly, and Godwin repeated the question in Danish. The seaman bared broken and blackening teeth and looked from Godwin to Brand and back again.

'He has gone to the king to claim what is due to him.'

Godwin drew breath sharply. 'How long since he went?'

The fellow stared insolently. His eyes travelled over Godwin, taking in the golden armbands and the jewelled rings on his fingers. 'How should I know how long I have slept?' He spat into the sand at Godwin's feet and lay back.

Godwin turned and hurried off. Brand eyed the seaman for a moment, and then followed. He heard the man call after him: 'Run after your master, old lap-dog.'

Godwin strode purposefully, seeing and hearing nothing. At the entrance to the hall, one of the king's housecarls barred the way.

'I must see the king. It is urgent,' said Godwin.

'The king is not well, lord earl. He will see nobody.'

'Has my son, Sweyn, been here?'

The housecarl grinned. 'He has, my lord. And it was after he left with a flea in his ear, that we had orders to admit no one else.'

Godwin swore a gutter oath and hurried back to his tent. Sweyn was there, sprawled on the bed. He rose to his feet as Godwin entered and the earl noted that he was as he remembered him — tall, broad and raven-haired. But there were unaccustomed lines on his forehead and the eyes were sunk deep into their sockets, darting and suspicious.

In Godwin's breast, love wrestled with anger, and lost.

'For God's sake, Sweyn . . . what have you done?'

Sweyn raised his eyebrows. 'Father, this is not the welcome I had expected after so many years.'

Godwin took his son's hands and pressed them between his own. 'It is good to have you back. But what passed between you and the king?' He became

81

aware that Sweyn's clothes were dirty and stinking.

Sweyn shrugged: 'The old fool . . . to be a king is man's work. He should go back to his abbey in Normandy.'

Godwin smiled. 'But what was said between you?'

Sweyn sighed deeply. 'I paid him my respects and asked for my earldom back. And he screamed at me in that woman's voice of his and said that I had no earldom, nor would I ever have while he was king. And he gave me four days to leave the country.'

Godwin was startled. 'Four days . . . ? God in Heaven, boy, what reason did he give?'

Sweyn shrugged again. 'I can only think he does not like my face.'

Godwin thought of all his efforts over the past months on Sweyn's behalf, and his anger returned. He said harshly: 'You should have let me speak to the king on your behalf. I had your earldom at my finger-tips — it was yours for the price of a moment's humility. Now, God knows how I can retrieve the chance.'

Sweyn answered sharply: 'I am a man — not a whimpering lad who needs someone to speak for him.'

'What you need,' said Godwin, 'is a wet-nurse and a man with a strong arm to teach you manners.'

Tempers rose, eyes blazed, nostrils flared, fists were clenched and words shouted that were never meant.

Godwin realised how it had been with the king. He swallowed his anger and said, after a pause: 'Come, Sweyn, this does no good. We must consider what is best.' He sent out for food and told a servant to fetch Harold, Tostig and Beorn.

They came while Sweyn was eating, and Godwin told them what had happened. Harold glanced at Tostig, and his eyes said, 'Well, what did you expect?' The good-natured Beorn gazed at Sweyn, his eyes full of compassion.

Sweyn greeted his brothers mockingly. Of his cousin, he said: 'What concern is this of Beorn's?'

'He holds half your old earldom,' said Godwin. 'Harold has the other half.'

Sweyn pushed the remains of the food away from him. 'Then the solution is simple,' he said. 'Harold and Beorn shall go to the king saying that they wish to give up their holdings to my benefit. What do you say to that, Harold?'

Harold folded his arms across his chest: as a boy, he had stood in awe of his elder brother, fearing the quick temper and the savage strength which had often put him to excruciating pain for no other reason than that Sweyn enjoyed inflicting pain. He could feel no compassion.

He said: 'I will give you fresh clothes, Sweyn, but not the earldom. Father knows the terms on which I will give that up.'

'Spoken like a brother,' sneered Sweyn. 'And it seems you are grown up enough to haggle with Father. Quite the little man.' He stared at Harold with contempt in his eyes.

Harold held his anger in check. 'And what have you ever done for me or for the family, except to cause trouble?'

Sweyn did not answer, but looked at his cousin. Beorn said that he would gladly help Sweyn by giving up his earldom, 'But what use is that,' he added, 'with the king in his present frame of mind?'

Sweyn laughed. 'Beorn should have been a priest. He offers hope with one hand and snatches it away with the other. And what does my brother Tostig have to say?'

Tostig, with his own chances of an earldom in mind, said: 'I am with Harold — I would not give Sweyn even a part of my earldom, if I had one.'

Sweyn raised his eyebrows. 'You too, Tostig? I had reckoned on some friendship from you. What axe have you to grind?'

Tostig flushed and bit his lower lip.

Throughout this talk, Godwin had been deep in thought. 'It seems to me,' he said at last, 'that it is pointless to argue over earldoms while Edward thinks only of exile. Was it a hasty decision, Sweyn? Or did he think before he spoke?'

'It came off his tongue like an arrow shot at random, trailing smoke from the heat of the moment.'

The earl nodded. 'In that case he can

be persuaded to change his mind. I shall go and see him in a day or two.'

'For God's sake, father,' said Sweyn irritably, 'I will not have you intercede on my behalf. I spoke my piece . . . and now I must pay the price.'

'And where will you go? Not back to Denmark, I think.' Godwin's voice was harsh with irritation.

'There are other places.'

Godwin banged his fist on the table so that the trenchers jumped and rattled. 'Listen to me, Sweyn,' he shouted. 'There is more at stake than your pride. Tomorrow at first light, you will sail your ship for Bosham. And there you will wait until I arrive within the week. Is that understood?'

Sweyn looked at his father for a moment as if to argue, then thought better of it and nodded. After a while, he left them to go back to his ship.

'You should have let him go into exile,' said Tostig. 'He will only cause more trouble here.'

Godwin did not answer. In his heart he thought that Tostig might be right.

The next morning, when he had watched Sweyn's ship leave the harbour and disappear out of sight, Godwin walked slowly back to his tent, feeling a mixture of emotions. There was relief that his dearest son was back in the country; pain at the enmity between his sons, and anger that all his carefully laid plans had been smashed to pieces. And there was hope that Sweyn might be allowed to stay, and that one day the pieces might be put back in place.

He sought an audience with the king, and when at last it was granted, the meeting was painful to Godwin, for he had no recourse but to swallow his pride. So, while Edward pontificated, the earl sat with downcast eyes, stifling the arguments that sprang to his tongue.

And how Edward could lecture when he had the whip hand . . . never had Godwin heard a man who could say the same thing in so many different ways. But he listened in silence, and when the king had at last exhausted himself, he ventured, very diffidently, to extenuate Sweyn's behaviour.

He related the story of the voyage from Denmark, adding a little detail here and there to heighten the effect. 'When he arrived here, the boy was exhausted — his brain was addled. How else could he have appeared before you in filthy clothes, ready to shout abuse?

'He was the same with me, and in the heat of the moment I could have whipped him. But, my lord king, to punish a man for being tired to the point of insanity . . . '

While Godwin talked, Edward was thinking. It seemed incredible to him that a man of the earl's shrewdness should waste time defending so uncouth a lout as Sweyn. It occurred to him that Godwin's love for his son was a Heaven-sent weapon: as long as Sweyn was in the country — as long as he had the chance of regaining his earldom, Godwin would be like wax in the king's hands.

He said: 'Did I punish him, earl Godwin?'

'My lord, you gave him four days in which to leave the country.'

'I had forgotten. It was said on

88

impulse. You may tell Sweyn that I shall not enforce it.'

'My lord . . . '

'But mark this, Godwin. There will be no earldom for him yet. I have seen enough of Sweyn to last me for many months.'

'My lord,' said Godwin, 'while he is in his present mood I would not press the point: he is not fit for the honour. But a year or two spent quietly in some far off corner of Wessex, behaving as a man of rank should — well, then . . . '

Edward nodded benignly. 'We shall see.'

His ascendancy over Godwin restored the king's interest in day-to-day affairs, and he was able to see that the size of the fleet at Sandwich must be reduced. Accordingly, a day or two later Godwin left Sandwich with most of his ships, hoping to make Bosham on the east wind. But when they were off Pevensey, the wind dropped and the sun went down behind a bank of clouds. The seamen foretold a westerly gale, so Godwin led the ships into the harbour.

They remained at Pevensey for several days, sheltering from storms and contrary winds, and during that time Godwin fretted and fumed, thinking of Sweyn and his crew of pirates at Bosham.

At mid-day on the fourth day, Sweyn appeared among them, having ridden from Bosham. It had rained continuously during his journey and he was wet to the skin and miserable when he came to Godwin.

'Father,' he said, 'the crew of my ship are growing restive: they ask to be paid off, and I have no money.'

'Give them the ship and tell them to go,' said Godwin.

'They say the ship is worthless. They want gold as well.'

'How much do they ask?'

When he heard the amount, Godwin became angry, but Sweyn told him that they threatened that unless they were paid what they asked they would take the ship and sail along the coast, looting and burning.

Godwin raged and cursed Sweyn for having associated himself with such a crowd of cut-throats. His son hung his head and admitted that he had been more than foolish, but that he had now learned his lesson. 'If God and the king allow it,' he said, 'I will settle down and mend my ways.'

Godwin was overjoyed to hear this. He told Sweyn of his audience with the king and that there was a chance that he might regain his earldom.

Sweyn's face brightened. 'How long must I wait?'

'Perhaps a year or two,' said Godwin.

Sweyn looked at the ground and bit his lip, as he had done when thwarted as a little boy. Watching him, Godwin felt the tears come to his eyes: it seemed to him that the Sweyn he loved had returned to him at last. He went to his treasure chest.

Sweyn stayed overnight and was pleasant in his talk, careful not to offend. Harold and Tostig watched covertly and exchanged glances: this was a Sweyn they had not known before. Beorn, whose good nature sprang from a warm heart, showed his delight and his cousin's change of heart and prospects of good fortune, talking and laughing with him as with an old friend.

After the evening meal, Sweyn took Beorn to one side.

'Cousin Beorn,' he said, 'you have shown that you are prepared to be my friend. My brothers are suspicious of me, and I cannot blame them — I was harsh to them in the old days. The king is the same: he thinks of me as wild and unruly, and it may take years to change his mind. How can he tell what I am like if he will not see me?

'What I need is a friend at Court other than my father. Will you ride with me to Sandwich to tell Edward that I am a changed man?'

Beorn was pleased at Sweyn's confidence in him. 'Not only that, cousin,' he said, 'but I will tell him that I shall willingly return to you my share of your earldom as soon as ever he shall give the word.'

'You are more of a friend than I deserve,' said Sweyn as they clasped hands.

When they told Godwin of their plan,

the earl at first looked down his nose, but at length he agreed to it, having first received promises from both of them that Sweyn should not go before the king unless he was sent for.

When Tostig heard of it, he was amazed. 'Father has gone mad,' he said. 'Can a man change his nature in a week?'

Harold said: 'I am sorry for Beorn: he will do himself no good at all.'

5

It was settled overnight: Sweyn and his cousin would ride at daybreak for Bosham to pay off the seamen, then to London, and if Edward was not there, they would take the road to Sandwich.

In spite of Sweyn's resolution to change his ways, Godwin was not happy as he stood in the early morning drizzle and watched the two men ride away towards the Downs. Brand, who stood beside him, tried to be soothing.

'They will have no difficulty, Godwin, in spite of the gold they carry. They will be all the more wary because of it.'

Godwin shook his head. 'No, Brand, it is the thought of Sweyn's men at Bosham that frets me. Would you trust them out of sight?'

'Huh . . . ' said Brand. 'If we could find enough horses . . . even a handful of armed men would be better than nothing.'

'Oh, they will leave Bosham with their gold like a flock of lambs. But where will they go, and what will they do? There are too many rich places along the coast for my peace of mind.'

Brand cast an eye to the west, where the sky was uncompromisingly grey. 'A couple of ships to stand sentry on them until they are out of temptation's way . . . But God, this weather . . . ' He spat forcefully on the ground.

But by mid-morning, the weather showed signs of improvement: the grey cloud lifted and broke, and far away to the west there was a streak of pale blue sky, and presently the wind softened and backed to the south.

Godwin spoke to Harold and Tostig, and was pleased to see their eyes shine with enthusiasm as he told them what they should do.

'With the two of us,' said Tostig, 'it would be easy enough to play the pirate — board them and take the gold. It is no more than they deserve.'

Godwin looked at him thoughtfully for a moment and then laughed. 'Spoken like a true son of your father, Tostig. But no . . . see them well away from the coast and then let them go. But if they seem likely to cause mischief, remember the gold. It would be a pity to waste it.'

It was early afternoon when Harold's ship *Dragon's Tail*, and Tostig's *Black Snake* pulled out of Pevensey and rowed easily along the coast until, at the white nose of Beachy Head, the land left them as they continued on southwards. When they reached the deep water, a long swell caressed the two ships, and they flowed smoothly across the contours of the sea, now a dark green, flecked by wind-raised wavelets and the scintillating reflections of a thousand suns.

At the tiller stood Harold, his head raised to the wind, enjoying the freedom and the challenge of the sea. Before him, the oarsmen grumbled and wheezed, because the inactivity of the previous weeks had let their muscles grow soft. Harold chided them for old women, and they bore it grinning ruefully, because they knew he was a good shipmaster and would not shirk taking his turn with an oar if it became necessary.

'It's all very well for you, with nothing else to do but lean on the tiller,' one of them called to him.

Harold joined in the general laughter: he knew that they would work at their oars until they dropped.

To port, and a little astern, *Black Snake* rode the swell like a gull floating the wind on outstretched wings, the carved snake's head at her prow dipping and rearing above the white frothing at her bows, rhythmic with each pull on the oars. Beside the steer board was Tostig, his auburn hair flowing behind him like a pennant, his teeth flashing white in the sunlight. Harold watched for a while, entranced by the beauty of the scene, and then gazed astern at the white cliffs as they receded and lowered in the water.

For several hours they rowed an easy pace southwards into the eye of the wind, until Harold, with an eye to the lowering of the sun, turned the ship to starboard towards the land and gave the order to hoist the sail. Thankfully the men shipped their oars, and the big square sail was run up the mast. Harold gave orders for the trimming of the sail, so that it filled with the wind and, leaning to starboard, the ship gathered speed so that the water creamed from the bows.

This was the best sailing of all, with the sail taut, the timbers creaking with the straining of the mast and the slapping and hissing of the sea as it made way before the prow. Harold stood at the tiller, his senses alert to every tremor and movement, balancing the ship with the wind so that she sailed smoothly and fast.

The sun sank lower, and the wind began to bite so that the oarsmen resting against the thwarts, pulled their cloaks around them, for the sweat was still upon them. Soon the coastline became visible as a faint purple blur on the horizon.

It was late when they beached their ships in a sandy inlet some miles north of Selsey Bill. Some put up the tilts of the ships while others made a fire on the shore from wind-dried driftwood, and made a stew of the salted pork and vegetables they had brought with them.

After they had eaten, and the seamen,

tired out by their exertions, had retired beneath the tilts, the two brothers sat by the embers of the fire and talked of their plans. Harold was for sailing straight into the harbour at Bosham, so that Sweyn's men could take warning.

But Tostig said: 'No, brother. We should wait for them out of their sight so that we can judge what they intend to do.'

Harold looked at him quizzically. 'Why should we do that, Tostig? Is it not better that they should be warned away by the sight of us?'

Tostig shook his head and looked meaningly at his brother. Harold met his gaze for a moment and then stared at the embers, thinking.

Suddenly he gave a little grunt of understanding: 'The gold . . . ' he said. 'Are you thinking of the gold?'

'What if I am?' said Tostig. 'Did you see it, Harold? Enough to keep a man in luxury for the rest of his life . . . why should Sweyn's scum have all this for the asking?'

'Perhaps they earned it, being at Sweyn's beck and call.'

Tostig scoffed. 'Birds of a feather.' And seeing a disapproving look on Harold's face, he added: 'It's all very well for you. With your estates, you have all the gold and silver you need at your finger-tips. I have to go cap in hand to father.'

'And is father ungenerous?' Harold's tone was slightly reproving.

'It seems,' Tostig said bitterly, 'that he is more generous to pirates.'

There was a silence. Tostig tried to wheedle his brother: 'It would be easy, Harold: one of us on each side of that rotten-timbered ship — we could crack it open like a nut, and leap aboard to seize the gold before it foundered.'

'And what of the crew?' said Harold, as if toying with the idea.

'What of them?' said Tostig, lightly. 'They will not be missed.'

'And the gold would be given back to father?'

'And father will laugh and be open-handed. Even half the gold, spread between us and our crews, would make our efforts well worth while.'

Harold got to his feet, laughing. 'We'll

do it,' he said, 'if we get the chance.'

'We'll make the chance,' said Tostig, still sitting.

Harold looked down at him. 'By God, Tostig,' he said. 'I learn more about you every day.'

'I hope you like what you learn,' said Tostig.

Harold walked back to his ship, frowning a little.

The next morning, they rowed south, giving the nose of Selsey Bill a wide berth because of the swift currents which flowed there. Harold had intended to lie-to off the lee shore of the Isle of Wight, to keep a watch on the mouth of the estuary which led to Bosham.

But hardly had they come abreast of the Foreland when Harold saw a dark shape upon the water about four miles to the north-east of them. Harold waved to Tostig and pointed, and his brother waved back that he also had seen the shape. Up went the sails, and the two ships gathered speed towards their quarry. Harold noticed that *Black Snake* was steering a more easterly course, widening the gap between them.

As *Dragon's Tail* drew closer, Harold could see that the shape was indeed a long-ship, a large one with as many as forty oars. It could only be Sweyn's ship.

Black Snake was well away from them now, almost ready to start its approach from the east, while Harold made his from the west. The nut, he thought, was about to be cracked.

He watched the longship with the concentration of a hunter stalking a deer, and became aware that it was moving faster than he had thought. Cursing himself for a fool, he edged the nose of his ship a point or two to the east. It was too much: *Dragon's Tail* heeled sharply to port and water poured in over the side. The sail lost the wind and flapped like prolonged thunder.

'Down sail!' roared Harold. 'Out oars!'

The sail came down, an untidy mass athwart the ship, and the oarsmen sought desperately to strike a rhythm before the ship lost way.

Harold swore a goatherd's oath. He had made a mess of it, and now there was nothing to be done but to row along in the longship's wake. It was no consolation to see that Tostig had made the same mistake and was now rowing on a course converging with his own.

He looked admiringly after the longship, now almost stern on, and noted the banks of oars on each side sweeping strongly, forcing the ship through the sea almost as though it was under sail. As soon as the shipmaster had seen what was in store for his craft, he had accelerated his pace and so eluded the trouble.

As he gazed at the figure of the man standing beside the tiller of the longship, he became aware that the outline was familiar. The height . . . the way the man stood . . . If he had not known that Sweyn was by now on his way to London with Beorn . . .

There was little chance of catching the longship, although for a time Tostig urged his seamen to enormous effort. With forty oars against the thirty of the two pursuers, it drew slowly but steadily further ahead, until first the hull and then the mast disappeared below the horizon.

By this time, the Isle of Wight was a distant smear on the northern horizon, and Harold signalled his brother to bring his ship in close.

Side by side, prows to wind, motionless except for the none too gentle undulations of the sea, the ships lay like amiable swans while the oarsmen rested on their oars and the shipmasters shouted through cupped hands.

'What to do next, Harold? He's half-way to Normandy by now.'

Harold shook his head vigorously. 'He'll not try for Normandy with this wind ... he'll double back, either north-east or north-west. Father can have the trouble if he goes north-east — we'll work along the coast to the west.'

Tostig shrugged, seemingly disinterested now that the chance had gone of taking the gold.

Harold cupped his hands to his mouth again: 'Did you note the shipmaster, Tostig?'

'Should I have done?'

'He had the look of Sweyn, I thought.'

Tostig's reply was half-angry and

half-resigned: 'To me he had the look of the Devil.'

Harold laughed and bade his men pull on the oars. When the ship was heading north-west, they shipped the oars and hoisted the sail.

They sheltered for the night at Swanage, and the following day set off to follow the coast westward, close inshore. The wind stayed in the south and the men were at the oars most of the day, but at each town or village with a harbour, one or other of the ships would put in, to make enquiries of the people concerning any strange longship recently sighted.

At the end of the second day, Tostig came to Harold in a peevish mood.

'How long must we carry on with this tedious business, Harold? I should like to eat good food again and spent a night in a comfortable bed.'

'So would I,' said Harold, thinking of his Edith. 'But there is a little voice in my ear saying that we have not seen the last of Sweyn's men.'

'Your little voice should also tell you that our men are tired and have been too long away from their homes,' said Tostig, testily.

Harold thought for a while, and then said: 'We should go as far as Plymouth. By that time, the wind should change to blow from the west, and we shall have a fast sail home.'

'And what if it blows a gale from the east?' Tostig's face had flushed red and the corners of his mouth were taut. 'I tell you, Harold, I'll sail west with you for one day more. Then *Black Snake* heads eastward.'

Harold looked at his brother, trying to keep the anger from his eyes.

'I shall not try to keep you, brother,' he said at last.

'You would be a fool to try,' said Tostig over his shoulder as he stalked off.

Harold watched him go, puzzled and angry.

During the morning of the following day, both ships put into the little harbour at the mouth of the Sid for food and water. There were pilchard fishermen there, busy about their boats, and Harold went over to question them.

Yes, they said, there had been a longship which had passed close by the previous morning, pulling southwards. Not only that, they said, but the same morning a shepherd had come down from the cliffs with the story that the previous evening foreign seamen had bought two sheep from him and taken them away. Being an inquisitive man, the shepherd had followed them in the dusk and had watched them carry the sheep to a longship beached in a sheltered cove below the cliffs.

Had it not been for the vigilance of his two dogs, the shepherd reckoned that the sheep would have been stolen and himself possibly murdered: as it was, they had paid for the animals with a gold piece, and since he had never had gold in his hand before, the shepherd had brought it with him to show to the people of the village.

Harold went back to the ships and hurried the loading of the provisions. To Tostig, he said: 'They have a day's start on us. We should hurry to Dartmouth, where there is a sheltered harbour where they might be tempted to spend more of the gold.'

'Or add to it,' said Tostig, darkly. News of the longship had revived his interest, and there was no trace in his manner of yesterday's bad temper.

They set off with as little delay as possible. During the day, the cloud lowered, and it came on to rain, after which the wind blew from the west and rose in strength.

Harold was pleased, thinking that a westerly wind would delay the longship's departure from Dartmouth and that they might yet have another chance at seizing the gold. He urged the oarsmen to great efforts, and sheltered from the wind and the turbulence of the sea by the high cliffs along the coast, the ships made good progress. But it was growing dusk as they made their way up the river, between the towering hills, which led to Dartmouth.

The village beyond the harbour seemed deserted as they made fast their ships. Harold strode to the nearest dwelling and hammered on the door. After a short time, he pounded it again, and a man's voice, faintly from within, said: 'Are you off the plague ship?'

'There is no plague on my ships. Open the door, you fool.' Harold was tired and wet from the rain, and his voice was harsh.

The door opened a crack, but before Harold could utter the words in his mouth, it was slammed shut again, and he heard the bar drawn across inside.

'God save me,' said Harold, wonderingly. 'What is the matter with the man?'

From beside him, Tostig laughed quietly. 'Your angry voice frightened him and your bulk terrified him. He thinks you are the Devil come for him. Let me try.'

He rapped on the door and said gently: 'You . . . fellow within there. We are the sons of Godwin, earl of Wessex. Open the door to us, if you please.'

The bar scraped back and the door opened, to frame a man, quivering like a jelly-fish and holding the door-post for support.

'My lords . . . your pardon. I had thought you were from the plague-ship.'

'What is this about a plague-ship?' said Harold.

The man almost fell over in his agitation. 'The priest,' he quavered, 'knows more about it than I.'

'Then take us to the priest,' said Harold, kindly.

They followed the man as he scurried up the hill, and led them to a house beside the church which loomed against the darkening sky.

The priest's house had candles and a pot, in which liquid simmered, over a low fire. Harold made himself known and the priest genuflected. Tostig sniffed appreciatively and pointedly at the pot, and a broth, made from vegetables was ladled into wooden bowls.

'The fellow that brought us here,' said Harold, 'prattled about a plague-ship. Is there truth in it?'

'Indeed,' said the priest. 'Last evening, some time before dusk, a longship came from the sea and stood to, just beyond the harbour. The shipmaster shouted across to the fishermen that he had the plague aboard, and that one of his men had died.'

'Did he speak in English?' said Harold.

'He would not have been understood otherwise,' said the priest. 'From the way he spoke, I would say he came from further east. He sounded much as yourselves.'

Harold nodded, and the priest went on, 'Hearing this, the fishermen came for me, and when I had got down to the harbour, the shipmaster shouted that, before he died the man had asked that he be buried in consecrated ground.

'My lords, what could I say? I told him that I could not risk the danger of infection — that no man from the ship, alive or dead, must come ashore. But he was persuasive, and in the end . . . '

'Did he offer you gold?' said Tostig, suddenly.

The priest looked at the ground. 'My lords, the gold shall be put to good works in the village,' he said, rather too quickly.

'And so they came ashore . . . ?' prompted Harold.

'At first light,' said the priest. 'The

111

villagers stayed bolted and barred indoors. Four men came ashore, two carrying the body, wrapped in sailcloth. I had left mattocks and spades for them in the churchyard, and with these they dug deep. After they had left, I said the last rites over the poor fellow's grave, and offered up prayers in the church for the rest of the crew, that God would spare them from the plague.'

'Is the longship still here?' said Harold.

'No, my lord. It left immediately the four men were aboard.'

Harold looked at Tostig. And Tostig looked at Harold. At length, Tostig said: 'Brother Harold, we must open that grave.'

The priest looked startled. 'What . . . would you desecrate the dead? And besides, the man died of the plague.'

Tostig said: 'If there is a man buried there, he did not die of the plague.'

Harold opened his eyes wide at Tostig, as though he could not believe his ears.

The priest said: 'My lords, I cannot allow it. If the bishop should hear of it . . . '

'The bishop,' said Tostig, 'will not hear of it unless you tell him.' He fumbled at his belt and tossed something in the air which glittered red as it caught the candelight. Tostig caught it and held it out for the priest. 'More gold for your good works in the village,' he said.

As they walked back to the ships, Harold felt bemused. He said to Tostig: 'Brother, what are you at?'

Tostig walked jauntily, whistling a little tune.

'Do you not see it?' he said. 'There was no man's body wrapped in that sailcloth. Under the sailcloth is a sheep's skin. And in the sheep's skin is father's gold.'

Harold stared at his brother, and his face betrayed his bewilderment.

Tostig laughed aloud, as much at his own cleverness as at his brother's astonishment.

'They suspect that we are after them for the gold,' he explained, 'so what better place to hide it than in the ground?'

'But why in a churchyard . . . and why this story about the plague.'

'What busybody of a priest will supervise the burial of a plague corpse? And who would dare to dig up a freshly buried body in a churchyard?' Tostig laughed aloud again. 'I'll lay a bet with you that at the next full moon Sweyn's crew will be back with their mattocks and spades at midnight. I'd give a lot to see their faces when they find the gold is gone.'

'My God,' said Harold. 'I would never have thought of that.' He looked at his brother admiringly.

Early the next morning they climbed the steep hill to the church with four of their men. The priest was already there with the digging implements: he looked pale and distraught, and gazed frequently at the sky as if expecting some Divine manifestation.

The four seamen dug into the freshly turned earth, heartily at first, and then more gently as the pit deepened.

Tostig said, under his breath: 'Look at the man of God, Harold. I think he knows what we shall find.'

The priest was gazing unseeingly over the river, his delicate hands folding and unfolding on themselves as if he would pray, but dare not.

One of the seamen gave an exclamation: his spade had uncovered a fold of sailcloth. They laid their tools aside and, with their hands, gently scraped away the loose earth from the whole length of the sailcloth. When it was done, they looked at Harold.

Tostig said: 'I will see to this.'

He smiled at Harold and stepped down into the pit. Stooping, he took a corner of the sailcloth and pulled it to one side; then another. There was laid bare a face as white as marble, the blue-lipped mouth agape, the open eyes staring through Tostig and beyond into the heavens.

The face was Beorn's, and his throat had been cut.

6

Beorn's body was brought to Winchester where it was buried in the old Minster next to the tomb of his uncle, Canute. He had been well-liked in his lifetime, and the manner of his death shocked and angered all those who knew him. Of Sweyn and his longship there was no trace and it was generally believed that Godwin's son was the murderer, and in his absence he was declared an outlaw.

For Godwin, it was a time of great humiliation. At first he held the faint hope that Sweyn was guiltless, or even that his murdered body might be found, for that would be preferable to the present disgrace. But Harold and Tostig were so convinced that Sweyn was the killer that his hope gradually faded, leaving a great sadness that his favourite son had duped him with promises of good behaviour, and a bitterness that with one stroke of a knife he had done more harm to his father than all his political enemies over the years. Gytha, sensitive to his misery, gently reminded him that he had other sons, but Godwin was inconsolable: there could be no substitute for his first-born.

In due course, Harold returned to Hereford. It had occurred to him that Beorn's estates were now untenanted and it might seem logical that they should once more be merged with his own. The idea did not excite him, for he was well content with things as they were.

The same thought occurred to Tostig who was land-hungry and saw it as the chance he had been waiting for. He asked his father to intercede with the king on his behalf. Godwin's vitality was at its lowest ebb: for the first time in his adult life he showed no interest in land or power for his family, and even the suggestion by Tostig that the vacant earldom might pass into hands hostile to the Godwin family did not seem to rouse him from his apathy. So Tostig pestered his father daily until the earl reluctantly agreed to make the journey to Westminster.

When he returned from his journey, Gytha had news for him.

'Sweyn is in Bruges,' she told him.

Godwin stared at her. Hope flickered and was firmly snuffed out.

'A messenger came from Count Baldwin. He asks you to go to see Sweyn as soon as possible.'

Godwin flung his riding cloak to the floor. 'I shall not go,' he said, angrily. 'I have had enough of Sweyn.'

Gytha watched him stride across the hall with all his old resolve. 'If only you meant it,' she said, softly to herself.

For several hours, Godwin kept to himself, so engrossed with the message from Bruges that he had forgotten that he had been to Westminster. Tostig, who had been pacing the floor as though it was red hot, could no longer contain his anxiety, dared to seek him out and ask the question which was burning his tongue.

Godwin looked at his auburn-haired son for a moment before answering.

'The honour is already granted,' he said, gruffly.

'To Harold?' There was bitterness in Tostig's voice, and the colour rose to his cheeks.

'To Ralf of Mantes.' Godwin watched his son's expression change to one of puzzlement. He added, 'The king's nephew . . . and a Frenchman.'

'A Frenchman . . . ' Tostig was angry again. 'God in Heaven! We have Norman bishops and abbots . . . and now a French earl. Are we to be ruled by foreigners?'

Godwin approved of Tostig's anger. 'There are those who wish it,' he growled. 'And some of those who could prevent it cannot see beyond the ends of their noses. Pray God that their eyes are uncrossed before it is too late.'

Tostig began to laugh, silently and with his hand across his mouth.

'What is so funny?' snapped Godwin.

Tostig controlled himself. 'I had a sudden thought of Harold . . . will he like his new neighbour, do you think?' He began to laugh again.

Godwin watched him unsmiling. 'It is

time you were married, Tostig. You and I will go to Bruges to make the arrangements with Baldwin.'

★ ★ ★

The news of Beorn's murder had been brought to the king not long after he had returned to London from Sandwich. Shocked though he was by the senseless savagery of the crime, he approved the outlawing of Sweyn with some regret, since it removed his hold on Godwin before he had had the chance to use it.

His wife, the lady Edith, wept when she heard the news, and Edward, who had treated her distantly of late, felt sad for her. He comforted her, saying that Sweyn was unworthy of her tears.

Edith dried her eyes with a silken kerchief. 'It is not for Sweyn that I weep: it is for Beorn, who loved life, and for my father who loved both Beorn and Sweyn.'

Edward wondered how it was that in the same family there could be such diverse characters as Edith and Sweyn. Presently he said: 'Why do you think

Sweyn should have done this?'

Edith shook her head. 'There is only one person who can tell you that. And I doubt that he knows the true answer himself.'

The king nodded his understanding. 'He is a strange man,' he said. 'He came to me at Sandwich and gave me the rough edge of his tongue.'

Edith listened while her husband told her what had passed between himself and Sweyn, and how afterwards Godwin had come to see him. 'I tell you,' he finished ruefully, 'that with one thing and another, Sandwich was not a happy place for me.'

She questioned him further and he told her of the gales and contrary winds, of the troubles in the town and the country around, and how in the end he had had to disperse the fleet because of the lack of provisions. 'It was God's way of teaching me that I am neither a seaman or a leader of men,' he said smiling. 'The lesson is learnt: in future I shall leave such undertakings to those who know best.'

It warmed his heart to see her smile with him, and he leaned forward and took her hand. 'There was another thing I had to bear, far worse than all those put together.' He spoke to her of what bishop Robert had told him concerning her chaplain, Ralf. She looked at him with pain in her eyes and would have withdrawn her hand, but he held it tightly between both his own.

'Did you believe this gossip, my lord?'

Edward shook his head. 'Never . . . but in my darkest hours the thought of it returned to me, and I raged that there should be servants of mine so disloyal as to slander my beloved lady.'

'What shall you do with them?'

'Bishop Robert has already sent them away. Think of missing faces among the servants and you will know who had the long, ugly tongues.'

Edith smiled. 'Then it is well: we are as we always have been.'

Edward stood up and went to the table to pour wine for them both. Edith tried to remember what faces were missing among the servants. And when she could think of none, she began to wonder about bishop Robert.

If Robert could have known what was passing through the lady Edith's mind, he would not have worried overmuch. More and more, Edward was turning to him for guidance, not only in Church matters but in the affairs of State. Concerning the disposal of Beorn's earldom, the king had been loth to return it to a member of the Godwin family, but he lacked the courage to take it from them in favour of the family of the ascetic earl Leofric.

In this state of indecision, he spoke to Robert, who was not one to waste an opportunity of furthering his designs.

'It is simple, Sire. The honour should go to one who owes allegiance neither to Godwin nor Leofric and can therefore reserve his loyalty for yourself.' Robert had several names in mind, each as Norman as his own.

But Edward did not ask for names. 'I have it,' he said. 'My nephew Ralf, who hold Mantes of the French king. I shall give it to him for my sister's sake.'

Robert was not displeased. He knew Ralf to be as French as his father and a hard man, not given to sentiment. His place in the Councils would give a voice, not for Edward, but for Robert.

In addition, Robert knew that Edsig, Archbishop of Canterbury for many years, was failing in health and being old, could not last much longer. Robert prized Canterbury for himself: it would give him power, prestige and wealth, and he knew that Edward would not keep it from him. And the man he had in mind to succeed himself as bishop of London would add yet another Norman voice in the Councils of the realm.

And best of all, in Sweyn's disgrace and the lowered prestige of the Godwins, Robert saw that the way was clear for the setting up of his plans for the final overthrow of the family.

★　★　★

Count Baldwin welcomed Godwin and Tostig to Bruges without reserve and told them that Sweyn was not himself and would not stir from his room.

They found him staring listlessly out of the window, and as he came towards

124

them, Godwin noticed that his face was pale and gaunt and that his frame seemed in some way smaller than when he had last seen him.

Father and son greeted one another with a wordless clasp of the hands, but Tostig stood aloof, looking anywhere but at his brother.

'You think me a murderer . . .' Sweyn's voice was cracked with tiredness and emotion.

'I did not say so,' Godwin answered gently, and drew up chairs so that they could all sit at the table. Tostig drew his chair away and sat so that he could watch the faces of both the others.

'Come now,' said Godwin, 'tell us how it was.'

Sweyn told of the ride to Bosham and how, arriving before mid-day, he had suggested going straight to the harbour to pay off his crew. 'Beorn said it was none of his business, and that he would go straight to the hall. But since he had half the gold under his cloak, I persuaded him. I wish to God I had not . . . none of this would have happened.'

Of how they had gone on board the ship and handed over the bags of gold, and how, when it had been counted, one of the seamen had said, 'It is not enough.'

'I told them that they would get no more: at which this man said, 'We shall see about that,' and before we could make a move to defend ourselves, we were both thrown down, bound and gagged. And at the same time, the ship put to sea.'

He told how, when they were well out at sea, they were untrussed and told that they were to be taken to Ireland and held captive until more gold was paid for their ransome.

When the ship put ashore at night, they were bound again, and it was on one of these occasions that Beorn, having managed to slip his bonds, tried to jump ashore.

'They were too watchful, father. They caught him before he had left the ship, but he struggled and fought like a madman, while I had to lie and watch. There was enough noise and hullaballoo to waken the dead . . . and suddenly the flash of a knife blade, and it was all quiet again. Poor Beorn . . . '

'How did you get away?' asked Godwin.

'They let me go as soon as they heard that I had been outlawed. They told me I could join them as a seaman, but I would sooner have flung myself from a cliff. And, father, I could not let you think that I had killed poor Beorn.'

Sweyn's eyes were pleading. Godwin stroked his beard while he considered. The story had a ring of truth, and Sweyn's manner in telling it had been sincere. Yet there were details that had to be put to the test. He looked at Tostig.

Tostig drew a deep breath and leaned forward in his chair. 'Tell me, brother, who was the shipmaster on this voyage?'

'It was a man who called himself Aylmar . . . an Englishman from Dover,' Sweyn answered, readily enough.

'A short, fat man with yellow hair?'

Sweyn gave the ghost of a smile. 'He was as tall as myself and had dark hair.'

'As dark as your own,' said Tostig evenly. 'After we had discovered the body at Dartmouth, we closely questioned the

127

priest, and he remembered that the shipmaster wore a cloak secured by a clasp set with a dark red jewel. It is strange, is it not, that this English shipmaster, Aylmar, as tall and powerful as yourself, with hair as dark as yours, should wear a jewel identical to the one you wore that day you came to us out of the rain at Pevensey?'

Sweyn looked down at the table, his lips thin. 'It is not strange at all,' he said quietly. 'It was my clasp that he wore. He took it on the first day of the voyage, and for all I know he still has it.'

'Oh, of course,' said Tostig. 'I should have thought of that for myself.' He looked at the ceiling, whistling softly between his teeth.

Save for the tuneless whistling, the room was silent. Tostig, conscious that the other two were watching him closely, leaned back in his chair.

'There is one more thing that puzzles me,' he said. 'If I had killed a man on board ship I would have cast the body overboard with a weight to its feet. This Aylmar . . . was he so pious that he had to bury the body of a man he had murdered in consecrated ground?'

Sweyn swallowed hard, and looked at his father. 'It is easy for Tostig to be scathing. He believes me guilty — he will believe nothing that I say.'

'It is a good question,' said Godwin. 'Answer it.'

Sweyn licked his lips. 'Beorn was more to me than a cousin — he was a good friend. When he was killed, it was as though I had taken the knife in my own throat, and when they were going to tip him overboard it was more than I could bear . . . I went on my knees to them, pleading for a decent burial for him.

'They laughed at me, so I told them that he had the blood of Canute in his veins and that my father would pay much gold if the body were to be buried where it could later be found. So they fell to discussing among themselves how it could be done and eventually agreed on the story that he had died from the plague.' He looked at them in turn, his eyes pleading.

There was a long silence. Finally,

Godwin said: 'Well, Tostig? Do you believe your brother?'

Tostig looked at the ceiling again. 'It is as good a story as any,' he said carelessly, 'and better than no story at all.'

Sweyn leaped to his feet and flung his arms wide in a gesture of appeal.

'Tostig! I swear before God . . . '

Tostig laughed quietly. 'I have not called you a liar, Sweyn. What does Father say?'

Godwin had no hesitation. 'I believe that Sweyn has been unjustly accused and punished.'

'So be it,' said Tostig. 'That is what I believe.'

Sweyn gave a little moan of relief. Godwin leaned across the table and patted his shoulder and noticed that there were tears in his son's eyes.

'There are things to be done,' he said, 'and pleas to be made. Until it is settled you must stay here with Baldwin. But it will not be for long.'

Sweyn looked his father in the eyes. 'I have no wish to return to England. I shall make a pilgrimage to the Holy Land.'

Godwin smiled: a kind father humouring a tearful son. 'Be easy — a few weeks of good food and plentiful rest and you will feel differently.'

Tostig watched them, his eyes thoughtful. There was one more question to be resolved — and it could not be asked of Sweyn.

7

The winter that followed was the mildest for many years, but shortly after the time of Christmas there was a period of incessant rain which went on into February, so that men slipped and slithered on the sodden ground and prayed for a drying wind or a hard frost. And when they went into the warmth of their homes, their clothes steamed like the flanks of a hard-ridden horse, and the dampness seeped into everything, even the straw of their beds. The rivers burst their banks and the roads became quagmires, making long journeys impossible, while even a short journey had the quality of a nightmare with the constant sucking of the mud at the horses' hooves and legs. So it was not until well into March that the Great Council was able to convene at Westminster.

This was the occasion for which Godwin had been preparing since his return from Bruges, and he sat impatiently through a great deal of what seemed trivial business before he could raise the matter of Sweyn's outlawry.

The Council listened to Godwin's eloquent version of Sweyn's story with attitudes ranging from polite indifference to ill-concealed scepticism, and the earl judged, with a certain amount of relish, that he was in for a long, hard fight before he got his way. He was amazed when, after he was finished, the king spoke up to say that as there was no proof in either direction, the most just course was to give Sweyn the benefit of the doubt, and he therefore intended to revoke the sentence of outlawry.

Godwin was not the only one to be amazed: later in the day, bishop Robert spoke to Edward, querying his decision. The king gave a crafty smile and told Robert of the thought that had occurred to him at Sandwich.

Robert shrugged the matter off: if his plans went as he intended, not only Sweyn but the rest of the brood would cease to bother him before very long.

Leofric of Mercia, his nose seeming longer and thinner than usual because he felt piqued, grumbled to Siward of Northumbria: 'Godwin has charmed the king out of his senses. While he was speaking that nonsense about his precious son I was reminded of the Council when Harthacanute accused him of causing the death of Alfred the Atheling.'

'Aye,' grunted Siward. 'But it took more than words to convince Harthacanute . . . a fully manned longship, if my memory is correct.'

'With a gold-plated dragon's head on the prow, and a chest full of gold beside the tiller.' Leofric had a memory for such things.

Siward spat on the floor and muttered to himself.

The newly honoured earl Ralf, the king's nephew, was at the Council, and Godwin saw that he spent much time with bishop Robert and the other Normans. He asked Harold what sort of a man Ralf was.

Harold shrugged. 'We have not spoken together, but I have heard that he is a great man for the hunt. There is a rumour that his favourite quarry is a man.'

Godwin looked sharply at his son, but Harold was not joking. He went on: 'I have it as the truth that he means to build a stone castle on his estate.'

Frowning, Godwin watched Ralf and noted the bull neck, the close cropped hair and the pig-like eyes. Things had gone far enough, he decided. England should be for the English.

In May, Tostig was married to Judith at Bruges. The celebrations went on for the best part of a week, with as much food and drink as anyone could wish for and with entertainments which included musicians, jugglers, wrestlers and story-tellers, and there was hunting and hawking in the countryside around for those who had the energy.

When the time came for Godwin and Sweyn to leave, Baldwin took the earl on one side. He had known Sweyn in the old days and he knew of Godwin's concern for the future.

'Sweyn,' he said, 'is a changed man. He would not disgrace a monastery — butter would not melt in his mouth.'

Godwin's pleasure at hearing this was tinged with a certain regret. Watching his son during the past celebrations, he had found himself thinking of a castrated bull.

When they returned to Winchester, Harold was waiting for them, having travelled from Hereford a few days previously. The two brothers greeted each other without enthusiasm, for Harold could not forget the figure of the man at the tiller of the longship, and Sweyn could sense Harold's hostility towards him.

That evening, when Godwin and Gytha were alone, Harold came to them with the news that Edith, his wife, was with child. For a while there was gay chatter and laughter, until Harold made a plea for the earl to take Edith into the family.

He judged that because of the coming of their first grandchild, his mother would add her pleading to his own, and he was not disappointed. But Godwin was adamant: wearily and a little sadly, he repeated his reasons, and for a long time the argument went back and forth but without rancour, for Harold had the greatest respect for his father.

At last, he said: 'But what power shall I ever have, except in Hereford? And that I would gladly give up for Edith's sake, now that Sweyn is back in favour.'

Godwin held up his hand. 'Sweyn is back,' he said, 'but he is not in favour, and I doubt that he ever will be. Besides, he talks of a pilgrimage to Jerusalem before he goes into a monastery.'

Harold burst out laughing. 'Sweyn in a monastery? He cannot be serious!'

Godwin did not smile. 'He is more serious than I would like. I shall try to dissuade him, but you must be prepared to take over the responsibilities of an eldest son.'

Harold fell silent. The news which should have pleased him had struck a chill in his heart.

After a day or two, he rode miserably back to Hereford. Edith Swan-neck, his wife, saw his mood at a glance.

'Come, now,' she said, lightly, 'is the whole world against you?'

'I have done my best, but Father will

137

not change his mind.'

'Did he say why?'

Harold did not answer. He could not bring himself to tell her the reason for the earl's obstinacy.

'Never mind,' said Edith, as though it was of no account. 'We shall still have each other.'

He looked at her for a moment, seeing the sparkle of her smile and the light of love in her eyes. He knew that he would rather die than betray her.

'Yes,' he said fiercely, 'we shall always have each other.' He picked her up in his arms and held her close to him.

'My love,' said Edith, laughing. 'You have forgotten that I am fragile.'

Gently, he set her down and smiled at her. 'I should not worry — mother is on our side, and she can twist father around her little finger when she has the mind to.'

But in his heart he knew that nothing would change his father's mind.

Harold was conscientious on behalf of his people. As often as possible, he journeyed around his earldom, meeting his reeves and mixing with the common people, and every man, however humble, knew that he had the ear of the earl and that any wrong would be set right. Also, the Welsh raiders who, in the past, had often pillaged deep into the shire, now sought their plunder elsewhere through fear of Harold's housecarls. For these reasons, he was well-liked and respected, so that he was able to travel the countryside with only a few of his men as companions.

That summer, one of his journeys took him and his three men close to the eastern boundary of his earldom. They were riding a path through thick wood-land when, faintly, there came the sound of baying dogs and the thin note of a hunting horn.

Harold cocked an ear, and the horse beneath him jigged with excitement.

'Who hunts this forest?' said Harold.

'We shall soon know ... they are coming closer,' said Aldred, who rode beside him.

They rode on slowly, listening. The sounds of the chase waxed and waned among the trees, until suddenly, to the baying of the dogs was added the whooping of excited men. Ahead of them there was a sudden crashing in the undergrowth.

Straining his eyes for a sight of the quarry, Harold did not at first see the horsemen as they galloped round the corner ahead, until a voice, hoarse with urgency, shouted: 'You there . . . out of the way!'

Harold reined in his horse and turned it so that the path was blocked. The huntsman slowed to a stop a few paces away: his red face showed a mixture of anger and surprise.

Harold said: 'Who hunts my forest without leave?'

Red face stared. 'Your forest . . . ?'

Harold said nothing, but looked him up and down.

From behind Red Face, another horseman forced his way to the front: a dark, thick-set man with cropped hair and pig's eyes.

'What is this nonsense?' he said forcefully.

'Greetings, earl Ralf,' said Harold with

a pleasantness he did not feel.

The Frenchman looked startled, then laughed — a harsh, unhumorous noise.

'Harold Godwinson . . . brother of the infamous Sweyn. Did I hear you claim this forest as yours?'

The tone was offensive to the point of insult, and Harold felt the warmth rising to his cheeks, but he answered evenly: 'In the valley to the east there is a stream — cross it, and you can hunt your own boar.'

Ralf looked at him from beneath his black eyebrows. 'If this is your land . . . which I doubt . . . would you grudge a neighbour some sport?'

'That depends,' said Harold icily, 'on the neighbour.'

From his bull-neck to his hairline, Ralf flushed an angry red. 'By God . . . will you be so haughty, Harold Godwinson, when you have no land?'

'Whoever takes it from me will be a better man than you.'

Ralf spat on the ground and turned his horse with a vicious flourish. Harold watched with pursed lips as the party disappeared from sight.

Beside him, Aldred was staring past Harold to a thorn thicket. 'Unless I am much mistaken,' he said softly, the boar they were hunting was two-legged. Hold my horse while I make sure.'

He dismounted and walked slowly to peer into the depths of the thicket. Presently, he beckoned the other two housecarls to join him, and Harold watched as they hacked at the under-growth with their swords. Then they laid aside their weapons and gently drew out a man. His clothes were in tatters and his face was lacerated and stained with blood.

They helped him to his feet, and Aldred told him gently that he was among friends and would not be hurt, while Harold eyed the gashes on his face and pronounced them to look worse than they were. So they mounted him behind Aldred and rode on until they came to a stream, where they washed his face and head clean of the dried blood.

His name, he said, was Hodda and he had been a swineherd until yesterday, when two of earl Ralf's men had seized him and told him that he was charged with poaching deer from the earl's forest. Hodda had laughed at them, saying that if they could find meat, skin or bone anywhere near his hut he would plead guilty and cut his own throat. But he was taken before earl Ralf, who told him that on the next day he would be tried by ordeal.

He told of the desperate, breathless chase across country, when fear gave strength to his legs, making for the stream which he knew as the ending of Ralf's lands, using every trick that he knew to throw the dogs from the scent — tearing his way through the brambles and thorns of the densest part of the forest to delay the men on horseback. And finally, the despair and horror when he realised that Ralf recognised no boundaries.

'That last thicket . . . the one you dragged me from . . . I could never have made my own way out.'

Harold had listened with growing anger, but he also marvelled at the courage and strength of purpose of the swineherd. To Aldred, he said: 'This is a brave man. What can we do for him?'

Aldred looked at Hodda. 'Do you know anything of horses?'

'I was born in a stable.'

'Then you shall work in mine,' said Harold.

Hodda smiled his thanks although the gashes in his cheeks made him wince with the pain of it.

* * *

In October, Archbishop Edsig died. He was known as a good and kind man and there was much sadness, even among the common people, when the news of his passing became known.

Robert did not lament: he went straightaway to the king and made his claim to the Archbishopric.

Edward raised his eyebrows at Robert's haste. 'Did you fear that I would give it to anyone else?'

'Sire,' said Robert, 'such a thought never entered my head. But the attainment of this office has been my ambition

144

for many years. Besides,' he added, 'Edsig was very old, and old men grow lax in their work. There are many things which should be done urgently.'

As much as he loved Robert, Edward did not like to hear such things said of Edsig, for whom he had had a great respect. Nevertheless, he smiled at Robert and told him to go to Rome as soon as possible to receive his pallium from the Pope.

Robert did not waste an hour. It had been inconsiderate of Edsig to die in the autumn because the road to Rome led through a pass in the mountains which, more often than not, was impassable in winter. But he thought that if he travelled in haste he would be able to return before the worst of the winter set in.

As it happened, the snow came early that year, and Robert was forced to winter in Rome. This galled him because he had much to do in England, but he spent the time as profitably as he could, although since the politics at the Papal Court were extremely complex it was difficult to discern who might or might not be of use to him in the future. But so that he should not be quickly forgotten, he made many rich gifts to the countless churches in the city.

As soon as it was possible, he started on his homeward journey, but made a detour to the west, to Caen in Normandy where he sought an audience with Duke William.

The Duke listened to what he had to say without interruption, although he was sceptical.

'I have heard it said that my cousin Edward cannot father children,' he said, 'but I had thought it no more than a jest. But surely he will name a man of his own race as his successor?'

'My lord,' said Robert, 'the country is divided — the North against the South. Edward keeps it so: it is the only way he can rule, playing one off against the other. But now, the Great Council contains a third faction — those who would have you as their next king, and I have long worked to turn Edward himself to this way of thinking.'

William furrowed his dark brows in

thought. England was a rich prize which he had long coveted, but it had always seemed out of his reach because he had only the flimsiest of claims.

'Surely the English will unite to fight for a king of their own choosing?'

'The rift is too deep,' said Robert. 'Each side is filled with distrust of the other. But there is one man who would fight, even though the rest stood by and watched: Godwin of Wessex, who covets the crown for himself or one of his sons.'

William had heard much of Godwin, of his great wealth and the respect he commanded in the South of England.

'Believe me, Robert of Canterbury,' he said, 'I have more than enough fighting on my hands already, against my own barons.'

Robert smiled and spread his hands. 'My lord, your accession will be bloodless. I have a plan to deal with Godwin which will make it seem as though he and his sons had never been.'

Duke William was not a man to believe in miracles or magic. He gave Robert a stare from under his brows which would have turned a lesser man to jelly. But Robert was not abashed.

'It will not be easy,' he said, 'for the man holds much power and his daughter is the king's lady. But if God wills that you be king of England, I shall have His firm guidance.'

'If it is possible,' said William, 'then do it.'

After Robert had gone, William sent for his friend and adviser, Lanfranc, and told him what had been said. 'This Archbishop Robert — either he is a windbag or he is too clever. If it is one, he is a nuisance; if the other, he is dangerous. We must wait to see the truth.'

Robert made his way to Boulogne, but before he took ship for England, he spent some time in discussion with Count Eustace, a friend of long standing who agreed to help him in the way he required.

In Canterbury, his arrival was expected, and the long-prepared plans for the ceremony of his installation as Archbishop were put into effect within two days. But Robert's head was so full of his plans for the downfall of the Godwin family that he barely noticed the great pomp and magnificence, and immediately after the ceremony he set off for London.

At Rochester, where he stopped for the night, was Spearhafoc, a rotund and placid English priest who was known to Robert as the abbot of Abingdon Priory and a man of no account. Spearhafoc had heard of Robert's return and was on his way to Canterbury: he was delighted that he would not have to continue the journey, for he was not fond of travel. He sought out Robert and gave him a parchment bearing the king's seal.

Robert broke the seal, and as he read the Latin, his eyes widened and he became angry, for the message was that he should consecrate Spearhafoc as Bishop of London.

Robert raged and beat his temples with his clenched fists: that Spearhafoc should be bishop nullified all his plans, for he believed the abbot to be one of Godwin's creatures. But it was enough that he was English, and he shouted at Spearhafoc as though he were a stray dog.

That night, Robert lost much sleeping time, mulling over what had occurred. The shock of learning that his carefully laid plans were at risk had caused him to lose his temper and act in a manner which he now knew to have been foolish. Not one to concern himself with remorse, he set about thinking of a way to set matters right, and early the next morning he continued his journey to London.

Edward welcomed him warmly, and questioned him about his dealings with Pope Leo and his long stay in Rome. When the conversation turned to affairs at home, and Spearhafoc was mentioned, Robert complained gently that the decision had not been deferred until his return.

'You were so long gone, Robert. And the abbot is a good and wise man who seemed the natural choice.'

Robert stared at the floor, biting his lip as though embarrassed. At length, he said: 'It is unfortunate, Sire, but I had another name in mind. And Pope Leo approved of my choice.'

Edward raised his eyebrows. 'What name was that?'

'Brother William, Sire. Your chaplain.'

'William . . . ?' Edward was plainly taken aback.

Robert was a smooth liar. 'When I mentioned brother William as my successor as bishop, the Pope asked many questions concerning his ability. And then he told me that he had faith in my judgement and that I should consecrate William as bishop.'

Edward looked away from Robert in case he should see the annoyance in his eyes. The Pope, he ruminated, had the final word in the choice of an Archbishop, but the appointment of a bishop was the king's prerogative. A surge of obstinacy swept through him: it was right that he should make a stand as a matter of principle.

'As a chaplain,' he said, 'I am well satisfied with brother William, but he lacks experience as an administrator. Spearhafoc has proved his worth in that respect — that is one of the reasons why I appointed him.'

151

'Sire, it is not too late to change,' said Robert, doggedly.

'I will not disappoint him, Robert. He shall be bishop.'

Robert saw the obstinacy in the king's expression, and he felt the anger well up within him. But he swallowed hard and hid his face by inclining his head.

'As you wish, Sire, but in view of what has gone before, I must ask that a message be sent to the Pope explaining what has occurred. When his reply is received I shall feel able to consecrate Spearhafoc with a clear conscience.'

Edward shrugged. He had won a little victory, but he could see that he had hurt Robert's feelings. He became conciliatory. 'You have deferred to my wishes, Robert, now I shall defer to yours. Send your message — Spearhafoc must wait.'

Robert withdrew not dissatisfied. Until he was consecrated, Spearhafoc could not sit in the Great Council, and as things were, Robert could still implement his plan.

8

No more than a week later, Count Eustace of Boulogne arrived in London. A heavily-built man, florid of face with deep-set eyes, he had ridden from Dover at the head of a retinue of forty men, French and Norman, with byrnies under their cloaks and war-swords hanging from their belts. By his side rode Alan, the captain of his guard, whose face was scarred with the marks of battles and brawls.

Edward received his brother-in-law without enthusiasm. He had known Eustace for many years and had never liked him, for the two men were opposite in nature, the one gentle and pious, the other brash and fun-loving — and Eustace's idea of fun had often caused Edward to wince and avert his eyes. Nevertheless, he accepted the gift of saintly relics with good grace and kept to himself the thought that there was more

153

to the visit than mere courtesy.

Only to the lady Edith did he mention his doubts.

'I shall be glad when he is gone,' he finished wearily. 'The more I see of him, the less I like him.'

'Patience, my lord,' said Edith. 'He will soon tire of our company. I fancy that self-restraint does not come easily for him.'

It was as Edith had said: on the evening of the second day of his visit, Eustace made his farewells, and early the next morning he set out on his return journey.

It was the evening of the following day when he halted his men a mile or two from Dover.

'Alan,' he said. 'We shall rest for the night in Dover.' He bared his teeth, and Alan grinned back, knowingly.

'Take two good men,' went on Eustace, 'and ride on ahead to arrange our billets. Good billets, mind you — none of your barns and stables.'

'None but the best, Sire.' Alan knew what was to be done and was looking forward to the fun.

'And Alan . . . be not too gentle in your manner. They are only English peasants.'

Laughing, Alan signed to two of his bulkiest men to follow him and rode off towards the town. Briefly, he told them what was expected, and when they came to the first houses, squat in the gloom, with thatched roofs crouched upon walls of wattle and daub, he drew rein and dismounted, leaving his companions astride their horses.

He selected a house at random and banged noisily on the door. It opened a crack and Alan kicked the bottom of it hard, so that it flew open. The man holding it staggered back, his face showing surprise and anger.

'Hey, there,' said Alan loudly, 'we want shelter for the night.'

The man tried to slam the door, but Alan took the force of it on his shoulder and seized the man's arm.

'What are you at?' he shouted. 'Have you no manners?' He forced his way into the doorway and gave the man a push which sent him sprawling. There was a flurry of skirts on the far side of the room, and the light from the fire reflected on a white, frightened face.

'You . . . Woman . . . ' bellowed Alan, taking a step towards her.

The man on the floor picked himself up and, crouching low, he came at Alan like a ball of fury. Seeing the glint of naked steel, Alan grabbed for the hilt of his sword, but before he could draw the blade the man was on him like a soundless whirlwind, his right arm flailing. Alan felt a sharp pain in his left forearm and another in his left thigh, and felt the hot blood trickle. Using his strength and weight, he managed to push the man away from him for a second or two, but it was like grappling with a mad dog — he could gain no respite to collect himself. He became aware that the woman was screaming — an unceasing, high-pitched screech, deafening in the confined space. And that unless he could get out of the wretched hovel he was going to be badly mauled — or worse.

It was easier than he thought: using his fists and forearms to fend off his attacker, he was inching his way gradually towards the doorway when an unusually heavy butt from the little Englishman threw him off-balance and he staggered back, to crash heavily on his back on the earth outside. Shocked and surprised, he prepared to meet another attack, but to his relief the door was slammed shut, and he heard the bar slide across.

As he picked himself up from the dust, relief changed to annoyance. Inside the hovel, there had been no time for anger — his first feeling of mild amusement had given way to irritation, but now that he had been literally thrown out — and by a man half his size and weight — a red rage seized him, and he drew his sword with a savage curse.

His two companions were still on their horses, staring down the road which led into the town. Beyond them, in the dusk, Alan could make out a semi-circle of figures, motionless but menacing, like wolves attracted by a camp fire in the forest.

'Drive them off,' he shouted in a voice harsh with anger. 'Ride them down . . . '

As he turned away, he heard the thud

of hooves as heels drove into flanks: then he fixed his attention on the door. It was made of stout oak and after a cut or two with his sword he knew that only an axe would make any impression on it. Frustrated, he slashed at the thatching: it was tinder-dry — it would burn like a torch . . .

The commotion down the road reached a sudden crescendo — men shouting — somebody screaming. Alan stepped back and peered into the gloom: he could make out the two horses — riderless — rearing and bucking, while on the ground were two indistinct heaps which seemed to writhe and change shape in the half-light. He was reminded of skinners at work on slaughtered deer.

The anger left him and he felt the short hairs at the back of his neck begin to prickle. His horse was where he had left it, its ears laid back as it pawed nervously at the ground. Some of the English were taking an interest in him — approaching slowly along each side of the road, keeping close to the buildings. Without taking his eyes off them he moved quickly to the horse and mounted it, the action making him aware that the knife wounds were more than pin-pricks. With a last look at the bodies of his two companions, he wheeled his horse and forced it into a gallop along the road to Canterbury.

Count Eustace was where he had left him, mounted at the head of his men. He looked quizzically at Alan, noting his torn garments and the wet blood.

'They are stirred up, then?'

'A hornet's nest . . . but I lost my two men to them.'

Eustace chuckled deep in his throat. 'A cheap price . . . but I think we should teach these peasants a lesson.' He drew his sword and turned in his stirrups, shouting to those behind: 'Follow me closely . . . Any Englishman is fair game . . . a silver piece to every man who bloods his sword.'

They rode through the town like a whirlwind, stones and dust flying from the horses hooves. The English in their path melted into the deep shadows between the hovels, and when they reached the deserted harbour, not one man had blood on his sword.

Eustace, sweating slightly from his exertions, looked back at the town and said, 'God, what cowards . . . ' and spat on the ground as a measure of his contempt for all things English. Then he gave the order to return the way they had come.

It was easier said than done: as they rode a hail of stones and sharp flints descended on them from each side and there were jeers and catcalls from dark passageways. When this became unbearable, hot-headed Frenchmen would force their horses into narrow alleyways where men with knives and oak staves and even pitchforks waited for them.

Eustace, his cheek cut by a flying stone, rode grimly on, the thought uppermost in his mind to get his men clear of the town. Progress was difficult, because now the English rolled round stones and wooden casks amongst the horses, and to the uproar of shouts and howls was added the shrill whinneying of frightened beasts.

At last, distant enough for safety, they turned their horses and waited for stragglers. Eustace dabbed at his face with his sleeve, while Alan strained his eyes into the darkness and counted his men as they came cantering up. Not one of them was without a cut or bruise, and Alan could not remember a time when he had seen men so sullen and subdued after an action.

The night became silent, and a cold wind caused them to shiver a little. Alan turned his horse and rode to where Eustace waited.

'All told, Sire, we are seventeen men short.'

Eustace whistled between his teeth and looked at Alan, whose eyes were hard and expectant, revealing what was in his mind.

'No, Alan,' he said. 'Enough is enough. We have done what was asked of us — now we shall rest the night in Canterbury. And tomorrow, you and I will ride for London, to show our scars to the king.'

Alan stared towards the town. 'We should not forget this place, Sire.'

The Count growled at the back of his

throat. 'I shall make sure that this place does not forget Eustace of Boulogne.'

Edward listened to Eustace's version of what had occurred with eyes widened in horror and incomprehension. He sat for a while, staring at the floor and shaking his head from side to side. Then the colour rushed to his face, his fists clenched and he began to rant in a loud, shrill voice.

Eustace watched him with a secret amusement. He had seen children work themselves into noisy rages, and sometimes a woman, but never had he watched a grown man — and a king at that — let loose such a storm of shrill temper. When at last the tempest had blown itself out, and Edward sat speechless and white with fury, Archbishop Robert stepped forward and placed his hand on Edward's shoulder.

'Sire . . . be easy,' he said, soothingly. Edward leaned back in his chair and shielded his eyes with his long white hand.

'This is Godwin's doing,' said Robert, quietly.

Edward looked at him sharply. 'Godwin?

Why do you say that?'

'Sire, it is well known that he was greatly angered when you gave Beorn's earldom to Ralf instead of to Harold or Tostig. Since then, he has been raising his voice against the number of honours given to men of French and Norman birth. This ... massacre ... is an expression of his resentment — he has incited the people of Dover to rebellion.'

The king's temper began to rise again. 'By all the Saints, Robert ... can it be proved against him?'

The Archbishop shook his head. 'I think not. There will be some cock and bull story of provocation by Count Eustace's men ... ' He stopped speaking and looked fleetingly at Eustace, who fingered the cut on his cheek to hide the twitching at the corners of his mouth.

'I have it ... ' Robert spoke as though suddenly inspired. 'Godwin shall proclaim his own guilt.'

Edward was at a loss for words. He looked appealingly at Robert.

'It is simple, Sire. The men of Dover must be punished — the town must be razed to the ground. Now, if your own men carry out the burning, there's the end of the matter . . . crime committed, punishment exacted. And no doubt Godwin will secretly recompense his people for their losses. But suppose you command Godwin to carry out the punishment himself?'

The king began to understand: he leaned forward in his chair, his eyes alert.

'If he is innocent . . . ' Robert went on, 'If he had no foreknowledge, then he will do as he is bid. But if he is guilty . . . '

'He will refuse.' Edward looked at Eustace, a slow smile spreading across his face. 'By Heaven, Robert, it is masterly. A refusal, and we shall know him for a traitor and a rebel . . . Have the order written on a parchment, Robert, and it shall be sent to him under my seal.'

Robert gave the wording of the command much thought, for he wanted to anger Godwin. And when, later, Eustace praised him for the way he had manipulated the king, he gave a rare smile.

'It was not difficult, for the king has

always hated Godwin. Sometimes the hate lies dormant, but it is easily stirred with the right spoon.'

'Suppose,' said Eustace, 'that Godwin does as the king bids him?'

Robert shook his head. 'You do not know Godwin. He shouts 'England for the English' in the market places, and he will not martyr Dover for striking a blow in his cause. Especially,' he added looking hard at Eustace, 'since by the time he receives the king's command he will have heard a different version of the affair.'

Eustace laughed. 'I feel almost sorry for the fellow.'

'Do not waste your pity. He is as wily as a fox, and for that reason, I want him to act hastily in anger.' He was thoughtful for a moment. 'To add insult to injury, I know the very man to carry the message.'

'Good Robert,' said Eustace, 'I have done as you asked, and I have lost seventeen good men in the doing of it. You will not forget what you promised at Boulogne?'

'The earldom of Kent? You shall have it

as a mark of my gratitude — and Edward's.'

'Must I wait long?' Eustace was thinking of the humiliation he had suffered at Dover: the smarting would remain until he had the power to avenge it.

'Be patient,' said Robert. 'The game has just begun, but the action will be fast. The Godwin family should be cornered by the end of the summer. Be patient until the new year.'

Robert's chosen messenger was Otto of Bernay, fourth son of a Norman baron who had shown Edward some kindness when he was a young man in exile in Normandy. Otto had crossed the Channel because the small estate he held of his father could not support his extravagances, and he had heard that there were rewards of land to be had from Edward's hands.

Robert knew him to be a forthright young man who made no secret of his contempt for the English, and he instructed him carefully as to what was at stake and what was expected of him.

Early the next morning he set out in high spirits for Winchester.

As it happened, a few weeks earlier Godwin had been stricken with an ailment of the stomach which, although it was soon dispelled, left him lifeless and depressed, prey to gloomy thoughts of the present and future. There was Sweyn, for example . . . once he had been gay — reckless and feckless, perhaps, but alive and full of vitality. Now, he was no more than a shell — a dull, morose person who did as he was bid with his lack-lustre eyes on the ground, and spoke like a decrepit old man of a pilgrimage, and life in a monastery.

And there was the state of the country . . . full of arrogant foreigners flaunting their rank, encouraged by a king who, since he could produce no heir, was no more than an unlovely ornament . . .

Gytha listened to him and nodded sagely. She knew these moods of his, and, like his stomach ailment, she guessed they were the product of too much work and worry. She persuaded him to go with her to Bosham, where there was peace and quiet, and the tang of the sea air.

After a while, Godwin's spirit improved and he began to think objectively of his problems, so that when a ship from Dover arrived in the harbour bringing two of the town's leading citizens for an audience with the earl, he received them courteously and listened while they told him of the recent affray.

As the story unfolded, Godwin felt his temper rise: clearly, it was a case of provocation on the part of arrogant foreigners, a symptom of the malaise that was afflicting the country, and he promised the two men that he would lay their complaint before the king and endeavour to obtain some compensation for the townsfolk.

By the time his visitors left the following morning, he had made up his mind to use the Dover incident as the first shaft in a campaign to curb the growing influence of the French and Normans. It would not be easy, for the canker had grown roots, but if he could persuade Leofric and Siward to open their eyes to the danger, it was certain that Edward would have to do more than listen to their complaints.

He made preparations to return to Winchester, but before he could set out on the journey, Otto of Bernay arrived.

Taking stock of his visitor, Godwin felt the slow burning of annoyance in his throat. That the man was a Norman was obvious, both from his name and from his looks, and the shaven face accentuated his youth. More than that, there was something in his manner which was almost insolent.

Keeping his irritation in check, the earl unrolled the parchment and sent for a clerk to read it.

'No need for that,' said Otto, 'I know the message by heart.'

Godwin stared at him, too astonished to say what was on his mind. Unabashed, and apparently unaware of the anger in the earl's eyes, Otto went on: 'The king is incensed by the behaviour of the men of Dover towards his kinsman, Count Eustace of Boulogne. He instructs you to bear in mind that seventeen men were slain by the townsfolk, and his command is that you shall lay waste to the town and hang no less than thirty-four of the inhabitants.'

Godwin stood as if turned to stone, the parchment quivering in his hand.

'I shall accompany you,' continued Otto, 'to see that the retribution is carried out, and to report to the king accordingly.'

A roar of berserk rage echoed round the chamber, and the clerk who had just entered turned and scurried out, his robe flying in his wake. Godwin pounded the parchment into a ball between his fists and flung it from him with all his force. His cheeks were bright red and his eyes blazed.

'Get out . . . ' he bellowed. 'Get out . . . go back to Normandy where you belong . . . '

Otto stood with a smile on his face. 'Is that your answer to the king?' he sneered.

Godwin moved close, as if to strike him. 'No . . . ' he said between his teeth. 'Go back to the king and tell him that when he sends a courier fit to bear his message, I will give him an answer.'

Otto stood his ground. 'You will not carry out the king's command?' he persisted.

'No,' snarled Godwin, 'I will not . . . not until it is proved that my people were at fault. Which will be never.'

Otto had the answer he wanted. He turned on his heel and left.

Godwin stayed alone for several minutes. He muttered to himself and paced up and down as though trampling his enemies underfoot, while his cheeks burned and his heart pounded.

Gytha came to him: she had heard from one of the servants that the earl was in a tantrum, and she found him still excited, waving his arms about as he told her what had happened. With her perceptive mind she saw that his fury had blinded him to the implications of the situation, and when he announced that he would be leaving for Westminster immediately, she held up a warning hand.

'My lord, that would not be wise.'

Godwin was taken aback. 'How so, Gytha?'

'If the messenger had been English and

well-mannered, would you have acted in the same way? Or would you have ridden back to Westminster with him, to wheedle the king into your way of thinking?'

Godwin had lost his anger. He nodded, smiling a little.

'Well, then,' said Gytha, 'it seems to me that Edward has been unusually tactless. Or perhaps he wishes you to refuse his command.'

The smile disappeared from Godwin's face. 'By God, I believe you are right.' He gazed at her for a moment, pulling at his beard. 'This is too subtle for Edward: it stinks of Robert. And I,' he added bitterly, 'have walked right into his trap.'

He stood staring at the ceiling, puffing out his cheeks in exasperation, while Gytha watched the colour ebb from his cheeks.

'Tell me what I should do, my love. I cannot think straight for myself.'

Gytha smiled. Godwin the earl, she respected; but it was Godwin the forlorn little boy that she loved.

'Nothing, my lord, except return to Winchester where you shall exercise your patience once again.'

Godwin nodded slowly. It could be said
— would be said that he was in rebellion,
and to ride to his enemies would be
madness. No, Gytha was right, as usual
. . . Winchester it should be. Winchester
. . . and patience. He did not think he
would have to wait long.

9

Godwin was wrong. Daily, he expected a summons to Westminster and daily, when it did not arrive, his impatience grew, and he began again to think of taking the bull by the horns. But Bishop Stigand, in a voice which had the scratchy dryness of a quill on parchment, advised against it. Whatever the truth about Dover, he said, Godwin had put himself in the wrong, and it would be more than foolish to walk into the lions' den.

'Who plays the part of the lion?' asked Godwin.

'There are two of them,' said Stigand. 'One roars and shows his teeth while the other, the more dangerous, prepares to spring.'

Godwin knew that Stigand's sources of information were impeccable, and he became worried. In his more sanguine moments he had been pleased to imagine that the whole affair might blow over or, at worst, come to a head in an outburst of harmless rage from Edward. But now, there was no knowing how it might end.

He spent the days cursing himself for an impulsive fool, and became peevish and difficult to please. Even his favourite sport of hawking could not divert his thoughts from his predicament.

At last, there came a courier from the king. Godwin broke the seal of the parchment and listened impatiently while the clerk translated the preamble.

'Come on, man,' snapped the earl. 'Get to the collop of it.'

The clerk flushed, and fumbled at the parchment with trembling fingers. His lips moved wordlessly as he scanned the closely written lines. 'There is to be a meeting of the Great Council at the king's manor of Tetbury in Gloucestershire on the fourth day of September,' he said fearfully.

Godwin stared at him. 'Is that all?' he demanded incredulously.

'There is no more, my lord.'

'Are you sure? Read the whole thing again from beginning to end.'

The clerk did so, enunciating each word carefully and occasionally glancing at the earl, who listened intently, smoothing his moustaches with his fingers.

The clerk had been right: there was no more. Godwin gave a little crow of laughter and dismissed the man, telling him that he was a good fellow and should go to Heaven when he died.

A meeting of the Great Council, indeed! A mile of talk and an admonition from Edward! He felt as though a great weight had been lifted from his shoulders.

Stigand, who came to see him the same day, was not so cheerful.

'What did you expect, my lord? A man as eminent as yourself cannot be thrust out of the servant's door . . . he has to be ushered from the main entrance with due ceremony. Besides, it is not only yourself, but all your sons as well.'

Godwin was shocked. 'My whole family to be exiled over so trivial a matter?'

'That is what the two lions have set their heart on.'

Godwin bit his lower lip and felt the skin tighten over his cheekbones.

'It is not possible,' he said, after a pause.

'I shall show you that it is,' said Stigand, evenly. From within the folds of his robe, he took a bundle of evenly cut slivers of wood and placed them on the open palm of his hand.

'Each piece,' he said, 'represents one member of the Great Council.' He recited the name of each member, and as he did so, placed a sliver on one of two well separated places on the table. Godwin watched fascinated as the piles grew; first one was the larger, then the other. His heart began to beat a little more quickly than usual.

Stigand spread his empty hands on the table and looked at the earl.

'You have forgotten Spearhafoc,' said Godwin.

The priest shook his head. 'Spearhafoc does not count — Robert refuses to consecrate him on some flimsy excuse, but his reasons are obvious when the pieces on each pile are counted.'

Godwin eyed the two piles as though they were venomous snakes. Stigand placed his hand over one pile and said: 'This pile — which I shall call Robert's — has one more sliver than the other.'

The earl looked at him from under his brows. 'One is not enough on an issue of this importance, Stigand,' he growled.

Stigand shrugged and carefully took three slivers from the Godwin pile and held them up. 'Three churchmen,' he said, 'who are ambitious enough to forget their allegiance at a whispered promise.' He dropped the slivers on to the other pile. 'Now the deficiency is seven. And there may be more like them.'

'Who are they?' Godwin was suddenly angry.

'Does it matter?'

'Two can play at that game, Stigand.'

'I think not, earl Godwin. At the moment, you have nothing to offer.'

Godwin rose to his feet and kicked the chair away from him so that it fell on its side. He paced the room, his cheeks flushed with anger, the muscles of his jaws working. Stigand sat watching, his fingers playing among the wood pieces.

'Stigand,' said Godwin at last, 'I am grateful to you. When the game is played out I shall not forget your kindness.' He added fiercely, 'I am not beaten, Stigand, until I am dead, and I shall live to see these foreigners fleeing from England like whipped curs.'

Stigand inclined his head. 'If it can be done,' he said, 'then you are the one man who can do it.'

Godwin did not sleep that night, and in the morning he sent for Sweyn, who was in Basing on the earl's business, and for Tostig, who was at his manor at Wilton, savouring the sweet afterglow of his honeymoon with Judith. It fretted him that Harold was at Hereford, for he had come to realise that, of all his sons, Harold had the great store of good sense.

There was still a coolness between Sweyn and Tostig, but on the day following their arrival, Godwin took them into a private room, where he told them what was afoot and of his talks with bishop Stigand. He did not gloss over his own foolishness, and spoke frankly of the possible outcome of the Great Council meeting.

Sweyn listened quietly, his eyes downcast, but Tostig asked many questions, and when his curiosity had been satisfied Godwin asked him what he thought should be done. Tostig was silent for a while, and then replied that the nub of the matter was not whether the men of Dover should be punished, but whether England was to be ruled by the king or by Robert of Canterbury. If the earl of Wessex was to be treated as a rebel, then he might as well merit the reputation. Tostig was for raising an army of levies and marching to Westminster, to demand of the king that Robert and the other foreigners holding high office should be banished from England. 'If we act quickly, father, we stand a good chance of success. If we fail — well, at least we shall have earned our exile.'

Godwin looked at his auburn-haired son with a new respect: the plan was a bold one, and it appealed to his instincts. But to raise the levies would take time, and there was more than a chance that

Robert would learn what was afoot and take steps to counter the plan.

He turned to his other son. 'What say you, Sweyn?'

Sweyn shook his head. 'I am the last person you should ask for advice. It is on my conscience that I am more than partly to blame for what has happened. Had I been a dutiful son . . . '

Godwin held up his hand. 'All that is in the past, my son, and we must think of the future. Tell me what I should do.'

'I can only tell you what I would do . . . go before the Council and admit that in anger I had been discourteous to the king. And I would say that I would gladly make atonement for the insult.'

The corners of Tostig's mouth twitched at the thought of his father humbling himself before his enemies. Godwin stared at Sweyn for a moment, his face impassive, before rising to his feet and thanking them both for their advice.

At the doorway, he turned and smiled. 'I shall ride alone on the Downs for an hour or two.'

After he had gone, Sweyn made as if to

leave, but Tostig said: 'Do not go, brother. I would talk with you for a while.'

'What can you have to say to me?' said Sweyn.

Tostig leaned back in his chair and stretched his shoulders. His green eyes were full of curiosity.

'That you have changed,' he said. 'Changed more than I would have thought possible. When you spoke to father just now, you sounded like a monk.'

Sweyn looked earnestly at him. 'I would to God I was a monk.'

'A whim of the moment, perhaps. Be patient, Sweyn, father has weathered worse storms than this before: he will emerge as the greatest man in England. There will be an earldom for you yet.'

Sweyn leaned forward. 'Tostig . . . believe me . . . I want no earldom. I have no place in this country — wherever I go people call me Sweyn Godwinson, but their eyes call me Sweyn, killer of Beorn. And they shun me as if I had some disease.'

Tostig scoffed. 'It is all in your mind.

People have short memories for what does not concern them.'

Sweyn shook his head. 'I cannot live in England. Soon, I shall set off for the Holy Land — not as a pilgrim by horse and ship, but as a penitent. There is a road which passes through Europe and over the mountains to Byzantium and thence across deserts to Jerusalem. They say that only sinners can survive the journey there, and only saints return the same way.'

'I have heard of it,' said Tostig. 'Have you told father?'

'He laughs at me. He says I should travel as befits my rank, and cannot understand that such a journey would be pointless.'

Tostig nodded his sympathy. 'It is a pity,' he said, 'that we have not talked together like this before. We might have been good friends. Now tell me the truth about Beorn.'

Sweyn glanced at him sharply, but did not answer.

'I swear that it shall go no further, Sweyn.'

Still there was no answer.

'For the good of your soul, brother.'

Sweyn closed his eyes and sighed deeply. 'You do not believe the story I told you and father?'

'For a day or two I believed it. Until I questioned Brand, who said that there was no Englishman among your crew.'

Sweyn was silent for a full minute. Then, for the first time, he looked his brother straight in the eyes.

'So be it,' he said. 'You shall know the truth. There was no Aylmar from Dover — I was the shipmaster. It was I who lured Beorn aboard my ship at Bosham, and it was I who turned my back when he pleaded for his life. I could have saved him, Tostig, with one word — but I turned my back.'

The look in Sweyn's eyes was one that Tostig had never seen before in any man. The horror in him turned to pity. 'But why . . . ?' he said, softly.

Sweyn shrugged. 'At that time I thought it was for gold. But when the knife went into Beorn's throat, it was as though my eyes were suddenly opened.

Ever since I can remember, there had been a devil in me . . . a mad, black devil, urging me to destroy, torture and kill.'

Tostig remembered the day at Sandwich and the feel of Harold's throat in his tightening grasp. 'I know that devil,' he said.

'Then guard against it. Or it will destroy you as it destroyed me.'

When Godwin returned from his solitary ride, his mind was made up. He sent for his two sons and for Brand, the captain of his housecarls.

To Sweyn, he gave the task of riding to Axbridge in Somerset, where, with the help of the Shire Reeve, he was to raise a token force of levies. Tostig was to do the same in the county of Wiltshire, and Brand was to ride to earl Harold at Hereford and bid him raise as many men as he could in the time available.

'We shall all meet,' he said, 'on the first day of September at Malmesbury.'

Brand, who had the furthest to go, set off that day, but the two brothers started their journeys together early the next morning. As they rode, Tostig was very much alive to the calm beauty of the summer morning and the cool breeze which caressed his hair and carried the scent of the country to his nostrils. His eyes sparkled as he thought of Judith, and he whistled a tune between his teeth.

Sweyn was morose. 'I do not like this venture,' he said. 'It is ill-fated: last night I dreamed of carrion crows and bodies rotting in the sun.'

Tostig laughed at him. 'You ate too much pork at supper,' he said, and added: 'Father knows what he is doing.'

'He is putting himself further into the wrong. The spear may be aimed at Robert, but it will strike Edward as well. The king should not be threatened with violence.'

Tostig threw back his head and laughed with delight. 'You are a fine one to talk . . . what was it you called him to his face at Sandwich?'

Sweyn relapsed into a glum silence and would not respond to Tostig's affable high spirits. As they came to the parting of their ways, he said: 'Tostig . . . that matter we discussed yesterday . . . if father knew the truth he would be deeply hurt.'

Tostig gazed about him as if seeking for something. 'What matter was that, Sweyn? I have forgotten, but if, by chance, I should remember, I shall pass it on to no man. You have my word on that.'

They clasped hands and went their ways.

Brand made good time to Hereford and found earl Harold in fine fettle and anxious to show off two new possessions of which he was very proud. The first was his son, born the previous November, and named Godwin, after his grandfather.

The past months had been a busy period in the earl's life, for scarcely a week passed but some refugee from Ralf's earldom arrived in Hereford with a tale of tyranny and oppression, and it became obvious that the Frenchman and his companions had no regard whatever for the native English or their laws.

Also, it was said that the stone castle was nearly built, and Harold made it his business to ride that way, inconspicuously dressed and with only two companions, for a sight of it. The cold hostility of the building on its man-made mound, alarmed and depressed Harold, and he rode back to his own land deep in thought.

He knew earl Ralf to be a rogue without scruples or conscience; a man who, although he paid lip service to the king of the English, recognised no man as his overlord. That being so, sooner or later there would be trouble and Harold, remembering Ralf's last words to him when they had met in the forest, resolved that he would be ready for it.

Without delay, he set about trebling the number of his housecarls, letting it be known that he would pay handsomely to those who served him. There were many applicants, and from these Harold chose each man personally for he wanted only the best men. One of his first recruits was Hodda, the man he had saved from earl Ralf's huntsmen, and who had proved himself capable of better things than cleaning out stables, for his physical strength was great, and his loyalty to his lord was beyond doubt.

Throughout the spring, Harold and his housecarls' captain, Aldred, were hard at work training the new men. They had to be able to ride distances at great speed, be expert with sword and throwing spear, and the strongest man of every three was trained to use the great war axe which, well-used, could slice through armour, man and horse at one blow.

By August, they had reached the high standards which Harold required, and he was half-wishing for an enemy to fight when Brand arrived with Godwin's message.

So Brand admired baby Godwin, who, he said, was a credit to his mother; and he admired the housecarls at their drill — a credit, he said, to any king.

Harold was happy: such words from Brand were praise indeed. And there was a chance of an opportunity to test the skill of his housecarls.

It was the last day of the month when Godwin arrived at Malmesbury. Tostig and his band of levies had arrived a few hours earlier, a motley collection of young men armed with spears and swords which had seen better days. Godwin's house-carls, in the manner of all professional soldiers when confronted with amateurs, pursed their lips and looked the other way.

Godwin took his son on one side and said, 'For the love of God, Tostig . . . have you snatched these children from their mothers' arms?'

Tostig flushed with resentment. 'It is the time of year, Father. I brought the young because I did not want to delay the harvest.'

Godwin gave a grunt. He would have preferred some quality with the quantity, and Sweyn's contingent, when it arrived the next day, was more to his liking. But when Harold rode in at the head of his housecarls, his admiration made itself shown.

'You make me feel like a pauper,' he said, eyeing the fine horses with their rich trappings, and the burnished accoutrements of the men.'

Tostig's nose was severely out of joint. He said to Sweyn: 'Who does Harold think he is — the Emperor of Europe?'

That evening, Godwin discussed his plans with his sons until well into the night. And in the morning, the force set off along the rough, unfrequented tracks which led through the hills to Tetbury.

Edward's manor lay in a fold of the hills, a sprawling complex of barns, outbuildings and dwellings, dominated by the hall built of timber, weathered to a silver grey, under its roof of golden new thatch. Godwin led his men in a wide detour to the south, arriving on the crest of the hill to the west of the manor during the afternoon of the day before the meeting.

He ordered that an encampment should be formed and that stocks of fuel should be collected from the woodland for many more fires than were necessary, which were to be lit at sundown.

When everything was done to his satisfaction, he called for Harold, and together they rode down the hill to the manor.

10

Everything was ready: the trap was set, the jaws poised ready to shut. The quarry, enmeshed in an unbreakable web, could move only in one direction — into the trap. Robert felt a glow of satisfaction at a difficult task well done as he stood by the side of the king, watching the great hall fill with the dignitaries and magnates of England as they came from their allotted quarters, hungry for the supper which they could smell roasting in the kitchens. They formed into groups among the tables, and there was the dull hubbub of chatter, and snatches of conversation in English and Norman came to his ears as the assembly waited their turns to pay respect to the king.

There was Leofric of Mercia, stiffly erect and slow moving, like a man walking on ice: as an old enemy of Godwin, Robert knew he could be counted on, and he nodded and smiled as the earl took the king's hand. There was his son, Alfgar, who bore the weight of his father's thumb so that the resentment showed only in his eyes: he would be dutiful and follow his father.

And there was the battle-scarred warrior, Siward of Northumbria: he also received a smile from the Archbishop. But when Stigand of Winchester came to the king, Robert stared frostily over his head, avoiding the shrewd, hooded eyes of the bishop.

There was earl Ralf, who greeted the king in the Norman tongue, and almost winked at Robert as he passed by. And as the bishops came and went, many of them Norman, Robert counted in his head the number of those who would support him.

When at last Godwin and Harold presented themselves, Robert looked at them stonily, and neither smiled nor avoided their eyes.

Godwin sought out Leofric and Siward, who were talking together. 'Archbishop Robert,' he said, 'stands there as though he rules the king.'

Leofric looked down his long nose at Godwin and would have ignored him, but the earl went on: 'And these other foreigners — they breed like flies on a rotting corpse. Soon they will outnumber the English.'

Siward cleared his throat as if to spit, but thought better of it. 'Court favourites,' he said. 'Morsel-snappers. They do not signify.'

'Be not too sure of that,' said Godwin. 'In the land of the foxes, the fox rules. What say you, Leofric?'

Leofric sought for words, but before he found any, Godwin added: 'The king should beware lest the foxes turn to wolves.'

Leofric watched him go, and then glanced questioningly at Siward.

'He is a fox himself,' growled Siward. 'But we shall miss him.'

'It will be a good miss,' said Leofric. He expected that when Wessex was split up there would be shares for himself and Alfgar.

It was then that one of the king's servants burst into the hall and hurried to his master's side to whisper in his ear. The man's haste caught attention, and conversation died away as heads turned towards the king.

Edward rose to his feet. 'What fires are these?' he said, hurrying towards the doors.

The assembly swarmed after him, and in the press Robert found his way barred: but Godwin was at the king's side.

To the west, the ridge was silhouetted black against the sun's afterglow, and in the heart of the blackness was a myriad of twinkling fires, each with a spire of smoke rising in the still air and dark against the yellow sky.

There was a silence as men stared with awe and superstition in their eyes.

'What is this?' said Edward, at last.

Godwin pitched his voice so that it would carry to those behind. 'They are my followers, lord king,' he said. 'I thought it unfit to burden your household with their appetites. They cook their meat and warm themselves against the night air.'

Edward was aghast. It seemed as

though there was an army encamped below the ridge. 'Your followers . . . ?' he said, looking hard at Godwin.

'My own and earl Harold's . . . with a few levies whose feet were in need of hardening.' He took Edward's arm and turned him towards the door. 'The night grows cold, my lord . . . '

Supper was taken in a subdued mood. There was no laughter or light-hearted talk, but each man realised the implications of the encampment on the ridge and spoke quietly to his neighbour. There were many glances at the earl of Wessex as he sat at the top table at the left hand of the king.

Robert, who sat on the other side of the king, was more thoughtful than most. He estimated that there might be as many as fifteen hundred men on the ridge, and one thing was painfully clear to him: no action against Godwin could be taken by the Great Council on the next day — the meeting would have to be postponed.

At his side, Edward ate without realising what he was doing; his fingers plucked meat from the bone and transferred it to his mouth and he was only vaguely aware that the act of swallowing seemed likely to choke him. His turmoiled mind could grasp only that Godwin had been too clever for him.

Godwin ate with a heartiness that belied his wariness. Sensitive to the tense atmosphere, he was well aware that the first part of his plan had given him the whip in his hand. Now he was alert for the opportunity of using it.

It came suddenly. Edward reached boiling point and, red in the fact, flung the half-cleaned bone on to the table with a loud clatter. Conversation ceased abruptly.

'Earl Godwin . . . ' Edward's voice was loud and querulous ' . . . you should send your men home at first light.'

Godwin looked at him as if surprised. 'Why so, my lord? Is it not usual to bring followers to a meeting of the Council?'

'You have too many,' snapped Edward.

Godwin wiped the grease from his hands and mouth with a cloth. He took his time over it, and when he spoke he pitched his voice so that it would carry to all parts of the hall.

'My lord, those men are here to protect you.'

For a moment, the silence seemed to intensify; then a low murmuring arose from the body of the hall, like approaching thunder. Above it, a voice called, 'You should explain yourself, earl Godwin.'

Godwin rose to his feet. 'My lords . . . ' He paused to look round the hall and along the length of the top table. The silence became absolute.

'My lords — which of you here are loyal to the king?'

The hush was broken by an almost unified shout of assent. Then, slowly, as if to accentuate the ensuing silence, Godwin gazed about him.

'In that case, some of you are liars.'

It was as though a thunderbolt had struck. In an instant, turmoil broke out. Men jumped to their feet, overturning chairs and benches, and everyone shouted at once, so that it was impossible to hear what any one man was shouting.

Startled, Edward gazed around him,

wide-eyed and open-mouthed, and then turned to Robert, mutely questioning. But for once, the Archbishop seemed bemused, his eyes flitting from Godwin to the far corners of the hall and back to Godwin, who stood with his arms upraised, appealing for quiet.

The loudness of his voice quelled the last of the shouts. 'You ask who the traitors are . . . but I will ask another question. Most of you will know why we are here — to argue over some trifling affray at Dover, where Englishmen dared to defend their homes against marauding foreigners. For which, it will be said, they must be punished with hangings and burning. Yet what is done to restrain earl Ralf . . . ' Godwin pointed dramatically at the Frenchman ' . . . who hunts Englishmen as though they were wild boars, and enslaves free Englishmen to build his stone castle?'

This time, the noise was deafening, and Edward put his hands to his ears. Ralf was on his feet, red in the face with anger and embarrassment. He advanced on Godwin, hand on the knife at his belt, shouting, 'He lies . . . Godwin lies in his teeth . . . '

From the other end of the table there came the large, angry figure of earl Harold, all muscle and sinew, shouting: 'It is no lie — there are men on the ridge to prove it . . . '

Adroitly, Robert left his place and stepped between the two men. He faced Ralf, placing his hands on his chest, and shouted angrily: 'For God's sake, man . . . go back to your place and be still.'

Ralf stared at him for a moment, and then turned on his heel. Harold, towering over the Archbishop, watched him go with regret and then went back to his own chair.

Still standing, Godwin surveyed the scene in the hall. English and Normans were standing almost toe to toe, barking like dogs at each other. It amused him to see the men of God behaving like fighting cocks: only Stigand sat hunched over his table, his fingers playing with a goblet. For a moment their eyes met, and Godwin fancied that the bishop winked at him. Well satisfied with his work, he sat down.

Gradually the noise died down, and Godwin turned to the king who sat white and shivering.

'My lord king — I beg your forgiveness . . . but there are things which must be brought into the open. There is much happening that you cannot know of.'

Edward looked at him, his eyes filled with loathing. 'Earl Godwin, you have said more than enough.' His lips were tight against his teeth, as though he would spit in the earl's face.

Godwin bowed his head. 'In that case, my lord, have I your permission to retire?'

The king nodded, not trusting himself to speak, and Godwin rose and walked the length of the table, tapping Harold lightly on the shoulder as he passed. Together the two men walked across the hall amid a deathly silence.

At the door, Godwin turned. 'My lords,' he said, 'I fear I have spoiled your appetites. But it is a small price to pay. We English, and those who truly serve England must stand together against those who would work evil on her.'

The Normans groaned and jeered, but the English sat silent, staring at the closing doors.

Immediately, Edward left the hall, feeling unwell, and the assembly broke up to go to their apartments, for they had lost the taste for food.

Siward found himself close to Leofric and reached out to take his arm. 'Man,' he said, 'that had all the makings of a fine brawl. I was beginning to flex my muscles, but it ended too soon.'

'On which side,' said Leofric, 'would you have fought?'

Siward gave a wheezy laugh. 'I am a Dane,' he said, 'but I have shed more than a little blood for England. I would not give a drop for the Normans.'

'Would you go against the king's wishes?' said Leofric, thinking of the next day's business.

'The king,' said Siward quietly, 'loves the Normans too much. He treats them like brothers.'

'Even so, he is still king of the English.'

'Until he is dead. And what then, old friend?'

Leofric was puzzled and unhappy. A short while ago, the issues had seemed clear cut — Godwin would be exiled. But now ... Was the Norman faction planning to seize power? And if so, who would be the next to fall from favour?

He felt suddenly tired and a little afraid. In his bones, he knew he would get no sleep that night.

The king sent for Robert to come to his private chamber. Now that the storm was over and the trembling and sickness had passed, he felt so weak that his knees would scarcely support his body. But the turmoil remained in his mind, and there were matters which had to be discussed.

Robert's face was grim. 'Godwin,' he said, 'has many things to answer for. I would not be in his shoes on Judgement Day.'

Edward wiped his clammy forehead with the palm of his hand: 'He said many things which I did not understand.'

'Half-truths and whole lies, Sire. He is a master at twisting the truth to suit his own ends. He says one thing and means another.'

'He implied a plot against the Crown,' said Edward, uncertainly.

Robert scoffed. 'You should pay no attention to such babblings. It is a figment of his imagination conceived to provide an excuse for bringing an army to Tetbury.'

Edward clenched his fist, and the colour rose to his cheeks. 'Intimidation . . . lies . . . And what was it he said against earl Ralf?'

'More lies, Sire. He seeks to divide the English from your Norman subjects and set himself up as the champion of the English. He is a danger to the peace of the country.'

Edward bit his lower lip. 'He must be got rid of, Robert. It is more essential now than ever before.'

They talked far into the night. It was plain that the presence of Godwin's army on the ridge made the Council meeting on the morrow impossible, therefore they plotted when and where it should be held so that the earl of Wessex could not again use the threat of force. By dawn, the problem was solved: they had a plan which was proof against everything — even the Devil himself.

Harold had slept badly and was early astir. As the sun rose, he sought his father and found him combing the tangles from his hair and beard, having sluiced himself with water from a nearby spring. The process was painful, and he greeted his son tersely.

Harold sat down beside the earl and began to trace patterns on the dry earth with a stick. 'Father, are you satisfied that the Council will not go against us today?'

Godwin did not answer at once, but finished his combing and then stretched his arms and filled his lungs with the morning air. Upwind of him, fowls were being roasted on a spit and the aroma reminded him that his stomach was hollow. His mood began to improve.

'Our chances are better than they were this time yesterday,' he observed.

Harold erased his drawings with a sweep of his foot and broke the stick between his hands. 'Chance . . . ' he said. 'Would you gamble your earldom — and mine — on the toss of a coin?'

Godwin looked at him. 'Come, now — it is not as desperate as that. Besides, what other choice have we?'

Harold said nothing, but glanced meaningly towards where the housecarls and levies were busy about their bivouacs. Godwin caught his meaning and stared across the valley where the sun was highlighting the mist above the trees.

At last, he said: 'No, my son. Never use force where persuasion will suffice. At the moment, I believe the bulk of the Council to be with us, but if we draw our swords there will be cries of 'treachery' and every man will turn against us.'

Harold leaned forward earnestly. 'It would not be treachery, father. We are not against the king. We should ride down with our housecarls and, in the name of the king, we should summon every Norman to surrender himself. They are all there — Archbishop, bishops, earl Ralf . . . There are ships at Bristol and they could be on their way to Normandy by nightfall.'

Godwin gazed at Harold for a long time. Then the corners of his mouth began to twitch and he threw back his head and burst into laughter.

'By God, Harold,' he said. 'Canute would have liked you . . . ' and he laughed again.

Tostig stood beside them. 'It takes a good joke to make Father laugh so early in the morning. I should like to hear it.'

Godwin wiped the tears from his eyes. 'Your brother,' he said, 'has a wish to play with his new toy.'

Harold flushed red with vexation and flung the sticks far into the valley. 'You laugh now,' he said, 'and I hope you will still be laughing tomorrow.'

Early in the forenoon, the two earls rode the path down to the manor, Harold silent, still smarting from his rebuff, while Godwin hummed a song to himself, seemingly at ease. On the way, they passed close to the stables, and Harold was surprised to see grooms busy with the saddling of horses.

The great hall was not as they had expected: of Edward and Robert there was no sign, but there were numerous men of God together with Leofric and

Alfgar, and they were all dressed for travel. As Godwin gazed about him, Stigand hurried over.

'Lord earl,' he said. 'There will be no meeting — the king is not himself.'

Godwin smiled a little. 'Nothing worse, I trust, than a draught playing about his feet?'

Stigand came close to the earl. 'It is put about that the chill is on his stomach, but I think you may be nearer the truth.'

'Did I do well last night, Stigand?'

'Better than you could have hoped, lord earl. Siward is for you, also Leofric and Alfgar. And the English bishops are quick to see the way the wind is blowing.'

Godwin clasped his hands and gave a crow of delight. 'The danger is past, then?'

Stigand touched his lips with his forefinger. 'Not quite, my lord. The Great Council meets at Westminster in fourteen days.'

Godwin nodded thoughtfully. 'Fourteen days . . . time enough for tempers to cool and minds to change.'

'Just so,' said Stigand. 'It would be as

well for you to cultivate your new friendship with earl Leofric and his son.'

They joined the group on the far side of the hall, where Godwin spoke to Leofric and Siward in his most charming manner, while Harold talked for a while with Alfgar. But his head was full of private thoughts, and as soon as he could, he excused himself and left the hall for the courtyard where he paced up and down.

He was not happy: he did not like to hear his father claim victory in a battle that was only half-fought. At the back of his mind, there was a warning voice, but what it was saying he was not sure.

So deep in thought was he that he did not notice the arrival in the courtyard of earl Ralf with Otto of Bernay as his companion.

Otto nudged his friend. 'See what we have here, Ralf — the fox's cub.'

Ralf growled in his throat. 'Leave him alone, Otto,' he said, and made as if to walk on. But Otto stood where he was, and as Harold drew close, he said loudly and mockingly, 'Harold of Hereford . . . good morning, lord earl.'

Harold stopped and looked at Otto, whom he did not know, and then at Ralf. It was a cold look because he did not like the tone of the stranger's voice. He turned on his heel.

Otto clicked his tongue. 'Come now,' he said. 'You and Ralf were close to a brawl yesterday — have you nothing to say to each other?'

Harold turned to face him. 'What is there that either of us should say?'

'He called your father a liar. I did not hear him retract it.'

'Perhaps,' said Harold, looking at Ralf, 'he would like to repeat the accusation while there are none to keep us apart.'

Ralf stared back at Harold and saw the width of his shoulders and guessed the strength in his arms. The blood rushed to his cheeks but he said nothing.

'Or perhaps,' said Harold, looking down on Otto, 'you would care to strike a blow on his behalf.'

Otto eyed him up and down, smiling a little. 'They tell me,' he said, 'that Hereford is a beautiful town, full of lovely women. If earl Ralf can spare me from

Westminster, I have a mind to visit it. I am sorry that you will not be there, earl Harold.'

Harold said, after a pause: 'I do not know your name, but I shall remember your face.'

Still smiling, the Norman inclined his head. 'Otto of Bernay, lord earl. Keep it in mind, for you shall hear it again.'

Harold turned away and walked to the furthest part of the yard. When he was out of earshot, Ralf said to Otto: 'You fool . . . for a moment I thought it would come to a fight.'

'Not he,' scoffed Otto. 'He is like all the English — slow and stupid. You would have to spit in his eye before he would fight. Besides . . . ' he added, grinning, 'what did I say that could have annoyed him?'

Harold was still puzzled and still a little angry as he rode up towards the ridge beside his father. Godwin, however, was in good spirits.

'It is over and done with, Harold. Even Leofric is firmly against the Normans. He agrees that at Westminster we should warn Edward of the danger of granting favours and power to the foreigners.'

Harold set his jaw. 'Father,' he said earnestly. 'Westminster is fourteen days hence, and much can happen in that time. The iron is hot now — and we should strike before it cools.'

The earl looked at him. 'Are you still riding that horse? Be sensible — it is all settled.'

When they reached the encampment, Godwin called for Sweyn and Tostig, and after telling them what had happened, bade them send the levies home and prepare to return to Winchester.

'Shall we raise fresh levies for Westminster?' asked Tostig.

Godwin smiled. 'No, my son. There is no more need for levies, thank God. A score of housecarls will suffice for that meeting.'

Harold heard this with relief, for he had taken his whole force to Tetbury and he was worried lest it should become known to the Welsh. Also, in spite of himself, he wondered what mischief Otto of Bernay could be contemplating. He called for

Aldred and, having put him on his guard, sent him back to Hereford with all but a dozen of his housecarls. These, with Hodda in command, he intended to take to Westminster.

11

In Winchester, Hodda moved around as though in a dream. It was the finest town he had ever seen — bigger and more splendid than Hereford, and the air did not smell of cattle; the merchants wore fine clothes and carried pieces of gold and silver in their purses, and the women seemed more beautiful.

He marvelled at the size and richness of Godwin's hall, gazed in wonder at the rounded greenness of the Downs, which seemed to stretch for ever into the purple autumn haze, and caught his breath at a glint of silver on the southern horizon, staring entranced when someone told him that it was the sea.

But the most wonderful thing of all was the Minster, built of stone, with a great square tower which reached up into the sky. Hodda had never seen anything so awe-inspiring, and as he stared at it he tried to remember everything that he had been told about God. Because, surely, nobody but God could have contrived such a building.

God . . . who held court with his angels in the sky and gazed with disapproval on sinners like Hodda. Or did he . . . ? Hodda allowed that it was earl Harold who had saved his life and given him the security of a bed in his stables. And it was earl Harold who had raised him to a position of trust and responsibility such as he had never dreamed of in the old days. But who, if not God, had directed him to the thorn bush at the earl's feet?

Hodda looked at the Minster and felt humble.

Godwin was anything but humble: he had tasted success at Tetbury and the fumes had gone to his head. Confident of the support of all the English members of the Great Council, he scoffed at those, like Bishop Stigand and Harold, who counselled caution.

His confidence was not shared by Harold, whose mind was full of forebodings; so much so that his face reflected his thoughts, and Tostig set off for Wilton and

215

Judith, saying that one glum face about the place was bad enough but two were insufferable. For Sweyn was as unhappy as ever, and had no interest for anything except his journey of atonement to Jerusalem.

For Gytha, sensitive to the varied moods of her menfolk, these few days were something of a strain, and she was not sorry when the time came for her husband and Harold to start their journey to Westminster.

With eighteen housecarls, they set off and rode briskly throughout the day. Harold had expected to spend the night at Guildford, but Godwin seemed determined to press on, and it was not until late in the afternoon that, tired and dusty, they arrived at the hall of Heremund.

Heremund was taken aback when they arrived, for his hall was not large and he was unused to entertaining such as the earl. Godwin interpreted the look on his face and roared with laughter.

'There are only a score of us,' he said. 'We shall not eat you into poverty.'

Heremund laughed his relief and sent

one of his servants for ale for the housecarls and mead for the two earls.

'I am surprised, lord earl. I should have expected ten times that number.'

Godwin looked at him with curiosity. 'Why so? We go to Westminster, not to fight a war.'

Heremund raised his eyebrows. 'Have you not heard that the Shire levies have been called?'

It was Godwin's turn to be taken aback. He glanced quickly at Harold, and when he spoke his voice was terse.

'How long since?'

Heremund fingered the chin under his beard. He had a great respect for Godwin's temper and wished he had kept the news to himself.

'It was two days ago. I saw the parchment myself — it carried the king's seal. The levies are to assemble at Kingston.'

Godwin cursed under his breath, and Heremund excused himself on the pretext that he had arrangements to make.

For a while father and son stared wordlessly at each other; then Godwin began to laugh quietly. 'You see how it is, Harold. They expect us to repeat our Tetbury tactics, and the Surrey men have been called as a counter. There will be some red faces in London when we arrive with our eighteen men.'

Harold was not reassured.

The next morning as they rode towards Kingston, both the earl and his son were silent in deep thought. The feeling of tension spread among the housecarls and they also were silent and wary, with the exception of Hodda, who rode beside Brand and was excited at the prospect of seeing the king's palace at Westminster. Often he smiled with pleasure at the thoughts which passed through his mind.

'What are you grinning at, young fellow?' growled Brand.

Hodda laughed. 'I am pleased to be alive,' he said. 'Were you not the same, the first time you came to London.'

Brand could not remember. He said: 'You may be fortunate to get to London this time.' And, after a pause, added, 'And even luckier to return.'

Hodda scoffed. 'Who would dare stop

earl Godwin and earl Harold on their lawful journey?'

Instead of answering, Brand pointed ahead. They had turned a corner and, lounging at ease by the side of the road, was a party of men. Hodda looked at them with interest: they were much the same as the levies he had seen at Tetbury, except that they were less youthful and carried more weapons among them. They rose to their feet as the column approached.

Godwin sat erect in his saddle, muscles tensed, brain like ice. As soon as they drew close, he called, 'A fine morning . . . Was your harvest good?'

They answered all at once, a confused sound like the lowing of cattle. A voice louder than the rest called out: 'Good luck to you, earl Godwin.'

The column rode on at the same even pace. Godwin looked at his son with raised eyebrows, and Harold replied with a shrug of his shoulders.

Hodda said to Brand: 'There . . . so much for your gloom. We shall get to London.'

'Hodda,' said Brand, patiently. 'When you set a trap, do you bar the entry before the quarry is inside?'

Hodda did not answer, but looked over his shoulder.

When they came close to Kingston, there came towards them a party of six horsemen. they were unarmoured, and Godwin recognised their leader as one of the king's thanes. As soon as they were close, the thane halted and greeted the two earls.

'I have a message from the king, earl Godwin,' he called, dismounting from his horse.

Godwin also dismounted. 'The meeting is not put off again?' he said, smiling.

'No, lord earl. The message is that you should leave your own escort in Kingston and make the rest of the journey with an escort provided by the king.'

Godwin's smile disappeared and his face became set and angry. He stood back from the thane and folded his arms across his chest.

'Now what nonsense is this? Are my men not good enough for Westminster?'

The thane shrugged. 'It is the king's wish, my lord.'

Godwin beckoned Harold off his horse, and they stood together out of the thane's hearing.

'It is one of two things,' said Godwin. 'A studied insult to raise our tempers so that we refuse to attend the meeting; or Edward fears another Tetbury.'

'Or,' said Harold, 'it is Robert's way of making us his prisoners.'

Godwin stared at him for a moment. 'We must find out which.'

Together they went back to the thane, who stood shuffling his feet in the dust. Harold indicated the thane's men.

'Are these to be our escort?'

'Indeed not, earl Harold. There is a fitting escort of fifty men at present on their way from London. They should arrive by mid-day.'

Harold looked meaningfully at his father.

'In that case,' said Godwin, 'ride to the king and tell him that our escort is only of eighteen men, but that it is sufficient for our dignity. Tell him that we ask his permission to bring them to Westminster.'

The thane looked startled. 'But, lord earl, it will be well into the afternoon before I can bring a reply.'

'Even so,' said Godwin, looking him in the eye, 'do as I command. It is a fine day, and we shall stay here by the river until you return.'

The thane would have argued, but he could not match Godwin's eye. Red in the face, he led his men towards Kingston.

The housecarls dismounted, and having tethered their horses spread themselves at ease along the bank of the river. Some pulled off their footwear and dangled their feet in the water, and there was talk of swimming. Godwin, whose anger had not died away, heard the chatter and called the men around him.

'By God,' he said, 'this is no holiday. Soon you may be fighting for your lives. Every one of you must stay armed and alert for trouble, and let there be no more talk of swimming or sleeping.'

As the housecarls sheepishly made themselves more like soldiers, he took

Brand on one side.

'I have been a fool, Brand. Stupid enough to walk into what may be a well-set trap.'

Brand grinned. 'It is a long time since we fought in anger, Godwin, but I doubt that we have lost the knack.'

Godwin smiled. 'Take off your cloak and sword, old friend, and stroll along the river into Kingston. Find out the lie of the land . . . and send a man to talk to the levies we passed this morning.'

Time dragged by. News came that the levies had gone from their position and were not to be found. Brand came back with a different story: the town, he said, was full of levies, and there was an attempt at a barricade across the road where it led into the market place. But it was not manned, and the townsfolk were grumbling because many of the levies were drunk and making a nuisance of themselves. 'We should have no trouble forcing our way through, if we had a mind to,' he concluded, looking at Godwin.

But the earl shook his head. What he had heard made him believe that Edward was at pains to prevent a repetition of Tetbury. Even Harold became more cheerful.

The sun passed its zenith. The day was warm, and now that the tension had relaxed, the housecarls were allowed to sprawl on the river bank, drowsing and talking in the autumn sun.

Hodda walked slowly along the bank, gazing intently into the water. Presently, he found what he was looking for — a deep pool among the shallows, shaded by the overhanging branches of a tree. He stood very still, staring intently into the dark water.

Harold, who had been idly watching him, wandered over to join him.

'What is it, Hodda?'

Hodda put his finger to his lips. 'A pike,' he whispered.

Harold looked hard. 'I see nothing.'

Hodda drew him away from the bank. 'Do you fancy a pike for supper, my lord?'

Harold smiled ruefully. 'If we had a hook and a line . . . '

Hodda shook his head. 'We have all the

line we want. And we can do without a hook.' He drew his knife and cut a length of branch from a sapling, tested its suppleness and cut a groove around one end of it. Then he went to the nearest horse and deftly plucked four or five hairs from its tail. The horse flicked its tail from side to side and stamped its hind hoof on the ground in irritation.

'Too late, my friend,' said Hodda.

Harold watched, grinning. He saw Hodda join the lengths of hair together and secure one end into the groove in his rod. The other end he formed into a slip-knot. Harold's grin became derisive.

Glancing up, Hodda grinned back.

'A month's extra pay if I land him?'

Harold laughed. '*If* you land him . . . '

At that moment, Godwin's raised voice split the afternoon stillness. 'Stand to arms . . . Stand to . . . '

Hodda dropped his rod and ran to his horse, cursing. Harold hastened to his father, who pointed down the road.

'Here they come . . . our escort from the king.'

A long column of mounted men at a

fast trot, raising a dust cloud. The sound of hoof-beats was like distant thunder.

Harold drew in his breath, mounted his horse swiftly and loosened his sword. His heart beat faster and his mouth was suddenly dry. He stared hard at the leader.

'By God,' he heard himself say. 'Do you see who commands them?'

It was Otto of Bernay.

They came on almost at a canter, closer and closer. Sunlight glinted on the burnished tips of the upright spears, and the thunder of the hoof-beats was deafening.

His horse began to dance a jig beneath him, and Harold had the impression that the column meant to crash into the housecarls, scattering them like chaff in the wind. He reined in his horse hard and turned in his saddle.

'Stand firm . . . ' he shouted. He glimpsed Hodda, wide-eyed; and Brand — solid dependable Brand, who turned in his saddle and repeated the order.

At the last possible moment, Otto raised his arm high in the air and pulled his horse to a stop. The column came to a clattering and dusty standstill, so close that Harold could have leaned forward and touched the nose of Otto's horse.

There was silence for a moment, then the Norman threw back his head and laughed.

'Greetings, my lords,' he said, 'and apologies for our late arrival.'

Godwin glared without answering. He remembered his last meeting with this young puppy and resolved that, whatever the effort cost him, he would not lose his temper.

'My lord earl, I am to have the pleasure of escorting you to Westminster.'

Godwin shook his head. 'I think that you and I will never ride together. Last time, it was to be to Dover . . . Now it is to Westminster . . . ' He shook his head again.

'Those are my orders,' said Otto, blandly.

'From whom?' Godwin snapped. 'The king? Or Archbishop Robert?'

'Does it matter?'

'To me it does,' said Godwin harshly.

'Young man, take your men back whence you came. I expect permission from the king to go to Westminster with my own men.'

Otto laughed and fumbled at his belt. 'I have the answer to that with me.' He held up a roll of parchment. 'A bit out of shape and travel-stained, but it still bears the king's seal.'

Godwin stared at the object, then glanced towards the sun.

'That cannot contain the answer since the question has barely reached Westminster.'

'It will not reach Westminster,' said Otto. 'I met up with the messenger and told him not to waste his time but to go home to his wife.'

In spite of himself, Godwin's rage boiled over, and he cursed Otto until Harold laid his hand on his arm. But Otto merely laughed, saying that the earl should take care lest he be harmed by his own passion.

Harold spoke between his teeth. 'We have no clerk with us. What is the message on the parchment?'

'I have already told you,' said Otto. 'You are to ride with me to Westminster.'

'That we shall not do. We shall await a reply to the request we sent to the king.'

Otto waved the parchment to and fro before his face. 'It also says that unless you do as the king commands . . . ' he spat out the words like cherry stones ' . . . you have five days in which to leave the country.'

There was a sudden cold silence, broken only by a horse blowing the dust from its nostrils.

'You have the eyes of a liar. I do not believe you.' Staring at Otto, Harold had an impulse to smash his fist into the dark, impudent face.

The Norman flashed him a sharp look and flung the parchment on the ground. 'Take it to a clerk, if you will. But waste no time doing it . . . five days will soon pass.'

'I believe him,' said Godwin. 'It bears the king's seal, but they are Robert's words.' He was gazing past Otto at the men ranged behind him. 'And the men are Robert's — not an English face or a beard among them. Would you trust them with your freedom, Harold?'

Harold sought to spit on the ground, but his mouth was bone dry and his lips felt like sandstone to his tongue's touch. 'Not I,' he said.

Godwin sighed. 'There is a lot to be lost and gained,' he said. 'We will ride with you on one condition.'

'There can be no conditions,' said Otto, flatly.

Godwin glowered at him. 'Is your name Robert or Edward?' he snapped. 'Go to your lord, whoever he is, and say that we will ride with you provided that twelve Normans or Frenchmen of good standing are delivered into the charge of my housecarls, to be held hostage at Winchester against the safe return of my son and myself.'

'There is no time for such fripperies. The Council meets tomorrow.'

'It can be postponed for a day or two.'

For the first time, Otto's face showed his irritation. 'You ride with me now or not at all,' he said brusquely.

Pale faced, Godwin sat very still for a while, staring at Otto and trying to swallow the taste of defeat, all the more bitter because he had convinced himself of victory. Otto had quickly gained his composure, and he returned the earl's gaze with an insolent smile.

'Well . . . ?' he said at last.

'Ride to Westminster,' said Godwin, 'and tell the king I wish him well. As for Archbishop Robert, warn him that he has not seen the last of me.'

'As you wish.' Otto looked at Harold and smiled. 'It seems we shall not meet in Hereford,' he said mockingly.

'Count yourself lucky,' growled Harold. 'The next time we meet there will be no talking.'

Otto laughed and turned his horse. Well pleased with himself, he led his men towards London.

Godwin watched them out of sight, then turned to Harold. 'We should have done as you suggested at Tetbury,' he said bitterly.

Harold shrugged. All that was past, and he had thoughts only for his Edith and

231

their baby son. Five days . . . and there were plans to be discussed at Winchester.

He signalled for Hodda to ride beside him.

12

When Otto arrived back at Westminster, dirty and dust-covered, Robert had only to catch the triumphant gleam in his eye to know that the plan had gone well. Nevertheless, he questioned him closely before hurrying to the king.

'Sire,' he said, 'they have chosen exile.'

Edward clapped his hands in delight. 'At last . . . all those years since he had my brother killed . . . ' He was ecstatic, pacing the floor with short, jigging steps, almost dancing in his excitement. His face showed the spiteful pleasure of a vindictive child.

He wagged a finger at Robert: 'He will go to his friend, Baldwin, at Bruges. He must not be allowed back . . . ever.'

Robert nodded his agreement. He was pleased with himself, but he did not delude himself that the success was complete, for Godwin was not the man to spend the rest of his days pining in

Bruges. Steps would have to be taken . . .

But that was for the future. Now there was a pressing matter which should be raised at once.

'There is one other thing, Sire. The lady Edith . . . '

The king's expression changed; the pale eyes became wary, defensive.

'She is a Godwin, Sire.'

Edward looked away and stroked the side of his face for a moment. 'I have thought on this, Robert, and I cannot send her away. What harm has she ever done me?'

Robert pursed his lips and looked at the ground. 'It is who she is and what she may do that matters. The Godwins are a tight-knit brood.'

The king's eyes clouded. It seemed ironic that his moment of triumph should be ruined in this way. He knew that Robert was right, but Edith was to him all those things which his mother had never been.

'Sire,' Robert's voice was insistent, 'you must put her away from you. If you do not, she will become centre point of the

hopes of Godwin and his secret supporters in this country, and God knows what
intrigues and mischief will result.'

In spite of his misery, Edward felt
faintly amused. 'My dear Robert, she has
not the brain for intrigues.'

'Has she not?' Robert's growing irritation expressed itself in mild sarcasm.
'Sire, she is the daughter of her father,
and you must not convince yourself that
her loyalty lies only with yourself. And it
grieves me to remind you that there has
been one instance in which her integrity
was put in doubt.'

Edward turned on him angrily. 'That
was idle gossip — a wisp of smoke in the
wind. There was nothing behind it.'

'No smoke without an ember.' Robert
returned the king's angry gaze steadily,
and it was Edward who turned his head
away.

Desolation crept around him like a wet
mist. He chewed upon the knuckles of his
hand and felt the hot tears roll down his
cheeks.

'For God's sake, Robert . . . must I do
this thing?'

'You must, Sire. Believe me.'

Robert watched without pity. An old, white-haired man grieving for the young wife who could mean nothing to him. The sight sickened him, and he waited with growing impatience.

'Very well. See to it for me, Robert . . . I cannot face her.' Robert left, filled with relief. There were other urgent matters to be discussed, but to raise them would have been pointless. He took it upon himself to cancel the meeting of the Great Council, telling the assembly that the earl of Wessex had refused to attend, preferring instead to go into exile.

The Englishmen present received the news in an incredulous silence and, while the Normans laughed and joked among themselves, they stared at each other with dazed eyes.

At length, earl Siward gave a long, low whistle.

'What now, Leofric?' he said.

Leofric shrugged. Inside him, he could not repress a feeling of pleasure. All that talk of Godwin's about a Norman plot . . . he had not been entirely convinced.

'Godwin was not king,' he said, 'and England is still England. I shall not lose much sleep over it.'

Siward blew through his lips as if he had suddenly felt the cold. He glanced over to where a group of Normans were particularly noisy in their jubilation.

'Hark at them,' he said. 'They are worse than a dozen Godwins.'

Leofric stared morosely. The foreigners had called for wine and were in the process of becoming uproarious. As he watched them, Leofric could not suppress a little shiver of revulsion.

Robert wasted no time in celebration, but sent for the lady Edith's chaplain and demanded an audience with her. She received him in her bower, tall, well-groomed and elegant, her auburn hair plaited to perfection. But from the way her mouth was set, it was plain that she knew that her father was in disgrace and that her own future was in the balance.

Robert did not mince words, but spoke directly, even harshly, for he loathed all the Godwin family. But he was soon aware that the calm, impassive face before him would not flinch or tremble, and that the cool green eyes did not fill with tears, but gazed into his own until he was forced to look aside.

Edith heard him out, then asked where she was to go.

'To your father at Bruges. Tell your women to pack whatever you need, and I will provide a ship to sail on the noon tide tomorrow.'

After he had gone, Edith sat with her chin in her hands. Her thoughts were for her husband: Robert had told her that he had no wish to see her, but she did not believe that and, besides, there was a request she wished of him.

She went to the doorway: she had expected a guard but there was none, and she made her way down the stairway, from where she could hear the shouting and laughter from the hall. Outside Edward's private room, the guard smiled and saluted her. Robert, she thought, was growing careless in success.

Her husband was sitting at the table, a half-empty glass goblet of wine in his hand and a flask on the table. He looked up as she entered and she noticed that his eyes were redrimmed and that he was unsteady as he rose to his feet. This concerned her, because she knew that he usually only drank sparingly because too much wine affected his stomach.

'My lord . . . think what you are at.'

He stared at her, blinking and holding the back of his chair for support. The candlelight glistened on his tear-stained cheeks, and his mouth opened but no words came.

Gently, she persuaded him back into his chair and sat down to face him, managing to smile encouragement.

'My lord,' she said. 'You must learn to take more care of yourself.'

He seemed at a loss for words. Like a small boy caught filching delicacies from the kitchen, he pushed the goblet away from him, wiped his mouth with the back of his hand and rubbed his cheeks with his fingertips.

Edith watched him sadly. Poor Edward, she thought. He would be lost without her.

'You must forgive me, my lord,' she said.

He raised his eyebrows. 'I . . . forgive you? For what?'

'Archbishop Robert said you had no wish to see me. But I have a favour to ask you.'

'A favour . . . ' He looked away as his eyes filled with tears, and blew his nose on a silk kerchief. 'Edith . . . believe me. This is not my wish. If I had my way you would stay with me.'

Edith nodded her understanding. At that moment she hated Robert with all her heart.

'Robert told me I am to go to Bruges to be with my father.'

'Is that not what you wish?'

She shook her head vehemently. 'Bruges is far away — an ocean would divide us. Let me stay in England, breathing the same air as yourself.'

Edward felt a great feebleness: throughout their life together, Edith had asked few favours and it was bitter that he could not grant this one final request.

'There is a nunnery at Wherwell,' she

240

said, 'not far from Winchester. I should not be too sad there.'

He looked at her. 'You would be a nun?'

Edith spread her hands. 'What else could I be if I am not to be with you?'

He sat silent for a while, staring at the wine in his goblet. As far as he could see, there was only one objection.

'Robert will not allow it,' he said, half to himself.

If he had been looking at Edith he would have seen the sudden blaze of anger in her eyes, quickly quelled. But the colour which had risen to her cheeks stayed.

'Robert is neither my husband nor the king of England,' she said quietly.

There was a rustling at the doorway and soft footfalls across the floor. Only one person would enter the king's presence unannounced. Edith did not look up.

'Robert . . . ' Edward shuffled himself erect in his chair. 'The lady Edith wishes to become a nun at Wherwell.'

There was a pause. Edith, staring at the

241

table-top, could imagine Robert pursing his lips and shaking his head.

'I can see nothing against it . . . ' Edward's voice was defensively shrill ' . . . therefore I have granted her request.' He rolled on his buttocks and looked away from the Archbishop, his mouth petulant. Robert stared at him for a moment then turned his head to look at Edith. She was looking up at him with the slightest of smiles, and her green eyes were eloquent.

Robert turned and left, furiously angry at the rebuff. True, it was of no consequence — the bitch could do no mischief in the nunnery, and he would give the Abbess strict instructions that she could have no favours. But his orders had been countermanded — and the victory had gone to a Godwin, at that.

Clenching his teeth, he swept into the great hall. It was empty but for a group of his countrymen, noisily convivial. Earl Ralf saw him and waved an arm.

'How goes it, lord Archbishop? Are we all rich and mighty yet?'

Robert saw that he was drunk, and his

lips grew thin. 'Do you expect to grow rich sitting on your backsides pouring wine down your throats?' he spat.

The grin faded from Ralf's face, and his mouth lapsed open as he tried to focus his eyes. The silence was broken by Otto, who had been drinking but was not drunk.

'Come, my lord,' he said reasonably, 'surely a victory deserves a celebration?'

'Victory . . . ?' Robert's tone was scathing. 'What victory? We shall have nothing to celebrate until Godwin and his brood are dead.'

'They have five days of grace,' said Otto. 'Perhaps on the sixth day . . . '

'On the sixth day they will be gone.' Robert thought for a moment, looking hard at Otto. 'Except, perhaps, for one.'

Otto's eyes became alert. 'Harold . . . ' he said. 'He has a wife and child in Hereford. He will not desert them.'

Robert gave the faintest of smiles. He approved of Otto as a man with a quick brain, prepared to think and work for his ambitions.

'He will need every minute of the five

days, and luck besides.'

Otto laughed and seized Ralf by the shoulder. 'Come on, my friend,' he said, shaking him. 'Find a bed and sleep off the wine — we have three days hard riding ahead of us.'

★ ★ ★

Dawn the next morning found Harold shaking the sleep from his eyes as he mounted his horse for the ride from Farnham to Winchester. His head was heavy on his shoulders and full of dark thoughts.

The previous afternoon, he had instructed Hodda to ride like the wind for Hereford, to gather Aldred and a hundred of the housecarls as escort to his wife and son on the journey to Bristol. Hodda was young, well-mounted and he knew what was at stake. He would not fail in his mission. But Harold grudged every step of the way to Winchester, and gazed longingly down every road and path which led to the west.

They arrived in Winchester well before noon, amid a cloud of dust that was not allowed to settle, for Godwin was like a man berserk: he took no rest or food, but set about organising the transportation of treasure and valuables, for he was determined that nothing of any worth should be left behind. He shouted orders, and servants ran like ants: any man who was slow in mind or movement felt the rough edge of his tongue, and within a few hours the first of the ox-drawn wagons began its slow and ponderous journey to Bosham.

He had sent Brand to fetch Tostig and Judith from Wilton, and in the late afternoon they arrived. Tostig affected to be amused at the commotion: he was pleased to be going back to Bruges, airily confident that Godwin would be recalled from exile as soon as the king came to his senses. As for Judith, she managed to charm Harold part of the way out of his black mood.

At last Godwin had done all he could for that day. He came to Gytha looking pale and drawn, his eyes deep set in their sockets. Gytha was concerned, but he waved her worries aside and called the family to him and outlined his plans for the future. Their exile, he said, could be no more than temporary, for there were larger issues at stake than family pride and possessions. Either common sense would return to the king, or they would have to fight their way back. In any event, they would be back in Winchester before a year had passed.

To Harold, he said: 'You leave for Bristol tomorrow to take ship with Edith and your son. Where shall you go?'

Harold had assumed that Godwin would not welcome his family at Bruges, and he had his answer ready.

'I shall go to Ireland, to the court of King Liam. He and I are good friends.'

Godwin nodded and smiled in a way that showed sympathy and respect. 'So be it,' he said, and would have passed on to another matter, but Leofwin spoke up.

'Why should not Harold bring his Edith and my nephew to Bruges?' he asked, with the directness of a twelve-year-old.

Godwin frowned at him. 'Harold knows the reason and accepts it. It is none of your business.'

'It is not fair,' said Leofwin, petulantly. 'If it must be so, then I shall go to Ireland with Harold.'

'I also,' said Gyrth, not to be outdone in defending his favourite brother.

Godwin glowered, but before he could say anything, Harold threw up his hands in mock embarrassment.

'Hold fast,' he said, laughing. 'It is a long journey to Ireland. And the Irish do not live in the way we do. You will be far more comfortable in Bruges.'

But the more he tried to dissuade them, the more they clamoured to go with him, until Harold looked question-ingly at his father.

'Very well,' said Godwin, 'but only one of you may accompany Harold. You must settle it between yourselves.'

They argued earnestly, and when it seemed as though it would end in a quarrel, Harold picked a rush from the floor and broke it into two uneven lengths.

'It will be quicker if you draw straws,' he said.

So it was that early the next morning, Harold set off for Bristol at the head of his five housecarls. Beside him rode Leofwin, breathless and bright-eyed, in spite of the early hour and the fact that he had hardly slept for excitement. That he was leaving his home and family for an indefinite period never occurred to him: he could only think that he was setting out on the greatest adventure of his young life.

Harold knew that the journey to Bristol could be accomplished in two days. This would leave a further two days in which to prepare the three ships which he knew were available in the harbour for the arrival of his family and the housecarls, who, he estimated, should reach Bristol during the final day of grace. But as he thought about it he became uneasy. Suppose that, for some reason, Hodda was delayed on his way to Hereford? Or, if he had done what was expected of him, there were a hundred things that could be amiss in Hereford to delay the start for Bristol.

The more he thought, the more he

worried, and the faster he urged the pace. His only consoling thought was that he was well-known and respected in Bristol, and the five days of grace might, with luck, be extended to six or seven.

But that night, he learned that such luck was not on his side. Wulstan, the thane in whose hall they lodged, had heard that a party of Normans, headed by earl Ralf, were heading westwards as though the devil were after them.

Harold drew air through his teeth. 'How many?'

Wulstan shrugged. 'Not many . . . a score, perhaps.'

Harold stared into the fire. If it came to a fight, even a score would be too many. He glanced at Leofwin, tired out and dozing in the warmth of the fire and a full belly. He wished he had not brought him with him.

They left at first light, speeded by Wulstan.

'God go with you, earl Harold, and bring you back soon.'

'We shall be back sooner than you

expect,' said Harold, with a confidence he did not feel.

The ships were where they should have been, and having sent two of his men to warn the sailors, he set about checking their seaworthiness, for he knew that the crossing to Ireland could be a severe test of a ship at that time of the year.

They spent two cold nights under the tilts of the ships, and on the morning of the final day of grace, Harold felt that he could sit waiting no longer. He told Leofwin that he would ride northwards to meet his family.

'I shall come with you,' said Leofwin.

'You will not,' said Harold, sternly. 'You will stay here with the men. It is better that I go on my own.' As an after-thought, he added, 'I shall not be long — but if, by chance, I have not returned by the time of the evening tide, you must set sail.'

Then, seeing the alarm on his brother's face, he said: 'Be easy — it was only a joke.'

Harold was in a sombre mood as he rode, filled with a sense of foreboding. At every vantage point he halted to scan the country ahead, looking in vain for a sight of what he most wished to see. At mid-day, he would have to decide whether to abandon hope of meeting up with his family and return to the ships, or whether he should press on northwards and sacrifice himself and perhaps Leofwin. As the sun approached its zenith, he favoured first one way and then the other, and his mood grew more and more black.

So encased was he in the armour of his thoughts that he failed to notice the horsemen who stood back from the road among the trees to the left and right of him, and he was brought to himself by a voice calling his name.

He looked up sharply, and reined in his horse.

Earl Ralf rode slowly towards him, showing his teeth in a smile. 'I had not expected you so soon — nor from that direction,' he said.

Harold stared at him. He was not deceived by the Frenchman's mild manner, and a brief glance about him made it clear that he had no chance if it came to a fight. To make a run for it would have been possible, but running away had never come easily to him.

'What of it?' he said, gruffly.

Ralf shrugged. 'You act oddly for a man sentenced to exile,' he observed.

'I may please myself until sundown tonight,' said Harold.

Ralf raised his eyebrows. 'By my reckoning,' he said, 'your five days of grace were ended last night.' His manner suddenly became menacing. 'Come, now . . . you have lived long enough, Harold Godwinson. But as you think that your five days end at sunset, we shall play fair and not hang you before then.'

The Normans had now surrounded them, blocking the road in both directions. Harold felt his mouth go dry.

'And what,' he said, 'do you think my housecarls will be doing in the meantime?'

Ralf laughed unpleasantly. 'What housecarls?'

Harold pointed northwards along the road. 'Look there . . . '

All heads turned. Harold bunched his

fist and hit Ralf hard across the mouth, at the same time kicking his horse's flanks. Like a startled hare, it plunged between the horses in its path, knocking them sideways. Harold regained his balance and urged his mount into a gallop; a backward glance showed the Normans in confusion and that he had gained a good start on them.

There was no way to go but straight on. Harold leaned forward over his horse's striving neck, his mind in a turmoil. It was useless to think of turning back — Leofwin would have to do as he thought best. As for himself, he would ride and ride until his horse dropped under him.

And then, suddenly, as he rounded a corner, there was Aldred at the head of the housecarls. And there was Hodda, cradling the baby Godwin in his shield. And, best of all, there was Edith.

13

When earl Ralf returned to Westminster and reported that Harold Godwinson and his family had set sail from Bristol, Robert was disappointed but not dismayed. The first of the autumn gales was shrieking its wild song along the eaves of the palace, stripping the last vestiges of summer from the oak trees and ruffling the placid water of the river into frothy wavelets. And Robert knew that close behind the gales would come the frost and snow of winter.

That Godwin would accept defeat was inconceivable: he would attempt a return, but it could not take place until spring at the earliest, and by that time Robert expected to have his house in order, proofed against any eventuality.

After the lady Edith had gone to Wherwell, Edward had become indifferent to the affairs of State. He became like a monk, spending much time in prayer and taking frugal meals in his private apartment. His sole concern was with the affairs of the Church and the building of the new Minster, which, he declared, was to serve as an indestructible monument to him after his death. It seemed to many that he was content to play the part of Archbishop to Robert's king.

Robert was happy with this state of affairs, since the king affixed his seal to whatever documents Robert set before him with only cursory interest. In this way, Harold's earldom was granted to Ralf, and the shires of Cornwall, Devon and Somerset, which had been Godwin's, were granted to Otto of Bernay, for Robert was well-pleased with the young man and had marked him down for a much higher place in the years to come.

It was in the matter of the disposal of the rest of Wessex that Edward first crossed Robert's path. In keeping with his promise to Count Eustace of Boulogne, Robert had suggested that the favour of Kent should be granted to the Frenchman. 'It would be recompense for the indignity inflicted on him by Godwin,' he said, expecting an easy agreement.

But Edward pondered for a while, biting on his knuckles and darting glances at Robert out of the corners of his eyes. 'Kent,' he said at last, 'is the threshold of my kingdom. It is best if I keep it for myself.'

Robert was taken aback but not deterred. 'Then may I suggest, Sire, that the shire of Sussex should be granted to Count Eustace?'

Edward's lips grew tight and the colour mounted to his cheeks. 'No, Robert,' he said firmly. 'Eustace may be my brother-in-law, but it was not by my choice. There is no love between us and I would rather he stayed on the far side of the Channel. As for the rest of Godwin's estates, I shall hold them forfeit.'

Robert felt a stab of annoyance, but he saw the set of the king's jaw, and knew that to argue the point would be time wasted.

So Eustace could whistle for his reward: Robert would lose no sleep over it. And when he reflected on the matter, he could see the advantages of Wessex being held in forfeit for the time being. For there were land-hungry men who would dance to Robert's tune at the prospect of a share in the riches of the south. Leofric, for example . . .

Taking all things into consideration, Robert had reason to believe that the tide of fortune was running strongly in his favour, and to take full advantage of it he sent a trusted messenger to Normandy with a parchment for the attention of Duke William.

The messenger found the Duke at Caen, where he was resting after a hard and bloody campaign against Geoffrey of Anjou. In private, William conferred with Lanfranc, whose advice he sought on most things.

'This Archbishop has proved himself to be no mere windbag,' he said. 'What do you read into his message, Lanfranc?'

Lanfranc shrugged. 'It is guarded. He says no more than that it may be to your advantage to visit the court of King Edward.'

William laughed shortly. 'It is vague enough to be interesting. Would to God I could spare the time. Perhaps this Robert can persuade our enemies to hold off for a while.'

'Sire,' said Lanfranc, 'you should go. A jewel lies glittering by the roadside — would you leave it to the next passer-by because you are tired and the hour is late?'

'Suppose the jewel turns out to be nothing more than a glow-worm?'

'Then no harm is done, and nothing is lost.'

'Except my dukedom, perhaps,' said William, morosely.

Lanfranc scoffed. 'Geoffrey has run to the king of France. They can do nothing until the summer. Go to London in the early spring and leave your affairs here in the hands of Roger of Montgomery. You need not be away for more than a month.'

The Duke thought for a while and then said: 'You must come with me, my friend.'

'I would not let you go alone,' said Lanfranc, smiling. 'Besides, I would see more of this Robert of Canterbury.'

The weather being favourable, early in March they landed in England and set off for London. William had brought with him a small escort of knights, and Edward, prompted by Robert, sent a king's escort, under the command of earl Otto, to meet them.

As William rode through the countryside, he noted the carefully tilled fields and holdings and stared thoughtfully at the plump cattle which grazed the common fields belonging to the villages and hamlets through which they rode. The land was rich and unmarked by war: in Normandy, one could not ride fifteen miles without coming across burnt and silent villages surrounded by the ashes of last year's crops. He looked at Lanfranc, his mind filled with the thought that, above all things, he wanted England for his own. Lanfranc looked back at him and nodded, as though he had read the Duke's thoughts.

He asked Otto many questions about the English and their government, and by the time they came to Westminster, he knew as much about the land as he needed.

It was many years since Edward had

seen Duke William, and he remembered him as a dark, brooding lad who said little but watched everything with resentful eyes. Edward had mistaken the surliness for shyness, and had been kind to the boy, and ever after William had remembered the strange young man with the white hair and peculiar eyes with an amused affection.

At supper that night, they spoke of old times, and Robert, who sat at the king's left hand, noted with satisfaction that Edward seemed completely at ease, and that his friendship for the Duke seemed to increase as the night wore on.

'Cousin,' said Edward. 'I would show you more of my kingdom: it is at its best in the early summer.'

'Alas, Sire, at home I have bad neighbours, and as much as I would like, I can only rest here for a few days.' William was eyeing the gold and silver plate and drinking vessels, calculating their worth.

Edward touched his hand lightly. 'War is an abomination. Nightly, I give thanks to God that there has been no fighting in this country since my coming, and I shall see to it that there will be none for many years after I am gone.'

William looked at the ceiling. 'Fortunate is the heir to this rich and beautiful country,' he said. 'To live in peace amid a happy and contented people should be the aim of every civilised man.'

Edward sighed and looked into his wine. 'I have no direct heir, cousin. My marriage was . . . not blessed.'

'You should marry again,' William turned to look at the king. 'You have time enough to produce a dozen heirs.'

'You are kind . . . but I shall not marry again.'

William did not fear to take the bull by the horns. 'Then who will follow you?'

'I have a nephew . . . the son of my half-brother, Edmund. He lives in Hungary and is known in England as Edward the Exile.'

Robert spoke up so that his voice could easily be heard by William. 'He is an old man, Sire, with less time to live than yourself.'

261

'He has a son, Edgar,' said Edward defensively.

'A puny child, Sire, weak in mind and body, so it is said. England will need a strong man to keep the peace.'

Edward shrugged. 'The Royal House,' he said to William, 'is not blessed with strong men since Godwin betrayed my brother.'

William thought that sufficient progress had been made for the time being, and turned the conversation to other subjects.

Edward took delight in William's company and spent the next few days escorting him through the countryside around London. William was impressed, particularly by the high regard which even the most humble of his subjects held for their king.

'In Normandy,' he said to Edward, 'when the peasants hear horsemen approaching, they run for cover like startled deer.'

Edward looked at the strong, well-defined features of the man who rode beside him and sighed for the Normandy he loved.

That evening there arrived a messenger from Roger of Montgomery with news that certain of the Norman barons, encouraged by William's absence, had banded together and were ravaging the land of a neighbour. Straightaway, William went to Edward.

'Sire, it grieves me, but I must leave for Normandy in the morning.'

Disappointed, Edward asked if the matter could not be dealt with later, but William would not delay.

'Normandy is like a barn full of dry straw — one spark, and you have a blaze.' He made a gesture of angry impatience: 'My barons are like unruly children — I must take the whip to them.'

Edward looked at him with unconcealed admiration: here was a man with the courage of Edmund Ironside and the strength of Canute.

'Cousin,' he said, 'we spoke the other evening of my successor. There is the old and decrepit father and the ailing son. But Robert is right — England is full of factions, and it needs a strong man to band them together. If I offered to name

263

you as my successor, what would you say?'

William looked at him for several moments, his dark eyes shining. 'Sire, there is nothing I would like better.'

'It shall be done, then,' said Edward, clasping the Duke's hand.

Later that night, William spoke in private to a triumphant Robert.

'Did I not tell you, Sire, when we met in Normandy a year ago?' said Robert.

William frowned. 'It has come about too easily. What could go wrong?'

'It was not easy to get rid of Godwin,' said Robert, testily.

The Duke's frown became a scowl. 'Even so, Robert, I am not king yet. Tell me what obstacles there may be.'

Robert gave a thin smile. 'There is only one — a mere pebble on the path: on the king's death, his chosen heir must be approved by the Great Council.'

'And if they decline to approve . . . ?'

'They will not,' said Robert. 'Not while I am alive.'

William studied the Archbishop in silence. He was much younger than the king, and seemed in good health.

'Very well,' he said at last. 'Archbishop Robert, you have done me great service: it shall not go unrewarded.'

Later, on board ship for Normandy, he asked Lanfranc for his opinion of Robert.

Lanfranc laughed. 'We hardly spoke more than a few pleasantries. He thought me beneath his dignity — he reserves his brain for the leaders of men.'

'He is a schemer — a contriver,' growled William. 'A dangerous man — I must rid myself of him. Besides,' he added, smiling, 'I cannot have two advisers when I am King of England.'

'If that day comes . . . ' said Lanfranc.

The Duke turned to look at him. 'It will come,' he said gravely, 'one way or the other.'

★　★　★

In Ireland, Harold fretted. He had received news from England that his earldom was now Ralf's, and he grieved for his people. The same messenger had told him that Otto held all the north coast of the western peninsular and was building himself a fine hall above the harbour at Porlock. The news added fire to his temper, for he disliked Otto even above Archbishop Robert, and Edith was hard put to soothe him.

'Be easy, my lord,' she scolded, 'now that the winter is gone you will surely receive news from your father.'

Harold grunted, stretching his arms and yawning. The winter had been the wettest he could remember — the roads had been unusable for weeks and one could hardly venture outside without risk of sinking up to the waist in a marsh. As a result, he and his men were out of condition and it would take many weeks of exercise before they were fit enough to call themselves soldiers.

Something would have to be done. He would consult with Aldred and Hodda . . .

He exploded into a laugh. 'Hodda . . . the voyage . . . have you ever seen a face so green?'

Edith shuddered, for she did not like to be reminded of that terrible voyage, with the wind shrieking overhead, and waves so enormous that they towered over the masthead, each one threatening to swamp the ship in a cascade of white, boiling foam. For two days and two nights she had sat, petrified with cold and fear, clutching baby Godwin wrapped in sailcloth, unable to think further than the next gigantic wave.

'Poor Hodda,' she said. 'On the way to Bristol he was so excited at the thought of going on the sea . . . After we had landed, he asked me if it was always thus.'

'What did you tell him . . . that it had been smoother than usual?'

'Shame on you for thinking of it.' said Edith.

Harold grew serious. 'It was an omen,' he said. 'I remember thinking that if we could live through that, we could survive anything. And every ship stayed afloat . . . it was a sign that God has not finished with us yet. But I am beginning to think that father has.'

The winter had passed slowly for Godwin, alternating between periods of depression because of the inactivity forced on him by the time of the year and interludes of anger and speculation whenever Bishop Stigand had contrived to send him news of events in England. In his mind, there was a half-formed plan of action, and he awaited the coming of spring like a hungry dog watching for its next meal.

Tostig had never passed a happier winter and, to him, England seemed part of a different world. To rile his father, he had once said that he had lost nothing by leaving, therefore there was nothing to be gained by returning. The remark had been facetious, but there were times when he believed in its truth.

Like his father, Sweyn awaited the first sign of spring, for it was then that he would start on his pilgrimage. As it happened, the day before he made his farewells, Godwin received news of Duke William's visit to England.

It was as though he had been bitten by a snake: immediately, he sent for Tostig.

'William of Normandy is at Westminster. Why, do you think?'

'How should I know?' said Tostig.

'You fool . . . he seeks the throne of England. And if Edward promises it to him you will have lost your country through your indifference.'

Tostig flushed bright red. 'I . . . ? Father, I was not serious when I said . . . '

'I did not suppose you were.' Godwin's face had relaxed into a smile. 'But neither does William joke, and Robert is deadly serious. No doubt he has weaved such a web that Edward does not know his head from his heels. By God, Tostig, we must start back before the damage is unmendable. This week . . . tomorrow.'

Tostig rubbed his forehead. He had been lazy, and he had eaten and drunk too much during the winter. But he did not think it had addled his brain.

'It will take months,' he said doubtfully, 'to raise an army and collect enough ships.'

Godwin laughed. 'You see? You have just begun to think. But I have been wrestling with this problem since we left England.' He watched Tostig's face with amusement. 'There will be no army, Tostig, because we want friends, not enemies. I am told that we still have many supporters in the south, and I shall go and test the quality of their friendship.'

Tostig did not fully understand, but he was dismayed at the thought of his father going alone to England. 'At least,' he protested, 'let me go with you.'

Godwin looked at his son and smiled. 'The colour of your hair shouts 'Tostig Godwinson'. No, my son, I shall take Brand as my companion. We shall be two old men together, and neither can run faster than the other.'

14

A lesser man than Archbishop Robert might have been content to rest on his laurels: the obstacles had been overcome, the opposition vanquished and there was nothing but time between him and his goal. But Robert could not rest easy while Godwin was alive.

Being the man he was, he had friends of convenience in most of the European states, and throughout the winter he received regular reports from Bruges on the activities of the Godwin family. When the coming of spring brought no news of the gathering of an army, he was not surprised, for he guessed that Godwin would be more subtle than to invade with an army of mercenaries, particularly as it had been reported to him that the people of Wessex were still loyal to their earl.

As soon as Duke William had left the country, Robert summoned the earls Ralf and Otto and sent them to Sandwich,

Otto to prepare and command a fleet of ships to defend the coast, while Ralf was to gather a force of mounted Normans, the presence of which, Robert hoped, would remind the people of the south-east that Godwin was no longer their lord.

Normally, these measures would have been submitted to the Council, for discussion and approval; but since Robert by now had sufficient adherents in both Councils to ensure that he had his way, it seemed to him that the old procedure would be a waste of time, and he therefore proceeded on the course of government by decree.

In his hall at Coventry, Leofric of Mercia was not happy. He thought of the old days, when the rivalry between himself and Godwin had been sharp to the point of bitterness. He remembered the feeling of achievement when he had gained a victory in the Council, and the anger and depression when he had been on the losing side. How often he had wished to see his rival discredited and disgraced. Now Godwin was gone — and so, it seemed, was the Council. He mulled over in his mind whether he preferred things as they had been, or as they now were; and, but for one consideration, the answer was undeniably clear.

The consideration was, of course, that the richest part of the old earldom of Wessex was going begging. Leofric knew that at the moment Edward held it, but he guessed that sooner or later it would be granted to some fortunate individual. The thought that the recipient might be some smooth-tongued Norman courtier was more than he could bear, and he rode to Westminster with the sole purpose of discussing the matter with Edward.

The king listened to what he had to say, but seemed disinclined to discuss the matter. Instead, the earl was treated to an unwanted lecture on the art of building in stone, and an invitation to hunt deer in the forest of Windsor. But as Leofric had no knowledge of and no interest in architecture, and his joints were too fickle to allow him to hunt, he turned, in a fit of frustration, to the Archbishop of Canterbury.

Robert was courteous — almost charming, in the manner of a predator not wishing to frighten away his next meal. It was true, he said, that the present arrangements were only temporary, and in due course the king would grant favours of land to deserving subjects. In the meantime, Robert would gladly whisper a word or two on Leofric's behalf.

The earl was slightly mollified but hardly at rest, while Robert smacked his lips as though he had partaken of some tasty morsel. As he had imagined, Leofric could be deemed a friend while the title of Wessex hung in the balance. He made a mental note that the king should hold Wessex until Leofric's goodwill was no longer necessary.

The weather turned wet and cold, and Leofric stayed at court until it should improve. While he was there, Earl Siward arrived, having made the journey from the far north with the object of assessing the worth of 'this Duke of Normandy' of whom he had heard so much. By the time Siward had overcome the bad weather and the atrocious roads, the Duke had

274

long since gone, and Siward, out of temper, vented his spleen to Leofric.

'God . . . look at them,' he said, indicating the assembled company, 'not an Englishman among them. And the food spiced enough to burn your stomach.' He belched loudly, as if to emphasise his point. 'Godwin,' he went on, 'may have been sharp enough to cut the beard from your face, but I'd rather have his brand of roguery than this lot of mealy-mouthed foreigners. What do you say?'

Leofric pretended not to have heard. He was tortured by the suspicion that, in spite of his smooth assurances, Robert would play him false, and that he would never count even a part of Wessex as his own. In which case he might as well agree with Siward. On the other hand, there was always a chance . . .

'I tell you this,' growled Siward, grinding a hand-cloth between his huge, greasy palms, 'if Godwin has any sense, he will land in Northumbria . . . among friends, with a readymade army to follow him.'

Leofric stared straight ahead. He was very unhappy.

Robert heard nothing of Godwin until the middle of April, when a monk of Canterbury sent a message to his master that a man reputed to be the earl had been seen in Dover. Robert frowned over the scrap of parchment: the information was third or fourth hand — probably nothing more than a piece of idle gossip.

He dismissed it from his mind until a week or two later when a report was brought to him that a pedlar who had recently arrived in London from the south had been heard to boast that he had actually spoken to Godwin. When he heard this, Robert's dark brown eyes flashed, and he demanded that the man be brought before him.

When at length he was traced, the pedlar proved to be a small, rat-like character, bewildered and afraid at being brought into the presence of the Archbishop. Robert delivered a stern homily on the advisability of telling the truth, and then began to question him soundly.

The pedlar had been in Hastings, and

attracted by the size of a group of fishermen, he had gone over to join them, hoping to make a few sales. In the centre of the group, talking and laughing, was Godwin. Yes, he was certain it was Godwin: he had seen him twice before, and there could be no mistaking him, even though on this occasion he had been wearing ordinary clothes instead of the usual finery.

When Robert asked what they had been talking about, the pedlar said he could not be sure because as soon as he had joined the group someone had made a remark about the presence of strange ears, and the group had broken up. He thought, however, that the talk had been of ships.

Robert gave him a piece of silver and sent him away. In his own mind he was convinced that Godwin was in England — that he had placed his head in a noose which must be jerked tight around his neck without delay. Immediately, he took horse for Sandwich to pass on what he knew to the earls Otto and Ralf.

Godwin was tired to the point of exhaustion. He had been in England for the best part of a month, and during that time, with Brand at his side, he had travelled all over the southeastern shires, from Dover to Selsey and inland as far as Dorking in Surrey. He had visited old friends, renewed acquaintances and, he hoped, made new friends. He had visited every harbour along the south coast, except for Sandwich, which he knew to be infested with foreigners, and he had talked to the seamen in their own language.

The incessant travelling had been tiring enough, but in addition it had been necessary to maintain a constant wariness, which had made the task doubly exhausting. But at last he was satisfied that he had done everything possible, and for the last time he turned his horse into the Forest of Andred to make his way to the home of Edric Cuthbertson, the outlaw.

Edric was alarmed when he saw the

ashy pallor of Godwin's face.

'For the love of God,' he said, 'you must rest here for a few days to recover your strength.'

Godwin slid thankfully from his saddle and gave a wan smile. To lay with his eyes closed on a bed of fresh straw seemed the most desirable thing in the world.

'A night's rest will suffice,' he said, without conviction.

Edric exchanged glances with Brand, who showed the whites of his eyes and felt tenderly at the sores from the rough saddle on his buttocks and thighs. It would be a day or two, he decided, before he sat on a horse again.

That night, when they had eaten, and while Godwin slept on his bed, Edric said to Brand: 'Is it all done, then?'

'It is, thank God. I would not like to have to start again.'

'Will it be worth the effort?'

Brand jerked his head towards Godwin. 'He says it will, and he is as good a judge of men as any. But I remind myself that what a man promises today he is liable to forget tomorrow.'

Edric stared at the earl's recumbent form. 'He is a man in ten thousand: the humble folk look to him as a father, and his thanes respect him as a god. They will do anything for him.'

Brand gave a rueful laugh and rose stiffly to his feet. 'He may be a god to some, but to me he is a mortal man — over the past weeks I have often wished that he would remember his age — and mine.'

It was several days before Godwin's will overcame his lethargy. He rose from his bed one morning and went outside to stretch his muscles and fill his lungs with air. The sky was blue, flecked by small white clouds, like swansdown, driven before a breeze from the south-west. He thought of the days he had lain idle, and cursed himself for a fool.

'I have been lazy for too long,' he said to Edric. 'We shall leave today for Pevensey, where there is a ship which will take us to Bruges.'

'Before you leave there are things you should know, Godwin.'

The earl looked sharply at his friend and grunted.

'Firstly,' said Edric, 'there are king's ships in the ports and harbours — one here and two there, and they change their harbours from day to day so that it is difficult to say where they are not. And secondly, there are parties of mounted men, Normans, scouring the coastal plain, offering pieces of silver for news of Godwin.'

Godwin rubbed his cheek, half-thoughtful, half-amused.

'Does anyone take their silver?'

Edric shrugged. 'Would you trust every man in Wessex with your life?'

Godwin laughed. 'I am not that much of a fool, Edric.'

'Then stay here for a while, until the Normans grow tired.'

But Godwin refreshed was like a hunter after a wounded quarry, and so later that morning he and Brand emerged from the Forest and set their horses' heads towards the south-east.

The day was warm, but they had a long way to go, and Godwin pressed forward at a trot, keeping to the most direct route.

Brand grumbled at the pace and urged caution, but Godwin scoffed at him, saying that they had wasted too much time already, and that there was no danger. But during the afternoon they rounded a bend in the road and saw ahead four horses tethered to the branch of a tree and their riders lounging on the grass in the shade. One of the men stood up and moved resolutely into their path, his arms outstretched.

Godwin noted the close-cropped hair and the beardless face, tensed himself to urge his horse into a gallop, but thought better of it and drew rein. The Norman grasped hold of the bridle and peered closely at Godwin.

'You travel fast on a warm day,' he said.

'I go to pay the rent for my holding,' said Godwin, tersely.

'Rent? It seems an odd time of year to be paying rent.'

'It is in arrears these past two months.'

The man laughed uproariously. 'You English . . . ' He fumbled at his belt and produced a silver penny, holding it up between his finger and thumb. 'Hard up, are you? You can have this for a small service.'

'What service is that?' said Godwin, his eyes on the silver.

'Tell me where I can find Godwin of Wessex.'

'Godwin . . . ' The earl eased himself in his saddle and looked fleetingly at Brand. He bent towards the man and spoke quietly. 'You might try Steyning,' he said, jerking his thumb towards the west.

'Steyning?' The Norman's eyes were suddenly alert. 'You have seen him there yourself?'

Godwin bridled. 'Not I . . . but I have spoken to a man who knows a man whose brother . . . '

'Oh, for God's sake . . . what sort of a story is that?' He let go of the bridle and stood back. 'Be off with you.'

Godwin made no move. 'What about the silver?' he said stubbornly. The Norman cursed and waved him on, and Godwin dug his heels into his horse's flanks.

Beside him, Brand gave way to laughter . . . a silent, shoulder-shaking laughter which turned his face bright red. Godwin watched him out of the corner of his eye.

'I shall treasure the memory of that,' he said. 'But I would have liked the silver penny as a keepsake.'

Brand at length controlled his laughter and drew air noisily into his lungs. 'Did you not recognise him?'

The earl looked startled. 'Should I have done?'

'He was one of Ralf's men. He has seen you often enough before . . . but not with that tangled beard and hair. You might be your own grandfather . . . ' He started to laugh again.

Godwin shivered down his back. He fingered his beard; and presently he, too, started to laugh.

They reached the heights above Pevensey well before dusk, and from there they could see that there was nothing as large as a king's ship on the water, so they rode down the slope and, having left the horses to graze where they would easily be found, set off on foot along the path which at low tide, wound its way through the marshes and mud flats to the shore.

Osred, the shipmaster, had kept the rendezvous for the past few evenings, and he sighed with relief when he recognised them, for he was beginning to think that they had been taken by the Normans. He would not listen to Godwin's apologies for his late arrival.

'That you are here is all that matters,' he said. 'The tide will float the ship in three hours and there will be enough wind to send us on our way.'

The next morning, the sun rose in a blaze of yellow from behind Boulogne, and as the morning mist cleared, Godwin could make out the coastline of both France and England. The west wind filled the sail and the prow of the ship dipped into the sea, slapping the waves so that the spray flew gleaming white in the sun. Godwin tasted the salt on his lips and felt the wind tug at his hair: suddenly, he felt carefree and wished that he could sail on and on before the wind for ever.

The helmsman shouted, and pointed over the port bow. Osred hurried past and Godwin followed him on to the helmsman's platform, placing his hand on the tiller to steady himself, feeling the strong, insistent vibration of the sea through the timber.

Osred turned to him. 'A warship,' he said.

Godwin looked at the long, low shape, sailless in the water, sunlight flashing on wet oar blades. He turned to Osred, who was looking at him questioningly, and shrugged: they could not outsail the longship and there was nowhere to hide.

As if Godwin had spoken, Osred took the tiller and altered course to pass behind the longship, which was making to cross their bows. Minutes passed: Godwin forgot the wind and spray as he stared at the graceful ship as it appeared to slide sideways past their starboard beam. The helmsman had turned to watch them: they could see the pink blur of his face framed in a mass of flowing red hair.

The longship turned sharply to port, the oars were shipped and the sail rose to the masthead and filled with wind. It came after them on a converging course as though they were motionless.

Godwin called to Brand: 'That man at the tiller — do you recognise him?'

Brand stared for a while and then smiled. 'With that hair . . . who else could it be but Thorkill the Red?'

'Turn into wind, Osred.' His relief made Godwin joyful.

Soon the two ships were side by side, in hailing distance. Godwin cupped his hands to his mouth.

'Thorkill . . . you old Viking . . . ' he roared.

The red-haired man was puzzled: there was a pause before they heard his voice: 'Who . . . are . . . you?'

'Godwin the Fisherman from Bruges . . . '

There was another pause before they saw him slap his thigh and double up with laughter. Then, adroitly, he brought his ship close.

'There are fifty gold pieces for the crew that takes you, Godwin.'

The earl made a gesture of disgust. 'Is that all? Your paymaster is a miser.'

'Worse than that . . . ' Thorkill's laughter crossed the water to them, and they could see the rest of his crew grinning their enjoyment.

'Thorkill . . . I'll double that. A hundred gold pieces for every crew that follows me when I call them.'

'Done . . . but make it soon, Godwin. We are all hard up.' Still laughing, Thorkill waved his farewell. The oars were unshipped and the longship fled into the wind.

Godwin beamed at Osred. 'Bruges,' he said. 'As fast as the wind will take us.'

15

It was not until July that a messenger from Bruges arrived at King Liam's hall with instructions from Godwin that Harold and his ships should meet up with those of his father off the southern shore of the Isle of Wight during the first week in August. Harold had spent the last few months fuming at the apparent inaction of his father. He had exercised his housecarls and seamen until they were even more efficient than they had been in England, but now that word had arrived at last from his father, his frustration exploded into a fury of energy and excitement.

His wife, Edith, half-amused by his mood, did her best to soothe him by saying that, even if the wind changed to blow from the east, there was more than enough time to reach the Isle of Wight. Harold smiled at her and said that he had fish to fry before he met his father, and two days later the ships set sail — not southwards towards the entrance to the Channel, but on a course which filled their sails with the westerly wind.

Early the following morning, a look-out posted on the cliffs above the mouth of the Lyn to watch for shoals of pilchard, saw the ships sailing eastward parallel to the coast. He was too young to have experienced the Viking raids, but he had listened to the stories told by his father, and there was something about these ships which disturbed him. He hurried to tell of what he had seen.

The news spread quickly along the coast and inland: men to whom the Vikings were no more than bogey-men threw down their tools and implements to seize what arms they had and chivvied their children and womenfolk to places of safety.

At Porlock, Fulk Blue Chin, the Norman steward of earl Otto's new hall, scoffed at the story of Vikings, but since the villagers were insistent he allowed the women and children to take refuge within the stout oak walls while the men prepared an ambush on the track which led inland from the harbour. From their hiding places they watched the ships sail into the bay, drop their sails and turn into wind. Presently, three of them rowed into the harbour and beached.

Harold jumped ashore ahead of his men and stared curiously about him: the village was like a place of the dead — no living thing to be seen and no reply to his enquiring shouts. He pushed open the door of one of the cottages: there was a fire on the hearth, and a half-gutted fish on the table. He began to laugh.

'By God,' he said to the man behind him, 'they think we are Vikings.'

From a concealed look-out place in the hall, Fulk watched the armed men as they roamed among the cottages below. A small, rotund man, he made up with the quickness of his brain for what he lacked in stature and bearing, and as he watched the strangers he noted an unusually tall and powerful man, obviously the leader. In a flash, he realised: these were no Vikings — the big man was Harold Godwinson, come from Ireland.

Swiftly, he left the hall and hurried to the lane where the village men had laid their ambush. At that point the track was steep and narrow, so that no more than two men could walk abreast, with steep grassy banks rising on either side. As he approached, a hand grasped his arm and pulled him into the shelter of some bushes, and a moment later he saw two men labouring up the track.

One of them, wearing a byrnie and helmet, seemed to be remonstrating with the other, who was unarmoured, tall, loose-limbed and slender; his beardless face was smiling and he shook his head vigorously so that his fair hair danced about his shoulders. Fulk watched, fascinated and breathless, as they walked into the ambush.

A second later, they were on their faces in the dust, borne down by two men who leaped from the banks above them . . . a moment of writhing, dusty struggle — the glint of steel in an upraised fist.

Fulk ran down the track, shouting.

'Stop . . . stop . . . Do not kill them . . . '

The struggling ceased, and the knife was lowered. Fulk was respected by the villagers as the right-hand man of earl Otto, and at his command the two strangers were pulled to their feet and held with their arms pinioned behind them.

'These men,' said Fulk, 'are as English as you are.' He looked at the fair-haired young man appraisingly. 'In fact, I should not be surprised if . . .'

'What is this?' A voice, loud and full of authority, interrupted him. Fulk looked down the track and saw the big man: his blue eyes were angry and his sword was in his hand. Behind him were more of his men.

Fulk bowed. 'Welcome to Porlock, Harold Godwinson. It would have been more courteous had you not been armed.'

Harold gestured with his sword. 'Let them go,' he said, curtly.

Fulk smiled and looked pointedly at the banks above where Harold and his men stood. Harold glanced up and saw the men looking down at him, some with swords or spears, some with nothing but cudgels. But they had the advantage, and Harold licked the sweat from his upper lip.

'Not yet,' said Fulk. 'First, I will bargain with you.'

'With a serving boy and a soldier as hostage?' Harold's voice was scornful.

'A soldier, perhaps,' said Fulk. 'But the other one . . . What serving boy wears gold armbands and a jewel about his throat? And look at his features . . . the nose . . . that chin . . . ' he looked from the lad to Harold and back again. 'I'll gamble that this lad is the son of your father.'

Harold swore under his breath, then raised his voice so that everyone could hear. 'If either of these two men is as much as scratched, I swear before God that there will not be a cottage standing in Porlock tonight.'

Hodda thought he detected a sudden lessening of the pressure about his arms, and he tried to jerk himself away from his captor. Quick as a flash, the man flung an arm across his chest: in his hand was a knife pointing straight up at Hodda's throat.

Fulk was still smiling. 'You may threaten, Harold Godwinson, but I hold the power of life and death over your brother. But I'll strike a bargain with you.'

'What do you want?' said Harold, gruffly.

'I want you,' said Fulk. 'King Edward will pay much gold for you. Throw down your sword and order your men back to their ships. Your brother and the soldier can follow them, but you will stay here.'

There was a silence: Harold licked his lips, and his eyes darted uncertainly between Fulk and Leofwin.

Out of the corner of his eye, Hodda could see Leofwin: he was leaning forward, leaving a slight gap between himself and the man who held him. Hodda remembered a trick of fighting he had learned as a boy: he was older now, and more stiff-limbed, but the distance was right. He thought, too, of the knife at his throat: he would have to take his chance — everyone had to die sometime, and if the knife went home, at least he would have paid his debt to Earl Harold.

He pressed fleetingly back and then

launched himself into the air, twisting his body so that his left foot smashed into the face of the man who held Leofwin.

'Run . . . ' he yelled.

The man released Leofwin's arms and pressed both hands to his broken nose, and Hodda saw Leofwin start forward like a hare. At the same time, the knife went into his throat.

He was surprised how little it hurt — no more than the pressure of a cold finger.

Harold pushed Leofwin behind him and stared wide-eyed at Hodda as he lay on the ground, the blood pumping from his throat. Then the world went red, and he started forward with a roar of rage, his sword raised.

Fulk saw him coming and ran back up the track, his short legs moving like a stoat's, and at that moment the men lining the top of the banks came down like an avalanche.

Harold impaled one on his sword and smashed another to the ground with his fist. The track became a seething, swearing, screaming mass of men. There was no room for sword-play: the house-carls were using their hilts, fists, knees and feet with savage effect, for Hodda had been well-liked.

Harold saw the way things were going and started up the hill. The villager he had knocked down was gathering himself on all fours, and as he passed, Harold cracked his skull with the flat of his sword and set off with long, purpose strides. He wanted Otto of Bernay. Or if he were not there, the little fat man would do.

As he ran, Fulk heard the noise from the track, like a fight between wolves and dogs. The result was foreseeable, and he ran as he had never run before, guided by some animal instinct towards the shelter of the hall.

The women and children had heard the noise of the fighting and were gathered in petrified groups. As he came in, some of them screamed, but he ran past without hearing, regardless of the hands that clutched at his clothes. He pulled a tapestry from the hall and, gasping for breath, red-eyed with terror, flung himself into an alcove and covered himself with the cloth.

Harold appeared in the doorway and stood for a moment accustoming his eyes to the gloom. This time the women did not scream, but shrank back in horror because his hands were red and there was blood on his sword. Ignoring the women, he walked slowly the length of the hall, his eyes darting here and there. The blood pounded in his ears and his fingers, tingling with resolve, clutched the hilt of his sword as though it was Otto's neck.

Suddenly, he saw the bundle in the alcove and swiftly pulled the cloth aside. Fulk looked at him through his fingers, his mouth drawn across his teeth.

'Otto . . . '

Fulk looked at the sword and saw the blood drying on the blade almost up to the hilt.

'No . . . ' he screamed. 'No . . . '

'Where is he?'

'No . . . no . . . ' Fulk's voice became a piercing shriek which penetrated his brain like a knife. He raised his sword and brought it down with all his strength.

The noise stopped. Harold threw the cloth down and turned away.

Harold prowled warily through the building, searching into alcoves and dark places. There was a fire in the kitchen, and bundles of straw and rushes, and as he thrust his sword into them his mind returned to normal, and he knew that he would not find Otto.

Most of the women and children had fled into the woods; those that were left were grey-faced, looking pleadingly at a group of housecarls, dusty and blood-spattered, who had entered thinking of loot. Harold cleaned his sword and sheathed it. Before he left, he told his men to burn the hall to the ground.

At the scene of the ambush, he looked for Hodda's body: someone had picked him up and laid him against the bank, so that his head hung forward on his chest, hiding the wound in his throat. But he was quite dead.

Harold picked the body up and walked down the hill into the village. Now that the fighting was done, he felt sad and wished he had not come to Porlock.

At the foot of the hill, Harold saw that his men were busy firing the cottages. The thatched roofs burned easily, with dark red flames that rolled and twisted, while the sombre grey smoke swirled and writhed about the shore before fleeing out to sea on the off-shore breeze.

Aldred came to him out of the smoke and took part of his burden. Together they laid the body beneath the steering platform of Harold's ship and covered it with sail-cloth.

'Get the men aboard as soon as maybe,' said Harold in a flat and lifeless voice. 'We have wasted enough time.'

He glanced up at the hall and saw the smoke billowing up. There was no satisfaction in the sight.

There was savagery in the air that summer. Godwin left Bruges with his longships and beat up-wind along the Channel. By the third day, their provisions were running low, and while it would have been easy to put ashore at one of the friendly harbours of the mainland, Godwin's sword had been in its sheath too long, and the blood of his father was strong in his veins. He remembered that Edward had a special fondness for the royal manor of Bembridge on the Isle of Wight, and he led his ships into Brading harbour, the nearest to Bembridge, and demanded the things he needed.

True to his lord, the king's thane refused, whereupon Godwin ordered the hall to be burned to the ground and the slaughter of any who resisted. After which, they took what they needed and much else besides.

It was the same at another royal manor on the Isle of Portland, and Gyrth, who knew his father as a kind man, was startled and a little shocked to see this side of his nature. But if Godwin was venting his pent-up spite, there was also a method in his madness.

★　★　★

By the middle of June, Archbishop Robert was prepared to accept that Godwin had eluded his net and made his escape from the country. It did not surprise him, for it confirmed what he already suspected — that Godwin was so beloved by the southern English that no man among them was prepared to risk his life by turning informer. What did surprise Robert was the fact that Godwin had apparently been unable to raise an army or entice any ships away from the harbours.

It was illogical; and because he could make no sense of it, he sent for Ralf and Otto to see if they could throw any light on the matter.

Earl Ralf vented his feelings: he and his men had expended much time and energy chasing will-o'-the-wisps and shadows. The English, he said, were as they always had been — stupid, sullen and obstinate, and on the whole they had been conscientiously unhelpful. Yet it was from this attitude of theirs that he had formed a strong impression that Godwin had been, and perhaps still was in the country. He added, with a little jerk of the chin, that if he had been allowed to use the whip he might have had more success.

Otto had much the same story. The

seamen had carried out his orders, but without the enthusiasm he had expected — after all, fifty gold pieces for the successful crew was no mean bait. And lately he had noticed that the attitude of the sailors — and even the shipmasters — had changed for the worse: ships became unseaworthy for obscure reasons — crews became afflicted with mysterious illnesses — orders were misunderstood. There was no mutiny, or even insubordination — just that it seemed that the seamen had grown weary and were declining to co-operate.

Robert rubbed the side of his nose and exhaled through his teeth. What he had been told alarmed him more than he could say, most of all that the seed of rebellion had been planted among the sailors of the king's fleet. It seemed to him that the shires of Kent and Sussex were like a thunder cloud, writhing and seething for a moment before the thunderbolt flashed from within to strike with tumult and destruction.

Godwin's plan had suddenly become plain: he would cross the Channel alone and raise his standard, to which men would flock as, no doubt, they had already promised to do. The thought of it sent a shiver down his spine, and he dismissed the two earls to wait for further orders, while he, himself, went straight-away to see Edward.

Preoccupied with his building and his labours for the Church, the king had almost forgotten the existence of Godwin, although he thought often of the lady Edith and prayed for her happiness. He listened to Robert's theories carefully, but after a little thought he was inclined to scoff. It was conceivable, he allowed, that the common people of the south-east might love Godwin more than they loved their king: but not so much more that they would be prepared to go into rebellion and fight battles which could only end in defeat. As for the fleet, it was ludicrous to think that any of the shipmasters, each one of which was known to him personally, would stoop to disloyalty: their indifference was not caused by any partiality for Godwin but by a dislike for the man over them. Otto was young and had had no experience of commanding Englishmen — he should be made to see where he was in error.

For a time they argued back and forth but, for once, Robert could not change the king's mind, and when he had left him, he sent for Ralf and Otto once more.

Half-convinced that Edward was right, he delivered to them a homily on the character of the English. 'Even the lowest of them are proud, stubborn and quick to sense an insult. Lead them by the nose and they become like mules: they must be coaxed and cajoled like thoroughbred horses.'

Otto was prepared to admit that he might have been at fault, but when he told Robert that eight of his ships were reputed to be in need of urgent repair, the Archbishop was quick to tell him that the work should be carried out in London. That way, he thought to himself, at least half of the fleet would be unable to defect to the rebel Godwin.

After the earls had set out for Sandwich, Robert rode to Canterbury, and from there he visited various parts of the shire so that he could judge for himself the temper of the people.

'When, at length, he returned to Westminster, he found Edward in a rage, for news had reached London of the killings and burnings at Bembridge, Portland and Porlock.

'It seems to me, Robert,' he said, 'that the old fox and his cub will come together in the West Country. We must call out the levies in the south and west, and send earl Ralf with his men to give them heart.'

But now Robert was certain that the main trouble would come from the south-east, and he strengthened his argument by telling the king what he had seen and heard during his recent travels in those parts. They talked the matter over for some time and eventually Edward was persuaded that the attacks in the west were a feint.

'In that case,' he said, 'our ships should be sent to intercept his fleet in the Channel.'

Earl Otto was in London at that time, angry over the burning of his new hall, and he was keen for the opportunity of revenge. But when the king explained to him what was to be done, his face fell.

'Sire, I have only eight ships ready for sea, and by all reports the combined rebel fleets are double that number.' He went on to explain that the remainder of his ships were being repaired in London.

'Then send those that are ready,' said Edward. 'Let them be based at Pevensey, where the remainder can join them as soon as possible.'

When Otto had gone, Edward and Robert discussed what other measures should be taken. A meeting of the Council seemed essential, and it was time that the levies of the north and east should be called out. But when it came to the levies of Wessex, they could not at first agree. Edward was for calling them. 'If they refuse to obey, then at least we shall know what we have to contend with,' he said.

'But, Sire, if they obey the order, we shall have done Godwin's work for him. He has only to place himself at their head.'

Edward thought it over in silence,

rubbing his cheeks and tugging at his beard. At last he said: 'Very well, Robert, it shall be as you say. And we must rely on the fleet to make sure that Godwin does not set foot in the south-east.'

Rely on the fleet . . . Robert felt his palms moisten. All his doubts and fears returned to him, and he reminded himself to pray for time and the northern levies.

Otto went to the shipwright who was entrusted with the repairs to the king's ships, and was appalled to find that the work had not yet started.

The shipwright, a man old enough to be Otto's father, was unashamed. 'Everything in its turn,' he said, in the manner of the old addressing the young.

'But the work is urgent — the ships are needed at once,' said Otto, aghast.

'Nobody told me that,' said the shipwright.

Otto swallowed hard and cursed himself for leaving the matter to the shipmasters. He asked if the ships were seaworthy as they were, and together they inspected each of the vessels as they lay on the strand.

Otto felt a chill wind blowing round his neck as the shipwright expounded. This one had rotten timbers below the water line . . . that one had rotting strakes . . . they all needed caulking . . . reasonably safe in sheltered waters, but . . . The old man's head never stopped shaking.

'How long . . . ?' Otto was getting desperate.

The shipwright went into a long rigmarole on how difficult it was to get good, reliable labour, at the end of which he cautiously intimated that they might be ready in three weeks, but more likely a month . . .

Otto's patience ran out, like sand out of a sieve. 'For God's sake,' he shouted, 'they must be ready inside a fortnight. See to it.'

The old man drew himself up. 'I'll not botch them,' he said fiercely. 'If that's what you want, you must find another shipwright.'

Otto thrust his face close to the old man's. 'Employ more men, you old fool . . . pay double wages if you have to, but get the work done quickly.'

He stalked off across the dark, muddy sand, muttering to himself about the stupidity of the English. If he had turned around he would have seen the shipwright watching him, hands on hips, shaking with suppressed mirth.

Otto set out for Sandwich, frustrated and angry. It was odd, he thought, that he, who had twisted Godwin around his finger like a piece of twine, should have failed with the shipmasters and that stupid old fool of a shipwright. Robert had told him that Englishmen should be coaxed: he had experimented on the shipmasters, and it had not worked — they were lazy, insolent, time-wasting pigs, whose only thought was to draw their pay and spend it in the ale houses and whore shops. Very well, he would try once more, but he could guess what their attitude to his orders would be.

At Sandwich, he called the shipmasters and their crews to him and, swallowing his evil mood, explained reasonably to them what was afoot and what was expected of them. He would, he said, join them at Pevensey with the remainder of the ships as soon as possible.

To his surprise, his mild manner seemed to please the men, and their faces lost the sullen look he was accustomed to. The senior shipmaster, Thorkill, announced that the ships were all ready to put to sea at once.

'And you can be easy in your mind,' he added, 'that these eight ships of ours will serve England well when the time comes for the drawing of swords.'

16

After the sacking of the king's manor at Portland, Godwin led his ships out into the Channel and turned eastwards, for the time of his meeting with Harold was drawing close. He returned to Brading where a camp was made and a look-out posted on the cliffs to watch for the arrival of his son's ships. Two days later, their sails were sighted and a ship was sent to lead them into the harbour.

To Godwin, this gathering together was far more than a family reunion: for the past ten months he had been living in a world that was half dream and half reality. Now the two parts were united, and whatever secret doubts he may have held about the outcome of his venture were banished from his mind. He knew that nothing short of death itself could bar him from success.

Harold observed him closely: whereas Tostig looked sleek and well-fed, Godwin was thinner than he remembered, and there were now lines about his eyes. But it seemed that the fire in his belly burned brighter than ever, and Harold, weary and a little dispirited, felt the glow and his resolve became firmer.

Gyrth was there, no longer a youth, but a young man with more than a trace of down across his upper lip. He and Leofwin were excitedly telling each other of their adventures. Godwin told Harold of his plans for the future and as he spoke Harold's eyes opened wider and wider.

Godwin laughed at Harold's perplexity. 'You do not believe we shall succeed?' he asked.

Harold rubbed his chin. 'How can we conquer without fighting?'

'There is no one to conquer,' said Godwin, 'but a handful of foreigners.'

The following day, the look-out on the cliffs sent a message to say that there were eight ships in sight to the east of the island. Godwin called the camp to arms and, with Harold and Tostig, hurried up the steep slope to the look-out. The ships were easily seen, eight low, black streaks on the wind-ruffled sea, pulling against the wind and making for the strait between the island and the mainland.

'They are king's ships,' said Harold, uneasily.

'Looking for us,' added Tostig.

Godwin did not reply, but stared hard at the longships, wishing he had the eyes of a hawk.

'Find Brand,' he said to Tostig, 'tell him to take a ship for a close look at those craft. He will know what to look for.'

Harold grumbled at his father. 'We should have let them pass by.'

Godwin shrugged. 'If the worst comes to the worst, there are only eight of them. Eight ships more for us and eight less for the king.'

They walked back to the camp in silence and Harold went to where he could watch the entrance to the harbour. Presently he saw Brand's ship appear — and close behind it were the king's ships. Harold jumped to his feet and would have called his men into ranks, but Godwin waved him to silence and ran down to the water's edge, for at the tiller of the leading ship he had seen the flaming red hair of Thorkill.

The ships beached and Thorkill jumped ashore, showing his teeth in a wide grin.

'What a man you are, Godwin. Holed up in the king's own harbour. I should have guessed it.'

Godwin held out his hand. 'I did not expect you so soon, my friend, but you are no less welcome.'

Watching them, Harold felt a grin spread across his face, and he began to understand why his father was so confident of success. He wondered what the king would say if he could see them.

If Edward had been able to see them he might have been happier than he was, for after Portland Godwin seemed to have vanished into thin air, and there was only the ominous stillness that precedes a thunderstorm.

With each day that passed without news, Edward became more and more convinced that he had been right — that the danger lay in the west country. But Archbishop Robert remained obdurate, and his confidence was enough to set the king's mind at rest for the time being — until the small hours when his brain, undistracted by other matters, churned the problem over and credited Godwin with superhuman cunning.

If Robert seemed calmly confident, he certainly did not feel it. He, too, lay awake at night, staring into the darkness, trying to pierce the veil which hid the future. Often he thought of the eight ships which were all that guarded the south coast; and sometimes he thought of the levies from Northumbria, Mercia and East Anglia which by now must be plodding their way towards London. Thousand upon thousand of them . . . he would not feel properly secure until they arrived.

Often he sent for Otto to give him a report on the progress of the work on the remainder of the fleet. At first, Otto had been confident that everything was as it should be, and that the ships would be seaworthy within a week. Then gradually his cocksure manner changed: things were not going well — some of the workmen had been taken ill, and there was a delay in obtaining materials, and some of the ships were in worse repair than had been thought.

Eventually, Robert looked Otto in the eye and put his suspicions into words: that the work was deliberately being held back. Whereupon Otto clenched his fists in anger and admitted that he was certain of it, but that he could find no way to put matters right. Offers of double, or even treble pay had no effect, and no other shipwright could be found to take on the work.

For a long while the two men stared at each other in silence. 'It seems,' said Robert, at last, 'that we must make do with the ships we have. Are you sure that the seamen are reliable?'

'They were keen enough to put to sea. I shall go to join them at Pevensey.'

But before Otto could set out, news came that Godwin was encamped at Brading, and that he had been joined by eight of the king's ships.

It was a dreadful blow for both of them: for Otto, there was the bitterness of defeat at the hands of a people he despised: For Robert, there was the realisation that his worst fears had come true.

But, he reminded himself, the battle could not have been won on the sea. And the levies from the north would soon arrive.

But before the levies, there came Leofric and Alfgar. Edward greeted the white-haired earl like a long-lost brother, for he remembered the long-standing enmity between Godwin and the earl of Mercia, and counted him as a staunch ally.

Leofric found such effusiveness embarrassing: it was not that he bore any ill-will towards Edward, but profound thought and the arguments of his son, Alfgar, had convinced him that, as things were, he had no chance of obtaining the favour of Wessex, or even a small part of it. The pickings would be reserved for the Norman favourites, and it was not improbable that Duke William would be honoured. That being so, he had come to the conclusion that it would be best if Godwin were allowed to return on his own terms.

Sooner or later, he would have to voice his opinion: he was not looking forward to it, and to have Edward pat his arm and call him 'old friend' made him feel a traitor of the most despicable kind.

Robert was anything but effusive. Leofric detected a change in the Archbishop which helped to confirm his decision. Gone was the pose of the trusted adviser, and in its place was the imperious manner of the ruler, with all the inborn ruthlessness laid bare.

'Where,' he demanded of Leofric, 'are your levies?'

The brusqueness of the question offended the earl, and he drew himself up and stared icily at Robert while he spoke of the time that was needed to assemble a force from an area as large as Mercia. This was true enough, and in fact the levies were assembling at a place not far from Bedford, but they had orders not to march further south without instructions from Leofric himself.

It was a plan conceived by Alfgar and himself, and when Robert asked the earl of East Anglia the same blunt question he received the same vague reply.

Earl Siward was more forthright when he arrived a day or two later. The King of the Scots was said to be raising an army on the far side of the border, and although Siward could not be certain that he intended to invade Northumbria, it would be a fool's game to denude the defences at this time. There would be no levies from Northumbria, said Siward. And he said it in a way that would brook no argument.

Robert sucked his teeth when he heard this. He could sense the way things were going — it was the attitude of the fleet seamen and the shipwright all over again, but on a far more dangerous scale. But Robert was not beaten: he knew Siward to be unreliable, therefore it was as well that he had brought no levies. But Leofric . . . he was a sitter on fences — he could be cajoled, he could be bought and he could be frightened. Robert decided to try the last two methods.

At the meeting which took place the following day, Edward took the chair at the head of the table, but there was no doubt as to who was in charge. Robert gave a lengthy account of all that had happened since the spring. He spoke of Godwin's secret journeyings in the south-eastern shires, enlarged on the happenings at Bembridge, Portland and Porlock and glossed over the defection of the fleet. Then he went on to explain what he expected to happen within the next week or two.

'This man Godwin will stop at nothing to get his way — not even the burning of English homes and the slaughter of Englishmen. He is nothing but a pirate who climbed to power through treachery and double-dealing over the bodies of his victims — among them the brother of our king. And he has finished as an arch-traitor. We must crush him with overwhelming force . . . '

Cleaning and paring his nails with a hunting knife, Siward listened with growing irritation as the voice ranted on, edging its way to a predictable climax. It irked him that a Norman should call on Englishmen to fight Englishmen to the last drop of blood to make the land safe for Normans. If Edward had been speaking it would have been bad enough, but this . . .

He finished his nails and sheathed his knife. As a rule, he spoke as rarely as possible at these meetings, for he had not the gift of words. But this time he had plenty to say.

Robert finished his diatribe with a final verbal flourish. For a moment there was silence, then Siward cleared his throat ominously. Robert ignored him, and looked at Leofric.

'Your comments, lord earl?'

Leofric sat upright in his chair. It had been a long speech, but it had aroused no passion in Leofric's breast, either for or against Godwin. But now the time had come when, in cold blood, he had to declare where he stood in the matter. He met the king's eye and looked hurriedly away. The words came from his throat, but left his tongue backwards and sideways. Conscious that he was making no sense, he looked appealingly at Siward.

'What earl Leofric is trying to say . . . '

Siward's voice was loud and his enunciation unusually clear ' . . . is that he believes — and I support him — that Godwin should be allowed to return to his old position as earl of Wessex.'

There was a horrified silence, broken by a little shriek of dismay from Edward, whose hands had flown to the sides of his face. His eyes were fixed on Leofric, who looked as though his boots had suddenly filled with cold water.

'Is this true?' Edward's voice was high-pitched with alarm.

With the cat out of the bag, Leofric found he could look the king in the eyes.

'That is what we believe, my lord king. Your feelings on the matter are known to us, and we are the first to agree that Godwin has his faults. But he is an Englishman, and we understand his ways.'

'Besides,' said Siward, 'I could see no real reason for his exile in the first place.'

Edward was speechless with horror, his cheeks pale. He looked at Robert for guidance.

Robert said nothing for a while, and

then rested his arms on the table with a sigh which might have expressed pity.

'You astound me,' he said, looking at Leofric. 'Knowing Godwin as you do, do you suppose that he will be content with his earldom of Wessex?' He paused, looking at each of the earls in turn. 'Wessex will be for the murderer, Sweyn . . . Mercia for Harold . . . Northumbria for Tostig . . . East Anglia for Gyrth.' He looked round the table again, showing his teeth in an unpleasant smile. 'As for Godwin, he has set his eyes on the Crown, itself.'

There was silence. Each man stared at him according to his feelings: only Siward's eyes showed disbelief.

'Do you doubt me?' Robert went on. 'Think of Tetbury — the stage was set and he had only to swoop down from the hilltop like a preying eagle. But God stayed his hand. And at Westminster we were ready for him and sent him into exile, but I can see now that we were too lenient . . . we should have killed him for his treachery.'

There was another long silence. Robert

saw Leofric exchange a glance with his son and knew that he had won the day. That Siward wagged his head in disbelief did not matter.

He rose to his feet. 'I hope I have made it clear that the king needs every single levy without delay,' he said, sternly.

When the earls had left the council chamber, Edward said: 'For the love of God . . . what are we to do.'

Robert smiled. 'Be easy, Sire. Leofric faltered, but he will not desert us. As for Siward, we know where his sympathy lies, and we shall not forget, once we have dealt with Godwin!'

'And Godwin . . . does he really covet my crown?'

'No man can doubt it. Not even Siward, in his heart.'

Edward smiled wryly. 'If it were any other man, he would be welcome to it and the loneliness it brings. But not Godwin . . . '

Robert became pensive. 'Sire,' he said. 'Leofric . . . now that his eyes are opened, I have no doubt that he will fight for you like a lion. But I think he would fight like two lions if he were promised some favour.'

'What do you suggest?'

'A part of your holding in Wessex would please him.'

Edward nodded. 'So be it. But not too generous, Robert . . . let him have Wiltshire. It is poor, chalky land, but he has enough wealth already. And what should we do for Alfgar?'

Robert smiled bleakly. 'Alfgar shall have his reward when his father dies.'

In the great hall, Leofric, Alfgar and Siward were grouped together in earnest conversation. For once, Siward was doing the talking, gesticulating with his large hands to drive home his point. The others listened attentively, Alfgar glancing from Siward to his father and back again, while Leofric tugged at his beard, his eyes thoughtful.

Siward was saying: 'And even if Robert is right, think of this: would you rather have Godwin as king, or William of Normandy? My friends, must you even think before you chose?'

Leofric shrugged. 'Put that way . . . '

Siward smiled. 'What other way can it be put? Come, my friend, do not be swayed by that Norman priest . . . let the English have the power in their own land.'

Leofric felt a hand on his arm. It was Robert, who drew him apart from the others.

'Lord earl,' he said. 'I had meant to tell you before . . . the king will be disposing of the favour of Wessex when Godwin is finished and done with. I have told him of your interest, and now that he knows he can count on your loyalty . . . ' he nodded, smiling.

Leofric's eyes lit up, so that for a moment the ice melted from them. He went back to Siward.

'My mind is made up,' he said, brusquely. 'Alfgar . . . send a messenger to command the levies to march to London.'

Siward watched him as he made his arthritic way across the hall. Then he hawked noisily in his throat and spat upon the floor.

17

The fleet pulled out of Brading harbour on the early morning tide. Banks of mist, grey against the rising sun, floated on the surface of a sea so calm that as it reflected the sun's light it seemed to the helmsmen as though they were sailing on molten gold. Presently, under the growing heat of the sun, the mist dispersed and a breeze blew from the west; softly, but enough to fill the sails.

Godwin steered close to the shore, because he wished it to be known that the hour of reckoning was not far off, and those who watched marvelled at the sight of the twenty-four ships of war led by Godwin's own magnificent longship, proud under the sail emblazoned with the emblem of Wessex, the water creaming from the stem under the carved dragon's head. At times they were close enough to land to make out the figures of men waving their greetings, and once they passed a cluster of fishing boats and the sound of cheering came thinly over the water.

Slowly, with the grandeur of a royal procession, they sailed eastwards. At night they put into harbour, to be welcomed with excited enthusiasm. Small children were held aloft to catch a glimpse of the earl and his sons; sheep and pigs were roasted whole over blazing fires, and the ale was plentiful and strong. And in the morning, when the fleet put out to sea amid cheers and good wishes, it was followed by ships from the harbour, sailed by men anxious to be able to tell their children and grandchildren that they had played their part in the return of the beloved earl.

By the time they reached Sandwich, the longships were well outnumbered by their followers, and when they were all beached, Tostig was reminded of that summer, three years since, when the king had commanded the fleet against Baldwin of Bruges. Laughing, he reminded Harold of it.

'I remember it,' said Harold, morosely.

'And I also remember that it was here that our troubles started when Sweyn came from Denmark to shout insults at the king.'

Tostig pulled a wry face. 'Why so sour, brother? Did you drink vinegar in mistake for ale last night?'

Harold was in no mood to be chaffed. The slow voyage by sea had tried his patience, and he thought how easy it would be to buy horses and lead his housecarls by road to London and settle his scores with Otto of Bernay and Ralf of Mantes.

But Godwin was firmly against it: Bishop Stigand had sent a messenger to Sandwich with news of the dissension in the Council, and he was determined that nothing should prevent him from taking full advantage of the situation.

'Forget your grudges,' he told Harold. 'There will be time for such things later.'

The next morning dawned calm and misty, but as soon as the sun rose a breeze sprang up from the east. The seamen cheered at this, because most of them had thick heads from the night's festivities

330

and they had dreaded the long pull up the estuary against the wind. Godwin shared their joy, for he saw the change in the wind as an omen of success.

As soon as the tide was right, they pulled out of the harbour and, once clear of the foreland, turned eastwards and hoisted their sails. Soon, the shoreline on both sides of the estuary could be seen, and as Harold watched the land converge ahead of them he could not stifle the feeling that they were sailing into the neck of a trap.

In the late afternoon they beached on the southern shore and made camp on a sandy spit of land. The area was deserted except for the seabirds which grudgingly made way for them. Inland, about four miles distant, there was a low ridge which marked the line of the road between Rochester and Sandwich, and for the first time, Godwin agreed with Harold that it would be as well to set up outposts to guard against a surprise attack.

That done, the earl called all the shipmasters to him and explained that on the morrow he expected to reach London shortly after noon. 'There is no certainty how we shall be received,' he said. 'The Mercian and East Anglian levies will be there — two or three thousand of them. Perhaps more, but at any rate enough to overwhelm us if it comes to a fight.'

'What of the men from the south-eastern shires?' Harold asked.

'They will be on the south bank of the river. They can do little to help, save look impressive.'

To Harold, this was madness, and he foresaw disaster. 'Father,' he said pleadingly, 'let me land my housecarls on the south bank — we can rally our men there and storm the bridge to gain a foothold on the north side. Otherwise you will stand no chance if it comes to a fight.'

Godwin shook his head. 'I know it. And that is why there must be no fighting. Not one of us must draw a sword, or even shake a fist.' He raised his voice so that all could hear plainly: 'When I and my four sons step ashore tomorrow, we shall be unarmed.'

There was an incredulous silence. Then a murmur of protesting voices rose in crescendo. Godwin held up his hand for silence, and as the noise died away a smile spread over his face.

'If you think me a fool, I forgive you. I reason the matter thus: our quarrel is not with the king, but with a handful of foreigners who have taken his power into their hands. I think that Englishmen will not fight Englishmen for the benefit of these men. If my judgement is right, we shall all be drinking good London ale by this time tomorrow.'

Planning an early start in the morning, they slept under the starlight. Towards dawn, Tostig awoke with the cold pressing into his bones. He sat up, and became aware that his father was standing close by, staring into the darkness.

Seeing that Tostig was awake, Godwin said: 'You heard it too, then?'

'Heard what?' said Tostig, irritably.

'Sweyn's voice.'

Tostig turned to look at his father. 'Sweyn is a thousand miles away. How can you have heard his voice?'

Godwin stood straining his ears for a break in the pre-dawn silence. 'Yet it was

333

his voice. Quite distinctly, I heard him call twice.'

There was something about his father's manner that disturbed him. He got to his feet and stood beside the earl. 'Seabirds squabbling at their roost . . . an owl hooting.'

'No . . . I am not mistaken. Twice I heard him call 'Father . . . help me' as though he were no more than a dozen yards away.'

Something that was not the cold made Tostig shiver. He took his father's hand and found it icier than his own.

'It was a dream, father. Go to your bed and cover yourself against the cold.'

Godwin pulled his coverings over him and lay shivering. It had been no dream — he knew that because he had hardly closed his eyes all night. And without a doubt, it had been Sweyn's voice.

He remembered the last time he had heard it: in his private chamber at Bruges. Sweyn had appeared in the doorway, his face pale in the candlelight.

'Father, I leave for Jerusalem at first light.'

His head full of his plans, Godwin had looked up slightly irritated at the breaking of his train of thought. If Sweyn wanted his paternal blessing he should have it at the proper time — at the moment of departure.

But as it happened, Godwin had slept late the following morning, and by the time he was himself, Sweyn had been many miles away. At the time, it had seemed unimportant — partings and absences were a part of Godwin's life, and he gave no thought to the matter. In fact, he had been so busy with his own pre-occupations that he had almost completely forgotten the existence of Sweyn.

For a moment he lay full of remorse and dark misgivings. But what was done was done — now there were more urgent things to contend with. As the warmth crept back into his bones he closed his eyes and relaxed his mind, striving for the sleep which would not come.

★ ★ ★

Archbishop Robert had followed God-win's progress up the Channel with tense interest. His intuition told him that the rebel would raise his standard at Hastings, because from there he would be within easy reach of the road which led through the eastern fringe of the Forest of Andred to London, and when he learned that the fleet had sailed from Hastings to Dover, his brows contracted in perplexity.

It was in a message from Sandwich that Robert had the first inkling of Godwin's intention, and after the first feeling of astonishment had passed off, he laughed, sure that the exile was playing into his hands, for by this time the Mercian and East Anglian levies had arrived in London. Even the knowledge that the men of the south-eastern shires were converging on London did not worry him since London Bridge was the only possible place to cross the river for many miles, and it could easily be defended.

For the first time that year, he ceased to worry about Godwin. All that nervous strain, all the fretting had been to no account: now, the only cause for concern was the loyalty of Leofric to the king. And Leofric, with the glittering prize of Wessex dangled under his nose, was the king's man from the top of his grey hair down to the stiffening joints of his toes.

Robert's air of confident good humour communicated itself to the king, whose stomach-workings, always sensitive to nervous tension, became settled. He was benign again, and spoke pleasantly to those around him, and Leofric, whose nose had been out of joint for so long, found it particularly pleasant to bask in the glow of the royal favour.

One man remained ill at ease. Earl Siward realised that he had committed himself so completely that his fortunes were bound up with those of Godwin — if he failed, Siward's disgrace would inevitably and rapidly follow. And it seemed to him that if Godwin did what was expected he could do nothing but fail — completely and miserably.

And yet . . . He had known Godwin for many years, and while the old fox was not infallible, he had never known him to make a mistake so obvious as the one he was apparently about to make now. Perhaps, he thought hopefully, there was more in Godwin's mind than anyone guessed.

From a distance, Robert's scouts kept an anxious watch on Sandwich, and when the fleet left they followed by road. News of Godwin's overnight camp reached London early the following morning, and at sunrise there was a call to arms and the levies began to move into their battle positions close by London Bridge.

The king was in an animated mood as he rode out from Westminster with Robert and all his earls to inspect the army, chattering and laughing as though he was on his way to the hunting field. In his elation, he lapsed into the Norman tongue which came more naturally to him, and Leofric, listening with distaste to the incomprehensible talk, began to feel out of place. Gradually he dropped back to ride beside Siward.

By that time, the fleet was well on its way to London. It had started at first light, and to allow passage under the bridge the masts had been unstepped, giving the ships the menacing look of beasts of prey about to spring.

Godwin stood on the steering platform of the leading ship, his arms folded, deep in thought. In spite of his sleepless night and the early start, his hair and beard were carefully combed and his eyes watchful. This was the final stride of a long journey, and within a few hours his theories would be put to trial. Failure was a possibility which he refused to admit, even to himself, but now that the test was approaching with every sweep of the oars, he realised that success was anything but assured. He had calculated the factors in his favour and he knew those which were against him, but at the last, there was one man who held the power of life and death over him — Leofric of Mercia.

His scalp prickled at the thought. Leofric — who felt nothing but loathing for him; who had spent the years opposing him in every possible way.

The ship moved on inexorably. The water, brown with mud stirred up from the shallows by the oar-blades, flowed past like time itself. A crane flapped its lazy way across the marshland to the south, and Godwin watched it for a moment, envying its freedom. He turned to look astern and saw Harold on the steering platform of his ship, talking to Gyrth and Leofwin. And beyond that was Tostig's ship.

Fool that he was, he should have paid more heed to Harold. March from Hastings to London, gathering his levies on the way . . . that had been Harold's advice. He should have taken it. And he should have taken Harold's advice at Tetbury . . .

The river narrowed and began gently to wind; the marshland was left behind and in its place there was woodland creeping closer and closer to the river banks. It was too late to turn back. Not that he would . . . if he was taken and killed it would not matter overmuch: he had lived his life and taken full value from it. But his sons . . . it seemed unjust that he should drag them to their deaths on a rope made of his own pride and stupidity, and he began to rack his brains for some good reason why the four of them should be sent back. But he knew it was useless — whatever excuse he gave, Harold's expression would change: his jaw would jut, the mouth become tight-lipped and the eyes seem like two pieces of blue marble. He would refuse to obey — and Gyrth and Leofwin would not leave their brother, and Tostig would smile indolently and say, 'I shall follow my brothers.'

So be it. Archbishop Robert would be delighted to have the whole of the Godwin family delivered into his hands. Except for Sweyn . . . Godwin winced as he remembered his favourite son, and heard again that forlorn, pleading voice of the night before.

The gentle curves of the river became great looping whorls, and through clearings in the trees could be seen the roofs of villages and drifts of smoke from burning stubble. And soon, in the distance, a great cluster of roofs which could only belong to London. As he gazed at them, Godwin straightened his back and turned to gesticulate to Harold in the ship behind. The oarsmen, with their faces to the rear, felt the increased tension and unwittingly increased the length of their stroke, as though they were racing for a prize.

Now the banks on both sides of the river were lined with men shouting their welcome and waving: the sound of their voices across the water came to Godwin like a gale of wind in the trees. Godwin waved back: the men on the south bank were his own people — they had marched from Kent, Sussex and Surrey, anxious not to miss this moment, and now they ran along the bank, striving to keep pace with the ships. But those on the north bank were Londoners, the king's people, and as he waved to them a great truth dawned in Godwin's mind: it was not Leofric who held the power of life and death — it was the people — the common people whose shouts of welcome rang in his ears.

He gave a great shout of laughter and waved both arms above his head. The steersman beside him looked askance for a moment, then concentrated on his task of aiming the ship between the massive black piles of the bridge which loomed above their heads.

Standing under the royal banner among his armour-clad earls, Edward had listened as the distant hubbub of voices grew louder until there was no mistaking its meaning. His face took on an expression of pained surprise that his own people of London should hold any opinion different from his own. He turned to Robert.

'They are cheering Godwin?' he asked, incredulously.

Robert's face was pale and tense. 'Those are his own men on the far bank who cheer,' he snapped.

Siward swore a Danish oath. 'Not so,' he said, loudly. 'The whole of London acclaims him. Lord king, this is no time for fighting . . . let us hear what Godwin has to say.'

Robert turned on him with a venemous look. 'He has said enough already. He is a murderer and a traitor.'

The cheering swelled in volume, and seemed to be coming from all around them. Suddenly, the din resolved itself into a recognisable chant — 'God-win . . . God-win . . . God-win . . . ' Along the lines of the Mercian and East Anglian levies, men stirred uneasily, peering uncertainly over their shoulders. Many laughed and joined in the chanting: only the housecarls drawn up in front of Edward's banner stood unmoving, as though they were deaf.

Edward put his hands over his ears to shut out the noise, and earl Ralf turned to Otto and raised his eyebrows. Otto shook his head and turned down the corners of his mouth.

At that moment, Godwin's longship came from beneath the bridge, followed closely by Harold's . . . Tostig's . . . another and another. The chanting was lost in a crescendo of shouting and cheering.

Siward took Leofric's arm. 'For God's sake . . . hold your men in check, or we shall have the whole of London about our ears.' He had to shout in Leofric's ear to make himself heard.

Leofric did not answer, but watched ship after ship as they came from under the bridge. He thought of the riches of Wessex, and his heart became heavy.

With deft oarsmanship, the three

leading ships had turned and were heading for the north bank. They beached opposite Edward's banner, and from their tall prows five men jumped to the shingly sand, and as if by magic the noise of the crowd died until there could be heard the lapping of water and the crunching of gravel underfoot.

Siward tightened his grip on Leofric's arm. 'They are not armed,' he said.

Edward, who had been staring as if fascinated, came to himself. 'Leofric . . . send your men to secure them.'

Leofric felt the grip on his arm tighten still further. He opened his mouth but no words would come.

'Earl Leofric . . . ' Edward's voice was shrill with impatience ' . . . have them brought to me fettered.'

Leofric shook his arm free of Siward's grip. 'My lord,' he said firmly. 'I will not do it. We must hear what Godwin has to say.'

Edward turned in a white fury, seeking the aid of the Archbishop, but there was emptiness where Robert had stood.

'Robert . . . where is Robert?' It was a cry of anguish.

But Robert had gone, and with him earl Otto and earl Ralf.

Godwin led his sons up the slope towards the housecarls who barred his way to Edward. He walked mechanically, seeing nothing, appalled by the silence which allowed him to hear the shortness of his breathing. Behind him, acutely aware that he lacked a sword, Harold glowered at the faces of the housecarls, wordlessly commanding them to open their ranks. The housecarls stared back with expressionless eyes and for a moment there was a battle of wills as the five men strode on without checking their pace. At the last moment, the ranks parted and the way was open to the king.

Godwin halted before Edward and sank on to one knee. He spoke loudly and slowly, so that as many as possible should hear.

'My lord king . . . we are here to ask your pardon.'

There was a long pause. Edward stared down at the man before him and Godwin was surprised to see that there were tears in his eyes.

Leofric cleared his throat. 'What else do you seek, Godwin?'

'Nothing . . . other than those things which were unlawfully taken from us by men who served a master other than our lord king.'

Leofric gave an audible sigh, and looked at the king.

'I would speak with Robert,' said Edward. 'Bring him to me.'

'The Archbishop,' said Leofric delicately, 'has taken his leave.'

Siward gave an impatient snort. 'He has run away,' he said brusquely. 'It was wise of him.'

Edward looked at him as though he could not believe his ears.

'As your chief advisers, my lord,' went on Siward, 'we urge that Godwin be allowed to stay, and that the Great Council should meet to decide what is fair and just.'

Edward did not seem to comprehend, but gazed about him searching for a familiar face. As the truth flooded into his mind, his manner changed and he made a gesture of resignation with his hands. But his face flushed with anger and his lips pouted.

Godwin had risen to his feet, and Edward stared at him for a moment, his eyes blazing with hatred.

'May you rot in hell,' he said through clenched teeth.

They watched in silence as he stamped away towards where the groom held his horse.

Siward shrugged expressively and stepped towards Godwin, his hand outstretched. 'If he will not welcome you, there are thousands of simpler folk who do.'

Harold brushed the dirt from his knees and looked at Siward.

'Otto of Bernay?' he asked quietly.

'Gone . . . with earl Ralf and the Archbishop.' He looked at Godwin and laughed. 'I doubt that there will be a foreigner of any consequence in London by this evening.'

Godwin gave a wan smile. For the first time in his life, and in the moment of his greatest triumph, he could not find it in himself to care. Frenchmen, Normans, kings, priests . . . they were as nothing to him. All he wanted was to sleep.

Tomorrow would be different. Tomorrow, he would care again.

Aftermath

Godwin died in the spring of the following year, in a manner and setting which he might have chosen for himself as being as dramatic and controversial as the rest of his life.

Edward, who had never forgiven him for the death of his brother, now blamed him for the loss of his friend and adviser, Robert of Jumièges, and relations between the two men were never better than frigid. But one of Edward's first thoughts after Godwin's return was to send for his beloved wife, the lady Edith, from Wherwell.

Now that Robert was gone, Edward needed a shoulder to lean on as he made his way through the snares and pitfalls of political decision. He had ceased to trust Leofric of Mercia, who, he thought, by one simple word of command, could have saved Robert from humiliation. And Siward of Northumbria was more of a soldier than a politician and, in any case, Robert had said that he was not to be trusted.

Of his earls, there remained Harold and Alfgar, and it was ironic that Edward came to rely on the son of his old enemy for political guidance. Ironic, too, that he formed a great liking for Tostig, the lady Edith's favourite brother, whose quick wit and handsome good looks were augmented at Court by the beauty and sweet nature of Judith, his wife.

As for Godwin, he had regained his position but he had lost his health. After the Great Council had agreed to the restoration of the family's estates, he became ill from exhaustion and lay for many days without the will to move or to eat and drink more than enough to keep himself alive.

By the middle of October, he had recovered sufficiently to make the journey to Winchester, where Gytha's joy at being home was stifled by the sorry state in which she found her lord. It seemed to her that he had lost his taste for life and the energy to live it. Saddest of all was that he knew this, and did not care.

As winter gave way to spring, a messenger came from overseas with the news that Sweyn was dead, killed by the cold on a mountainside in Smyrna when his party of pilgrims had lost their way in a sudden snowstorm. The man had survived the disaster and, when closely questioned by Godwin, said that it had taken place during the early part of September. Godwin thought of the voice he had heard calling that night on the sand spit. Although he had half-expected the news, the blow was not softened.

The king was persuaded to hold Easter Court at Winchester that year. It was thought that the time might be ripe for a reconciliation between him and Godwin, and for the occasion, the earl recovered something of his former spirit and zest. On the first evening of the festival when they were at supper, Godwin rose to his feet and hammered on the table with the handle of his knife for silence. When all were quiet and expectant, he raised his wine-cup and desired them to drink a toast to the king's health.

As he was speaking, the cup suddenly fell to the table: for an instant, Godwin stared in surprise at his empty hand, then, like a discarded cloak, he fell to the floor so that his head lay on the king's foot-stool.

His heart was still beating, so they carried him gently to his couch where, after a long while, he came to his senses, although unable to speak or move his limbs. Death was only a short time away, and his family gathered about him while Gytha and the lady Edith tried to massage some warmth into his cold hands and feet.

There, too, came king Edward to say farewell to his most powerful subject. With his wife and Godwin's family present, he dared not say what was in his mind, but probably Godwin saw the cold, smug smile on his lips and read the message in his eyes.

'Rot in hell, Godwin.'

Later that same month, strange lights were seen in the northern sky, and in Sussex it rained blood. Men said that these were portents of evil days to come.

Stroke in the Elderly
New Issues in Diagnosis, Treatment, and Rehabilitation

Ruth E. Dunkle, Ph.D. received her doctorate in the Social Sciences and her M.S.W. from Syracuse University. She taught at the School of Social Work at San Diego State University and the School of Applied Social Sciences at Case Western Reserve University before joining the faculty of the School of Social Work at the University of Michigan. Her research interests and publications have been in the areas of mental health, language impairment of the elderly, and service utilization for impaired elders. She is co-author of *The Older Aphasic Person: Strategies in Treatment and Diagnosis* and co-editor of *Communications Technology and the Elderly: Issues and Forecasts*, and *Food, Drugs, and Aging.*

James W. Schmidley, M.D. is an Assistant Professor of Neurology at Case Western Reserve University School of Medicine and an attending physician at University Hospitals of Cleveland. He attended college and medical school at the University of Virginia, then pursued postgraduate training in internal medicine at the New York Hospital–Cornell University Medical Center, and in neurology and electron microscopy at the University of California, San Francisco. Dr. Schmidley's principal scientific interest is the ultrastructure of the cerebral microvasculature; his chief clinical interest is cerebrovascular disease. He is a fellow of the Stroke Council of the American Heart Association, a councillor of the American Society for Neurological Investigation, and an investigator for the Canadian American Ticlopidine Study and Ticlopidine Aspirin Stroke Study.

STROKE IN THE ELDERLY
New Issues in Diagnosis, Treatment, and Rehabilitation

Ruth E. Dunkle, Ph.D.
James W. Schmidley, M.D.
Editors

Springer Publishing Company
New York

Springer Publishing Company, Inc.
536 Broadway
New York, NY 10012

87 88 89 90 91/ 5 4 3 2 1

Library of Congress Cataloging-in-Publication Data

Stroke in the elderly.

  Includes bibliographies and index.
  1. Cerebrovascular disease. 2. Aged—Diseases.
I. Dunkle, Ruth E. II. Schmidley, James W.
[DNLM: 1. Cerebrovascular Disorders—in old age.
WL 355 S9192]
RC388.5.S8526   1987   618.97'681   87-16301
ISBN 0-8261-5430-1

Printed in the United States of America

Contents

Contributors

Robert H. Binstock, Ph.D. Henry R. Luce Professor of Aging, Health, and Society, Department of Epidemiology & Biostatistics, School of Medicine, Case Western Reserve University, Cleveland, OH.

Louis R. Caplan, M.D. Professor and Chairman, Department of Neurology, Tufts University School of Medicine and New England Medical Center, Boston, MA.

Mark L. Dyken, M.D. Professor and Chairman, Department of Neurology, Indiana University School of Medicine, Indianapolis, IN.

Edward Ganz, M.D. Assistant Professor of Neurosurgery, Case Western Reserve University School of Medicine and University Hospitals of Cleveland, Cleveland, OH.

Gary Goldberg, M.D. Assistant Professor, Departments of Physiology and Physical Medicine and Rehabilitation, Temple University School of Medicine; Director, Electrodiagnostic Center, Moss Rehabilitation Hospital, Philadelphia, PA.

Amy Horowitz, D.S.W. Director, Research and Evaluation, New York Association for the Blind (The Lighthouse), New York, NY.

Thomas R. Price, M.D. Professor of Neurology, Department of Neurology, University of Maryland School of Medicine and Hospital, Baltimore, MD.

Marcus E. Raichle, M.D. Professor of Neurology and Radiology, Division of Radiation Sciences and the Department of Neurology and Neurosurgery, Washington University School of Medicine and Hospital, St. Louis, MO.

Robert A. Ratcheson, M.D. Professor and Chief, Division of Neurosurgery, Case Western Reserve University School of Medicine and University Hospitals of Cleveland, Cleveland, OH.

Warren R. Selman, M.D. Assistant Professor, Division of Neurosurgery, Case Western Reserve University School of Medicine and University Hospitals of Cleveland, Cleveland, OH.

Barbara Silverstone, D.S.W. Executive Director, New York Association for the Blind (The Lighthouse), New York, NY.

W. McFate Smith, M.D., M.P.H. Professor of Epidemiology, School of Public Health, University of California, Berkeley; Clinical Professor of Medicine, University of California, San Francisco, CA.

Robert T. Wertz, Ph.D. Chief, Audiology and Speech Pathology, Veterans Administration Medical Center, Martinez, CA; Adjunct Professor, Department of Neurology, University of California School of Medicine, Davis, CA.

Jack P. Whisnant, M.D. Professor of Neurology and Roy E. and Merle Meyer Professor of Neuroscience, Department of Neurology, Mayo Medical School, Rochester, MN.

Fay W. Whitney, Ph.D., R.N. Assistant Professor and Director, Primary Care Graduate Program, University of Pennsylvania School of Nursing, Philadelphia, PA.

Introduction

Stroke victims have historically been viewed as untreatable; this pessimism is attributable at least in part to the statistic that 85% of persons disabled by a stroke are over the age of sixty-five. Furthermore, prognosis for survival following stroke is limited. In 20% of all strokes, death occurs within 24 hours of onset. The long-term survivors of stroke have an annual death rate much higher than the rate in the general population, regardless of amount of time since the stroke occurred (Marquardsen, 1982).

Future trends in stroke offer opportunities for both pessimism and optimism. On the one hand, it is recognized that the incidence of stroke increases after age 65, and with the mean age of the population in Western countries advancing, there will be an increase in the absolute number of strokes. On the other hand, in Europe and North America, a dramatic decrease in the incidence of and mortality from cerebrovascular disease has been documented (Hachinski, 1983). Although there is little to suggest that the medical management of the completed stroke will affect the future course of cerebrovascular disease, greater benefit could come from identifying the stroke-prone individual and providing treatment before the stroke occurs (Schoenberg, Schoenberg, Pritchard, Lilenfeld, & Whisnant, 1983).

Those experiencing a stroke can suffer from an array of problems including affective disorders and mood changes, as well as cognitive, social, and physical impairment (Feibel, Berk, & Joynt, 1979). Typically, feelings of helplessness, fear, depression, and irritability result from the sudden loss of bodily function. Treatment of these disorders is one of the greatest unmet needs in the care of the stroke patient (Feibel et al., 1979; Robinson & Benson, 1981; Robinson & Szetela, 1981).

In rehabilitation programs for stroke victims success is usually measured in terms of the proportion of survivors who regain mobility and function in activities of daily life. It has recently been noted that a significant proportion of survivors manifest social disability despite complete or nearly complete physical rehabilitation (Labi, Phillips, & Gresham, 1980), and this social disability may be particularly severe for the older stroke victim.

We are confronted with a complex picture of diagnostic issues, risk factors, and rehabilitative concerns. Because stroke significantly changes the quality of life of older Americans, failure to apply the most recent knowledge about prevention, diagnosis, treatment, and rehabilitation could lead to greater physical and social isolation for large segments of the older population. The nature of vascular illness and its effects is such that biomedical and sociobehavioral issues are involved in effective care.

This book provides information on the most recent scientific and clinical approaches to the care of the older stroke victim within three major categories: risk factors, treatment, and rehabilitation.

PART I: RISK FACTORS

In Chapter 1 Dr. Dyken reviews the major risk factors in stroke and provides evidence that treatment of certain major risk factors can decrease the incidence of stroke. His presentation includes appraisals of the contribution of various risk factors to stroke, as well as their potential treatability. Next, Dr. Whisnant presents an overview of "Issues of Stroke in the Elderly," setting the stage for the remainder of the book. His presentation of the history of cardiovascular mortality from the turn of the century until the present addresses potential explanations for the fluctuations in mortality statistics. His major focus is on hypertension as a risk factor. Dr. Smith, in Chapter 3, provides a review of two major controversies in the treatment of hypertension and stroke prevention: (1) the effect of drug treatment on incidence of stroke and mortality in individuals with hypertension, and (2) the effect of treating isolated systolic hypertension.

PART II: TREATMENT

Chapter 4, by Dr. Raichle, deals with pathophysiology of ischemia and infarction. He itemizes the numerous disturbances in homeostasis initiated by ischemia which appear to contribute to further tissue damage. Among these are disturbances in calcium homeostasis and cellular acidosis due to accumulation of lactate within ischemic tissue. Dr. Ganz focuses in Chapter 5 on the diagnostic techniques utilized in preventing stroke as well as caring for the stroke victim. Computed tomography and nuclear magnetic resonance are two approaches that provide hope for stroke therapy. Next, Dr. Caplan's chapter on "A General Therapeutic Perspective on Stroke Treatment" provides an overview of present-day stroke treatment and does much to dispel the myth that stroke is an untreatable condition. Dr. Whitney follows in Chapter 7 with a discussion of "Using Physical and Neuropsychological Assessment in the Nursing Care of the Acute Stroke Patient." She combines information on predicting outcomes of rehabilitation procedures and nursing practice into an ongoing assessment plan in the acute phase of the stroke. Finally, in Chapter 8, "Surgical Therapy for Stroke," Drs. Ratcheson and Selman provide an excellent view of current surgical therapy for atherosclerotic occlusive disease, while acknowledging the lack of conclusive evidence that surgical treatment for carotid atherosclerosis is effective. They also note that the indications for and efficacy of surgery for vertebrobasilar insufficiency remain unclear.

PART III: REHABILITATION

Until recently, rehabilitation has not been held consonant with aging. The next three chapters deal specifically with critical aspects of rehabilition in stroke victims. Dr. Goldberg emphasizes the neurobiological dimensions of rehabilitation in Chapter 9. Dr. Wertz explores in Chapter 10 the efficacy of language treatment for the older aphasic person and demonstrates through a review of major research studies that treatment is successful for certain types of stroke victims. Dr. Price's chapter deals with depression, a major concomitant to the decline in physical functioning that results from stroke. He documents the research findings that support the relationship between stroke and depression and discusses diagnostic and treatment concerns. Chapter 12 addresses the need for social support for older stroke patients. Drs. Silverstone and Horowitz reappraise the family system in relation to the care of the elderly stroke patient, stressing the need for clinical strategies and rethinking of rehabilitative services to facilitate the relationships among the professional rehabilitation team, the family, and the stroke patient. In Chapter 13, Dr. Binstock provides evidence for a shift in the economic and political climate that may favor rehabilitation. He suggests that this shift may be short lived and that professionals should therefore seize the opportunity to discover what potential resides in rehabilitating the older stroke patient.

R.E.D.
J.W.S.

REFERENCES

Feibel, J., Berk, S., & Joynt, R. (1979). The unmet needs of stroke survivors. *Neurology, 29,* 592.

Hachinski, V. (1983). Prognostic indicants in cerebrovascular disease. In M. Reivich & H. Hurtig (Eds.), *Cerebrovascular disease.* New York: Raven Press.

Labi, M., Phillips, T., & Gresham, T. (1980). Psychosocial disability in physically restored long-term stroke survivors. *Archives of Physical Medicine Rehabilitation, 61,* 561–565.

Marquardsen, J. (1982). The natural history of ischemic cerebrovascular disease as background to therapeutic approaches. In F. Rose (Ed.), *Advances in stroke.* New York: Raven Press.

Robinson, R., & Benson, D. (1981). Depression in aphasic patients: Frequency, severity and clinical-pathological corrections. *Brain and Language, 14,* 282–291.

Robinson, R., & Szetela, B. (1981). Mood change following left hemisphere brain injury. *Annals of Neurology, 9,* 447–453.

Schoenberg, B., Schoenberg, D., Pritchard, D., Lilenfeld, A., & Whisnant, J. (1983). In M. Reivich & H. Hurtig (Eds.), *Cerebrovascular disease.* New York: Raven Press.

PART I
Risk Factors

Introduction

While the main risk factor associated with stroke is hypertension, other risks have also been noted. In Chapter 1, Dr. Mark Dyken, of Indiana University, enumerates and elaborates upon all of the various risk factors for ischemic cerebrovascular disease. These associations range from the well-established (hypertension) to the more speculative (alcohol use). Some risk factors—for example, hypertension—are imminently treatable; others—such as age, gender, and geographic location—are obviously not treatable but may give insights into the causes of stroke.

In Chapter 2, Dr. Jack Whisnant discusses the beneficial effects of aggressive screening and public education. He presents convincing evidence that the treatment of hypertension is effective both in the primary prevention of stroke and in the prevention of subsequent strokes in a patient who has already had an ischemic event.

Dr. William McFate Smith, of the University of California, Berkeley, continues in Chapter 3 on the theme of the benefits of treating hypertension. He briefly surveys the considerable clinical evidence that lowering of elevated pressures decreases the risk of stroke and of

1

death from stroke. In the second part of his chapter he examines the current controversy over the treatment of isolated systolic hypertension in the elderly and gives details about an ongoing trial that should determine whether such intervention reduces the risk of stroke and other cardiovascular morbidity. Just as important, he assesses whether these benefits are greater than the potential risks of adverse drug effects in the elderly.

J.W.S.

1

Symptoms, Epidemiology, and Risk Factors

Mark L. Dyken, M.D.

Stroke is the number-three cause of death in the United States and the number-one crippler. Its effects may be as minimal as a brief numbness of one side of the body and as major as total incapacity and death. In the next chapter, evidence is given that the effective treatment of hypertension is the major reason for the decrease in stroke mortality, although there are other factors that may also contribute. Regardless, the evidence is quite strong that the dropping death rates are related to prevention. Prevention, in turn, is most likely related to the improved recognition and treatment of risk factors. Therefore, it is imperative that these factors and their relative degree of risk be clearly identified. This is the focus of the present chapter.

ALCOHOL CONSUMPTION

Although the relationship of alcohol consumption to stroke has not been firmly established, an association with hemorrhagic stroke was observed in the Honolulu heart study and the Hisayama study in Japan (Kagan et al., 1974, 1976). In the Hawaiian study, however, the intake was related to coexistent hypertension. Several studies in Scandinavia have implicated alcohol intoxication as a precipitating factor in stroke, both for infarction and subarachnoid hemorrhage (Hillbom & Kaste, 1978, 1982; Lee, 1979; Taylor, 1982). The Framingham study suggested an association in men (Wolf, Kannel, & Verter, 1983). The problem is that there is not a clear-cut independent relationship. For example, alcohol consumption and cigarette smoking are known to be associated with hemoconcentration and increased hematocrit, and a rebound thrombocytosis occurs during abstinence from alcohol (Dintenfass, 1975). Cardiac rhythm disorders also have been associated with acute alcohol intoxication (Ettinger et al., 1978). Regardless of exactly how it contributes to stroke, alcohol intake as a risk factor can easily be modified.

ORAL CONTRACEPTIVES

Use of oral contraceptives is also a factor to be considered. Retrospective case control studies have reported that oral contraceptive use is associated with 4 to 13 times the relative risk of cerebral infarction (Collaborative Group for the Study of Stroke in Young Women, 1973; Handin, 1974; Layde, Beral, & Kay, 1981). However, when smoking is controlled as a risk factor, Petitti and his group found no independent effect except for subarachnoid hemorrhage (Pettiti, Wingerd, Pellegrin, & Ramcharan, 1979). It is suggested that the risk of stroke is further enhanced by coexisting hypertension, a history of migraine, age exceeding 35 years, prolonged use of oral contraceptives, presence of diabetes or hyperlipidemia, and, in particular, cigarette smoking. The risk, if it is present, seems to be greatest for women taking oral contraceptives rich in estrogen (Handin, 1974). A number of reviews suggest that the evidence for an association is inconclusive (Comer et al., 1975; Schoenberg, Whisnant, Taylor, & Kempers, 1970; Shearman, 1981; Stadel, 1981). In fact, the incidence for stroke in the 15-to-45 age group is no less in men than women. Further, there has been no substantial increase in stroke mortality in these age groups since oral contraceptives became available. In the recent review of risk factors by the Subcommittee of the Stroke Council of the American Heart Association, this was the most controversial of all subjects and there was no consensus (Dyken et al., 1984). Again, we have a risk factor that is suggestive but not conclusive.

SMOKING

Although cigarette smoking is an established risk factor for cardiac, pulmonary, and peripheral vascular disease, its relationship to atherothrombotic brain infarction is not as clear. In the Framingham study, smoking was an apparent risk factor for infarction only in men below age 65 (Wolf et al., 1983). Paffenbarger and Williams (1967) found smoking to be one of the risk factors in college students, who later developed fatal occlusive stroke at twice the rate of nonsmokers. Other studies, including Seal Beach, either showed no relationship or an inverse relationship (Stallones et al., 1972). Therefore, although there is some suggestion of a relationship, it is not as strong as most might assume. Regardless, nicotine addiction can be treated.

OBESITY, DIET, CHOLESTEROL, LIPIDS, AND SEDENTARY ACTIVITY

Other factors that are not well established are obesity, diet, elevated blood cholesterol, elevated lipids and sedentary activity. Obesity has not been established as a separate risk factor independent of hypertension and diabetes (Wolf et al., 1983). Obesity can be related to hypertension, and an increase in weight is often associated with an increase in severity of hypertension (Messerli, 1982). Obesity also contributes to impaired glucose tolerance. Therefore, although obesity is not a direct risk factor for stroke, it is for hypertension and glucose intolerance, which in turn increase the likelihood of stroke. Therefore, if a person has hypertension or glucose intolerance, the treatment of the obesity may, by eliminating these factors, greatly decrease the likelihood of stroke.

Reports of the relationship of stroke to elevated blood cholesterol and lipids are conflicting (Dyer et al., 1981; Editors, 1981; Farid & Anderson, 1972; Kannel, 1976; Ladurner, Ott, Dornauer, Schreyer, & Lechner, 1978; Mathew, Davis, Meyer, & Chander, 1975). In the Framingham study, an increased risk was present only in those under age 50 (Kannel, 1976). The Framingham study also suggested a relationship between sedentary work and stroke, but this was not statistically significant. In a study of longshoremen, those men with sedentary jobs had coronary death rates one-third higher than cargo handlers, while the rates for stroke were similar in both groups (Paffenbarger, Laughlin, Gima, & Black, 1970).

GEOGRAPHIC AND ECONOMIC FACTORS

Geographic location, season and climate, and socioeconomic factors as direct risks for stroke are also not well established, nor is treatment practical. Cerebrovascular disease is more common in certain areas, for example, the southeastern United States (Kuller et al., 1970; Nefzger, Acheson, & Heyman, 1973; Nefzger, Heyman, & Acheson, 1973). A general relationship has been reported between the frequency of stroke deaths and extremes in temperature (Bull, 1973; Haberman, Capildeo, & Rose, 1981; Knox, 1981; Rogot & Padgett, 1976). Studies relating stroke to socioeconomic status are conflicting. In England a weak but direct correlation between cerebrovascular disease and high socioeconomic status has been reported (Acheson & Fairbairn, 1971), while in one U.S. study of men who died because of stroke, poverty was found to be a risk factor (Acheson, Heyman, & Nefzger, 1973).

ASYMPTOMATIC BRUITS

Asymptomatic bruits are the most interesting and controversial of risk factors for stroke. The Framingham study reported that, in 171 patients with bruits who were prospectively followed, the risk of developing permanent stroke during eight years of follow-up was 2.6 times that of those without bruits (Wolf, Kannel, Sorlie, & McNamara, 1981). The rate was 1.25% per year for men and 1.5% for women. Yet, in only 6 of the 21 patients who had a stroke was there an atherothrombotic infarction in the arterial distribution in the artery exhibiting bruit. Therefore, in only 6 could the stroke have possibly been prevented if a lesion on the side of the asymptomatic bruit had been removed. In addition, cause of death in 34 of the 43 who died was cardiovascular.

Heyman and colleagues (1980) did a similar study in Evans County, Georgia, although it must be noted that the Framingham study was done in Massachusetts, in a northern, middle-class, white community, while Evans County is in the South and more than 40% black. The study surveyed 1,620 people and identified 72 with bruits. During a six-year follow-up, 10, or 13.9%, of these developed a stroke, compared to 52, or 3.4%, of the 1,548 without bruits. The calculated annual incidence rate was 2.4%. In only 3 of the 10 did a spontaneous stroke occur on the same side as the bruit. Therefore, both the Framingham and Evans County studies concluded an asymptomatic bruit was a major risk factor for stroke; however, because the stroke occurred randomly, it was unlikely that removal of a lesion producing the bruit would have affected the outcome.

Regardless, some recommend that because a bruit frequently indicates atherosclerosis of the artery at the site, individuals with a bruit should be completely worked up for a surgically accessible lesion and, if one is found, that it be removed. No prospective random studies exist to indicate the benefit or lack of benefit of endarterectomy for asymptomatic bruit. In fact, an early study of transient ischemic attacks reported in 1970 is the only prospective random study of endarterectomy for any condition (Fields et al., 1970). The results of this study are interpreted differently by different reviewers.

Using the data reported, Jonas and Hass (1979) calculated that for surgery to be beneficial, the maximum acceptable stroke complication rate for surgery would be 2.9%. Karis (1983) using the same type of analysis, noted that for stroke and/or death this should be no more than 1.4%, and Jonas (1983) agreed. For asymptomatic bruits, Chambers and Norris (1984) reported from a review of the literature and their own studies that surgical risk outweighed possible benefits, unless a subgroup with a spontaneous risk of at least 5% per year could be identified. The Framingham and Evans County studies indicate that the risk of asymptomatic bruits is far below this, at 1.25% to 2.4% per year.

Although some surgeons report extremely low morbidity and mortality rates, it cannot be assumed that this is true for all or even most. Some years ago, Easton and Sherman (1977) reviewed 228 consecutive patients operated upon by board-certified neurosurgeons and vascular surgeons in one community and found that the total operative stroke and death rate was 21.1%. For asymptomatic bruit, it was 18%. A follow-up study in the same community of 421 additional patients showed a considerable drop, but it was still more than 5% (Modi, Finch, & Sumner, 1983). In 1984, three similar studies were reported. In Cincinnati (Brott & Thalinger, 1984), of those operated on for asymptomatic bruit or stenosis, 7.7% had stroke and 3.1% died. At the Lehigh Valley Hospital (Slavish, Nicholas, & Gee, 1984) 743 consecutive endarterectomies were performed with a 2.7% death rate and a combined 4.4% permanent stroke or death rate. For the 190 asymptomatic arteries, it was 2.6%. In Helsinki (Muuronen, 1984) 10% of 110 endarterectomy cases had major stroke and/or death. These data do not appear to be isolated to one hospital. The National Hospital Discharge Survey (Dyken & Pokras, 1984) indicated that endarterectomies performed in private hospitals in the United States jumped from 15,000 in 1971 to 103,000 in 1984. Of these patients, 2.8% were listed dead at the time of discharge from the hospital, when surgery was performed. From these data, it appears that the combined death and stroke rate might average as high as 10%. Chambers and Norris (1984), in the Toronto

Asymptomatic Prospective Cervical Bruit Study, reported that 500 patients followed prospectively had a stroke rate of 1 to 2% per year and a cardiac death rate of 2 to 4% per year. Of the 24 patients who were withdrawn to have endarterectomy, there was a complication rate of 16.7%. Thus, asymptomatic bruit is a potent risk factor for stroke or death, but the value of specific therapy is not well established. Still, it is important to identify the patient with an asymptomatic bruit, since an aggressive approach may identify other risk factors that can be treated.

DIABETES, PREVIOUS STROKE, AND BLOOD DISTURBANCES

Diabetes mellitus is a major risk factor for the development of stroke, along with hypertension and heart disease. Much of the risk is because of coexistent hypertension, but there is a significant independent impact (Kannel, 1976; Schoenberg, Schoenberg, Pritchard, Lilienfeld, & Whisnant, 1980). Although diabetes should be treated, to date there is no evidence that this treatment will reduce the risk for stroke.

Once a stroke has occurred, the risk for recurrent stroke increases 10 to 20 times (Robins & Baum, 1981; Toole et al., 1975). Although it might at first appear to be too late, the knowledge of this increased risk offers the opportunity to institute vigorous therapy for associated diseases and other risk factors.

The Framingham study (Wolf, Kannel, Meeks, Castelli, & D'Agostino, 1985) and a Swedish study (Wilhelmsen et al., 1984) have recently reported that increased blood fibrinogen level has an independent relationship to stroke. Although cause and effect cannot be assumed, if there is such a relationship, a number of therapeutic interventions might be possible.

The occurrence of stroke associated with homozygous sickle cell anemia varies from as low as 2.4% to as high as 17% (Portnoy & Herion, 1972). Treatment of the neurological complications, once they occur, does not have a beneficial effect. The effectiveness of prophylactic therapy in preventing stroke has not been established.

GENDER AND AGE

Consider the following two statements. First, being a male carries a greater risk for stroke than being a female. The second, more women than men die each year from stroke in the United States. It would seem at first that both cannot be true, but both are. To understand this, it should be known that *age* is the most potent single risk factor for stroke. Therefore, to assess the effect of any other factor, one has to age-adjust for the general population. The stroke rate percentage more than doubles for each successive 10 years after 55 years of age (Kurtzke, 1980), and the National Survey of Stroke (Robins & Baum, 1981) reported that, in short-term general hospitals, for each 10-year period between 35 and 65, the initial stroke incidence rate was always higher for men than women. Before age 65 the number of men and women is almost equal. After age 65 there are approximately 150 women for every 100 men and this difference increases as age increases. Therefore, even though the men available have more strokes, there are so many older women at high stroke risk and so few older men, that more women die from stroke than men (Kurtzke, 1980; Wolf et al., 1983). In 1978, for example, 73,648 men died from stroke, compared to 101,981 women.

The greater risk to men has been thought to be connected to hormones. However, prospective studies comparing estrogens to placebo failed to demonstrate any beneficial effect on men with cerebral infarction (Veterans Administration Cooperative Study Group, 1972). Not only was stroke not affected, but there was a higher overall death rate, largely due to cancer and various other diseases. One can conclude that being male and being old are high risk factors for stroke but neither is treatable. Before we leave the subject of age, we should note that the National Survey of Stroke (Weinfeld, 1981) reported that 29.6% of strokes occurred before 65 years of age; therefore, youth does not necessarily prevent stroke.

GENETIC FACTORS

A number of studies have reported a marked excess of stroke deaths among parents and male and female relatives of patients with cerebrovascular disease (Gifford, 1966; Heyden, Heyman, & Camplong, 1969; Paffenbarger & Williams, 1967). While this is an established risk factor, it is not treatable.

Blacks, especially in the southeastern United States, have higher death rates for strokes than whites (Eckstrom, Brand, Edlavitch, & Parrish, 1969; Heyman et al., 1971; Nichaman, Boyle, Lesene, & Sauer, 1962; Ostfeld, Shekelle, Klawans, & Tufo, 1974; Parrish, Payne, Allen, Goldberg, & Sauer, 1966; Peacock, Riley, Lampton, Raffel, & Walker, 1972). This has been related to the higher prevalence of hypertension among blacks. Studies conducted in Japan and Hawaii strongly suggest that such racial variation may be environmentally and not genetically determined. In Japan the incidence and mortality rates for stroke among Japanese people have been very high for most of this century and exceed those for heart disease (Fusa, 1974; Hatano, 1976; Katsuki et al., 1964; Katsuki, Omae, & Hirota, 1964; Tanaka et al., 1982; Ueda et al., 1981). In Hawaii, however, stroke incidence rates for Japanese residents appear similar to those of Caucasian Americans (Kagan, Popper, Rhoads, & Yano, 1985; Kagan et al., 1976; Worth, Kato, Rhoads, Kagan, & Syme, 1975). Thus, if the death rates truly reflect stroke incidence in Japan, then environmental factors would be the most likely explanation for the differences.

CARDIOVASCULAR DISEASE

Although hypertension at any level is the most potent of all treatable risk factors, heart disease is the next most important factor. Independent of blood pressure, persons with cardiac impairment of any sort, whether symptomatic or not, have more than twice the risk of stroke than persons with normal cardiac function (Wolf et al., 1983). Coronary heart disease is also the major cause of death in stroke survivors as well as patients with transient ischemic attacks or carotid bruits (Toole et al., 1975). In the Framingham study (Wolf, Dawber, Thomas, & Kannel, 1978), patients with chronic nonrheumatic atrial fibrillation developed strokes more than five times as often as those without atrial fibrillation, and when atrial fibrillation accompanied rheumatic heart disease there was a 17-fold increase.

Transient ischemic attacks (TIA's) are significant risk factors for stroke (Schoenberg et al., 1980). But in the Framingham study (Wolf et al., 1983), patients with TIA's also exhibited other, more significant risk factors such as hypertension and cardiac disease. Therefore, TIA as a risk factor is greatly influenced by other stroke risk factors. This suggests that its risk for impending strokes might be greatly reduced by treating associated conditions.

There is increasing evidence that the risk for stroke can be appreciably decreased in individuals who have transient ischemic attacks. One of the most promising therapeutic approaches is related to what is assumed to be the platelet antiaggregating effect of aspirin. A number of studies (Canadian Cooperative Stroke Study Group, 1978; Fields, Lemak, Frankowski, & Hardy, 1977, 1978; Ruether & Dorndorf, 1978; Sorenson et al., 1983) have shown a decrease in stroke and death which in the Canadian men approached 50% (Canadian Cooperative Stroke Study Group, 1978).

High hemoglobin or high hematocrit are associated with an increased incidence of cerebral infarction. The Framingham study (Kannel, Gordon, Wolf, & McNamara, 1972) noted that this association was present even within the normal range and was directly proportional to the concentration. When they adjusted for blood pressure and smoking, the hemoglobin level as a separate risk factor was not statistically significant. Nevertheless, a Japanese autopsy study (Katsuki, Omae, & Hirota, 1964) and several clinical and radiological studies of patients with stroke (Pearson & Thomas, 1979; Tohgi, Yamanouchi, Murakami, & Kameyama, 1978) support these observations. Harrison, Pollack, Kendall, and Marshall (1981) found a direct correlation between hemoglobin levels and the size of brain infarcts. Elevated hematocrit can be treated acutely, but there is some doubt whether this is one of the treatable factors. Nevertheless, because of the potential, I have listed this with hypertension, heart disease and transient ischemic attacks which are established to be risk factors for stroke and are treatable.

COMBINATIONS OF RISK FACTORS

To this point, we have considered risk factors pretty much individually, but there is evidence that some become more important when in combination and some are only important when in combination with others. Much work needs to be done in this area. Wolf et al. (1983), from analysis of data from the Framingham study, have described a general cerebrovascular risk profile that can be used to identify the 10% of the population who will have at least one-third of the strokes. This risk profile consists of five factors: elevated systolic blood pressure, elevated serum cholesterol, glucose intolerance, cigarette smoking, and left ventricular hypertrophy by electrocardiogram. Paffenbarger and Williams (1967) reported that combinations of smoking, elevated systolic blood pressure, and low ponderal index were associated with an eight-fold increased stroke mortality rate. Body height, having a parent dead, and not having been a varsity athlete resulted in a four-fold increase. The most important single factor of the six was elevated blood pressure.

Longstreth and Swanson (1984), in an in-depth review, noted that much of the controversy concerning the relationship between oral contraceptives and stroke might be because most studies were of young populations with a lower incidence of stroke. Therefore, a multiple factor effect might be lost, particularly if an important component was age. They observed that most women who had strokes and were on oral contraceptives had other risk factors such as hypertension. They concluded that oral contraception, cigarette smoking, and age above 35 years are particularly potent in combination.

SUMMARY

The following list brings together all the known and potential risk factors we have discussed in this chapter.

1. Well established and potentially treatable; treatment reduces stroke risk:
   a. hypertension
   b. heart disease
   c. transient ischemic attacks
   d. increased hematocrit and hemoglobin
2. Well established and treatable; treatment has questionable effect on stroke risk:
   a. diabetes mellitus
   b. prior stroke
   c. increased fibrinogen
   d. sickle cell anemia
   e. asymptomatic bruit
3. Well established and not treatable:
   a. age
   b. gender
   c. heredity
   d. race
4. Not well established but treatable:
   a. obesity
   b. diet
   c. increased cholesterol and lipids
   d. cigarette smoking
   e. alcohol consumption
   f. use of oral contraceptives
   g. inactivity
5. Not well established and not treatable:
   a. geographic location
   b. season and climate
   c. socioeconomic status

The evidence reviewed indicates that stroke may be decreased significantly by treating certain major risk factors. Active programs need to be initiated and continued so that risk factors can be identified in the population at large. Upon identification, effective therapy should be initiated and maintained, particularly for hypertension.

REFERENCES

Acheson, R. M., & Fairbairn, A. S. (1971). Record linkage in studies of cerebrovascular disease in Oxford, England. *Stroke, 2*, 48–57.

Acheson, R. M., Heyman, A., & Nefzger, M. D. (1973). Mortality from stroke among U.S. veterans in Georgia and five western states. Part III. Hypertension and demographic characteristics. *Journal of Chronic Diseases, 26*, 417–429.

Brott, T., & Thalinger, K. (1984). The practice of carotid endarterectomy in a large metropolitan area. *Stroke, 15*, 950–955.

Bull, G. M. (1973). Meteorological correlates with myocardial and cerebral infarction and respiratory disease. *British Journal of Preventive and Social Medicine, 27*, 108–113.

Canadian Cooperative Stroke Study Group. (1978). A randomized trial of aspirin and sulfinpyrazone in threatened stroke. *The New England Journal of Medicine, 299*, 53–59.

Chambers, B. R., & Norris, J. W. (1984). The case against surgery for asymptomatic carotid stenosis. *Stroke, 15*, 964–967.

Collaborative Group for the Study of Stroke in Young Women. (1973). Oral contraception and increased risk of cerebral ischemia or thrombosis. *The New England Journal of Medicine, 288*, 871–878.

Comer, T. P., Tuerck, D. G., Bilas, R. A., Clow, S. F., Falero, F. Jr., & Raskind, R. R. (1975). Comparison of strokes in women of childbearing age in Rochester, Minnesota, and Bakersfield, California. *Angiology, 26*, 351–355.

Dintenfass, L. (1975). Elevation of blood viscosity, aggregation of red cells, haematocrit values and fibrinogen levels in cigarette smokers. *Medical Journal of Australia, 1*, 617–620.

Dyer, A. R., Stamler, J., Paul, O., Shekelle, R. B., Schoenberger, J. A., Berkson, D. M., Lepper, M., Collette, P., Shekelle, S., & Lindberg, H. A. (1981). Serum cholesterol and risk of death from cancer and other causes in three Chicago epidemiological studies. *Journal of Chronic Diseases, 34*(6), 249–260.

Dyken, M. L., & Pokras, R. (1984). The performance of endarterectomy for disease of the extracranial arteries of the head. *Stroke, 15*, 948–950.

Dyken, M. L., Wolf, P. A., Barnett, H. J. M., Bergan, J. J., Hass, W. K., Kannel, W. B., Kuller, L., Kurtzke, J. F., & Sundt, T. M. (1984). Risk factors in stroke. *Stroke, 15*, 1105–1111.

Easton, J. D., & Sherman, D. G. (1977). Stroke and mortality rate in carotid endarterectomy: 228 consecutive operations. *Stroke, 8*, 565–568.

Eckstrom, P. T., Brand, F. R., Edlavitch, S. A., & Parrish, H. M. (1969). Epidemiology of stroke in a rural area. *Public Health Reports, 84*, 878–882.

Editors. (1981). High-density lipoprotein. *Lancet, 1*, 478–480.

Ettinger, P. O., Wu, C. F., De La Cruz, C. Jr., Weisse, A. B., Ahmed, S. S., & Regan, T. J. (1978). Arrhythmias and the "Holiday Heart": Alcohol-associated cardiac rhythm disorders. *American Heart Journal, 95*, 555–562.

Farid, N. R., & Anderson, J. (1972). Cerebrovascular disease and hyperlipoproteinemia. *Lancet, 1*, 1398–1399.

Fields, W. S., Lemak, N. A., Frankowski, R. F., & Hardy, R. J. (1977). Controlled trial of aspirin in cerebral ischemia. *Stroke, 8*, 301–316.

Fields, W. S., Lemak, N. A., Frankowski, R. F., & Hardy, R. J. (1978). Controlled trial of aspirin in cerebral ischemia. Part II. Surgical group. *Stroke, 9*, 309–319.

Fields, W. S., Maslenikov, V., Meyer, J. S., Hass, W. K., Remington, R. D., & Macdonald, M. (1970). Joint study of extracranial arterial occlusion. Part V. Progress report of prognosis following surgery or nonsurgical treatment for transient cerebral ischemic attacks and cerebral carotid artery lesions. *Journal of the American Medical Association, 211*, 1993–2003.

Fusa, K. (1974). An epidemiological study of hypertension. A prospective study of incidence of cerebrovascular disease and myocardial infarction in an area in Tohoku District of Japan (author's translation). *Journal of the Japanese Society of Internal Medicine, 63*, 630–642.

Gifford, A. J. (1966). An epidemiological study of cerebrovascular disease. *American Journal of Public Health, 56*, 452–461.

Haberman, S., Capildeo, R., & Rose, F. C. (1981). The seasonal variation in mortality from cerebrovascular disease. *Journal of the Neurological Sciences, 52*, 25–36.

Handin, R. I. (1974). Thromboembolic complications of pregnancy and oral contraceptives. *Progress in Cardiovascular Disease, 16*, 395–405.

Harrison, M. J. G., Pollack, S., Kendall, B. E., & Marshall, J. (1981). Effect of haematocrit on carotid stenosis and cerebral infarction. *Lancet, 2*(8238), 114–115.

Hatano, S. (1976). Experience from a multicentre stroke register: A preliminary report. *Bulletin of the World Health Organization, 54*, 540–553.

Heyden, S., Heyman, A., & Camplong, L. (1969). Mortality patterns among parents of patients with atherosclerotic cerebrovascular disease. *Journal of Chronic Diseases, 22*, 105–110.

Heyman, A., Karp, H. R., Heyden, S., Bartel, A., Cassel, J. C., Tyroler, H. A., & Hames, C. G. (1971). Cerebrovascular disease in the biracial population of Evans County, Georgia. *Archives of Internal Medical, 128*, 949–955.

Heyman, A., Wilkinson, W. E., Heyden, S., Helms, M. J., Bartel, A. G., Karp, H. R., Tyroler, H. A., & Hames, C. G. (1980). Risk of stroke in asymptomatic persons with cervical arterial bruits: A population study in Evans County, Georgia. *The New England Journal of Medicine, 302*, 838–841.

Hillbom, M., & Kaste, M. (1978). Does ethanol intoxication promote brain infarction in young adults? *Lancet, 2*, 1181–1183.

Hillbom, M., & Kaste, M. (1982). Alcohol intoxication: A risk factor for primary subarachnoid hemorrhage. *Neurology, 32*, 706–711.

Jonas, S. (1983). Asymptomatic carotid artery disease. (Response to letter to the editor by Robert Karis). *Stroke, 14*, 443.

Jonas, S., & Hass, W. K. (1979). An approach to the maximal acceptable stroke complication rate after surgery for transient cerebral ischemia (TIA). (Abstract.) *Stroke, 10,* 104.

Kagan, A., Harris, B. R., Johnson, K. G., Kato, H., Syme, S. L., Rhodes, G. G., Gay, M. L., Nichaman, M. Z., Hamilton, H. B., & Tillotson, J. (1974). Epidemiologic studies of coronary heart disease and stroke in Japanese men living in Japan, Hawaii and California: Demographic, physical, dietary and biochemical characteristics. *Journal of Chronic Diseases, 27,* 345–364.

Kagan, A., Popper, J., Rhoads, G. G., Takeya, Y., Kato, H., Goode, G. B., & Marmot, M. (1976). Epidemiologic studies of coronary heart disease and stroke in Japanese men living in Japan, Hawaii, and California: Prevalence of stroke. In P. Scheinberg, (Ed.), *Cerebrovascular Diseases: Tenth Princeton Conference* (pp. 267–277). New York: Raven Press.

Kagan, A., Popper, J. S., Rhoads, G. G., & Yano, K. (1985). Dietary and other risk factors for stroke in Hawaiian Japanese men. *Stroke, 16,* 390–396.

Kannel, W. B. (1976). Epidemiology of cerebrovascular disease. In R. W. R. Russel, (Ed.), *Cerebral arterial disease* (pp. 1–23). Edinburgh, Scotland: Churchill Livingstone.

Kannel, W. B., Gordon, T., Wolf, P. A., & McNamara, P. (1972). Hemoglobin and the risk of cerebral infarction: The Framingham study. *Stroke, 3,* 409–420.

Karis, R. (1983). Asymptomatic carotid artery disease. (Letter to the Editor.) *Stroke, 14,* 443.

Katsuki, S., Hirota, Y., Akazome, T., Takeya, S., Omae, T., & Takano, S. (1964). Epidemiological studies in Hisayama, Kyushu Island, Japan. Part I. With particular reference to cardiovascular status. *Japanese Heart Journal, 5,* 12–36.

Katsuki, S., Omae, T., & Hirota, Y. (1964). Epidemiological and clinicopathological studies on cerebrovascular disease. *Kyushi Journal of Medical Science, 15,* 127–149.

Knox, E. G. (1981). Meteorological associations of cerebrovascular disease mortality in England and Wales. *Journal of Epidemiology and Community Health, 35*(3), 220–223.

Kuller, L., Anderson, H., Peterson, D., Cassel, J., Spiers, P., Curry, H., Paegel, B., Saslaw, M., Sisk, C., Wilber, J., Millward, D., Winkelstein, W. J., Filienfeld, A., & Seltser, R. (1970). Nationwide cerebrovascular disease morbidity study. *Stroke, 1,* 86–99.

Kurtzke, J. F. (1980). Epidemiology of cerebrovascular disease. In R. E. Siekert (Ed.), *Cerebrovascular survey report for Joint Council Subcommittee on Cerebrovascular Disease, National Institute of Neurological and Communicative Disorders and Stroke and National Heart and Lung Institute* (pp. 135–176). Rochester, NY: Whiting Press.

Ladurner, G., Ott, E., Dornauer, U., Schreyer, H., & Lechner, H. (1978). Lipid metabolism and angiologic findings in transitory ischemic attacks. (Authors' transl.) *Nervenarzt, 49*(2), 88–89.

Layde, P. M., Beral, V., & Kay, C. R. (1981). Further analyses of mortality in oral contraceptive users. (Royal College of General Practitioners' Oral Contraception Study). *Lancet, 1,* 541–546.

Lee, K. (1979). Alcoholism and cerebrovascular thrombosis in the young. *Acta Neurologica Scandinavica, 59,* 270–274.

Longstreth, W. T. Jr., & Swanson, P. D. (1984). Oral contraceptives and stroke. *Stroke, 15,* 747–750.

Mathew, N. T., Davis, D., Meyer, J. S., & Chander, K. (1975). Hyperlipoproteinemia in occlusive cerebrovascular disease. *Journal of the American Medical Association, 232,* 262–266.

Messerli, F. H. (1982). Cardiovascular effects of obesity and hypertension. *Lancet, 1,* 1165–1168.

Modi, J. R., Finch, W. T., & Sumner, D. S. (1983). Update of carotid endarterectomy in two community hospitals: Springfield revisited. (Abstract.) *Stroke, 14,* 128.

Muuronen, A. (1984). Outcome of surgical treatment of 110 patients with transient ischemic attacks. *Stroke, 15,* 959–964.

Nefzger, M. D., Acheson, R. M., & Heyman, A. (1973). Mortality from stroke among U.S. veterans in Georgia and five western states. Part I. Study plan and death rates. *Journal of Chronic Diseases, 26,* 393–404.

Nefzger, M. D., Heyman, A., & Acheson, R. M. (1973). Stroke, geography and blood pressure. (Editorial.) *Journal of Chronic Diseases, 26,* 389–391.

Nichaman, M. Z., Boyle, E. Jr., Lesene, T. P., & Sauer, H. I. (1962). Cardiovascular disease mortality by race, based on a statistical study in Charleston, South Carolina. *Geriatrics, 17,* 724–737.

Ostfeld, A. M., Shekelle, R. B., Klawans, H., & Tufo, H. M. (1974). Epidemiology of stroke in an elderly welfare population. *American Journal of Public Health, 64,* 450–458.

Paffenbarger, R. S. Jr., Laughlin, M. E., Gima, A. S., & Black, R. A. (1970). Work activity of longshoremen as related to death from coronary heart disease and stroke. *The New England Journal of Medicine, 282,* 1109–1114.

Paffenbarger, R. S. Jr., & Williams, J. L. (1967). Chronic disease in former college students. Part V. Early precursors of fatal stroke. *American Journal of Public Health, 57,* 1290–1299.

Parrish, H. M., Payne, G. H., Allen, W. C., Goldberg, J. C., & Sauer, H. I. (1966). Mid-Missouri stroke survey: A preliminary report. *Missouri Medicine, 63,* 816–821.

Peacock, P. B., Riley, C. P., Lampton, T. D., Raffel, S. S., & Walker, J. S. (1972). The Birmingham stroke, epidemiology and rehabilitation study. In G. T. Stewart (Ed.), *Trends in epidemiology: Application to health service research and training* (pp. 231–345). Springfield, IL: Charles C Thomas.

Pearson, T. C., & Thomas, D. J. (1979). Physiological and pharmacological factors influencing blood viscosity and cerebral blood flow. In G. Tognoni & S. Garattini (Eds.), *Drug treatment and prevention in cerebrovascular disorders: Proceedings of the International Seminar on Drug Treatment & Prevention in Cerebrovascular Disorders, Milan, Italy, May, 1979* (p. 33). Amsterdam: Elsevier North Holland.

Pettiti, D. B., Wingerd, J., Pellegrin, F., & Ramcharan, S. (1979). Risk of vascular disease in women. Smoking, oral contraceptives, noncontraceptive estrogens, and other factors. *Journal of the American Medical Association, 242,* 1150–1154.

Portnoy, B. A., & Herion, J. C. (1972). Neurological manifestations in sickle-cell disease, with a review of the literature and emphasis on the prevalence of hemiplegia. *Annals of Internal Medicine, 76,* 643–652.

Robins, M., & Baum, H. M. (1981). The national survey of stroke. Incidence. *Stroke, 12*(Suppl. 1), I-45–I-55.

Rogot, E., & Padgett, S. J. (1976). Associations of coronary and stroke mortality with temperature and snowfall in selected areas of the United States, 1962–1966. *American Journal of Epidemiology, 103*, 565–575.

Ruether, R., & Dorndorf, W. (1978). Aspirin in patients with cerebral ischemia and normal angiograms or non-surgical lesions: The results of a double-blind trial. In K. Breddin, W. Dorndorf, D. Loew, & R. Marx (Eds.), *Acetylsalicylic acid in cerebral ischemia and coronary heart disease* (pp. 97–106). Stuttgart, Germany: Schattauer.

Schoenberg, B. S., Schoenberg, D. G., Pritchard, D. A., Lilienfeld, A. M., & Whisnant, J. P. (1980). Differential risk factors for completed stroke and transient ischemic attacks (TIA): Study of vascular diseases (hypertension, cardiac disease, peripheral vascular disease) and diabetes mellitus. In R. C. Duvoisin (Ed.), *Transactions of the American Neurological Association* (pp. 165–167). New York: Springer.

Schoenberg, B. S., Whisnant, J. P., Taylor, W. F., & Kempers, K. D. (1970). Strokes in women of childbearing age: A population study. *Neurology, 20*, 181–189.

Shearman, R. P. (1981). Oral contraceptives: Where are the excess deaths? *Medical Journal of Australia, 1*, 698–700.

Slavish, L. G., Nicholas, G. G., & Gee, W. (1984). Review of a community hospital experience with carotid endarterectomy. *Stroke, 15*, 956–959.

Sorenson, P. S., Pedersen, H., Marquardsen, J., Petersson, H., Helteberg, A., Simonsen, N., Munck, O., & Andersen, L. A. (1983). Acetylsalicylic acid in the prevention of stroke in patients with reversible cerebral ischemic attacks. A Danish cooperative study. *Stroke, 14*, 15–22.

Stadel, B. V. (1981). Oral contraceptives and cardiovascular disease. *The New England Journal of Medicine, 305*(12), 672–677.

Stallones, R. A., Dyken, M. L., Fang, H. C. H., Heyman, A., Seltser, & Stamler, J. (1972). Epidemiology for stroke, facilities planning, Part I. (Report of the Joint Committee for Stroke Facilities.) *Stroke, 14*, 443.

Tanaka, H., Ueda, Y., Hayashi, M., Date, C., Baba, T., Yamashita, H., Shoji, H., Tanaka, Y., Owada, K., & Detels, R. (1982). Risk factors for cerebral hemorrhage and cerebral infarction in a Japanese rural community. *Stroke, 13*, 62–73.

Taylor, J. R. (1982). Alcohol and strokes. (Letter to the editor). *The New England Journal of Medicine, 306*, 1111.

Tohgi, H., Yamanouchi, H., Murakami, M., & Kameyama, M. (1978). Importance of the hematocrit as a risk factor in cerebral infarction. *Stroke, 9*, 369–374.

Toole, J. F., Janeway, R., Choi, K., Cordell, R., Davis, C., Johnston, F., & Miller, H. S. (1975). Transient ischemic attacks due to atherosclerosis: A prospective study of 160 patients. *Archives of Neurology, 32*, 5–12.

Ueda, K., Omae, T., Hirota, Y., Takeshita, M., Katsuki, S., Tanaka, K., & Enjoji, M. (1981). Decreasing trend in incidence and mortality from stroke in Hisayama residents, Japan. *Stroke, 12*, 154–160.

Veterans Administration Cooperative Study Group. (1972). Estrogenic therapy in men with ischemic cerebrovascular disease: Effect on recurrent cerebral infarction and survival. *Stroke, 3*, 427–433.

Weinfeld, F. D. (Ed.). (1981). The national survey of stroke (National Institute of Neurological and Communicative Disorders and Stroke). *Stroke*, *12*(Suppl. 1), I-1–I-91.

Wilhelmsen, L., Svardsudd, K., Korsan-Bengtsen, K., Larsson, B., Welin, L., & Tibblin, G. (1984). Fibrinogen as a risk factor for stroke and myocardial infarction. *The New England Journal of Medicine, 311*, 501–505.

Wolf, P. A., Dawber, T. R., Thomas, H. E. Jr., & Kannel, W. B. (1978). Epidemiologic assessment of chronic atrial fibrillation and risk of stroke—The Framingham study. *Neurology, 28*, 973–977.

Wolf, P. A., Kannel, W. B., Meeks, S., Castelli, W. P., & D'Agostino, R. B. (1985). Fibrinogen as a risk factor for stroke—The Framingham study. *Stroke, 16*, 139.

Wolf, P. A., Kannel, W. B., Sorlie, P., & McNamara, P. (1981). Asymptomatic carotid bruit and risk of stroke—The Framingham study. *Journal of the American Medical Association, 245*, 1442–1445.

Wolf, P. A., Kannel, W. B., & Verter, J. (1983). Current status of risk factors for stroke. In H. J. M. Barnett (Ed.), *Neurologic clinics* (Vol. 1, pp. 317–343). Philadelphia: W. B. Saunders.

Worth, R. M., Kato, H., Rhoads, G. G., Kagan, A., & Syme, S. L. (1975). Epidemiologic studies of coronary heart disease and stroke in Japanese men living in Japan, Hawaii and California: Mortality. *American Journal of Epidemiology, 102*, 481–490.

2

Issues in Stroke in the Elderly

Jack P. Whisnant, M.D.

It is easy to direct a discussion of issues concerning stroke to the elderly because stroke is largely a disease of old age. In our population-based studies, nearly 90 percent of the strokes occurred in people over the age of 55 and about 80 percent occurred in people over the age of 65. In this chapter I will focus on what has happened to stroke incidence and mortality over a long period of time. The mortality from stroke has gone down dramatically, and at a fairly consistent rate, from 1900 through 1978. Perhaps there has been a slightly greater rate of decline since 1970. Total cardiovascular mortality (which includes stroke mortality) gradually increased up until 1950, after which it gradually declined by about 33 percent. So, in 1970, total cardiovascular mortality was about the same as it was in 1900, when stroke mortality represented about 40 percent of all cardiovascular mortality. Since 1950, however, stroke mortality has consistently represented about 20 percent of all cardiovascular mortality (Whisnant, 1984).

The problems in interpreting data from national health statistics are many. First, we depend upon what is recorded on death certificates, so we must deal with revisions in codes, changes in terminology, and, very important changes in the fashion of diagnosis. It was common practice some years ago to record stroke on the death certificate if the death occurred fairly suddenly. This still occurs in some instances today, even though the majority of such sudden deaths are probably cardiac in origin. In most populations, there is quite a low autopsy rate and therefore a correspondingly low accuracy in diagnosis on death certificates. Thus, one is never quite sure what data compiled from death certificates mean.

The decline in stroke mortality could be due to a decline in case fatality (early deaths) because of more effective early treatment or less severe cases, or it could be due to a decline in the incidence of new cases of stroke. We need to have knowledge of the trends in mortality and in incidence of new cases and in case fatality during the same time and in the same population, to make a judgment about the relative contribution of each. If there is a change in incidence or case fatality, then one has to determine what factors might have produced that effect.

In Rochester, Minnesota, we have a unique resource that allows us to look at a whole population. This resource was made possible largely through the work of one of the pioneers at the Mayo Clinic, Dr. Henry Plummer, who designed a unit record system for the Mayo practice of medicine. This unit record system is for all hospital admissions and outpatient visits, emergency room visits, house calls, or any kind of medical care provided by the Mayo Clinic, all in a single system. This record system, mostly in handwritten form, dates back to the beginning of the Mayo practice in the early part of this century. It serves as the basis for the record system for the population and allows us to look back in time at various medical conditions, particularly chronic medical conditions, in order to examine trends. This is not simply the Mayo practice for referrals from all over the world, it is the practice of Mayo for people who are residents of Rochester or the surrounding Olmsted County. In about the last 15 years, we have tied other medical care units in the community into this record system so that those records are also indexed and linked with the Mayo system. Various diagnoses from these other medical care units can now be retrieved for study in the same way as Mayo records.

In Rochester, mortality rates for stroke among whites are lower in all age/sex groups than for the U.S. white population as a whole. The rate declined in Rochester from 1945 through 1979 for all age groups, by about 55% in each, including those over the age of 75 (Whisnant, 1984). In U.S. whites, the decline was less in all age groups and it actually increased by 3% in those over the age of 75 in the same period. We are fairly sure this increase in the rate for U.S. whites over 75 is an artifact, because the most inadequate information in the U.S. vital statistics probably comes from the oldest patients.

Our Rochester data from 1945 to 1979 cover about 1.5 million person years of observation, which allows us to look at incidence rates in a fairly reliable fashion. For women, from the mid 1950s through 1979, there was a gradual decline in the incidence of new cases of stroke (Whisnant, 1984). For men, this was not so dramatic; the rates showed little change until the end of the 1960s, after which there was a sharp decline of 44 percent from 1969 through 1979 (Whisnant, 1984). It appears that, in Rochester at least, the decline in incidence rates contributed substantially to the lower mortality observed. On the other hand, the case fatality rate for stroke in Rochester was relatively stable from 1945 through 1979, and almost exactly the same between 1945 and 1949 as it was from 1975 to 1979. This does not apply to long-term mortality following stroke, because patients have had increasingly better long-term survival after stroke, presumably due to better management of cardiac and respiratory complications.

Since cerebral infarction represents more than 80% of strokes, the foregoing comments relate to cerebral infarction as well as to all strokes. It is more difficult to judge other categories of stroke because death certificates generally provide quite inadequate information. We believe that the incidence rate and mortality rate for cerebral hemorrhage have dropped, but it is a little difficult to assess the rate for cerebral hemorrhage from our population because of the relatively small numbers and some confounding factors.

After the mid 1950s, anticoagulants were commonly used for a number of different conditions in various medical centers around the country, including Rochester. After the mid 1950s, there was a 20% higher rate of intracerebral hemorrhage, when all hemorrhages were considered, as compared to the rate when those on anticoagulants were excluded. For those individuals over the age of 50, where intracerebral hemorrhage is more common, there was about a 50% increase if you consider those on anticoagulants. So the use of angicoagulants makes it more difficult to interpret trends in cerebral hemorrhage. However, the overall picture does indicate a decline in incidence of new cases of cerebral hemorrhage, contributing greatly to the decline in mortality due to cerebral hemorrhage (Whisnant, 1984).

Subarachnoid hemorrhage is a different situation. It probably represents close to the same proportion of all strokes as does cerebral hemorrhage, but the mortality rate in the United States from subarachnoid hemorrhage gradually increased until about 1970, after which there was a small decline in both women and men. The increasing rate of aneurysmal subarachnoid hemorrhage is due, at least in part, to improvements in angiography in that period of time. In Rochester, because of the small number of cases, we must look at average annual mortality rates over a 10-year period. With this approach we have noted fairly flat mortality and incidence rates for subarachnoid hemorrhage. Certainly it does not appear that there has been a change in subarachnoid hemorrhage rates of a magnitude sufficient to contribute to a decline of stroke, so I shall not consider that further in this discussion.

We must consider what factors have contributed to this decline in incidence of stroke. Of the many factors that Dr. Mark Dyken discusses in Chapter 1, I shall consider primarily high blood pressure, as it relates to stroke occurrence.

When we examine the effect of a particular risk factor, we must consider both the prevalence of the risk factor in the population and the relative risk of stroke for that factor. *Relative risk* refers to the probability of a stroke occurring in the presence of that particular factor, compared to the probability of a stroke occurring in a normal population without that risk factor. The relative risk of stroke for high blood pressure is about 6. In other words, patients with the risk factor (hypertension) are 6 times as likely to have a stroke as those without the factor.

Persons with hypertension clearly have an ever-increasing risk of stroke, in all age groups and in both sexes. Those at greatest risk usually have the highest blood pressures. This is seen most readily from the Framingham study (Dawber, Wolf, Colton, & Nickerson, 1977). High blood pressure is also quite prevalent. It is very hard to get satisfactory data on the prevalence of high blood pressure in the era before effective treatment was available. At the present time, if you add hypertensive persons to those who are on treatment for hypertension, the prevalence of high blood pressure could be as high as 30% in the over-50 age group. Given the very high prevalence rate, the effectiveness of treatment for high blood pressure deserves close consideration in attempts to explain the decline of stroke.

Systolic hypertension also increases the risk of stroke and is the subject of an anticipated lengthy clinical trial in elderly patients to determine the extent to which treatment of systolic hypertension decreases the risk of stroke.

Although there were no good population-based studies of the prevalence of hypertension prior to the advent of effective treatment, since 1962 there have been several blood pressure surveys. I would like to focus on what these tell us about the percentages of hypertensives treated and controlled over the years. A 1960–1962 National Health Survey of 1214 hypertensives indicated that 16 percent had been treated and controlled (National Center for Health Statistics, 1966). In a Chicago industrial survey from 1967 to 1972, 20% of hypertensives were treated and controlled (Schoenberger, Stamler, Shekelle, & Shekelle, 1972). In a 1976 study of a very large group of patients with hypertension, 59 percent were treated and controlled (Berkson et al., 1980). Following a one-year educational campaign carried on in the same group, this figure rose to 71 percent. The corollary of that, of course, is that the percentage of persons with previously unknown and known but untreated high blood pressure had to change in the other direction.

All of these studies suggest that efforts at diagnosis, treatment, and control of high blood pressure are on the increase. These studies are not representative of the whole population, or any particular population, but they do give us some insight into attitudes toward control of high blood pressure.

A number of treatment trials, including some very good randomized treatment trials, have examined the effects of treatment of high blood pressure on the incidence of stroke and other vascular events. None of these treatment trials has shown a significant difference in stroke occurrence, perhaps because they excluded the patients with more severe disease, but also because stroke as a single end point did not occur with a high enough frequency so that it would be easy to detect a difference. The trials have shown a benefit from treatment when *all* vascular events were considered as end points.

It was not until the results of the Hypertension Detection and Follow-up Program (1982) were published that it was shown that systematic treatment of patients with hypertension resulted in their having significantly fewer strokes than patients referred to their own physicians for routine care. This study, which lasted five years and required nearly 11,000 persons, shared an overall stroke incidence of 1.9% in aggressively treated patients, compared to 2.9% in referred-care patients. This represented a 35% reduction in all strokes and a 44% reduction in fatal strokes. Total stroke rates were lower in the aggressive-care group than in the referred-care group, in all race/sex categories, but the greatest reductions were in black women and white men.

These observations do not seem to fit entirely satisfactorily with U.S. stroke mortality trends. There was little effective treatment available for high blood pressure prior to 1955, yet the rate of decline in mortality from stroke in the U.S. was about the same from 1920 to 1970, with a greater rate of decline after 1970. The most one could suggest might be that treatment of high blood pressure contributed to the increased rate of decline from 1970 on. Although there could have been some other effect of hypertension prior to effective medical treatment, we do not have data to indicate that hypertension was more prevalent in the several decades prior to antihypertensive treatment. What evidence there is would indicate that it may have been less prevalent.

Some other factor may account for the earlier decrease in stroke mortality, or, more likely, the U.S. stroke mortality trend may be an artifact. That is, there may have been more mixing of types of cardiovascular mortality, and stroke may have been cited more frequently on death certificates than was appropriate. It is fairly clear that a similar practice occurred in Japan in more recent years.

The observations on the effect of treatment of high blood pressure fit rather well with the trend of incidence of stroke in Rochester back to 1945; that is, we now have incidence rates for stroke in Rochester from 1935 showing that the stroke rates for women were stable from 1935 through 1954, after which there was a gradual decline. In men the decline was not appreciable until after 1969. These data reinforce the idea that the decline in stroke mortality prior to the 1950s in the U.S. is probably an artifact caused by diagnostic fashion.

Antihypertensive treatment was used rather frequently in Rochester after 1955, and we have now shown that it was used with increasing frequency from that time through 1979. We now also have data to indicate a decreasing prevalence of hypertension in the community and a gradually increasing use of antihypertensive medication in Rochester as a whole, and we have demonstrated that men have lagged behind women in regard to identification and treatment of hypertension, as has been shown in other studies.

In summary, the following points should be emphasized in regard to the effect of hypertension:

1. The clear demonstration of hypertension as a powerful risk factor for stroke
2. The declining incidence rate for stroke in Rochester, with the rates for men starting to decline much later than those for women

3. Decreasing blood pressure, over time, by age group, in the Framingham population sample, with a similar earlier effect in women
4. Increasingly effective treatment of high blood pressure and the earlier effect in women, shown both in hypertensive surveys and in the Rochester population
5. The extent of the decrease in stroke occurrence in the Hypertension Detection and Follow-up Program in five years, favoring carefully treated patients and showing comparable differences in men and women when both were managed in a similar fashion

All of these points collectively support the idea that treatment of hypertension is the major contributor to decreased stroke incidence and mortality. The available evidence would be consistent with the idea that it is the only contributor to the decline in stroke. Hypertension is prevalent enough and the effect of treatment would be powerful enough to account for the extent of the decline. This is not to indicate that management of other powerful risk factors such as transient ischemic attacks and cardiac disease, if clearly effective, could not have had some effect on stroke. The evidence for such an effect is not very strong, and I shall not consider those factors in this discussion.

Many unexplained areas remain in stroke prevention with regard to recognition and treatment of high blood pressure, especially in black populations. Systolic hypertension also deserves more attention.

REFERENCES

Berkson, D. M., Brown, M. C., Stanton, H., Masterson, J., Shireman, L., Ausbrook, D. K., Miles, D., Whipple, I. T., & Muriel, H. H. (1980). Changing trends in hypertension detection and control: The Chicago experience. *American Journal of Public Health, 70*(4), 389–393.

Dawber, T. R., Wolf, P. A., Colton, T., Nickerson, R. J. (1977). Risk factors: Comparision of the biological data in myocardial and brain infarctions. In J. J. Zulch, W. Kaufmann, K. A. Hossmann, & V. Hossman (Eds.), *Brain and heart infarct* (pp. 226–252). Berlin: Springer-Verlag.

Hypertension Detection and Follow-up Program Cooperative Group. (1982). Five-Year findings of the Hypertension Detection and Follow-up Program. Part III. Reduction in stroke incidence among persons with high blood pressure. *Journal of the American Medical Association, 247*, 633–638.

National Center for Health Statistics. (1966). *Hypertension and hypertensive heart disease in adults, US, 1960–2* (DHEW Publication No. 1000, Series 11). Washington, DC: U.S. Government Printing Office.

Schoenberger, J. A., Stamler, J., Shekelle, R. B., & Shekelle, S. (1972). Current status of hypertension control in an industrial population. *Journal of the American Medical Association, 222*(5), 559–562.

Whisnant, J. P. (1984). The decline of stroke. *Stroke, 15*(1), 160–168.

3

Hypertension: A Treatment Controversy

W. McFate Smith, M.D., M.P.H.

Two questions in the treatment of hypertension have been controversial in relationship to stroke and its possible prevention. The first, which can now be laid to rest with considerable confidence, while the second is only just now being properly addressed. The first controversy has to do with the question of secular change versus pharmacologic treatment of hypertension; that is, has the drug treatment of individuals with hypertension had a noticeable effect on stroke incidence and mortality in the population? The second controversy has to do with whether or not isolated systolic hypertension (ISH) should be treated.

SECULAR CHANGE VERSUS TREATMENT OF HYPERTENSION

First of all, the fact of declining national stroke mortality and incidence rates is not controversial. They have been going down since the beginning of the century (see Figure 3–1). In Rochester (Olmstead County), Minnesota stroke mortality declined 45% over the period from 1945 to 1974 (Garraway et al., 1979). The National Stroke Study, which reviewed hospital admissions from 1971 to 1976, revealed a downward trend for first strokes that paralleled the acceleration since 1972 of the long-term trend in age-adjusted stroke mortality rates (Weinfeld, 1981). Similar changes were seen in the Manitoba study (Abu-Zeid, Choi, & Nelson, 1975). It should also be noted that, as emphasized by Whisnant in Chapter 2, it is no longer controversial as to whether the pharmacological treatment of essential hypertension (diastolic hypertension) in controlled clinical trials prevents strokes.

What, then, has been the nature of the first controversy? There are at least three issues. First of all, there is disagreement as to whether there really was an acceleration in the trend of declining stroke mortality coincident with the advent of effective antihypertensive agents in the early 1950s, and whether therapy had anything to do with it. Second, the results in early studies of the effects of hypertension treatment on stroke survival were equivocal and inconsistent. Third is the question as to how the acceleration in the decline in stroke mortality noted between 1968 and 1979 (see Figure 3–2) might be related to the intensity of the public and professional educational campaign that resulted in more widespread control of serious hypertension. The evidence for the role of treatment in the changes in the trend of stroke mortality in the early 1950s is equivocal. Why was this the case if treatment that lowers arterial pressure is really helpful? In the first place, the proportion of the hypertensive population on therapy and controlled was low. Moreover, the early studies conducted during that era were for the most part studies of stroke recurrence or of survival after stroke recovery rather than interven-

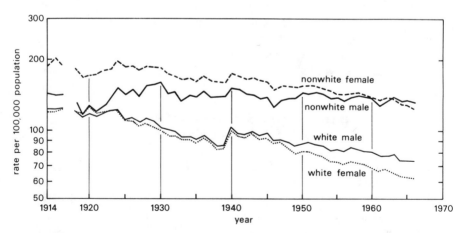

FIGURE 3-1. Trends in stroke mortality rate (top 2 lines) and stroke incidence rate (lower 2 lines) in the United States.

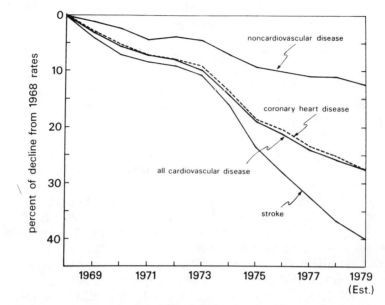

FIGURE 3-2. Decline in age-adjusted death rates for cardiovascular and noncardiovascular disease, 1968–1979.
Source: National Center for Health Statistics (1982).

tion studies. Even the intervention studies, with the exception of the Hypertension-Stroke Cooperative Study (1974), were not well controlled clinical trials. Nonetheless they suggested a reduced incidence of stroke, but no difference in survival. On the other hand, the evidence for the role of treatment in the changes in stroke mortality trends in the 1970s, as reviewed by Dr. Whisnant (Chapter 2) is very persuasive. The first controlled clinical trial in severe hypertension was that of Hamilton, Thompson, & Wisniewski (1964). That trial, plus the Veterans Administration Trial (1972), the U.S. Public Health Service Hospitals Cooperative Study Group (1977), and Oslo Study (Helgeland, 1980) that followed, consistently showed a reduction in stroke incidence and/or mortality at least in males, but all the studies were too small and the populations too selective to warrant generalization. In the Veterans Administration Trial, for example, the 563 individuals were all men and mostly black.

The more recent, large experimental epidemiology studies—the European Working Party on High Blood Pressure in the Elderly (1985), the Australian National Blood Pressure Study (Management

Committee, 1982), and the British Medical Research Council's study of mild hypertension (1985)—observed a 32 to 55% reduction in the incidence of stroke.

The EWPHE was a double-blind, randomized placebo-controlled trial of antihypertensive treatment conducted in 840 men and women (70%) over the age of 60. Entry criteria were diastolic blood pressure (DBP) 90 to 119 mmHg and systolic pressure (SBP) 160 to 239 mmHg. The 840 subjects were randomized to active treatment (hydrochloro-thiazide + triameterne) or to matching placebo. The study continued for 12 years with an average follow-up of over 5 years. In the double-blind part of the trial a 43% reduction in cerebrovascular mortality was observed ($p = 0.15$); by "intention to treat" analysis this percentage reduction was 32% ($p = 0.16$). Both systolic and diastolic arterial pressure had been substantially and significantly reduced in the active treated group, the difference varying between –21/–7 mmHg at year one and –19/–5 mmHg at year seven.

The Australian National Blood Pressure Study was a single-blind placebo controlled therapeutic trial of antihypertensive drug treatment of 3,427 men and women age 30 to 69, with mild hypertension, i.e., DBP 95 to 110 mmHg and SBP < 200 mmHg in a 2-stage screening schedule. The active treatment regimen was chlorothiazide supplemented by methyldopa, propranolol, or pindolol. Follow-up averaged 3 years on therapy and 4 years overall. The percentage reduction in cerebrovascular events in the active treatment group was 48% and 55% by "intention to treat." The average reduction in DBP was 5.6 mmHg greater in the treated group.

The aim of the British MRC trial was also to determine whether drug treatment of mild hypertension (90 to 109 mmHg) reduced the rates of stroke, of death due to hypertension, and of coronary events, in this case in men and women age 35 to 64 years. This study included 17,354 patients, was single-blind, and based almost entirely in general practices. Patients were randomly allocated at entry to take ben-drofluazide or propranolol or placebo tablets. Follow-up averaged nearly 5 years and blood pressure was significantly reduced by each of the active regimens compared to placebo. A 45% reduction in stroke incidence occurred in the combined treated groups, with ben-drofluazide having a greater effect than propranolol, especially in cigarette smokers. Cigarette smokers had higher rates in all groups.

These three separate, large, long-term placebo-controlled studies from different parts of the world, using similar designs, each observing a substantial reduction in stroke, provide incontestable evidence in support of treating hypertension for prevention of stroke. The

Hypertension Detection and Follow-up Program referred to earlier by Dr. Whisnant found that systematic treatment of patients with hypertension resulted in significantly fewer strokes than the referred or community control group (1982). This study, which had no placebo control group, involved 10,939 men and women who were randomly allocated to either aggressive, closely monitored Step-care or referred back to their usual source of medical care for routine management. The Step-care treated group's stroke rate was 35% lower and the stroke mortality rate was 44% lower than the referred control group, and this was true for all age, race, and sex categories. Thus, the evidence based on clinical trials is overwhelming that lowering diastolic blood pressure reduces the incidence of strokes and stroke deaths and that it is this treatment that has accelerated the already declining stroke mortality.

THE MANAGEMENT OF ISOLATED SYSTOLIC HYPERTENSION

Isolated systolic hypertension (ISH), defined as systolic blood pressure equal to or greater than 160 mmHg with a diastolic blood pressure less than 90 mmHg, is relatively common among the elderly. In cross-sectional studies, both systolic and diastolic blood pressure tend to rise with age. The rise of systolic pressure is disproportionate to diastolic, and this difference widens progressively with age. In fact, diastolic blood pressure tends to level off during middle age, while systolic pressure continues to rise through advancing years. As a consequence, the pulse pressure rises on the average of 20 mmHg over the age range of 60 to 90 years.

The prevalence of ISH is approximately 6 to 10% in the 60-and-over age group, with a steep age gradient such that the age group over 75 years is more than three times as likely to have ISH than persons aged 60 to 64 (Garland, Barrett-Conner, Suarez, & Criqui, 1983). At any age, ISH is more frequently found in blacks and women. These changes in blood pressure are attributable to the loss of elasticity and atherosclerosis of the aorta and major tributaries, with a consequent loss of distensibility.

The clinical importance of ISH relates to its being a potent predictor of cardiovascular risk, particularly for stroke. This is confirmed in numerous data sets (Colandrea, Friedman, Nickaman, & Lynd, 1970; Garland et al., 1983; Kannel et al., 1981; Shekelle, Ostfield, & Klawans, 1974). ISH carries a 2- to 3-fold excess risk of cardiovascular mortality, with the relative risk of stroke death in men varying from 2.5 to 6.0. Moreover, the HDFP (1986) has demonstrated that baseline SBP (and also pulse pressure) is predictive of 5 year mortality from all causes. A twofold increase in age-adjusted mortality rate across four SBP strata (I = < 140 mmHg, II = 140–159 mmHg, III = 160–179 mmHg, IV = 180+ mmHg) was noted, and this effect remained after other risk factors were controlled for by multivariate analysis. Baseline DBP was not predictive in this population.

Unlike the case for essential hypertension, the excess cardiovascular risk associated with ISH has not been shown to be favorably affected by antihypertensive treatment. Is there a reasonable basis for concern that the effect on cardiovascular risk of treatment of hypertension should be different for ISH than essential hypertension? First of all, the basic underlying pathophysiology of the two conditions is different. Since isolated systolic hypertension is a manifestation of the same underlying pathology to which the cardiovascular morbidity and mortality are attributed, and since no mechanism is known whereby lowering systolic blood pressure would favorably influence that underlying structural pathology, there is reason to be skeptical of the results of treatment. Of more concern, however, is the fact that the issue has not been adequately studied. Only two controlled studies have included isolated systolic hypertension in their treatment population (Ikeda, 1976; Priddle, Liu, & Breithaupt, 1968). Only Ikeda analyzed the ISH subjects separately from other hypertensives. In his study, in which the treatment was primarily diuretics, he found morbidity and mortality were two to three times higher in the placebo group. Thus the evidence that treatment helps in ISH is limited to two small studies, each numbering fewer than 200 subjects.

For this reason and in order to obtain an answer to the question before prevailing practices precluded conduct of a definitive study, the National Heart, Lung and Blood Institute, in conjunction with the National Institute on Aging and the National Institute of Mental Health, sponsored a pilot study to assess the feasibility of conducting a full-scale trial of ISH in the elderly (Smith, 1983). The central research questions addressed in the pilot study were (1) the feasibility of recruiting adequate numbers of elderly participants for randomization into a clinical trial, (2) participant compliance to the prescribed double-blind treatment regimens and to a regular visit schedule, (3) a comparison of the effectiveness of specific antihypertensive medications in reducing systolic blood pressure, (4) an analysis of the unwanted effects of specific antihypertensive medications, and (5) the development of methods for ascertaining stroke and other disease end points.

The subjects were 27,199 men and women aged 60 and over who were screened for eligibility in the study of ISH. Of these 2,910 (10.7%) were eligible for a three-visit evaluation process, from which 551 were randomized into a comparison study of chlorthalidone (25 to 50 mg daily) versus placebo. Each of five clinical centers successfully met their goal of recruiting over 100 participants in a 12-month period (Vogt, Ireland, Black, Camel, & Hughes, in press). Systolic blood pressure was successfully controlled in the treatment group, with a differential fall in systolic blood pressure between the two groups of 17 mmHg at one year (Hulley et al., 1985). Over 80% responded satisfactorily to the diuretic alone, with greater than 50% responding to the starting dose of 25 mg. Medications were very well tolerated, and compliance to the visit schedule and therapeutic regimens was high. No adverse impact on the quality of life was detected.

On the basis of this successful pilot study, the National Heart, Lung and Blood Institute and the National Institute on Aging are sponsoring a 16-center clinical trial for which recruitment began in March 1985 (Wittenberg, 1985). A two-year recruitment period is expected to enroll approximately 5,000 participants, half of whom will receive active pharmacologic therapy, the first of which will be the diuretic chlorthalidone. The other half will receive placebo on a double-blind basis. The primary end point for the study is the number of persons who suffer from a stroke. Total mortality, stroke mortality, cardiovascular mortality, and all other causes of death will also be recorded. The potential value of the study is the determination of whether or not the treatment of isolated systolic hypertension reduces the risk of stroke and other cardiovascular morbidity and mortality and whether these risks outweigh the potential risks of adverse drug effects and their impact on the quality of life.

SUMMARY AND CONCLUSIONS

There should be no doubt in anyone's mind concerning the merits of treating diastolic (essential) hypertension, regardless of age, race, or sex, as a means of reducing the risk of stroke in the individual and of reducing the incidence of fatal and nonfatal strokes in the community.

No comparable basis exists for recommending the treatment of isolated systolic hypertension. Given the potential of adversely affecting the quality of life of elderly persons by treatment with antihypertensive agents, it may be prudent either to limit treatment to nonpharmacologic methods or to low doses of diuretics given judiciously to those with systolic blood pressures 180 mmHg and above, while awaiting the results of the full-scale national clinical trial described in this chapter.

REFERENCES

Abu-Zeid, H. A. H., Choi, N. W., & Nelson, N. A. (1975). Epidemiogic features of cerebrovascular disease in Manitoba: Incidence by age, sex, and residence, with etiologic implications. *Canadian Medical Association Journal, 113,* 379–384.

British Medical Research Council. (1985). MRC trial of treatment of mild hypertension: Principal results. *British Medical Journal, 291,* 97–104.

Colandrea, M. A., Friedman, G. D., Nichaman, M. A., & Lynd, C. M. (1970). Systolic hypertension in the elderly. An epidemiologic assessment. *Circulation, 41,* 239–245.

European Working Party on High Blood Pressure in the Elderly. (1985). Mortality and morbidity results. *Lancet, 1,* 1349–1354.

Garland, C., Barrett-Conner, E., Suarez, L., & Criqui, M. H. (1983). Isolated systolic hypertension and mortality after age 60 years. A prospective population-based study. *American Journal of Epidemiology, 118,* 365–376.

Garraway, W. M., Whisnant, J. P., Furlan, A. J., Phillips, L. H. II, Kurland, L. T., & O'Fallon, W. M. (1979). The declining incidence of stroke. *New England Journal of Medicine, 300*(9), 450–452.

Hamilton, M., Thompson, E. M., & Wisniewski, T. K. M. (1964). The role of blood-pressure control in preventing complications of hypertension. *Lancet, 1,* 235.

Helgeland, A. (1980). Treatment of mild hypertension: A five-year controlled drug trial. The Oslo Study. *American Journal of Medicine, 69,* 725–732.

Hulley, S. B., Furberg, C. D., Gurland, B., McDonald, R., Perry, H. M., Smith, W. M., & Vogt, T. M. (1985). Systolic Hypertension in the Elderly Program (SHEP): Antihypertensive efficacy of chlorthalidone. *American Journal of Cardiology, 56,* 913–920.

Hypertension Stroke Cooperative Study Group. (1974). Effect of antihypertension treatment of stroke recurrence. *Journal of the American Medical Association, 229,* 409–418.

Ikeda, M. (1976). Prognosis and pathology of mild hypertension and systolic hypertension in the aged. In S. Hatano, I. Shigematsu, & T. Strasser (Eds.), *Hypertension and stroke control in the community* (pp. 248–257). Geneva: World Health Organization.

Kannel, W. B., Wolf, P. A., McGee, D. L., Dawber, T. R., McNamara, P., & Castelli, W. P. (1981). Systolic blood pressure, arterial rigidity, and risk of stroke—The Framingham Study. *Journal of the American Medical Association, 245,* 1225–1229.

Management Committee. (1982). The Australian therapeutic trial in mild hypertension. *Lancet, 1,* 1261–1267.

Priddle, W. W., Liu, S. F., & Breithaupt, D. J. (1968). Amelioration of high blood pressure in the elderly. *Journal of the American Geriatric Society, 16,* 887–892.

Shekelle, R. B., Ostfield, A. M., & Klawans, H. L., Jr. (1974). Hypertension and risk of stroke in an elderly population. *Stroke, 5,* 71–75.

Smith, W. M. (1983). Isolated systolic hypertension in the elderly. *Current Medical Research Opinion, 8*(Suppl. 1), 19–29.

U.S. Public Health Service Hospitals Cooperative Study Group. (1977). Treatment of mild hypertension. Results of ten year intervention trial. *Circulation Research, 40*(Suppl. 1), 98–105.

Veterans Administration Cooperative Study Group on Antihypertensive Agents. (1972). Effects of treatment on morbidity in hypertension. Part III. Influence of age, diastolic pressure, and prior cardiovascular disease; further analysis of side effects. *Circulation, 45,* 991–1004.

Vogt, T. M., Ireland, C. C., Black, D., Camel, G., & Hughes, G. (In press). Recruitment of elderly volunteers for a multi-center clinical trial: The SHEP pilot study. *Controlled Clinical Trials.*

Weinfeld, F. D. (Ed.). (1981). National survey of stroke. *Stroke, 12*(2), (Suppl. 1).

Wittenberg, C. K. (1985). Systolic hypertension therapy trial begins. *Journal of the American Medical Association, 253,* 1700–1701.

PART II
Treatment

Introduction

Dr. Marcus Raichle of Washington University begins this part with a succinct cataloguing of the overwhelmingly complex biochemical pathophysiology of nervous system ischemia. One's initial reaction, when confronted with this bewildering array of interlocking, interdependent events, is likely to be despair. However, like the general who, when surrounded by the enemy, announced, "We have them just where we want them, gentlemen; we can attack in any direction," physicians and basic scientists alike are presented with a plethora of opportunities for potential intervention, or at least further study of brain energy metabolism. The reader is also referred to Dr. Raichle's extended in-depth discussion of the same subject (1983).

Dr. Edward Ganz, of Case Western Reserve University, provides in Chapter 5 an overview of computed tomography (CT), positron emission tomography (PET), and nuclear magnetic resonance (NMR), also known as magnetic resonance imaging, (MRI). These techniques have already vastly improved our ability to care for stroke patients and promise to provide fresh insights into the diagnosis, pathophysiology, and potential therapy of stroke for decades to come.

These first two chapters serve to emphasize some of the unique problems confronted by those who seek to prevent or ameliorate the consequences of stroke. If we are to intervene and successfully reverse the metabolic consequences of ischemia, as outlined by Dr. Raichle, we must do so within the first few hours of the ischemic insult. This need for immediate action implies a similar need for rapid and extremely accurate diagnosis. CT scanning has already given us a tool with unprecedented resolution, permitting an exactitude of anatomical and pathophysiological diagnosis that was undreamed of only 15 years ago. MRI and PET are not in general use and, because of cost limitations, may never become as widely used as CT. They will, however, continue to be indispensable research tools.

The next two chapters, by Dr. Louis Caplan of Tufts University and Dr. Fay Whitney of the University of Pennsylvania, provide a general overview of the medical and nursing care of stroke patients. A central message of both chapters is that there is no such thing as a "generic" stroke patient. Stroke is a syndrome with a variety of causes, as outlined by Dr. Caplan, and an even larger variety of consequences, including physical, emotional, intellectual, and social disabilities. While the ultimate goal of all medical research on the cerebral vasculature is to prevent stroke or, failing that, to minimize the extent of ensuing damage, we must not lose sight of the fact that today's stroke victim needs appropriate care, delivered by humane and well-informed physicians, nurses, and therapists.

Chapter 8, the final one in this part, by Drs. Robert Ratcheson and Warren Selman of Case Western Reserve University, reviews the state of the art in surgical therapy for occlusive cerebrovascular disease. The authors review the historical background of the pathophysiology of strokes resulting from carotid atherosclerosis, give the essentials of clinical diagnosis and laboratory investigation of the problem, and describe the available surgical options for therapy. The ultimate goal of cerebrovascular surgery is the same as that of medical therapy and risk-factor management: the prevention of all strokes. Although many physicians are "believers" in carotid endarterectomy for selected patients with carotid atherosclerosis, the overall role of arterial surgery in the management of ischemic cerebrovascular disease has not been sharply defined. The recently published study of extracranial-intracranial bypass surgery (EC/IC Bypass, 1985), which is described in this chapter, has shown the medical community that surgical therapy for cerebrovascular disease can be examined in a dispassionate and scientific way. Trials of carotid endarterectomy for patients with symptomatic as well as asymptomatic extracranial carotid atherosclerosis are currently in the early stages and should provide long overdue information about the exact role of carotid surgery in these situations.

J. W. S.

REFERENCES

EC/IC Bypass Study Group. (1985). Failure of extracranial-intracranial arterial bypass to reduce the risk of ischemic stroke: Results of an international randomized trial. *New England Journal of Medicine, 313*(19), 1191–1200.

Raichle, Marcus E. (1983). The pathophysiology of brain ischemia. *Annals of Neurology, 13*(1), 2–10.

4

Stroke: The Ischemic Lesion

Marcus E. Raichle, M.D.

Protecting the human brain from ischemic damage is an important clinical problem. Most observers, whether clinicians or basic scientists, would agree that prevention of ischemia is, without a doubt, the most effective approach. However, despite much effort to detect pre-ischemic lesions, identify and combat risk factors, and educate the general public and the medical community, most patients suffering acute ischemic cerebral infarction are first seen only after signs and symptoms of focal or generalized ischemia have already occurred.

For many years the persistence of signs and symptoms of ischemia in a person for more than a few minutes was thought by clinicians to signify the presence of irreversible cellular damage to the brain. This belief was challenged when several laboratories demonstrated, in other mammalian species, that total cerebral ischemia for as long as one hour could be followed by at least partial recovery of the tissue. The realization that the mammalian brain may be more resistant to ischemia than previously thought has raised the possibility of intervening before damage becomes irreversible, and it has focused attention on the search for factors that might contribute to irreversible ischemic cell damage. Identification of these putative cytotoxic factors is crucial to development of a rational approach to the protection of brain threatened by ischemia. The picture that emerges from a

This research was supported by NIH Grants NS06833 and HL13851 and by the McDonnell Center for the Study of Higher Brain Function.

review of the extensive and often conflicting literature on the subject (Raichle, 1983; Siesjo, 1981, 1984) is a complex one: Interacting and cascading events tend to reinforce the initial ischemic insult and initiate biochemical reactions that ultimately destroy vital cellular elements. Before commencing an examination of the specific details of the ischemic lesion, I shall briefly summarize the major features of an ischemic insult to the brain, to orient the reader not familiar with the subject.

Interruption of cerebral blood flow results in loss of consciousness within 10 seconds and cessation of spontaneous and evoked electrical activity within successive 10-second intervals. Several minutes after the loss of electrical activity there are major disruptions of normal tissue *ion homeostasis*. Ion-sensitive microelectrodes placed in the extracellular fluid space of the brain record a marked increase in potassium concentration and a fall in sodium and calcium concentrations. The movement of sodium and calcium into the cell plus the release of calcium from mitochondria and endoplasmic reticulum results in a substantial rise in the intracellular sodium and free-calcium concentrations. Two important biochemical events occur as the result of anaerobic metabolism of glucose in ischemic brain tissue. First, *energy stores* of the tissue (i.e., phosphocreatine and adenylate energy charge) are depleted. Second, lactic acid is produced in excessive amounts and accumulates in the tissue, leading to *cellular acidosis*. Finally, alterations in the *blood-brain barrier* also occur. With the exception of the loss of consciousness and of electrical activity, all these events and those that they subsequently cause are thought to have important implications for cell survival. Let us consider each in turn.

ABNORMAL ION HOMEOSTASIS

Ischemia results in rapid accumulation of potassium in the brain extracellular fluid, followed by astrocytic swelling (Hertz, 1981). The result of this potassium-induced swelling of the astroglia is to increase significantly the diffusion distance for molecular oxygen from blood to the neuronal elements of brain tissue. This potassium-induced glial swelling, as well as with the known increase in tissue osmolality due to generation of so-called idiogenic osmoles and the accompanying increase in tissue water content, in all likelihood result in magnification of the initial ischemic insult and enlargement of a so-called ischemic penumbra, or zone of viable but functionally inactive cells at the borders of a cerebral ischemic lesion.

A second and related effect of the increase in potassium concentration in brain extracellular fluid is stimulation of brain metabolism. Thus, the ischemia-induced increase in extracellular fluid potassium ion concentration begets more ischemia through a process that both adversely affects oxygen delivery to the tissue by causing elements of the tissue to swell and increases the metabolic demand of that tissue in the process.

In addition to the rise in extracellular fluid concentration of potassium just discussed, ischemia results in a fall in the extracellular fluid concentration of calcium and sodium (Farber, Chien, & Mittnachit, 1981). Data from a variety of sources strongly implicate calcium in the pathogenesis of irreversible ischemic cell injury. In order to understand the role of calcium in ischemic brain damage, it is necessary to review briefly some aspects of intracellular calcium regulation in ischemia as well as the effect of calcium on membrane phospholipid metabolism.

Ischemia causes membrane depolarization and a rise in the intracellular concentration of free calcium. This increase in intracellular calcium is vigorously combated by several defense mechanisms available to the cell. Only one of these defense mechanisms, however, is available to the ischemic, energy-depleted cell, namely, mitochondrial sequestration of calcium at the expense of oxidative phosphorylation (i.e., uncoupling of oxidative phosphorylation). Thus, the ischemia-induced intracellular accumulation of calcium results in diversion of a limited supply of available oxygen from much-needed energy production to an ineffectual recycling of ions across mitochondrial membranes. As others have noted, however, energy failure alone cannot explain irreversible ischemic cell injury. It is important, therefore, to consider the other consequences of a persistently elevated intracellular free-calcium concentration.

A rise in intracellular free-calcium concentration is associated with the breakdown of membrane phospholipids and the release of free fatty acids, including arachidonic acid, from these membrane phospholipids (Wolfe, 1982). The calcium-induced loss of membrane phospholipids probably alters the equilibrium between the membrane protein and the remaining lipid such that membrane calcium permeability is drastically altered. This increased permeability permits an additional massive influx of calcium into the ischemic cell. It has been suggested that the presence of these high concentrations of calcium within the cell prevents the recovery from a number of important ischemia-induced mitochondrial abnormalities. When calcium influx is blocked during reperfusion following ischemia, cell survival is greatly enhanced, and this is correlated with complete recovery of mitochondrial function. Although mitochondrial calcium toxicity is a simple, straightforward explanation for irreversible ischemic cell damage, it ignores the potential damaging effects of free fatty acids and their metabolites, both of which accumulate in ischemic tissue.

Free fatty acids are known to have a variety of detrimental effects on brain structure and function, primarily due to their ability to disrupt cell membranes. In addition to the adverse effect of free fatty acids on cell membranes, potential damage also follows the intracellular accumulation of their metabolites (e.g., thromboxane, leukotrienes, and prostacyclin). An additional important result of the disruption in fatty acid metabolism is the accumulation of active oxygen species in the ischemic tissue (often referred to as "free radicals"). Because these compounds have the capacity to initiate destructive reactions in biological membranes and other cell structures, they have assumed importance in discussions of the pathophysiology of ischemic cell damage (DelMaestro, 1980; Siesjo, 1981).

During complete ischemia, free radicals cannot contribute greatly to irreversible cell injury. However, it has been suggested (DelMaestro, 1980) that, during periods of anoxia, alterations may occur in the elaborate cellular defenses against free radicals which then permit an increase in the concentration of these reactive molecules during states of partial or incomplete ischemia. Such a hypothesis has naturally prompted a number of investigators to search for evidence of damage by these compounds. Controversy and conflicting claims surround the results of these studies, which have for the most part failed to support the claim that free radicals damage ischemic brain tissue. Because of the complexity of the brain's defenses against free radicals, because of the limited data available at present, and because of our inability actually to measure free radicals in tissue samples from ischemic brain, one should reserve final judgment about their role in irreversible ischemic cell damage.

DEPLETION OF STORES

Energy depletion, defined in terms of the tissue concentrations of phosphocreatine, adenosine triphosphate, adenosine diphosphate, and adenosine monophosphate, occurs in ischemic brain tissue, making it attractive to suggest that energy failure is a major determinant of irreversible cell injury. Available evidence, however, does not support this hypothesis. Many investigators have noted a poor correlation between evidence of cell damage and the level of cellular energy metabolism.

CELLULAR ACIDOSIS

Ischemia is invariably accompanied by an increase in the tissue lactate concentration in the adult brain, due to anaerobic metabolism of glucose and the slow clearance of lactate from adult brain tissue, and a fall in tissue pH. Considerable evidence suggests that tissue lactacidosis is an important determinant of ischemic cell death in the adult brain, and the preischemic tissue level of glucose is the important determinant of the level of tissue lactacidosis.

BLOOD–BRAIN BARRIER ALTERATIONS

Studies of the blood-brain barrier in anoxia and ischemia have traditionally focused on the change in permeability to large tracer molecules such as radiographic contrast materials and Evans blue dye. These studies have shown classically a breakdown in the blood-brain barrier to these molecules occurring hours to days after an ischemic insult. The actual relevance of such changes to recovery of tissue is not clear. More recently studies have indicated that major changes in glucose transport may occur well in advance of a general breakdown of the blood-brain barrier (Betz, Gilboe, & Drewes, 1974; Gjedde & Siemkowicz, 1978). Such changes may impair substrate delivery to a failing brain.

CONCLUSIONS

Our understanding of the pathophysiology of brain ischemia and infarction has advanced considerably over the past decade. Several important observations have emerged. First, a disturbance in calcium homeostasis within the ischemic cell may be essential to the ultimate death of the cell. The exact biochemical and metabolic events initiated by disordered calcium homeostasis that are responsible for cell death remain undetermined.

Second, cellular acidosis due to accumulation of lactate within ischemic tissue appears to have a deleterious effect. Excessive accumulation of lactate may, in fact, contribute directly to irreversible cell damage. This fact may have important implications for the management of patients. Thus, in the adult, elevated blood glucose levels preceding infarction may well predispose to a worse outcome because higher tissue glucose levels lead to greater accumulation of lactate when the brain must resort to anaerobic glycolysis.

Third, a variety of factors initiated by ischemia appear, in turn, to contribute to further tissue damage. These include (1) the rise in extracellular fluid potassium concentration, which paradoxically stimulates metabolism while further impeding substrate delivery by causing cell swelling; (2) the release of excitatory neurotransmitters (Rothman & Olney, 1986) capable of stimulating metabolism; and (3) the release of a variety of vasoactive substances capable of disrupting blood flow in relation to the metabolic needs of the tissue.

REFERENCES

Betz, A. L., Gilboe, D. D. & Drewes, L. R. (1974). Effects of anoxia on net uptake on unidirectional transport of glucose into isolated dog brain. *Brain Research, 67*, 307–316.

DelMaestro, R. F. (1980). An approach to free radicals in medicine and biology. *Acta Physiologica Scandinavica, Suppl. 492*, 153–168.

Farber, J. L., Chien, K. R., & Mittnachit, S. Jr. (1981). The pathogenesis of irreversible cell injury in ischemia. *American Journal of Pathophysiology, 102*, 271–281.

Gjedde, A. & Siemkowicz, E. (1978). Effect of glucose and insulin pretreatment on cerebral metabolic recovery after ischemia. *Transactions of the American Neurological Association, 103*, 1–3.

Hertz, L. (1981). Features of astrocyte function apparently involved in the response of the central nervous system to ischemia-hypoxia. *Journal of Cerebral Blood Flow and Metabolism, 1*, 143–154.

Raichle, M. E. (1983). The pathophysiology of brain ischemia. *Annals of Neurology, 13*, 2–10.

Rothman, S. M., & Olney, J. W. (1986). Glutanate and the pathophysiology of hypoxic-ischemic brain damage. *Annals of Neurology, 19*, 105–111.

Siesjo, B. K. (1981). Cell damage in the brain: A speculative hypothesis. *Journal of Cerebral Blood Flow and Metabolism, 1*, 155–186.

Siesjo, B. K. (1984). Cerebral circulation and metabolism. *Journal of Neurosurgery, 60*, 883–908.

Wolfe, L. S. (1982). Eicosanoids: Prostaglandin, thromboxanes, leukotrienes and other derivatives of carbon-20 unsaturated fatty acids. *Journal of Neurochemistry, 38*, 1–14.

5

New Imaging Techniques for Stroke Detection

Edward Ganz, M.D.

Tomographic imaging has come to have a profound effect on the diagnosis and treatment of stroke. Since the introduction of x-ray computed tomography (CT), sophisticated current-generation scanners are able to render both ischemic and hemorrhagic lesions of the central nervous system in superb anatomical detail, with excellent sensitivity, especially if iodinated contrast agents are used. The basic methodology of computed tomography, the synthesis of an anatomical cross-section from a series of many projections or views taken around an object from different angles, is common to the individual modalities of positron emission tomography (PET), single photon emission computed tomography (SPECT), and nuclear magnetic resonance imaging (MRI). The physical principles upon which each is based however, significantly differ from those of x-ray CT.

The image created by CT can best be thought of as a finely detailed map of regional x-ray attenuation coefficients. It is determined by measuring the absorption of x-rays emanating from an external source by using a ring of sensitive detectors placed around the object to be imaged. In PET, the tomographic section depicts the local concentration of an injected radionuclide that decays to a stable form by emitting a positron (Powers & Raichle, 1985). Any volume element within the plane of section represents the amount of radionuclide that has been deposited at that site. The physiological processes that govern the rate of deposition and ultimate accumulation of the labeled compound vary greatly. For instance, the regional blood volume can be determined using red cells labeled by trace quantities of oxygen-15 containing carbon monoxide. Thus, the image produced by the positron tomograph reflects function rather than merely depicting anatomical structure. The ability to model various physiological processes accurately ultimately determines the quantitative precision of positron tomographic data.

SPECT (Royal, Hill, & Holman, 1985) is similar to PET in that the image produced is a spatial mapping of the quantity of some radionuclide marker deposited regionally. The two techniques differ in that the radionuclides used in PET scanning eject a positron that is quickly converted to a *pair* of photons, whereas in SPECT the radionuclide decays to stability by emitting a *single* photon instead of a pair. The characteristics of such single-photon-emitting radionuclides differ significantly from those that emit positrons.

Certain nuclei, when placed in a strong magnetic field and exposed to radiofrequency energy, will absorb and re-emit signals at a very specific, narrow frequency which can be detected with a sensitive receiver (Budinger & Lauterbur, 1984; Pykett et al., 1982). This phenomenon is known as nuclear magnetic resonance. Applications have included NMR spectroscopy, utilized by the chemist to identify compounds, and NMR imaging, which has come to be called magnetic resonance imaging (MRI). The tomographic image of the brain generated by an MRI scanner is a synthesis of many projections taken around the object, from different angles of view, of the emitted radiofrequency signal. The intensity of that signal, which can be recorded from small regions of the brain, is a function of the local concentration of hydrogen nuclei as well as their interaction with one another and with their physical and chemical environment. NMR spectroscopy, on the other hand, does not produce images but is a sensitive and noninvasive *in vitro* technique for the identification and quantification of a variety of metabolites undergoing chemical reaction.

The purpose of this review will be to summarize briefly the physical principles upon which PET, SPECT, and NMR imaging are based, and to cite representative applications of these techniques to the detection and study of stroke.

POSITRON EMISSION TOMOGRAPHY

Certain radionuclides decay from the unstable state by emitting a positron (positive electron.) After a few millimeters of travel in tissue, the positron encounters an electron and the two undergo a particle/antiparticle annihilation, with the production of two high-energy photons. The two photons (or gamma rays) fly away from one another at the speed of light in opposite directions, almost exactly 180 degrees apart. If the object to be scanned, such as the brain of a patient, is surrounded by an array of suitable detectors, the photons produced can be identified. Because each positron encounter results in the production of a pair of photons, the method of detection employed is to look for the coincident arrival of each of the two photons at two separate detectors. When this event occurs and is identified, it is then known that the nucleus that emitted the positron is located on a line connecting the two detectors that are simultaneously struck. It is then possible to sum up the activity between all possible pairs of detectors. The resulting data set characterizes the emitted activity for the radionuclide distributed in the object as viewed from many angles around the periphery. Such data are similar to those obtained from an x-ray CT scan and can be synthesized to form an image using computer algorithms similar to those developed for CT scan reconstruction.

It is important to recognize that a PET image thus formed is a map of the local accumulation of some tracer that has been labeled with a positron-emitting isotope. It is possible to be precisely quantitative about the amount of radionuclide present in each small volume of brain thus depicted. Positron emission tomography then, is a modality of imaging that emphasizes function, much as x-ray CT emphasizes structure.

Positron-emitting isotopes that have proved to be useful in tomography include oxygen-15, nitrogen-13, carbon-11, fluorine-18, and rubidium-82. The first four species listed are important elemental building blocks of organic compounds. As such, synthetic schemes that can incorporate one of their number into a molecule of interest have been developed so that the compound becomes a tracer whose fate is observable using the PET scanner. Fluorine-18 is particularly valuable due to the large number of organic compounds to which it can be attached. Because it undergoes many physical and chemical reactions similar to potassium, rubidium-82 has been used as a potassium analog, particularly as an ion usually excluded by the blood-brain barrier.

Positron-emitting isotopes characteristically have a short half-life. This ranges from 75 seconds for rubidium-82 to 1.7 hours for flourine-18. Isotopes are produced in a cyclotron by bombardment of a stable atomic species with the particle beam. It is thus necessary, for experiments using the shorter half-life isotopes, to have a cyclotron immediately accessible to the scanner where the studies are carried out. The short half-lives put a premium on the development of biochemical syntheses that proceed not only with high purity and reasonable yield, but also very quickly.

Once having synthesized the radiopharmaceutical, it is possible to administer such an agent to a patient and use the PET scanner to measure its accumulation regionally within the brain. The relationship of that local accumulation of radionuclide to a physiological parameter being measured, such as regional cerebral blood flow or regional cerebral metabolic rate for glucose, depends entirely upon the prior development of a suitable model. Such a model, which requires extensive testing and validation, enables one to transform the image from raw data expressed in microcuries of radionuclide per gram of tissue, to a physiologically interesting quantity such as milliliters of blood flow per gram of brain tissue per minute.

Most methods for measuring regional cerebral blood flow with PET use oxygen-15 (^{15}O) labeled water (H_2O) as the flow tracer (Ackerman et al., 1981; Fox, Mintun, Raichle, & Herscovitch, 1984; Huang et al., 1983; Jones et al., 1985; Mintun, Raichle, Martin, & Herscovitch, 1984; Raichle, Martin, Herscovitch, Mintun, & Markham, 1983; Ter-Pogossian & Herscovitch, 1985). $H_2{}^{15}O$ is desirable in this application for several reasons. Because water is a naturally occurring body constituent, it has no undesirable side effects of either pharmacological or physiological nature. It is chemically stable in the body and the radio-labeled form can be synthesized in large quantities. Due to the short half-life of oxygen-15 (two minutes), relatively large amounts of activity can be administered while keeping the total radiation exposure to the patient within very acceptable limits. The model that defines regional cerebral blood flow stems from one that describes the behavior of inert, freely diffusible tracers developed by Kety and his collaborators (Kety & Schmidt, 1948). In brief, the rate of change of tracer concentration in a tissue region is equal to the difference in the rate at which tracer is transported to the tissue in the arterial blood and the rate at which it is washed out in the venous blood. This relationship can be evaluated in a number of ways using ^{15}O-labeled water and can yield a steady-state solution to the Kety relationship. Another technique is to infuse a bolus of labeled water and simultaneously measure the time-activity curve of radionuclide in the circulating blood. Both these approaches are capable of yielding accurate results in the determination of regional cerebral blood flow and have been instrumental in the application of PET to the study of stroke.

By employing the radionuclide, $C^{15}O$, it is possible to label the red blood cell mass with tracer quantities of carbon monoxide and thus to measure regional cerebral blood volume. Such determinations have been particularly valuable in the analysis of the ischemia associated with cerebral vasospasm accompanying subarachnoid hemorrhage (Grubb, Raichle, Eichling, & Gado, 1977). Also amenable to measurement in the positron emission tomograph is the oxygen extraction ratio for individual regions of the brain. Such measurements have yielded data about the magnitude of actual tissue extraction of oxygen by marginally perfused areas, as opposed to merely measuring the flow. Finally, it is also possible to determine the regional metabolic rate for glucose within the brain. Because virtually all cerebral energy production results from glucose utilization, this ability to measure cerebral metabolic rate (CMR) glucose closely approximates measuring the regional cerebral energy metabolism. Glucose metabolic rate can be determined using the model developed initially by Sokoloff (1981) and his collaborators for autoradiographic applications, by employing 2-deoxyglucose. In the case of positron emission tomography, this compound is labeled with flourine-18 (^{18}F). The model consists of three metabolic compartments linked by four rate constants, and the distribution of 2-deoxyglucose trapped in tissue is a function of the regional cerebral glucose metabolism. When combined with the flow, volume, and oxygen extraction data, the metabolic rate for glucose has proved a powerful tool for studying cerebral infarcts and the normal brain around them, as well as the transitional zones which may include brain that is ischemic but yet capable of functional recovery (Ackerman et al., 1981; Baron et al., 1984; Lenzi, Frackowiak, & Jones, 1982; Powers, Grubb, & Raichle, 1984).

SINGLE PHOTON EMISSION COMPUTED TOMOGRAPHY

The success of positron emission tomography in studying the human brain stimulated a revival of interest in single photon emission computed tomography for the same purpose. The techniques differ in that the detection of photons in the SPECT instruments is performed by collecting single events rather than photon pairs in coincidence, as in PET. The angular sampling is achieved by either a single or, more commonly, multihead camera that rotates about the patient, thus providing the necessary angular sampling. Reconstruction of the image is performed in a fashion similar to that of CT or PET scanning. In general, the radionuclides that have been used for SPECT are long-lived and do not require on-site preparation with a cyclotron. SPECT instrumentation is less amenable to accurate attenuation correction than is PET, but recent advances have made regional quantification of deposited isotopes more feasible (Ackerman, 1984). The biggest impetus for the application of single-photon techniques to the study of stroke has been the development of a class of compounds the distribution of which reflects cerebral blood flow (Hill et al., 1984; Holman, Lee, Hill, Lovett, & Lister-James, 1984; Kung, Tramposch, & Blau, 1983). An example of such a compound is N-isopropyl iodoamphetamine (IMP) labeled with iodine-123 (^{123}I). This compound is very lipid soluble and has a high first-pass extraction by the brain, so that its regional distribution is strongly a function of flow. When coupled with an efficient single-photon tomograph, images that represent a mapping of regional cerebral blood flow are obtained which are comparable in many respects to those generated by the more sophisticated but more elaborate PET system.

Phenylalkylamines labeled with ^{123}I, such as iodoamphetamine, differ from freely diffusible compounds such as water in that they become trapped in tissue. Because they do not wash out readily, relative regional cerebral blood flow can be evaluated by quantifying the distribution of the trapped tracer after an initial uptake period, in a fashion similar to flow analysis using microspheres. It is thus possible to estimate regional cerebral blood flow using SPECT with less elaborate instrumentation and fewer specialized personnel than required for PET.

Unless a cerebral infarct is hemorrhagic, a CT scan will frequently be normal for one to two days after the inital symptoms are manifest. On the other hand, ^{123}I-iodoamphetamine images are abnormal almost immediately (Drayer et al., 1983). Instances have been well documented where SPECT studies performed four hours after the onset of symptoms clearly demostrated large perfusion defects in regions that were initially normal on CT, but which became abnormal after several days and coincided with the defect delineated early by the ^{123}I-IMP. While such information was initially not of great utility due to the lack of therapeutic options available for intervention in the acute ischemic stroke, current interest is very high in techniques that may influence the course of such ischemia. Under such circumstances, it is clearly advantageous to demonstrate perfusion defects as early and accurately as possible. The prospects for highly extracted lipophilic agents such as ^{123}I-IMP, used in conjunction with SPECT, are most promising.

NUCLEAR MAGNETIC RESONANCE IMAGING

Nuclear magnetic resonance imaging (NMRI or MRI) differs dramatically from the radionuclide emission tomographic techniques previously described. It is based on the fact that the hydrogen nucleus, a single proton, has an associated magnetic field that is similar to that of a miniature bar magnet or magnetic dipole. This field is present because the proton may be considered to spin on its axis like a top and that spin is associated with a small magnetic moment. If a strong static magnetic field is imposed upon a population of these protons, such as exist in tissue, they tend to align themselves such that their spin is parallel to the lines of magnetic force of the imposed field. If their axis of rotation is displaced from parallel, they behave like a spinning top in the earth's gravitational field and wobble or precess at a characteristic rate that is a function of the strength of the applied field. This precession occurs in the radio-frequency portion of the electromagnetic spectrum and can be detected with a sensitive radio receiver.

To initiate the resonance phenomenon, a short pulse of radio-frequency energy is applied to the specimen at the precession frequency of the nuclei. The nuclei then tip away from their parallel alignment and will continue to depart from that orientation for as long as the radio-frequency pulse is applied. If the pulse is applied for enough time to cause a tip of 90 degrees, it is referred to as a 90-degree pulse. If the radio-frequency energy is then turned off and the receiver activated, an exponentially diminishing radio signal, called the free induction decay, is recorded. The characteristics of the signal are determined by physical parameters known as "relaxation times." The overall magnitude of the signal is a function of the number of nuclei present in the sample, the longitudinal relaxation time (T1), and the transverse relaxation time (T2). The T1 relaxation time characterizes the way in which the nuclei lose energy to their environment or "lattice" and is frequently designated the "spin-lattice relaxation time." The T2 relaxation time reflects the progressive dephasing or loss of synchrony of the precessing protons after they have been tipped away from parallel alignment with the principal magnetic field. It reflects interaction between spins of adjacent nuclei and is often termed the "spin-spin relaxation time." Both T1 and T2 are important in the imaging process and tissue characterization because they are often markedly different in magnitude from one another, under circumstances where the overall hydrogen concentration in normal and abnormal tissue is the same.

In order to generate tomographic images successfully, based upon the magnetic resonance phenomenon, some form of spatial encoding is necessary. Such information can be obtained by imposing a magnetic field gradient across the sample such that the resonance frequency is slightly different in different portions of the object to be imaged. Because the resonance frequency is a function of magnetic field strength, different loci within the subject will have slightly different resonance frequencies, due to the small imposed gradient field. By rotating this gradient about the patient, a data set similar to the multiple views of CT or PET scanning can be obtained and image reconstruction performed.

Important differences exist between MRI and the other forms of imaging previously discussed. One is that the applied gradient field can be imposed in any desired orientation with respect to the object or organ to be scanned. Therefore, not only transaxial but coronal or sagittal sections can be easily obtained. While reformatted images of x-ray CT scans can be obtained in these additional planes, the spatial resolution of the coronal or sagittal sections is not equal to that in the transaxial plane. This is not a problem in MRI. Another important difference is that the inherent image contrast between different tissues, such as gray and white matter, is very high compared to the small difference between the two seen in x-ray CT. As a result, with MRI it is possible to see striking differentiation between gray and white matter rendered with excellent anatomical detail. Because bone produces a negligible MRI signal, the characteristic "beam-hardening" artifacts produced by x-ray CT are totally absent from MRI scans. This is particularly valuable in examining the base of the brain and posterior fossa.

In general, any magnetic resonance signal used for image synthesis contains information related to nuclear concentration, or T1 and T2 relaxation times. Certain methods of image acquisition, or "pulse sequences," tend to emphasize one or another of these parameters and are becoming more standardized in the clinical imaging domain. A currently popular mode of imaging is the spin-echo technique with which T1-weighted, T2-weighted, or mixed images can be generated.

Certain paramagnetic ions such as manganese and gadolinium are able to modify relaxation times as a function of their local concentration. By taking advantage of this effect, it has been possible to develop contrast agents for MRI that serve a function analagous to the iodinated contrast agents used in x-ray CT (McNamara et al., 1986; Wehrli, MacFall, Shutts, Breger, & Herfkins, 1984). They have been useful, for instance, in delineating areas of enhanced blood-brain barrier permeability. The application of magnetic resonance imaging to evaluation of clinical stroke syndromes has been extremely fruitful (Buonanno et al., 1983; Kato, Kogure, Ohtomo, Izumiyama, et al., 1986; Kato, Kogure, Ohtomo, Tobita, et al., 1985; Sipponen, 1984; Sipponen et al., 1983). It has been possible to identify ischemic regions with a high degree of sensitivity soon after perfusion ceases. Characteristic signal parameters associated with blood and heme products make possible the identification of hemorrhagic infarction and intracerebral hematoma with a high degree of sensitivity (Bryan, Willcott, Schneiders, Ford, & Derman, 1983; DeWitt et al., 1984). While experimentation continues with the most appropriate pulse sequences to be used for both sensitive detection and accurate characterization of lesions, it is apparent that T2-weighted images, generally obtained from the long spin-echo delay pulse sequence, are the most revealing for the analysis of ischemic infarction.

The data available from nuclear magnetic resonance imaging combine high sensitivity with excellent spatial resolution. Specificity has thus far been less impressive, but work in that area has been extremely productive in a very short period of development time. While much of the emphasis in NMRI has concentrated on the proton or hydrogen nucleus, chiefly associated with intra- and extracellular water in the brain, significant steps have been made in depicting other biologically important nuclei, such as sodium. While the sensitivity for such nuclei is much lower than for that of hydrogen, the possibility of significant functional or metabolic data emerging from this approach has continued to encourage investigators.

Another aspect of nuclear magnetic resonance in the study of stroke does not involve imaging, but rather spectroscopy. In general, the frequency spectrum of an NMR signal for a specimen in which all the nuclei are subjected to the same magnetic field should consist of a single narrow peak. For a collection of protons in a sample of pure water this is, in fact, what is observed. In more chemically complex compounds, however, such as those associated with a living cell, the signal observed is a collection of peaks of varying amplitudes and frequencies. This is due to the fact that the magnetic field in the immediate vicinity of some nuclei is altered by shielding currents associated with the electrons around adjacent atoms. These variations in field cause a change in the resonance frequency, which is known as a chemical shift. The spectra contain significant information about the molecular structure in which the nuclei participate. It is possible, using this technique, to measure noninvasively the concentration of selected metabolites almost in real time. In the past this was generally done with cell suspensions or components in a test tube placed within an NMR spectrometer. In recent years, however, it has been shown that it is feasible to make quantitative determinations of certain metabolites within the brains of experimental animals and human subjects placed within large spectrometers using magnets similar or identical to those used for imaging. For example, by analyzing the phosphorus spectra, the ATP-ADP ratios and relative amount of creatine phosphate may be identified and followed as a function of substrate concentration, oxygenation, or other environmental parameters.

While both the sensitivity and spatial resolution of these studies, performed on living subjects using surface coils external to the skull, have been poor compared to results with NMR spectrometers, the promise is evident. The potential for identifying unique metabolic changes associated with ischemia and infarction in a noninvasive fashion is most intriguing. Of particular interest is the promise of being able to determine whether various forms of intervention are effective as they are tried, rather than having to wait to see whether ischemic changes have become irreversible and produced a region of unsalvageable infarction.

CONCLUSION

In this chapter we have briefly discussed three imaging modalities—positron emission tomography, single photon emission computer tomography, and magnetic resonance imaging—and described the physical principles upon which each is based. It will be evident that these techniques complement one another and the more familiar CT scanning in several important ways. In the radionuclide emission techniques, it is function rather than structure that is visualized. NMRI is largely structural at this point but has sensitivity and inherent image contrast unmatched by x-ray computed tomography. The promise exists for both NMR spectroscopy and the emission tomographic techniques to yield new and important information about the pathogenesis of stroke as well as its detection and differential diagnosis. In combination, these imaging techniques constitute a powerful multifactorial approach to a more complete understanding of stroke and hopefully will lead to progressively more effective prevention and treatment.

REFERENCES

Ackerman, R. H. (1984). Of cerebral blood flow, stroke and SPECT. *Stroke, 15*(1), 1–4.

Ackerman, R. H., Correia, J. A., Alpert, N. M., Baron, J. C., Gauliamos, A., Grotta, J., Brownell, G. L., & Taveras, J. M. (1981). Positron imaging in ischemic stroke disease using compounds labeled with oxygen-15. Initial results and clinico-physiologic correlations. *Archives of Neurology, 38,* 537–543.

Baron, J. C., Rougemont, D., Soussaline, F., Bustany, P., Crouzel, C., Bousser, M. G., & Comar, D. (1984). Local interrelationships of cerebral oxygen consumption and glucose utilization in normal subjects and ischemic stroke patients: A positron tomography study. *Journal of Cerebral Blood Flow and Metabolism, 4,* 140–149.

Bryan, R. N., Willcott, M. R., Schneiders, N. J., Ford, J. J., & Derman, H. S. (1983). Nuclear magnetic resonance evaluation of stroke. *Radiology, 149,* 189–192.

Budinger, T. F., & Lauterbur, P. C. (1984). Nuclear magnetic resonance technology for medical studies. *Science, 226,* 288–298.

Buonanno, F. S., Pykett, I. L., Brady, T. J., Vielma, J., Burt, C. T., Goldman, M. R., Hinshaw, W. S., Pohast, G. M., & Kistler, J. P. (1983). Proton NMR imaging in experimental ischemic infarction. *Stroke, 14,* 178–184.

DeWitt, L. D., Buonanno, F. S., Kistler, J. P., Brady, T. J., Pykett, I. L., Goldman, M. R., & Davis, K. R. (1984). Nuclear magnetic resonance imaging in evaluation of clinical stroke syndromes. *Annals of Neurology, 16,* 535–545.

Drayer, B., Jaszczak, R., Friedman, A., Albright, R., Kung, H., Greer, K., Lischko, M., Petry, N., & Coleman, E. (1983). In vivo quantitation of regional cerebral blood flow in glioma and cerebral infarction: Validation of the HIPDM-SPECT method. *American Journal of Neuroradiology, 4,* 572–576.

Fox, P. T., Mintun, M. A., Raichle, M. E., & Herscovitch, P. (1984). A noninvasive approach to quantitative functional brain mapping with $H_2^{15}O$ and positron emission tomography. *Journal of Cerebral Blood Flow and Metabolism, 4,* 329–333.

Grubb, R. L. Jr., Raichle, M. E., Eichling, J. O., & Gado, M. H. (1977). Effects of subarachnoid hemorrhage on cerebral blood volume, blood flow, and oxygen utilization in humans. *Journal of Neurosurgery, 46,* 446–453.

Hill, T. C., Magistretti, P. L., Holman, B. L., Lee, R. G. L., O'Leary, D. H., Uren, R. F., Royal, H. D., Mayman, C. I., Kolodny, G. M., & Clouse, M. E. (1984). Assessment of regional cerebral blood flow (rCBF) in stroke using SPECT and N-isopropyl-(I-123)-p-iodoamphetamine (IMP). *Stroke, 15*(1), 40–45.

Holman, B. L., Lee, R. G. L., Hill, T. C., Lovett, R. D., & Lister-James, J. (1984). A comparison of two cerebral perfusion tracers, N-isopropyl I-123 p-iodoamphetamine and I-123 HIPDM, in the human. *Journal of Nuclear Medicine, 25*, 25–30.

Huang, S. G., Carson, R. E., Hoffman, E. J., Carson, J., MacDonald, N., Barrio, J. R., & Phelps, M. E. (1983). Quantitative measurement of local cerebral blood flow in humans by positron computed tomography and ^{15}O-water. *Journal of Cerebral Blood Flow and Metabolism, 3*, 141–153.

Jones, S. C., Greenberg, J. H., Dann, R., Robinson, G. D. Jr., Kushner, M., Alavi, A., & Reivich, M. (1985). Cerebral blood flow with the continuous infusion of oxygen-15-labeled water. *Journal of Cerebral Blood Flow and Metabolism, 5*, 566–575.

Kato H., Kogure, K., Ohtomo, H., Izumiyama, M., Tobita, M., Matsui, S., Yamamoto, E., Kohno, H., Ikebe, Y., & Watanabe, T. (1986). Characterization of experimental ischemic brain edema utilizing proton nuclear magnetic resonance imaging. *Journal of Cerebral Blood Flow and Metabolism, 6*, 212–221.

Kato, H., Kogure, K., Ohtomo, H., Tobita, M., Matsui, S., Yamamoto, E., & Kohno, H. (1985). Correlations between proton nuclear magnetic resonance imaging and retrospective histochemical images in experimental cerebral infarction. *Journal of Cerebral Blood Flow and Metabolism, 5*, 267–274.

Kety, S. S., & Schmidt, C. F. (1948). The nitrous oxide method for the quantitative determination of cerebral blood flow in man. *Journal of Clinical Investigation, 27*, 476–483.

Kung, H. F., Tramposch, K. M., & Blau, M. (1983). A new brain perfusion imaging agent: [I-123]HIPDM:N.N.N'-Trimethyl-N'-[2-Hydroxy-3-Methyl-5-Iodobenzyl]-1,3-Propanediamine. *Journal of Nuclear Medicine, 24*, 66–72.

Lenzi, G. L., Frackowiak, R. S. J., & Jones, T. (1982). Cerebral oxygen metabolism and blood flow in human cerebral ischemic infarction. *Journal of Cerebral Blood Flow and Metabolism, 2*, 321–335.

McNamara, M. T., Brant-Zawadzki, M., Berry, I., Pereira, B., Weinstein, P., Derugin, N., Moore, S., Kucharczyk, W., & Brasch, R. C. (1986). Acute experimental cerebral ischemia: MR enhancement using Gd-DTPA. *Radiology, 158*, 701–705.

Mintun, M. A., Raichle, M. E., Martin, W. R. W., & Herscovitch, P. (1984). Brain utilization measured with 0-15 radiotracers and positron emission tomography. *Journal of Nuclear Medicine, 25*, 177–187.

Powers, W. J., Grubb, R. L. Jr., & Raichle, M. E. (1984). Physiologic responses to focal cerebral ischemia in humans. *Annals of Neurology, 16*, 546–552.

Powers, W. J., & Raichle, M. E. (1985). Positron emission tomography and its application to the study of cerebrovascular disease in man. *Stroke, 16*, 361–376.

Pykett, I. L., Newhouse, J. H., Buonanno, F. S., Brady, T. J., Goldman, M. R., Kistler, J. P., & Pohost, G. M. (1982). Principles of nuclear magnetic resonance imaging. *Radiology, 143*, 157–163.

Raichle, M. E., Martin, W. R. W., Herscovitch, P., Mintun, M. A., & Markham, J. (1983). Brain blood flow measured with intravenous $H_2{}^{15}O$. Part II. Implementation and validation. *Journal of Nuclear Medicine, 24*, 790–798.

Royal, H. D., Hill, T. C., & Holman, B. L. (1985). Clinical brain imaging with isopropyl-iodoamphetamine and SPECT. *Seminars in Nuclear Medicine, 15*(4), 357–376.

Sipponen, J. T. (1984). Visualization of brain infarction with nuclear magnetic resonance imaging. *Neuroradiology, 26,* 387–391.

Sipponen, J. T., Kaste, M., Ketonen, L., Sepponen, R. E., Katovuo, K., & Sivula, A. (1983). Serial nuclear magnetic resonance (NMR) imaging in patients with cerebral infarction. *Journal of Computer Assisted Tomography, 7*(4), 585–589.

Sokoloff, L. (1981). Localization of functional activity in the CNS by measurement of glucose utilization with radioactive deoxyglucose. *Journal of Cerebral Blood Flow and Metabolism, 1*(1), 7–36.

Ter-Pogossian, M. M., & Herscovitch, P. (1985). Radioactive oxygen-15 in the study of cerebral blood flow, blood volume, and oxygen metabolism. *Seminars in Nuclear Medicine, 15*(4), 377–394.

Wehrli, F. W., MacFall, J. R., Shutts, D., Breger, R., & Herfkins, R. J. (1984). Mechanism of contrast in NMR imaging. *Journal of Computer Assisted Tomography, 8,* 369–380.

6

A General Therapeutic Perspective on Stroke Treatment

Louis R. Caplan, M.D.

Stroke treatment has advanced a great deal during the last three decades. Newer technology; advances in the understanding of stroke mechanisms, pathology, and pathophysiology; and the availability of more physicians interested in and experienced with the care of stroke patients have led to large gains in diagnosis. Unfortunately, this improvement in diagnosis has not been paralleled by quite so rapid gains in management or treatment. Academicians and stroke experts have not had great success in transmitting new knowledge to the army of practitioners giving care on the front lines or to stroke patients and their families. Though the public is now reasonably knowledgeable about heart disease and cancer, there is unfortunately little general sophistication about stroke (American Heart Association, 1984, 1985).

My task in the present chapter is to provide an overview of present-day stroke treatment. This is clearly a very complex subject. There are four basic aspects of treatment: (1) general care aimed at preventing complications and promoting the comfort of the patient, (2) rehabilitation, (3) prevention of future symptoms and signs of vascular disease, and (4) specific treatment aimed at the specific type of stroke present in that individual patient. The first two categories are relevant no matter what the cause of the stroke, and as recently as four decades ago they were the only treatments available. The third category, prevention of future vascular disease, depends on individual risk factors operant in the individual patient and on the stroke mechanism itself. In the last category, treatment is dependent on accurate diagnosis of stroke subtype; it is in this area where the major recent gains in treatment have been made. Treatment of stroke subtypes is the most complex of the areas mentioned and so will be given the most attention.

GENERAL CARE

An important task of all physicians is to limit suffering, give comfort, and prevent complications. Stroke victims often are at least partially immobilized and may not be able to care fully for their bodily needs during the acute period. Examples of the types of problems encountered are listed in Table 6–1, along with the general types of treatment. Key goals are maintenance of nutrition; prevention of contractures and pressure palsies; and prevention of thromboembolic,

TABLE 6-1 Typical Problems and General Treatment in Stroke Cases

Problems	General Types of Treatment
Nutritional maintenance (especially if patient has dysphagia)	Intravenous fluids, nasogastric tubes, gastrostomy
Immobility (body, 1 or more limbs)	Range-of-movement exercises, prevention of pressure palsies and dislocations
Pulmonary complications (aspiration, pneumonia, atelectasis, pulmonary emboli)	Care in or avoidance of oral feeding; pulmonary toilet; respiratory therapy; early antibiotic treatment; anticoagulants ("mini-heparin")
Urinary tract complications (bladder distension, infection)	Catheterization if needed; careful antiseptic techniques; surveillance for infection and early treatment
Skin (decubiti)	Careful turning and positioning and skin surveillance
Psychological (depression and apathy)	Positive outlook, team & family approach, antidepressants

pulmonary, urinary, and skin complications. Perhaps just as important as these physical problems is maintenance of a positive outlook in patients and their physicians and families.

REHABILITATION

In general, this type of treatment is limited to patients with residual handicaps. Therapy depends not upon the subtype of stroke but upon the type of handicap, for example, paralysis, speech problems, intellectual deficits, visual disturbances, and the like. To be most effective, rehabilitation should focus on the individual patient, taking prior capabilities and circumstances and future needs into consideration. Rehabilitation succeeds via an educational process, training the person to understand the handicap and to devise strategies for overcoming it. Sometimes a well-learned task, such as walking or sitting on a toilet, must be done in a different way and the patient must be instructed or trained in this new approach. To be successful, the rehabilitation process must be shared with the patient's family and significant others so that they can carry on and amplify the gains once the patient returns home or to a new facility. Again, a kind, personal, understanding, positive approach is essential. Rehabilitation should start during the acute stroke.

PREVENTION

The patient's visit to the doctor or to the hospital gives the physician an opportunity to look at the whole person and his or her environment. In the hurry of the crisis of the acute stroke, general preventive measures are often overlooked. Death in patients with stroke is most often due to associated coronary artery disease. While the specific subtype of stroke is being investigated and treated, a search for risk factors should be made and measures should be instituted to deal with them (Dyken et al., 1984; Longstreth, Koepsell, Yerby, & Van-Belle, 1985). Some of these factors are listed in Table 6–2. If attention to these factors is not given early in the patient's hospital stay, they are often forgotten later or at discharge.

In most of the specific stroke subtypes, treatment also includes prevention of recurrences. Examples include prevention of a second cardiogenic cerebral embolus, a rebleed from an aneurysm or arteriovenous malformation, or a new episode of cerebral ischemia

TABLE 6-2 Prevention: Risk Factors and Their Management

Risk Factor	Management
Hypertension	Dietary and drug treatment
Heart disease	Evaluation and treatment
Smoking	STOP
Unhealthy lifestyle	Advise on exercise, rest, etc.
Elevated blood lipids (cholesterol, triglycerides)	Dietary and drug management
Drug use (amphetamines, cocaine)	STOP
Oral contraceptives	Advise
Elevated hematocrit	Appropriate treatment
Diabetes	Dietary and drug treatment

from known extracranial occlusive disease. Particular treatment strategies will be discussed in the following section on stroke subtypes.

MANAGEMENT OF INDIVIDUAL STROKE SUBTYPES

There are two general categories of stroke—hemorrhage and ischemia. Hemorrhage damages the brain by disconnecting and disrupting tissues and by exerting pressure on vital areas. Ischemic damage occurs due to a lack of blood flow and nutrition to focal regions of the brain, with the threat of permanent death of brain tissue. Thus, hemorrhage—the presence of too much blood—is the polar opposite of ischemia—too little blood. It requires little imagination to understand that treatment of these two categories would be quite different, if not opposite.

The general category of hemorrhage is divided into (1) *subarachnoid hemorrhage* (SAH), which involves bleeding into the cerebrospinal-fluid-containing spaces around the brain, and (2) *intracerebral hemorrhage* (ICH), which is bleeding directly into the brain substance. The causes and associated problems in these two subtypes of hemorrhage are quite different.

The general category of ischemia is customarily subdivided according to the cause of lack of blood flow. *Thrombosis* usually means that the deprivation of blood flow is due to a focal lesion within an artery supplying the ischemic brain region. That process can be due to a gradual narrowing of the artery or to clot formation obstructing the artery. Either can affect large arteries in the neck; medium-sized arteries on the surface and within the brain; and tiny, microscopic arteries deep within brain substance. *Embolism* is diagnosed if the substance blocking the artery did not arise *in situ* within the artery as in thrombosis but instead developed further downstream within the heart, the systemic or pulmonary veins, or within a more proximal large artery. The embolus then broke loose and lodged more distally, causing the ischemia. *Hypoxic-ischemic* damage refers to a circulatory and respiratory insufficiency causing rather widespread damage instead of an obstruction within the vascular system. Each category of ischemia is also distinct and requires quite different treatment.

Subarachnoid Hemorrhage (SAH)

SAH is a very serious subtype of stroke that has a very high morbidity and mortality. The usual cause is rupture of a saccular or "berry" aneurysm which releases blood on the brain's surface. The bleeding is instantaneous and under the high pressure of arterial circulation. Less often, SAH can result from a leaking arteriovenous malformation, bleeding diathesis, trauma, or drug abuse. The physician sees the patient with aneurysmal SAH after the leakage has stopped, as continued bleeding would have been fatal. The major task of the treatment is prevention of another possibly fatal rupture. Nearly all experts, whether they be neurologists or neurosurgeons, agree that the best way to do this is surgically. Surgical techniques include tying the aneurysm neck, clipping or coating of the aneurysm, or tying feeding arteries. The choice of surgical technique will depend upon the size, shape, and location of the aneurysm and the experience of the individual surgeon. The use of the operating microscope and improved neuroanesthesia has greatly improved the neurosurgeon's capabilities. Physicians try to get the patient in the best condition for surgery, hoping that definitive surgical treatment can be accomplished before the next bleed. A number of complications often require management along the way. These include

1. Systemic hypertension
2. Intracranial hypertension
3. Heart arrythmias and failure
4. Hemorrhage (rebleeding)
5. Hydrocephalus

6. Hypoperfusion (spasm or delayed ischemia)
7. Hyponatremia
8. Hematoma within the brain

Unfortunately, many SAH patients arrive at the neurologist or neurosurgeon's doorstep too ill to be saved. Some of these patients have had warning or sentinal leaks that went unheeded (Drake, 1981). Either the patient had not sought medical advice or physicians had missed the significance of the symptoms of headache, vomiting, and inability to function. The flu, tension, or migraine are the most frequent erroneous diagnoses. A high index of suspicion for the diagnosis of SAH and more liberal use of lumbar puncture and CT are required in these patients.

Intracerebral Hemorrhage (ICH)

Bleeding into the brain substance is most often caused by hypertension. Bleeding diathesis (especially iatrogenic, in patients taking anticoagulants), trauma, arteriovenous malformations, drug abuse (especially amphetamines and cocaine), amyloid angiopathy, and aneurysms are less common causes.

Treatment depends on the cause, size, and locale of the hemorrhage. Control of hypertension and reversal whenever possible of a bleeding diathesis are important. In general, small hemorrhages will resorb by themselves, while massive hemorrhages usually prove fatal or very disabling even before the patient presents for medical treatment. Mortality is due to the increase in intracranial pressure produced by the expanding lesion. Treatment of medium-sized (2.5–5 cm) lesions includes medical decompression with steroids and osmotic agents such as mannitol and glycerol and surgical decompression of the hematoma when it is located in a part of the brain that is accessible to surgery (Caplan, 1979). CT, by allowing accurate definition of the locale and size of the lesion, has greatly improved the diagnosis and treatment of ICH.

Hypoxic–Ischemic Encephalopathy

In this subclass of ischemia, the brain lesion is caused by a circulatory disturbance usually involving the heart. Arrhythmia is probably the most common such disturbance, but acute myocardial infarction, gastrointestinal bleeding, and pulmonary embolism are other etiologies. Recognition that the problem is cardiopulmonary is key to directing appropriate treatment, since the patient usually presents to the physician or hospital stuporous or, if awake, complaining of dizziness, blurred vision, weakness, and other generalized neurological symptoms. In other cases, physicians are asked to evaluate and treat patients after known cardiac arrest. Research centers around possible protection of the endangered brain in an attempt to reduce the ischemic damage caused by poor circulatory supply.

Cerebral Embolism

Formerly considered rare, we know now that embolism accounts for approximately one-fifth to one-fourth of all strokes (Caplan, Hier, & D'Cruz, 1983; Mohr et al., 1978). In past times, diagnosis of cardiogenic cerebral embolism was reserved for patients with a known cardiac source, such as rheumatic mitral stenosis with atrial fibrillation, or acute myocardial infarction with sudden onset of neurological deficit and evidence of systemic embolism. However, results from prospective studies have increased the range of diagnosis. They have shown, first, that many cardiac sources underly embolism. These include atrial fibrillation without known valvular disease, mitral valve prolapse, mitral annulus calcification, prosthetic and calcific valves, myocardiopathies, ventricular aneurysms, and marantic endocarditis. Second, neurological deficits are not always sudden or maximal at onset (Caplan, Hier, & D'Cruz, 1983; Mohr et al., 1978). Third, systemic embolism is rarely recognized (Mohr et al., 1978). Newer cardiac technologies such as echocardiography, radionuclide scanning, and Holter monitoring have aided immensely in the detection of potential cardiac embolic sources. Yet the fact that cardiac thrombi are often very small and leave their nesting place to migrate distally means that many potential cardiac sources still go undetected. Studies of treatment of patients with cardiogenic embolism have documented the usual safety of immediate anticoagulation. Complications arise mostly in hypertensive patients, those with large infarcts, or those excessively anticoagulated. The therapeutic goal is prevention of another embolus.

Artery-to-artery emboli are also common. Direct surgical removal (endarterectomy of the arterial embolic source), drugs that decrease platelet aggregation (e.g., aspirin, dipyridamole, sulfinpyrazone), and standard anticoagulants such as heparin and warfarin have all been used to prevent interarterial embolism. We need more studies to compare the relative effectiveness and risks of these therapies.

Thrombotic Stroke (*in situ* occlusive disease)

This is the largest single category of stroke, and unfortunately therapy for this problem is the least well studied. In my opinion, two very misguided strategies have led to decades of nearly fruitless research within this stroke subtype. The first is a search for a panacea. A single treatment has been sought for the entire group of patients with brain ischemia. We now know that this disorder is quite heterogeneous and is caused by a great array of vascular pathologies and mechanisms. A single cure is quite unlikely. The second mistaken strategy uses treatment trials based solely on the temporal pattern of the ischemia (TIA, progressing stroke, etc.). The temporal pattern of stroke is not specific for any of the different vascular pathologies. These terms refer only to the changing pattern of the neurological findings. I have considered in detail elsewhere (Caplan, 1983) why these terms are often misleading and difficult to define and why studies based on them are likely to produce very incomplete data.

Table 6–3 illustrates the diversity of pathological processes underlying thrombosis by listing several major types. Penetrating artery disease is usually caused by hypertension. The resulting small, deep brain infarcts are usually called "lacunes" or "holes," after Marie and Fisher (Fisher, 1965). The arterial lesion is primarily medial hypertrophy with gradual narrowing of the lumen. There is very little if any intimal or lumenal change. In striking contrast are the irregular, often ulcerated plaques that jut directly into the lumen of an atherosclerotic large artery such as the internal carotid artery in the neck. These plaques form and serve as a nidus for release of cholesterol crystals, fibrin-platelet clumps (so-called "white clots"),

TABLE 6-3 Types of Vascular Pathologies in Thrombotic Stroke

Large artery stenosis or occlusion due to progressive atherosclerosis

Small penetrating artery occlusion due to hypertension

Vascular irregularity without severe stenosis
  Atherosclerotic plaques
  Dissections
  Fibromuscular dysplasia
  Hemorrhage in the plaques
  Arteritis
  Aneurysms

Clotting due to polycythemia, thrombocytosis, hypercoagulable states, cancer, etc.

and red clots made of red blood cells and thrombin. The small artery lesion is well beyond reach of surgery, whereas a neck lesion is accessible. Strategies aimed at prevention of red or white clots are not likely to help the medial hypertrophy in such small arteries.

Not only are the pathologies different, but the pathophysiology of ischemia is heterogeneous. Ischemia in an area of the brain can be due to poor perfusion caused by severe obstruction of flow at the stenosing lesion. Years ago, physicians did not have safe technology to evaluate the arterial lesion. Epidemiological studies now give us data about the most frequent locations of vascular disease in patients of different race and gender (Caplan, Gorelick, & Hier, in press). Noninvasive technology using various techniques (real-time ul-trasound imaging, Doppler ultrasound probes, oculoplethysmography) can now safely yield accurate data about the extracranial arteries. Digital subtraction angiography can also yield useful images of the large arteries. Conventional arterial angiography by catheter insertion has become safer because of the advent of newer contrast agents and equipment and the performance of the procedure by specialists experienced in its use. It is now possible to define the underlying vascular process and its locale and severity in most patients with thrombosis. CT and MRI have made it possible, along with the traditional neurological examination, to define the location and extent of brain ischemia. We have all the tools to embark on a careful evaluation of the different treatments in patients with well-

TABLE 6-4 Treatment of Ischemic Stroke: Some Strategies

Direct surgical repair of arterial lesion (endarterectomy)

Management of coagulation cascade to prevent clot formation, clot propagation, and clot embolization
    Standard anticoagulants (heparin, warfarin)
    Platelet antiaggregant medicines (aspirin, indocin, dipyridamole, sulfinpyrazone)
    Foods that decrease platelet activity (eicosopentanoic acid and chinese tree fungus)

Medical augmentation of flow (increasing blood pressure, alteration of viscosity of blood by hemodilution, vasodilatation, etc.)

Increasing the brain's resistance to ischemia (manipulation of blood sugar, calcium channel blockers, antioxidants, etc.)

Surgical conduits bypassing the lesion (extracranial to intracranial shunts)

Transluminal arterial manipulation (angioplasty) or injection of material (for example, fibrinolysins)

---

defined vascular lesions (Caplan, 1984, 1985a, 1985b). The various treatment strategies are listed in Table 6–4. It is hoped that the next decades will uncover rational therapeutic principles for the treatment of individual patients with "thrombotic stroke."

REFERENCES

American Heart Association. (1984, October). *Public awareness survey*. (Study No. 62202). San Francisco: Author.
American Heart Association. (1985, March). *Stroke awareness study SRI*. New York: Research Center, Inc.
Caplan, L. R. (1979). Intracerebral hemorrhage. In H. R. Tyler & D. Dawson (Eds.), *Clinical neurology* (Vol. 2, pp. 185–205). Boston: Houghton-Mifflin.
Caplan, L. R. (1983). Are terms such as completed stroke or RIND of continued usefulness? *Stroke, 14*(3), 431–433.
Caplan, L. R. (1984). Treatment of cerebral ischemia—Where are we headed? *Stroke, 15*(3), 571–574.
Caplan, L. R. (1985a). Management of ischemic cerebrovascular disease. *Family Practice Survey, 1*, 139–143.
Caplan, L. R. (1985b). New stroke diagnostic techniques for patient management of ischemic stroke. *Comprehensive Therapy, 11*, 47–55.
Caplan, L. R., Gorelick, P. B., & Hier, D. B. (in press). Race, gender, and occlusive vascular disease. *Stroke, 17*.
Caplan, L. R., Hier, D., & D'Cruz, I. (1983). Cerebral embolism in the Michael Reese Stroke Registry. *Stroke, 14*(4), 530–536.
Drake, C. G. (1981). Progress in cerebrovascular disease. Management of cerebral aneurysm. *Stroke, 12*(3), 273–283.
Dyken, M., Wolf, P., Barnett, H. J., Bergan, J., Hass, W., Kannel, W. B., Kuller, L., Kurtzke, J., & Sundt, T. (1984). Risk factors in stroke. *Stroke, 15*, 1105–1111.
Fisher, C. M. (1965). Lacunes: Small deep cerebral infarcts. *Neurology, 15*, 774–784.
Longstreth, W. T., Koepsell, T., Yerby, M., & VanBelle, G. (1985). Risk factors for subarachnoid hemorrhage. *Stroke, 16*, 377–385.
Mohr, J. P., Caplan, L. R., Melski, J. W., Goldstein, R. J., Duncan, G. W., Kistler, J. P., Pessin, M. S., & Bleich, H. V. (1978). The Harvard Cooperative Stroke Registry: A prospective registry. *Neurology, 28*, 754–762.

7

Using Physical and Neuropsychological Assessment in the Nursing Care of the Acute Stroke Patient

Fay W. Whitney, Ph.D., R.N.

One of the joys of caring for acute stroke patients is that you can rarely be accused of "nursing the machines." Patients are seldom on life-support systems, but they are deeply in need of support in their lives. Following the initial event, nurses need to care physically for the patient who suddenly loses ability to carry on basic activities, help the patient discover and use individual strengths and coping mechanisms as recovery occurs, and maximize potential for optimal rehabilitation and health. Acute stroke patients differ in their immediate needs, depending upon the type, extent, and location of insult suffered and existing comorbid and premorbid conditions. The array of deficits seen can be overwhelming. The variability among patients, or between two patients with similar kinds of stroke, is often confusing. But the lack of ability to characterize the "generic

This work was begun while the author was attending the University of Pennsylvania School of Nursing as a Robert Wood Johnson Clinical Nurse Scholar.

stroke patient" should not deter nurses from developing a systematic approach to assessment and intervention in the acute phase of illness. Carefully organized and skillfully delivered nursing care at that time can be the foundation upon which others in the rehabilitation process build. Ultimate return of the patient to active participation in life may depend upon it. Throughout the acute and rehabilitative phases, nurses are the most constant and consistently present caregivers. The overriding principle must be that rehabilitation begins as soon as the stroke occurs.

Space prevents an exhaustive review of the many important nursing activities in the acute phase, so our discussion will begin with a focus on the most important of these. The main purpose of this chapter is to highlight the role of physical and neuropsychological assessment by nurses who care for acute stroke patients. We will also discuss the usefulness of combining present knowledge of predictors of rehabilitation outcome with present nursing practice to produce an active, ongoing assessment plan in the acute phase. Finally, we will have a look at how nurses can help patients to cope with stroke.

MAJOR NURSING ACTIVITIES IN ACUTE STROKE

Between initial impairment and recovery, crises that threaten both body and mind occur. For example, patients with hemmorhagic stroke may die if progressive symptoms are not detected immediately. Intervention requires constant, focused assessment and action. Less immediate, but no less important, may be subtle changes in behavior or level of consciousness. Initial confusion and slowness in comprehension may later give way to affective disorders and behavioral problems which, if they are not identified and attended to from the beginning, may seriously alter the patient's recovery potential.

To interact effectively with patients and families in crisis, nurses must try to (1) enter their world, (2) identify and deal with their losses, (3) substitute for actual deficits, (4) support and encourage natural coping mechanisms, and (5) help regain and retain functional independence. Nurses who are truly effective in caring for acute stroke patients need large stores of knowledge, competence, compassion, realism, enthusiasm, and humor. In addition, they must be able to organize thinking and activities in many areas concurrently. The major nursing issues in caring for the acute stroke patient are shown in Table 7–1.

TABLE 7-1 Major Nursing Activities in Care of Acute Stroke

Physical assessment and management
  Safety and comfort: protection from sensory overload
  Nutrition
  Pain control
  Bowel and bladder management
  Skin and circulatory integrity
  Medications
  Neurological deficits (motor and sensory)
  Preparation for tests and monitoring results
  Prevention of intercurrent disease and illness

Neuropsychological assessment and management
  Behavioral assessment and monitoring changes
  Cognitive deficits
  Memory deficits
  Conceptual deficits
  Management of aberrant or demented behavior
  Crisis intervention with patient and family

Communication needs
  Language deficits: assessment of physical and emotional barriers to production and comprehension of language
  Establish functional communication techniques
  Establish functional communication networks:
    among professionals and patient/family;
    between patient and family;
    between patient and community at large

Rehabilitation needs and assessment
  Physical and mental parameters (measurement)
  Family needs and deficits
  Financial concerns

Community health and discharge planning
  Coordination and location of resources
  Teaching and preparation of family and patient for discharge
  Follow-up planning for ongoing medical and nursing needs

The activities involved in physical assessment and management change over time. Yet, it is important that *serial evaluation* of the acute stroke patient become an ongoing process from admission, where rapid changes occur, through periods where less change occurs and the patient stabilizes, until the patient leaves the acute setting. The rapid changes that occur in the first hours may reflect worsening that requires emergency intervention. Accurate and swift assessment is important to make sure the patient does not die of transtentorial herniation, hemmorhage, or acute cardiac/respiratory complications.

Equally important is continuing assessment following the acute stage, where progress is measured daily, rehabilitation starts, and planning for discharge is begun.

Neuropsychological assessment is essential in managing the interplay of psychological deficits and the effects of the anatomical and physiological lesions on mood, cognition, and behavior. Stroke patients present a confusing array of behaviors which are often assessed by observation and self-report, but practicing nurses have not found these two major methods to be universally reliable. Consequently, interventions have not always produced optimal outcome. For the nurse who spends so much time providing physical care to stroke patients, concurrent assessment of the mental and emotional health of the patient is also important. At the present time, nurses have little information about the interplay of these factors, or even how to measure them effectively. The majority of this chapter, therefore, will concentrate on the areas of physical and neuropsychological assessment, in an effort to provide a better understanding of how they can be incorporated into practice.

It is tempting to spend a great deal of time on the area of communication needs. Nurses in acute care know only too well the consequences of disturbed communication in the stroke patient. Aphasias and dysarthrias, two common communication disorders in stroke, cause interminable problems in helping patients and families understand and deal with the impact of the stroke. Caregivers are often frustrated in trying to understand and be understood as they work with patients. But it is the patient who suffers most from what is sometimes called a "lack of humanness." Many believe it is the ability to think and communicate that separates humans from other animals. As important as this topic is to nurses and patients, the scope of the problem cannot be covered in this chapter. (See R. T. Wertz, Chapter 11 of this volume; Lezak, 1983, pp. 312–341; Mesulam, 1985, pp. 193–238.)

The final topics, rehabilitation needs and assessment and discharge planning, are covered in this chapter as they interact with the major activities in physical and neuropsychological assessment and management. The section on predictors of rehabilitation outcome also contains examples of nursing activities in the acute phase that have direct effect upon discharge and rehabilitation. From these few examples, it will be obvious that nursing care of the stroke patient should always be directed toward these later activities. Early planning and intervention with families and patients is obligatory if plans for transition to rehabilitation units or home are to become reality.

HISTORICAL, PHYSICAL, AND NEUROPSYCHOLOGICAL ASSESSMENT

In order to intervene effectively and plan for recovery of the patient, nurses need to develop, use, and continue to update a patient data base. A standardized approach to this endeavor is not only possible but essential. It is important to consider simultaneously the physical, behavioral, and emotional aspects of the stroke. Several methods of quantifying physical findings in relation to stroke disability have been used by physicians (cf. Hachinski & Norris, 1985, pp. 16–19). Although the various scales developed have been questioned in terms of their research validity, tracking patient progress by using a standardized recording system has empirical value. Likewise, systematic, periodic neuropsychological tracking, using brief mental status exams,[1] serves as a quantitative check against the observed and self-reported behavior encountered by nurses caring for acutely ill stroke patients. When assessments are standardized and used consistently, everyone caring for the patient has a straightforward view of what is occurring. The development of a flow sheet on which to record the results of these assessments and by which to maintain a serial picture of the changes in the patient as he or she passes through stages of recovery can add depth to interpretations of needs and progress as well as an accurate record of events.

Historical Assessment

Table 7–2 presents the basic elements of historical and physical assessment that should be included in serial examination of acute stroke patients. During the acute admission, history taking may be brief, related to the acute event, and directed toward physical deficits, medical management, and acute nursing interventions. It is important that a second, detailed history be taken to enlarge and corroborate the data base obtained during the acute admission. All of the diseases and risk factors listed in Table 7–2 are health problems related to stroke, so information about them should be sought systematically (Hachinski & Norris, 1985; Meyer & Shaw, 1982; Mohr et al., 1985).

Taking a second history of the present episode is important. In particular, information about other similar occurrences that may

---

[1]Abbreviated mental status exams and their sources include the following: Mental Status Checklist (Lifshitz, 1960); Geriatric Interpersonal Rating Scale (Plutchik et al., 1970); Mini-Mental State (Folstein, Folstein, & McHugh, 1975); Memory Loss Scale (Markson & Levitz, 1973); and Mental Status Questionnaire (Kahn & Miller, 1978).

TABLE 7-2 Historical and Physical Elements of Assessment of the Acute Stroke Patient

History:

Patient and/or family history of:
hypertension, coronary heart disease, diabetes, thyroid disease, valvular heart disease, atherosclerosis, stroke, seizures, collagen vascular disease, TIA's

Patient risk factors:
smoking, alcohol excess, drug use, birth control pills

Present episode:
time and onset of *first* episode, number and pattern of previous attacks, loss of consciousness, changes in mood or behavior, changes in speech and other neurological deficits, current medications (prescribed and over-the-counter), recent acute medical and/or surgical illness, concurrent illness, presence of pain

Social and family constellation:
financial arrangements, recent losses, family aggregation, primary relationships, community activities, hobbies, work, leisure activities

Physical Exam:

Cardiac exam: include all major vessels for pulse pressure and bruits; heart for murmurs, enlargement, arrythmias

Chest and lung: include breath sounds, quality and depth of respirations, adventitious sounds, dullness

Vital signs: blood pressure (include right and left measurement, attention to all three positions), temperature, respirations

Neurological exam: include all cranial nerves, fundoscopy, range of motion and mobility, motor strength, sensation, balance, abnormal movements, reflexes and pathological reflexes, mental status, speech, bowel and bladder function

Skin integrity: general and areas of dependent pressure, edema, rashes

Pain: presence, location, and effects of drug therapy and comfort measures

---

have been forgotten by the patient or family during the acute admission needs to be sought. Careful questioning may elicit information about premorbid events or conditions that will aid in determining a final diagnosis or management regimen. Of particular importance is distinguishing among seizures, common syncopal episodes, and transient ischemic attacks (TIA's). While TIA's are a common precursor of stroke (Meyer & Shaw, 1982), adult-onset seizures or simple syncope may herald other important medical problems that need to be investigated.

Physical Assessment

Table 7–2, as noted already, also lists the items of the physical assessment that should be done serially. It is clear that limited neurological checks for level of consciousness and mental status are not sufficient in this phase of care. Nurses should be active in assessing all of the items listed in the table. Nursing activities relating to prevention of concurrent illnesses and management of stroke consequences are determined by accurate assessment, cooperative efforts with medical management, and determination of the short- and long-range goals of individual patients and their families. Development of a longitudinal assessment sheet (flow chart) that is individualized to each patient but contains major, common categories will aid in this effort.

Upon acute admission, the nurse encounters a patient who has experienced the sudden loss of function. If the setting is an emergency room, physical assessment will be centered on level of consciousness, airway patency and respiration, possible hemorrhage, and safety measures. Rapid, serial reassessment, often called the "neuro check," is instituted, mainly to identify a rapid decline in level of consciousness or worsening neurological deficit that heralds active cerebral hemorrhage, overwhelming cerebral edema, or progressive thrombosis. Many activities will be related to the diagnostic work-up, including blood and urine tests; computerized tomography (CT), positron emission tomography (PET), or magnetic resonance imaging (MRI); multiple neurological examinations by the medical staff; and the administration of drugs to control blood pressure, fluid and electrolyte balance, or cerebral edema. Nursing assessment is used to monitor the outcome of these activities. Death related to the cerebral event itself occurs most often in hemorrhagic stroke, or stroke where cerebral edema is severe, perhaps causing transtentorial herniation. Cardiac complications may occur in the hours and weeks following stroke, and myocardial infarction is the most common cause of death in patients surviving an acute stroke (Whisnant, 1983).

The patient is usually transferred to an inpatient floor and carefully monitored until "stabilization" occurs. This usually means the stroke has been "completed" and no further neurological worsening is seen or expected. Often this is a period where nursing activities are concerned with safety, standard physical care, and measures designed to prevent complications (see Hickey, 1981; Sahs, Hartman, & Aronson, 1976).

In addition to the standard physical assessment items mentioned, nurses must have knowledge of the common treatment modalities and tests used with acute stroke patients. This information is vital to understanding the medical regimen and the concurrent assessments needed to monitor it. Teaching families and patients about the course of the illness and probable outcomes also means that nurses must have current and reliable data as well as research resources for patient reference.

Generally, drugs are not used in the long-term treatment of stroke, but they are sometimes used in the acute phases to reverse potentially life-threatening situations and later to maintain homeostasis and/or prevent recurrence (Hachinski & Norris, 1985). The drugs used fall into six major categories: (1) drugs used in blood pressure control and electrolyte balance, (2) sedatives and/or antidepressants, (3) anticoagulants, (4) drugs used in osmotherapy, (5) vasodilators and vasoconstrictors, and (6) experimental drugs.

The most common problem for nurses in the acute phase is to monitor and regulate concurrent use of blood pressure medications (e.g., beta blockers, thiazides) and intravenous therapy to hydrate and/or provide nutritional and electrolytic balance. Drugs used in osmotherapy (hypertonic glucose, urea, glycerol, or mannitol) to reduce brain edema also require frequent regulation and assessment. Variations in hematocrit and glucose levels can occur, producing variations in orientation and exacerbation of existing diabetes and hypo- or hyperglycemia (Hachinski & Norris, 1985; Mohr et al., 1985). Patients should be carefully monitored by following results of laboratory tests and serial testing of level of consciousness and mental status. It is important that confusional states be appropriately assessed, since they can be a result of the stroke, drug intervention, and/or changes in electrolyte and glucose levels. As Hachinski & Norris (1985) suggest, with tongue in cheek, "Although cerebral infarction may cause confusion, the confusion more often lies with the physician than the patient" (p. 98). Nurses share in this confusion, but careful evaluation and reevaluation around the clock can help clarify the interaction of drugs, disease, emotional, and other intervening variables so that adjustments can be made. When experimental therapies are used, they should be discussed with the physicians who have initiated them so that appropriate monitoring can be instituted.

The tests that are generally ordered for stroke patients include cerebral scanning by CT, PET, or MRI; selective angiography, echocardiography, and cardiac monitoring for probable source of emboli; noninvasive vessel studies; and occasionally EEG (electroencephalogram). These studies are important in determining the location and size of the lesion. They can be used for prognostication and as aids in corroborating clinical assessments of behavior and severity of neurological deficit. Nurses who understand both the method and the result of the testing can more accurately assess the behavioral and neurological deficits observed. They can then explain to patients and families the purpose, performance, and meaning of the results of tests; these explanations will facilitate understanding and promote cooperation with the overall management plan.

For nurses, systematic physical assessment and longitudinal recording encourage logical yet individualized development of interventions and evaluation of their efficacy. An extra advantage lies in the easily accessible, concise, 24-hour record of the patient's condition for use by all members of the health team.

Neuropsychological Assessment

Lezak (1983) writes,

> Like all other psychological phenomena, behavioral changes that follow brain injury are determined by multiple factors. The size, location, and kind of lesion certainly contribute significantly to the altered behavior pattern. Another important predisposing variable is the duration of the condition. The patient's age at the onset of the organic disorder, the pattern of cerebral dominance, background, life situation, and psychological makeup also affect how the patient responds to the physical insult and to its social and psychological repercussions. Moreover, these changes are dynamic, reflecting the continually evolving interactions between behavioral deficits and residual competencies, the patient's appreciation of his strengths and weaknesses and family, social, and economic support or pressure. [p. 204]

The common behavioral characteristics of conscious patients following stroke include (1) impaired retention and short-term memory loss, (2) impaired concentration and attention, (3) emotional lability, and (4) fatigability (Lezak, 1983). The study of affective disorders (i.e., depression, anxiety) following stroke is an area of brisk investigation and discussion. Since early studies by Gainotti (1972) describing differences in affective response between right- and left-hemisphere-damaged patients, there has been continuing debate about the relationship of laterality, handedness, and affective response following stroke. Some investigators strongly suggest that affective differences are a function of altered perceptual and/or expressive capabilities with respect to affectively intoned speech and language processing (Folstein, Maiberger, & McHugh, 1977; Heir, Mondlock, & Caplan, 1983; Ley & Bryden, 1982; Ross, 1981). Other investigations are concerned with differences in ability to recognize or verbalize emotion in regard to right- or left-hemisphere damage (Robinson, Starr, Kubos, & Price, 1983; Sackheim et al., 1982). The newer neurodiagnostic techniques (e.g., CT and PET scan and cerebral blood flow) have allowed neuroscientists to explore intra- and inter hemispheric function and structure with more precision *in vivo* (Alavi, Reivich, Jones, Greenberg, & Wolf, 1982; Reivich, Gur, & Alavi, 1983). It is clear that both observed behavior and self-report of mood and affect are not always reliable in the stroke population. Nurses caring for these patients should be familiar with neuropsychological tests that can be performed simply and serially.

Lezak (1983, p. 577) suggests that neuropsychological assessment include the following areas: (1) appearance; (2) orientation; (3) speech; (4) thinking; (5) attention, concentration, and memory; (6) intellectual functioning; (7) emotional state; (8) special preoccupations and experiences; and (9) tests of insight. Although some of these functions can be monitored in daily discourse with patients, we have already mentioned the unreliability of this method alone. Abbreviated mental status exams that have been used with brain-damaged patients were suggested earlier, in footnote 1. Nurses can easily become familiar with these tests, which can be performed simply, quickly, and serially. Scores obtained are readily interpretable. One test should be chosen and used consistently, for best results. The information obtained can add immeasurably to the efficacy of planning patient care.

PREDICTORS OF POSITIVE REHABILITATION

The optimal goal in caring for the acute stroke patient is to return her or him to the highest level of function possible. It is essential that nurses caring for the acute stroke patient be aware of the factors that most often impede the rehabilitation process in later recovery phases.

Hachinski and Norris (1985) state, "Continuous nursing care in acute stroke units prevents and minimizes complications such as pneumonia, pulmonary ebolism, thrombophlebitis, urinary tract infection and septicemia, decubiti and sudden death" (p. 22). Prevention of intercurrent disease and illness in the acute phase directly and substantially affects both the outcome and timing of recovery (Hachinski & Norris, 1985; Stonnington, 1980; Wade, Wood, & Hewer, 1985). It is obvious that the physical assessment and management activities outlined in Table 7–1 are vital in prevention of intercurrent illness, which will retard the rehabilitation process.

Other predictors have been studied by a variety of investigators (Feigenson, Gitlow, & Greenberg, 1979; Gibson & Caplan, 1984; Hachinski & Norris, 1985; Henley, Pettit, Todd-Pokropek, & Tupper, 1985; Levy et al., 1984; Stonnington, 1980; Wade, Wood, & Hewer, 1985). Although each investigator studied specific variables under different methodological designs, there is general consensus on the relationship of the following factors to poor prognosis:

1. *Advanced Age:* Older stroke patients generally have poorer outcomes, although age alone is not a strong predictor.

2. *Continence:* Persistence of bowel or bladder incontinence beyond four weeks was a strong predictor of poor prognosis in most studies, with bowel management more difficult than bladder management.

3. *Sensory loss, spatial and constructional loss:* This includes persistent inability to locate oneself in space, denial of or hemi-inattention to motor loss, visual field loss, and perceptual loss.

4. *Persistent negative behavior and attitude:* This was a poor indicator regardless of whether the observed behavior/attitude was premorbid or a consequence of the stroke (i.e., a cognitive or mood dysfunction).

5. *Presence of pain:* This indicator related both to actual muscle/bone pain in paralyzed limb.

6. *Low premorbid functional level:* This relates to physical inactivity and low motivation prior to stroke.

7. *Impaired motor ability:* Continued ability to walk and loss of motor strength on one side only were related positively to recovery. Dense motor loss of an upper extremity or confinement to a wheelchair are not necessarily related to poor prognosis for independent function.

8. *Communication deficits:* When global aphasia is interpreted as a defect in cognition, more weight is given to this predictor. Ability to communicate was cited as a variable interdependent with self-esteem, mood, motivation, and ability to learn by some investigators (cf. Gibson & Caplan, 1984; Hachinski & Norris, 1985; Heilman, Scholes, & Watson, 1975; Stonnington, 1980).

These predictors, so vital to rehabilitation in the later stages of recovery, are *greatly* influenced by nursing care in the acute setting. Two specific examples follow.

Considering the importance of continence in predicting good rehabilitation outcome, nurses should concentrate on this area of care. Bowel and bladder training, with attention to preventing infection, can be started immediately following the stroke. For example, frequent toileting to prevent the need for indwelling catheters, the loss of bladder tone, or getting an infection, may prevent urinary incontinence as active rehabilitation begins. When patients have cognitive deficits that cause bowel incontinence, it may be possible to retrain and recue their cognitive patterns. Cognitive stimulation techniques have been used successfully to increase functional abilities in patients with other cognitive problems (Trexler, 1982; Young, Collins, & Hren, 1983). If incontinence is caused by loss of cognitive awareness, this technique might be eminently successful in retraining stroke patients, removing a major stumbling block in successful rehabilitation.

A second example comes from a recent study by Henley et al. (1985), who found that having a partner was significantly related to positive rehabilitation outcome. Interrupting persistent, negative behavior and attitudes, plus providing motivation for increased activity may be part of the reason why partners are important to patients' recovery from stroke.

Nurses who obtain early history of premorbid behavior and coping mechanisms from family, friends, and the patient may provide valuable clues for successful future relationships with helping partners. Nurses can foster the care, concern, and interest of partners early in the stroke episode, adding further strength to the bond that will benefit the patient who returns home. These points emphasize the need for the nurse in the acute-care setting to be fully aware of, and actively working toward, the goals and activities related to rehabilitation. It is far easier to foster strengths that are discovered early than to uncover them when they have been nearly buried by despair, frustration, and inattention.

HELPING PATIENTS TO COPE WITH STROKE

Major nursing activities, especially serial physical and neuropsychological assessment, have been highlighted here as part of the care of the acute stroke patient and family. A more general but perhaps equally important activity is to aid them in the process of coping. Characteristics of adequate coping include the ability (1) to contain distress within personally tolerable limits, (2) to maintain self-esteem and role identity, (3) to preserve interpersonal relationships, (4) to convert unfamiliar to familiar, (5) to meet the conditions of new circumstances, (6) to control and predict situations, and (7) to maintain meaningful human attachments. Yet Hachinski and Norris (1985) state, "Many physicians are therapeutic nihilists concerning stroke, creating a vicious circle in which lack of knowledge retards the search for effective therapy, generating even more negative attitudes" (p. 13). Nurses and other members of the therapeutic team in an acute setting share some of the same nihilism. It seems that both the patient and the caregivers are overwhelmed with the catastrophic change: a once-healthy person who now cannot care for self, often cannot communicate, and seems disinterested in the world. Caregivers from acute-care hospitals often express surprise at the eventual progress of patients whom they encounter who have been through intensive programs in rehabilitation units. Perhaps they would be less pessimistic if there were better avenues of exchange between the two types of nursing units, an activity nurses can and should foster.

It takes a great deal of optimism for stroke patients to work through sudden loss of functions that change patterns of living and individual roles within families. Our ability to help people through the acute phase of stroke rests partially in meeting our personal despair and frustration as we actively meet the demanding nature of our work, developing conviction that what we are doing is vital to the patient's future. The potential for rehabilitation lies not only in our ability to diagnose, test, and treat the stroke, but in our ability to assess and then help the patient cope with disabilities, whether physical, mental, or emotional.

Many of the nursing activities outlined in this chapter fulfill this purpose. The nurse in acute care holds many of the keys to maximizing rehabilitation potential. One of these is adequate, accurate, serial assessment of physical and neuropsychological well-being. Flexible, sound interventions based on current practice, research, and updated diagnostic and treatment techniques are another. In speaking about rehabilitation, Stonnington has said, "At all times, the happiness of the patient and of his family must be kept in mind, and their ability to love and be loved should be maintained" (1980, p. 102). Perhaps this is the most important key—working to find the love and happiness that exist in even the most chaotic of situations, knowing that these are the fragile tools stroke patients and their families need to build a different life in the future.

REFERENCES

Alavi, A., Reivich, M., Jones, S. C., Greenberg, J. H., & Wolf, A. P. (1982). Functional imaging of the brain with positron emission tomography. *Nuclear Medicine Annual* (pp. 319–322). New York: Raven Press.

Feigenson, J. S., Gitlow, H. S., & Greenberg, S. D. (1979, Jan./Feb.). The disability oriented rehabilitation unit—A major factor influencing stroke outcome. *Stroke, 10*(1), 5–8.

Folstein, M. F., Folstein, S. E., & McHugh, P. R. (1975). Mini-mental state: A practical method for grading the cognitive state of patients for clinicians. *Journal of Psychiatric Research, 12,* 189–198.

Folstein, M. F., Maiberger, R., & McHugh, P. R. (1977). Mood disorder as a specific complication of stroke. *Journal of Neurology, Neurosurgery and Psychiatry, 40,* 1018–1020.

Gainotti, G. (1972). Emotional behavior and hemispheric side of lesion. *Cortex, 8*(1), 41–55.

Gibson, C. J., & Caplan, B. M. (1984). Rehabilitation of the patient with stroke. In T. F. Williams (Ed.), *Rehabilitation in the aging* (pp. 145–159). New York: Raven Press.

Hachinski, V., & Norris, J. W. (1985). *The acute stroke.* Philadelphia: F. A. Davis.

Heilman, K. M., Scholes, R., & Watson, R. T. (1975). Auditory affective agnosia: Disturbed comprehension of affective speech. *Journal of Neurology, Neurosurgery and Psychiatry, 38*(1), 69–72.

Heir, D. B., Mondlock, J., & Caplan, L. R. (1983, March). Recovery of behavioral abnormalities after right hemisphere stroke. *Neurology, 33,* 345–350.

Henley, S., Pettit, S., Todd-Pokropek, A., & Tupper, A. (1985). Who goes home? Predictive factors in stroke recovery. *Journal of Neurology, Neurosurgery, and Psychiatry, 48*(1), 1–6.

Hickey, J. V. (1981). *The clinical practice of neurological and neurosurgical nursing.* Philadelphia: J. B. Lippincott.

Kahn, R. L., & Miller, N. E. (1978). Assessment of altered brain function in the aged. In M. Storandt, I. Siegler, & M. Elias (Eds.), *The clinical psychology of aging* (pp. 43–69). New York: Plenum Press.

Levy, D. D., Scherer, P. B., Lapinski, R. H., Singer, B. H., Pulsinelli, W. A., & Plum, F. (1984). Predicting recovery from acute ischemic stroke using multiple clinical variables. In F. Plum & W. Pulsinelli (Eds.), *Cerebrovascular diseases* (pp. 69–75). New York: Raven Press.

Ley, R. G., & Bryden, M. P. (1982). A dissociation of right and left hemispheric effects for recognizing emotional tone and verbal content. *Brain and Cognition, 1*(1), 3–9.

Lezak, M. D. (1983). *Neuropsychological assessment* (2nd ed.). New York: Oxford University Press.

Lifshitz, K. (1960). Problems in the quantitative evaluation of patients with psychoses of the senium. *Journal of Psychology, 49,* 295–303.

Markson, E. W., & Levitz, G. A. (1973). A Guttman scale to assess memory loss among the elderly. *The Gerontologist, 13,* 337–340.

Mesulam, M. M. (1985). *Principles of behavioral neurology.* Philadelphia: F. A. Davis.

Meyer, J. S., & Shaw, T. (Eds.). (1982). *Diagnosis and management of stroke and TIA's.* Redwood City, CA: Addison-Wesley.

Mohr, J. P., Rubenstein, L., Edelstein, S. Z., Gross, C. R., Heyman, A., Kase, C. S., Kunitz, S. C., Price, T. R., & Wolf, P. A. (1985). Approaches to pathophysiology of stroke through the NINCDS data bank. In F. Plum & W. Pulsinelli (Eds.), *Cerebrovascular diseases* (pp. 63–68). New York: Raven Press.

Plutchik, R., Conte, H., Lieberman, N., Bakur, M., Grossman, J., & Lehrman, N. (1970). Reliability and validity of a scale for assessing the functioning of geriatric patients. *Journal of the American Geriatrics Society, 18,* 491–500.

Reivich, M., Gur, R., & Alavi, A. (1983). *Positron emission tomographic studies of sensory stimuli: Cognitive process and anxiety.* New York: Springer Verlag.

Robinson, R. G., Starr, L. B., Kubos, K. L., & Price, T. R. (1983). In M. Reivich & H. I. Hurtig (Eds.), *Cerebrovascular diseases* (pp. 137–152). New York: Raven Press.

Ross, E. D. (1981). The aprosodias: Functional-anatomic organization of the affective component of language in the right hemisphere. *Archives of Neurology, 38*(9), 561–569.

Sackheim, H. A., Greenberg, M. S., Weiman, M. A., Gur, R. C., Hungerbuhler, J. P., & Geschwind, N. (1982). Hemispheric asymmetry in the expression of positive and negative emotions. *Archives of Neurology, 39,* 210–218.

Sahs, A. L., Hartman, E. C., & Aronson, S. M. (Eds.), (1976). *Guidelines for stroke care.* (DHEW Report No. HRA 76-14017). Washington D.C.: Bureau of Health Planning and Resources.

Stonnington, H. H. (1980, March). Rehabilitation in cerebrovascular diseases. *Primary Care, 7*(1), 87–106.

Trexler, L. E. (1982). *Cognitive rehabilitation: Conceptualization and intervention.* New York: Plenum Press.

Wade, D., Wood, V. A., & Hewer, R. L. (1985, January). Recovery after stroke—The first 3 months. *Journal of Neurology, Neurosurgery, and Psychiatry, 48,* 7–13.

Whisnant, J. P. (1983). The role of the neurologist in the decline of stroke. *Annals of Neurology, 14*(1), 1–7.

Young, G. C., Collins, D., & Hren, M. (1983). Effect of pairing scanning training with block design training in the remediation of perceptual problems in left hemiplegics. *Journal of Clinical Neuropsychology, 5,* 201–212.

8

Surgical Therapy for Stroke

Robert A. Ratcheson, M.D.

Warren R. Selman, M.D.

Although there has been a recent decline in the incidence of stroke, cerebral ischemia remains one of the leading causes of death and disability in the United States. The devastating effects of stroke, however, can be avoided for many patients who are recognized as having premonitory symptoms of occlusive cerebrovascular disease. Although surgical therapy for stroke also encompasses the management and treatment of cerebral aneurysms and arteriovenous malformations, in elderly patients the neurosurgeon is mostly concerned with the treatment of atherosclerotic occlusive disease.

EPIDEMIOLOGY AND RISK FACTORS

Stroke therapy and prevention have as their origin an appreciation of the significance of clinical phenomena. In 1893, Gowers identified the frequent occurrence of certain symptoms preceding cerebral infarction (Gowers, 1888). Chiari, in 1905, recognized that thrombi in intracranial blood vessels were secondary to emboli from atheromatous plaques located near the carotid bifurcation. In 1914, Hunt emphasized the importance of carotid occlusion in the pathogenesis of stroke. Modern efforts toward stroke therapy and prevention awaited the observations of Miller Fisher (1951), who suggested that disease of the internal carotid artery played a major role in cerebral infarction. He noted that carotid occlusion was often the result of thrombosis superimposed upon an enlarging subintimal atheroma and that thrombotic fragments could embolize to the intracranial circulation. In addition, he stressed the occurrence of premonitory fleeting symptoms including monocular blindness and hemiplegia (Fisher, 1952). His later, direct observations of retinal emboli during episodes of transient monocular blindness suggested that similar emboli might also lodge in cerebral vessels (Fisher, 1959). In 1955, Millikan and Siekert further defined the syndrome of carotid artery insufficiency by emphasizing the occurrence of transient ischemic phenomena. Later, Martin, Whisnant, & Sayre (1960) demonstrated that atherosclerosis was more prominent and severe in the extracranial carotid arteries than in the intracranial cerebral vessels.

The prevention of cerebral infarction in the patient with transient manifestions of cerebrovascular disease requires early recognition of the signs and symptoms of carotid artery atherosclerosis and an appreciation of their significance. Although symptoms that frequently precede cerebral infarction can be identified, because of the variability of long-term outcome, there is debate regarding the appropriate treatment of patients with transient ischemic attacks (TIA's).[1] A TIA does not invariably lead to cerebral infarction, nor are all transient ischemic symptoms the result of carotid atherosclerosis. Indeed, cerebral infarction in patients with carotid atherosclerosis is not uniformly heralded by a TIA. In persons 60 years or older, approximately 6% have an asymptomatic occlusion of one internal carotid artery, and in almost all persons 65 years of age or older, fibrous plaques are seen in the region of the carotid bifurcation (Solberg & Eggen, 1971). These plaques may remain stable for long periods, and it is unknown exactly why they may become "active," causing stenosis, ulceration, and subsequent platelet aggregation and thrombosis.

The epidemiology of stroke and the identification of risk factors are covered in other sections of this volume. In spite of this information, the percentage of cerebral infarctions that are preceded by warning episodes (TIA's) remains unclear, although some authorities have placed this figure as high as 50%. There is no detailed information

---

[1]TIA's are defined as a loss in neurological function or vision of sudden onset that clears within 24 hours. Most episodes last for approximately 15 minutes, rarely as long as an hour; they usually clear rapidly. Symptoms that persist after 24 hours are presumptive evidence that infarction has occurred.

available that permits correlation between anatomical manifestations of a TIA and the risk of subsequent infarction in the same
carotid distribution. It is known, however, that cerebral infarction
may be preceded by hundreds of TIA's or, more frequently, by only
one or two such events. A stroke may occur within one day to one
week of the first TIA but can be delayed for weeks or months. Symptoms may cease spontaneously without further difficulty. In a study
of 3,788 cases presenting with cerebrovascular symptomatology, the
role of extracranial vascular disease in cerebral infarction was
documented (Fields et al., 1968). Lesions involving a surgically
accessible portion of either the extracranial carotid or vertebral
arteries were found in 41.2% of the patients in this study. Although
another 33% had lesions in accessible areas, they also had one or
more inaccessible (intracranial) lesions. Ninety percent of carotid
occlusions occurred at the common carotid bifurcation, with less
than 8% occurring in the region of the carotid siphon. A smaller
portion occurred in the supracavernous or petrous segment. Stenosis
or occlusion in other parts of the internal carotid artery is rare.
Radiographic studies (Houser, Sundt, Holman, Sandok, & Burton,
1974) have demonstrated close correlation between carotid ischemic
symptoms and the degree of carotid atherosclerosis seen on angiography. These studies have indicated a high correlation between the
incidence of symptomatology, such as transient monocular blindness, and the presence of demonstrable extracranial carotid disease,
but it was not possible to differentiate angiographically those lesions
causing transient ischemic episodes from those causing cerebral infarction. Although stenotic carotid artery lesions that reduce the
arterial lumen to 2 mm in diameter (or the cross-sectional area to 2 to
5 mm^2) may produce decreased cerebral blood flow (Brice, Dowsett,
& Lowe, 1964), other lesions are nonstenotic and hemodynamically
insignificant, yet have the potential to produce cerebral ischemia due
to distal embolization. Although both mechanisms play important
roles in the production of cerebral ischemia and infarction, embolization is thought to be the dominant factor in the carotid system. In
symptomatic patients treated by endarterectomy, ulceration commonly occurs superimposed upon an area of stenosis, and virtually
all symptomatic patients having nonobstructive plaques will have
ulceration identified at operation (Ratcheson & Grubb, 1982).

Without therapy, over 50% of patients believed to have transient
ischemic episodes are normal after 4 to 5 years (Whisnant, 1974). In
some cases, it is possible that the original diagnosis was spurious. In
other patients, the danger resolves, either because the involved vessel
becomes occluded (i.e., there is cessation of embolization in the pres-

ence of adequate collateral blood supply), or because a nonstenotic ulcer heals. However, in the majority of cases, there is no way to determine which symptomatic patients are at greatest risk of cerebral infarction. The presenting symptomatology can provide such information in a few instances (Marshall & Wilkinson, 1971). Symptoms such as clustering or crescendo transient ischemic episodes are an ominous indicator of impending infarction, making rapid therapy imperative. Patients who exhibit warning signs of cerebral infarction and are safely treated by carotid endarterectomy have a smaller subsequent risk of cerebral infarction in the distribution of the operated artery than similar patients who have been treated by other means.

Once cerebral infarction occurs, little can be done to alter the course of the disease. The key to helping those threatened by stroke lies in prevention. This requires an accurate diagnosis of carotid atherosclerosis. The information needed to make a decision about further, invasive evaluation can be obtained by careful history. The physician must make specific inquiries, as patients often will not recall brief and evanescent symptomatology. Questions should be directed toward symptoms of focal retinal or cerebral ischemia. The infrequency of symptomatology should not lead to a false sense of security, as infarction can occur following a single attack or without prior warning. The signals of carotid artery disease are ipsilateral monocular visual loss, contralateral limb weakness and sensory change, and dysphasia when the dominant hemisphere is involved. Bilateral symptomatology, cortical visual impairment, diplopia, dizziness, or sudden loss of consciousness are not signs of carotid disease and should lead one to suspect involvement of the vertebrobasilar system. Dysarthria or homonymous hemianopsia are rarely products of carotid system disease. Confusion should not be attributed to disease of the carotid artery unless it accompanies a focal neurological deficit.

While most symptoms allow identification of the region of the brain involved, pinpointing specific arterial lesions is quite difficult. For example, occlusion of the carotid artery may occur without producing symptoms or signs, or it may present with transient ischemic episodes or with signs identical to middle cerebral artery thrombosis. In the typical case, there is a sudden onset of variable severity. Irrespective of whether the neurological symptoms are transient or permanent, they usually evolve over a few seconds, minutes, or, rarely, hours. A sudden apoplectic onset is characteristic of embolism, with the onset of thrombosis being more variable, chiefly due to the potential for collateral blood supply to develop. Recurrent emboli originating at the carotid bifurcation, as distinguished from the heart, are thought capable of producing stereotyped episodes of cerebral or retinal ischemia. Eighty percent of emboli are thought to lodge in the middle cerebral artery distribution (Penry & Netsky, 1960). In the case of a tight carotid stenosis with superimposed platelet fibrin aggregates, the distinction between embolic or thrombotic etiology becomes difficult.

History-taking should be directed toward obtaining enough information to differentiate the presence of disease in the carotid as opposed to the vertebrobasilar system, the specific arteries to be investigated, and the patient's medical condition and suitability for surgical treatment. Carotid artery disease produces symptoms of retinal and cerebral ischemia which may be transient (TIA's), longer lasting, or permanent. Although the great majority of symptoms due to ulceration or stenosis of the cervical and intracranial carotid artery are those of unilateral hemispheric dysfunction, other symptoms—some clear and some of questionable significance—have been ascribed to carotid artery atherosclerosis. In certain circumstances the following conditions may be indicative of carotid artery disease: First, a condition of generalized cerebral ischemia, perhaps associated with lightheadedness or a sensation of impending faint, may occur. Frequently there is difficulty walking, and rarely a dimming of vision. These symptoms, which are often postural, are believed to be the result of decreased cerebral perfusion due to bilateral carotid artery stenosis or occlusion. The actual incidence of this condition is unknown. To make a diagnosis of this generalized hypoperfusion syndrome, the carotid disease must be bilateral and severe, and symptoms should not be confined to dizziness. In general, surgical therapy to reverse these symptoms is indicated only when all the major cerebral feeding arteries are involved. Second, dementia may result from severe bilateral carotid occlusive disease. The information that would enable one to determine which patient actually benefits by operation in this setting is quite difficult to evaluate. It is believed that many cases in which cerebrovascular reconstructive surgery for this condition has failed to benefit patients have not found their way into the literature.

Because of the variability of collateral blood supply, each individual suffering transient ischemia or infarction, regardless of clinical presentation, must be evaluated separately. Proper care requires a detailed analysis of neurological symptomatology and its relationship to specific pathophysiology and anatomy. In many instances, patients with identical clinical symptoms will benefit from different therapies.

New arterial imaging techniques can provide an anatomical diagnosis with increased safety. More asymptomatic patients with preocclusive lesions are being brought to the neurosurgeon's attention, making it crucial to define further the indications for surgical therapy. Unless a further definition of the risk represented by a particular arterial lesion or lesions evolves, the amount of carotid surgery performed may exceed its considerable benefits. The common occurrence of carotid artery plaques in the asymptomatic aged person indicates that the presence of an anatomical irregularity does not by itself constitute an indication for surgical therapy. A decision for a specific therapeutic course must rely upon an accurate correlation of clinical symptomatology and angiographic findings based upon a thorough understanding of the influence of anatomical variations on cerebral circulation and upon a knowledge of the pathophysiology of extracranial and intracranial occlusive disease.

CAROTID ENDARTERECTOMY

At the present time, surgical therapy of symptomatic common carotid bifurcation lesions offers the most direct and efficient mechanism for removing the source of cerebral emboli and for restoring blood flow when a lesion produces a critical stenosis. As previously indicated, not all lesions of the carotid artery represent a significant risk to an individual patient. The decision to perform carotid endarterectomy must therefore rely upon an accurate correlation of clinical symptomatology and angiographic findings. Medical and surgical factors that increase the risk of surgery must also enter into the decision whether to perform carotid endarterectomy or to treat the patient medically.

The primary indication for carotid endarterectomy is the angiographic demonstration of a stenotic or ulcerated lesion in the extracranial carotid artery that is compatible with the patient's cerebrovascular symptomatology. The symptoms, previously described, are transient monocular blindness, central retinal artery occlusion, carotid distribution TIA's, prolonged reversible ischemic neurological deficits, and mild to moderate fixed neurological deficits. These represent a spectrum of diseases that have in common the important fact that the patient's cerebral hemisphere remains at risk for further ischemic damage. In many instances appropriate therapy can prevent a devastating stroke, so each patient should be evaluated in a direct and prompt manner. The specific risk of stroke in an individual patient should be determined. Those patients at greatest risk, including patients with frequent TIA's, stuttering-stroke symptomatology, or an acute onset of mild to moderate neurological deficit, should be evaluated on an urgent basis. Patients having infrequent cerebral episodes are at unknown risk but should be evaluated without undue delay. The evaluation of each patient should include an assessment of surgical risk factors for carotid endarterectomy. There is no noninvasive test that can reliably detect all the conditions of the cervical carotid artery that may be responsible for cerebral symptomatology. At the present time, cerebral angiography is the only reliable study that will accurately demonstrate extracranial and intracranial vascular lesions and, therefore, a definitive angiographic study should not be delayed by noninvasive testing unless there is evidence to implicate an etiology other than extracranial or intracranial vascular disease.

Angiography should be performed immediately after appropriate medical evaluation and computerized tomographic (CT) scanning of the head. Although in most instances the administration of intravenous heparin will prevent further ischemic episodes until angiography can be performed under optimal conditions, such therapy does not guarantee that a patient will not suffer additional symptoms and permanent sequelae. If stenosis with a residual lumen less than 1 mm is found, or if intraluminal thrombus is found, surgery should be performed on an urgent basis. If ulceration or plaque formation is demonstrated in the appropriate carotid artery, a patient without neurological deficit should undergo surgery at the next elective opportunity. When the cervical carotid artery contains a nonstenotic lesion with only shallow ulceration, the patient may be treated with warfarin anticoagulant therapy. On occasion, despite adequate anticoagulation, such patients will have persistent symptoms and will require carotid endarterectomy.

The indications for surgical therapy in those with asymptomatic cervical bruits, asymptomatic angiographic lesions, and vertebrobasilar symptoms associated with carotid artery stenosis are controversial. The natural history of patients with asymptomatic bruits is not clearly defined (Fields, 1978; Hammond & Eisinger, 1962; Heyman et al., 1980). In general, these patients are currently studied with digital subtraction angiography and lesions of a preocclusive nature are routinely recommended for surgery. Frequently, the neurosurgeon must decide whether to treat an asymptomatic lesion that has been demonstrated angiographically during investigation of a contralateral symptomatic lesion. With the exception of unusual circumstances, dictated by the pattern of collateral circulation or accessibility of the lesion, treatment should be directed toward the symptomatic side. As the natural history of asymptomatic lesions also is not well defined (Johnson et al., 1978; Levin, Sondheimer, & Levin, 1980; Moore, Boren, Malone, & Goldstone, 1979), carotid endarterectomy should be restricted to those lesions having a residual lumen of 2 mm or less or lesions with evidence of multipe intraluminal irregularities that could produce flow disturbances that interrupt the normal laminar flow pattern and predispose the lesion to further ulceration and thrombus formation. On infrequent occasion, patients with symptoms of vertebrobasilar insufficiency will benefit from carotid endarterectomy if it can be demonstrated that posterior circulation blood flow will be augmented by removing a critical carotid stenosis. These patients must be carefully evaluated to determine the competence of the circle of Willis and other sources of collateral blood flow.

Good-quality angiography is an absolute necessity in evaluating patients for carotid endarterectomy. It is important that the origin of the cerebral vessels in the thorax and the cervical and intracranial distribution of the carotid arteries are all well visualized. Neurological consequences are not proportional to the size of a carotid lesion, and the angiographic appearance is often an unreliable predictor of the presence of active ulceration with shallow erosion of endothelium and the accumulation of thrombus and debris. In our surgical experience, more than 90 percent of the atherosclertoic plaques in carotid arteries ipsilateral to symptomatic hemispheres or eyes will be ulcerated and contain platelet aggregates and thrombus (Ratcheson & Grubb, 1982). When surgery is performed for asymptomatic cervical carotid lesions, irregularities identified angiographically are often found to be smooth and endothelialized.

Carotid endarterectomy should be performed with an overall operative mortality and major morbidity of less than 4%. However, those patients at greatest risk for stroke—that is, those who are neurologically unstable—will also have the highest rate of neurological complications following operation. The long-term outcome of carotid endarterectomy is difficult to evaluate. Wide variation in severity of preoperative neurological deficits and the natural history of improvement of stroke without treatment make it difficult to assess the role of endarterectomy in neurological recovery. In selected patients with mild, stable strokes, carotid endarterectomy appears to lower the incidence of recurrent strokes and may be responsible for improvement in neurological function beyond that expected from the natural course of the disease. The role of carotid endarterectomy in patients with TIA's is better defined. Carotid end-arterectomy is effective in relieving the symptoms of TIA's and in lowering the incidence of stroke in selected patients. The majority of late deaths in patients undergoing carotid endarterectomy are of cardiac origin. While at the present time no increase in survival rate of surgical patients compared with control patients can be demonstrated, it is believed that the avoidance of stroke significantly improves the quality of life.

SUPERFICIAL TEMPORAL/MIDDLE CEREBRAL CORTICAL ARTERY BYPASS

A number of significant atherosclerotic lesions responsible for cerebral ischemia involve either the internal carotid artery at sites inaccessible to extracranial surgical approaches or the intracranial arteries (Blaisdell, Clauss, Galbraith, Imparato, & Wylie, 1969; Fields et al., 1968). While many of these lesions are hemodynamically insignificant and produce cerebral ischemic symptoms due to embolization from diseased intima, others occlude vessels and obstruct blood flow to the cerebral hemispheres. During the past two decades, neurosurgeons have developed increasingly sophisticated microvascular surgical techniques that should logically lead to the effective treatment of cerebrovascular lesions previously not amenable to surgical correction. The most popular of these operations has been the extracranial/intracranial (EC/IC) arterial bypass procedure, which was first conceptualized by Fisher (1951) and brought to practical technical development by Donaghy (1967) and Yasargil (1967). The first operations on humans were performed in 1967 (Donaghy, 1972; Yasargil, 1969), and following that the operation was performed with rapidly increasing frequency as a logical treatment for a brain threatened with an insufficient supply of blood. In some patients the added collateral blood flow provided by this operation has been demonstrated to be capable of returning diminished cerebral flow and deranged cerebral oxidative metabolism to normal (Grubb, Ratcheson, Raichle, Kliefoth, & Gado, 1979). However, the natural history of specific anatomical cerebral vascular lesions is poorly understood and the indications for EC/IC bypass remain to be fully defined. A recently concluded cooperative study was unable to demonstrate any benefit (EC/IC Bypass Study Group, 1985). At the present time, clear indications for this operation exist only in certain cases of vascular trauma or surgically planned vascular occlusion, where the augmentation of blood supply to the brain by an EC/IC anastomosis may provide an added degree of safety. This technique has been successfully used in the treatment of giant aneurysms at the base of the skull and arteriovenous malformations. It has also been applied in cases of carotid-cavernous fistula. While it remains logical to assume that some patients will require added blood flow to diminish the risk of stroke, appropriate selection of these patients has proven elusive.

VERTEBROBASILAR ISCHEMIA

Ischemic symptoms in the vertebrovascular system, as opposed to the carotid circulation, are more commonly due to thrombosis superimposed on pre-existing stenosis. The symptomatology associated with these lesions has been described earlier in this chapter. Extracranial and intracranial bypasses have been utilized in the treatment of vertebrobasilar ischemia. These operations remain experimental and are of unproven efficacy. The surgical options include anastomoses of the occipital artery, either to the posterior inferior cerebellar artery or to the anterior-inferior cerebellar artery. Anastomoses can also be performed between the superficial temporal artery and either the superior cerebellar artery or the posterior cerebral artery. These procedures are also augmented by use of vein bypasses. Posterior circulation bypass, as well as other measures designed to augment blood flow (including vertebral artery endarterectomy and vertebral-artery-to-carotid-artery transposition), should be employed only in the patient with deficient collateral supply to the posterior circulation. Anomalies of the circle of Willis, which could result in incompetent collateral supply, are seen in as many as 20% of autopsy series. Thus, careful detailed angiography of both the anterior and posterior circulation is needed to determine the appropriateness of surgical therapy. In patients with appropriate clinical symptoms and evidence of deficient collateral supply, an occipital to posterior inferior cerebellar artery (PICA) bypass may be considered for bilateral intracranial vertebral artery occlusion or stenosis proximal to PICA, while anastomoses to the superior cerebellar or posterior cerebral artery are considered for occlusion or stenosis of the basilar artery.

SUMMARY

Surgical treatment for cerebrovascular disease is preventive in nature. A decision to operate is influenced by the risk-versus-benefit ratio in a specific surgical candidate. The patient's age, however, is never a barrier to good treatment or good judgment. Carotid endarterectomy appears to be most beneficial in appropriately chosen symptomatic patients, while extracranial/intracranial bypass is of value only in cases with planned vascular occlusion. Surgery for vertebrobasilar insufficiency is performed occasionally and with some increasing frequency, but the precise indications for its use and proof of its efficacy remain to be determined. Carotid atherosclerosis commonly occurs in asymptomatic elderly patients, and an anatomical irregularity in itself is not an indication for surgical therapy. Despite the unproven nature of surgical therapy, it is frequently the only option in caring for symptomatic patients threatened with the risk of stroke.

REFERENCES

Blaisdell, W. F., Clauss, R. H., Galbraith, J. G., Imparato, A. M., & Wylie, E. J. (1969). Joint study of extracranial arterial occlusion. Part IV. A review of surgical considerations. *Journal of the American Medical Association, 209,* 1889–1895.

Brice, J. G., Dowsett, D. J., & Lowe, R. D. (1964). Haemodynamic effects of carotid artery stenosis. *British Medical Journal, 2,* 1363–1366.

Chiari, H. (1905). Über das Verhaltern des Teilungswinkels der Carotis, communis bei der Endarteriitis chronica deformans. *Verh. Dtsch. Ges. Pathol., 9,* 326–330.

Donaghy, R. M. P. (1967). Patch and bypass in microangional surgery. In R. M. P. Donaghy & M. G. Yasargil (Eds.), *Micro-vascular surgery* (pp. 75–86). St. Louis: C. V. Mosby.

Donaghy, R. M. P. (1972). Neurologic surgery. *Surgery, Gynecology, and Obstetrics, 134,* 269–271.

EC/IC Bypass Study Group. (1985, November). Failure of extracranial/intracranial arterial bypass to reduce the risk of ischemic stroke. Results of an international randomized trial. *New England Journal of Medicine, 313*(19), 1191–1200.

Fields, W. S. (1978). The asymptomatic carotid bruit—Operate or not? Current concepts of cerebrovascular disease—Stroke. *Stroke, 9,* 269–271.

Fields, W. S., North, R. R., Hass, W. K., Galbraith, J. G., Wylie, E. J., Ratinov, G., Burns, M. H., Macdonald, M. C., & Meyer, J. S. (1968). Joint study of extracranial arterial occlusion as a cause of stroke. Part I. Organization of study and survey of patient population. *Journal of the American Medical Association, 203,* 955–960.

Fisher, C. M. (1951). Occlusion of the internal carotid artery. *Archives of Neurological Psychiatry, 65,* 346–377.

Fisher, C. M. (1952). Transient monocular blindness associated with hemiplegia. *Archives of Opthalmology, 47,* 167–203.

Fisher, C. M. (1959). Observations of the fundus oculi in transient monocular blindness. *Neurology, 9,* 333–347.

Gowers, W. R. (1888). *A manual of diseases of the nervous system.* Philadelphia: Blakiston.

Grubb, R. L. Jr., Ratcheson, R. A., Raichle, M. E., Kliefoth, A. B., & Gado, M. H. (1979). Regional cerebral blood flow and oxygen utilization in superficial temporal-middle cerebral artery anastomosis patients: An exploratory definition of clinical problems. *Journal of Neurosurgery, 50,* 733–741.

Hammond, J. H., & Eisinger, R. P. (1962). Carotid bruits in 1,000 normal subjects. *Archives of Internal Medicine, 109,* 109–111.

Heyman, A., Wilkinson, W. E., Heyden, S., Helms, M. J., Bartel, A. G., Karp, H. R., Tyroler, H. A., & Hames, C. G. (1980). Risk of stroke in asymptomatic persons with cervical arterial bruits: A population study in Evans County, Georgia. *New England Journal of Medicine, 302,* 838–841.

Houser, O. W., Sundt, T. M. Jr., Holman, C. B., Sandok, B. A., & Burton, R. C. (1974). Atheromatous disease of the carotid artery: Correlation of angiographic, clinical, and surgical findings. *Journal of Neurosurgery, 41,* 321–331.

Hunt, J. R. (1914). The role of the carotid arteries in the causation of vascular lesions of the brain with remarks on certain special features of the symptomatology. *American Journal of Medical Sciences, 147,* 704–723.

Johnson, N., Burnham, S. J., Flanigan, D. P., Goodreau, J. J., Yao, J. S. T, & Bergan, J. J. (1978). Carotid endarterectomy: A follow-up study of the contralateral non-operated carotid artery. *Annals of Surgery, 188,* 748–752.

Levin, S. M., Sondheimer, F. K., & Levin, J. M. (1980). The contralateral diseased but asymptomatic carotid artery: To operate or not? An update. *American Journal of Surgery, 140,* 203–205.

Marshall, J., & Wilkinson, I. M. S. (1971). The prognosis of carotid transient ischemic attacks in patients with normal angiograms. *Brain, 36,* 395–402.

Martin, M. J., Whisnant, J. P., & Sayre, G. P. (1960). Occlusive vascular disease in the extracranial cerebral circulation. *Archives of Neurology, 3,* 530–538.

Millikan, C. H., & Siekert, R. G. (1955). Studies in cerebrovascular disease. Part IV. The syndrome of intermittent insufficiency of the carotid arterial system. *Proceedings of the Mayo Clinic, 30,* 186–191.

Moore, W. S., Boren, C., Malone, J. M., & Goldstone, J. (1979). Asymptomatic carotid stenosis. Immediate and long-term results after prophylactic endarterectomy. *American Journal of Surgery, 138,* 228–233.

Penry, J. K., & Netsky, M. G. (1960). Experimental embolic occlusion of a single leptomeningeal artery. *Archives of Neurology, 3,* 391–398.

Ratcheson, R. A., & Grubb, R. L. Jr. (1982). Surgical management of diseases of the extracranial carotid artery. In H. H. Schmidek & W. H. Sweet (Eds.), *Operative neurosurgical techniques: Indications, methods, and results* (Vol. 2). New York: Grune and Stratton.

Solberg, L. A., & Eggen, D. A. (1971). Localization and sequence of development of atherosclerotic lesions in the carotid and vertebral arteries. *Circulation, 43,* 711–724.

Whisnant, J. P. (1974). Epidemiology of stroke: Emphasis on transient cerebral ischemic attacks and hypertension. *Stroke, 5,* 68–70.

Yasargil, M. G. (1967). Experimental small vessel surgery in the dog, including patching and grafting of cerebral vessels and the formation of functional extra-intracranial shunts. In R. M. P. Donaghy & M. G. Yasargil (Eds.), *Micro-vascular surgery* (pp. 87–126). St. Louis: C. V. Mosby.

Yasargil, M. G. (1969). Anastomosis between the superficial temporal artery and a branch of the middle cerebral artery. In M. G. Yasargil (Ed.), *Microsurgery applied to neurosurgery* (pp. 105–115). Stuttgart: Georg Thieme Verlag.

PART III
Rehabilitation

Introduction

Little attention, even among gerontologists, has been given to rehabilitation of the older stroke victim. This traditional picture of rehabilitation being relevant to the younger disabled population has been changing, fueled by the economic incentives of the national efforts at health care cost containment. Hospitals have become more involved in long-term care as an additional source of revenue from Medicare and other health care payers, since medically authorized rehabilitation remains an open-ended source of revenue.

Dr. Gary Goldberg, in Chapter 9, "Principles of Rehabilitation of the Elderly Stroke Patient," deals with the medical dimensions of function and disability as they relate to rehabilitation. He examines current issues of rehabilitation of the elderly stroke patient as a complement to acute medical care. Three conceptual issues are explored: prevention of complications or recurrence, restitution of function, and substitution of alternative strategies. While noting that the magnitude of the problem of stroke itself could be reduced through a basic understanding of its etiology and an understanding of primary prevention, Dr. Goldberg does not feel that this is likely in the near future. Some hope is seen in a decrease in the incidence of stroke through better identification and management of risk factors, as well as improvement in the acute management of the stroke patient. He does propose that the neuro-psychobiological study of dynamic change in the nervous system will produce insights into rehabilitation of brain-damaged patients. New insights into the relationship of the brain to behavior will need to be evaluated and integrated by the clinical rehabilitationist, to provide new knowledge for utilization in the care of patients with focal brain lesions. New medical knowledge, in conjunction with an understanding of the psychosocial and cultural factors in the provision of health care, will ultimately affect the social reintegration of the elderly stroke patient.

Dr. Robert Wertz's chapter on the "Efficacy of Language Therapy for Aphasia" reviews the debate on whether or not language therapy affects aphasia. He notes the many complications that thwart treatment trials, such as spontaneous recovery; problems with defining an acceptable nontreatment group; and the inability to control biographic, medical, and behavioral variables that may influence response to treatment. In this light, he reviews two studies that used random assignment of patients to treatment and nontreatment groups, to answer the question. While both investigations controlled some of the variables that may influence response to treatment, the results of the studies were dissimilar. Wertz analyzes the design and methodologies of the two studies in assessing whether or not they are relevant to the efficacy of therapy for aphasia. Dr. Wertz concludes by qualifying his case supporting the efficacy of speech therapy for aphasic patients. His positive results were obtained in men who suffered a single, left-hemisphere thrombo-embolic infarct and who received 8 to 10 hours of treatment each week by a speech pathologist for 12 weeks during the first 6 months post-onset. Whether other groups of patients—for example, those with multiple infarcts—will benefit or whether other regimens of therapy will prove beneficial remains to be determined by further well-designed trials.

Chapter 11, "Depression and Stroke," written by Dr. Thomas Price, emphasizes the fact that depression after stroke is a common condition. With little information in this area, a systematic study of depression following stroke was begun by the author and Dr. Robert Robinson. They found that depression was a common problem both soon after a stroke and later on. Lesion location was also examined, and it was found that rate of depression was significantly greater in those with left anterior lesions and that severity increased with proximity to the frontal pole in this group. Dr. Price also notes the difficulties in diagnosing post-stroke depression. He recommends asking the patient about it directly and forthrightly, but also emphasizes the utility of reliable research scales in identifying and following such patients.

Drs. Barbara Silverstone and Amy Horowitz contribute their view of "Issues of Social Support: The Family and Home Care" in Chapter 12 of this section. They contrast the situation of the chronically impaired elderly to elderly stroke patients, citing sudden onset, potential for recovery, and communication problems as the major differences. Further, they note needed research, identify appropriate clinical interventions, and examine the existence and adequacy of formal rehabilitation services.

With a political economy focused on "reducing the deficit," the provision of rehabilitative services has become subject to economic and political forces. While other chapters in this part focus on specific areas of interest to the rehabilitation of the older person who has suffered a stroke, Dr. Robert Binstock presents a view of the rehabilitation process within this broader context. He notes the challenges facing those professionals who champion the delivery of rehabilitative services to the older stroke victim: (1) research initiatives to explore the efficacy and costs of stroke rehabilitation, (2) guarding against rehabilitative "creaming," that is, selecting only those most likely to do well in rehabilitation; and (3) vigilance against rehabilitative fraud and neglect. The author concludes on the optimistic note that the economic and political climates in this country now encourage the promotion of rehabilitation on a larger scale, using Medicare resources.

The authors balance issues of formal and informal social support in providing services to the older stroke victim, noting the necessity for both types in short- and long-term rehabilitation. Emphasis is placed on the necessity of making rehabilitation available to the elderly stroke victim on an ongoing or extended intermittent basis. This approach allows for follow-up evaluations and reinforcement of relearned skills. Silverstone and Horowitz conclude by identifying weaknesses in health care delivery systems to stroke victims and urge rethinking of the continuum of care in order to develop further an integrated system of service.

R.E.D.

9

Principles of Rehabilitation of the Elderly Stroke Patient

Gary Goldberg, M.D.

DEFINING THE PROBLEM

Epidemiology of Disability Due to Stroke in the Elderly

Among people over 70 years of age, stroke is the second most frequent cause of death. Around 75% of strokes occur in people over the age of 65. Well over one quarter of all strokes affect the "very old"—i.e. people over the age of 75. While the overall incidence of stroke appears to have been decreasing for some time (Garraway et al., 1979; Levy, 1979; see chapter by Whisnant), in the very old, the incidence of stroke is probably continuing to increase (Haberman, Capildeo & Rose, 1978). This is of particular importance in view of the continuing disproportionate increase in the aged, particularly the very old, in the population of most western societies.

Supported by a grant from the Moss Rehabilitation Hospital Research Fund. The author wishes to acknowledge gratefully the support of J. T. Demopoulos, M.D., and the board and administration of Moss Rehabilitation Hospital, Philadelphia, PA. Valuable suggestions and comments were made on earlier versions of the manuscript by Nathaniel Mayer, M.D. and William Jenkins, Ph.D. The author would also like to thank Marian Schmier and Barbara Jermyn for editorial suggestions and technical assistance.

The overwhelming majority of stroke patients survive the initial hospitalization (Sacco, Wolf, Kannel, & McNamara, 1982). Of these approximately 30% become dependent upon the assistance of other persons for their daily needs, about 15% require long-term institutional care, and 70% are left with a significant functional disability in the realms of mobility, activities of daily living, social integration, and gainful employment (Gresham et al., 1975). Only 10% of the stroke survivors in the Framingham study had no discernible functional disability as a result of their stroke (Sacco et al., 1982).

There are about 2 million people living in the United States today with the residua of stroke. Well over half of these people are over the age of 65. The economic burden to society and to the affected individuals and their families is quite obviously immense. More important, an indeterminate but equally immense toll is taken in human suffering. While stroke is a major cause of death in the elderly, it is *the major cause of permanent neurological disability*. After the acute phase of medical care, the long and arduous process of dealing with the multifaceted functional sequelae is only beginning, not just for the patient but also for the multi-layered social system—family, friends, community, employer—of which the patient is an integral part. This chapter will address the general question of how the health care system can and should respond to the needs of the elderly stroke survivor with significant functional disability. A comprehensive treatment of this topic would properly occupy the pages of a substantial monograph (see, for example, Kaplan & Cerullo, 1986). In this chapter, it will not be possible to examine current practice issues in stroke rehabilitation. These are reviewed in a separate work (Goldberg, 1986a). An attempt will be made, rather, to convey a theoretical and experimental justification for the application of rehabilitation therapy to patients with stroke. This will be prefaced by an introduction to basic issues in rehabilitative care.

Rehabilitative Care versus Acute Medical Care

Standard acute medical care, based on a traditional structurally oriented model of disease, focuses on identifying and curing or minimizing primary pathology. In contrast, rehabilitation has been defined as a "therapeutic program specifically directed toward restoring the optimum level of function available to patients with severe permanent disabilities" (Perry, 1983, p. 799). In rehabilitation, disease is viewed in terms of its operational consequences, and treatment is developed in this context. In that rehabilitation embraces an operational or performance-based view of disease, its scientific perspective is more akin to that of physiology than to that of anatomical pathology. Physiology, the study of dynamic, operational mechanisms in living systems, is a key source of basic science information for the rehabilitationist, whose primary goal is the optimization of function.

Rehabilitative care can be viewed as complementary to acute medical care and comes into play when a pathological process cannot be completely reversed with short-term measures, and a prolonged course of recovery associated with long-term impairment ensues. The nature of the impairment sustained in stroke is related to the pathophysiological function of the damaged brain. How this impairment translates into disability is an immensely complicated issue related to the larger problem of brain/behavior correlation (Popper & Eccles, 1977; Kandel, 1985a). How the dysfunction at a personal level ("disability") translates into "handicap" is an even more complicated issue.

A hypothetical and oversimplified example can help to illustrate these points. Suppose we consider a patient who has an infarction of the inferior frontal convexity of the dominant hemisphere producing an inability to speak fluently. Suppose further that this is an isolated impairment. Rehabilitation might focus on both restorative and substitutive techniques. A restorative approach would emphasize methods for facilitating verbal output, while in substitutive treatment, the patient would be taught to utilize alternative forms of communication such as gestures, selection of symbols or words from a "communication board," facial expressions, or writing. Since rehabilitation encompasses both the restorative and the substitutive approaches, critical treatment decisions involve determining the extent to which these approaches are emphasized. Clearly, complete restoration of lost function is preferable to resorting to less efficient and less socially acceptable alternatives. Unfortunately, while some recovery of function following stroke can be expected, complete restoration is less frequent and less predictable. The processes underlying the recovery of function following brain damage and basic principles of neuroplasticity in the adult, and particularly the older individual, remain poorly understood, although important insights are being gained through basic science efforts (more on this later). Regardless, the disability associated with this stroke in our patient with an isolated nonfluent expressive aphasia would translate into a much greater vocational *handicap* for an individual who had been employed as a telephone operator than for an individual who had been making a living as a mime artist. Handicap, then, is seen as the consequence of disability in terms of departure from a social norm.

Defining Function and Disability

To understand rehabilitation and rehabilitative care, one must have a clear understanding of the terms *function* and *disability*. *Function* can be conceptualized as the ability to solve "motor problems" (Bernstein, 1967) or, equivalently, to achieve desired outcomes through action. The solutions to a motor problem are hierarchically organized, goal-directed, complex behaviors (Bernstein, 1967; Pickenhain, 1984a, 1984b). Solutions to a multitude of subproblems must be linked together (Mayer, Keating, & Rapp, 1986) to permit the individual to perform independently those tasks essential to everyday life: dressing, grooming, feeding, moving about, carrying out vocational and avocational activities, participating in social relationships with others, and so forth.

Disability represents loss of ability to perform such multifaceted routines of daily living (Wood & Badley, 1978). It can be measured by determining the level of independence with which the patient is able to perform particular tasks (see Table 9-1). The measurement and documentation of level of disability is referred to as "functional assessment" and is obviously a critically important area of investigation (Granger, 1982). Functional assessment provides the rehabilitationist with a way of following patient progress and documenting rehabilitation outcome.

A goal-directed behavior proceeds within constraints imposed both by the biological limitations on performance and by environmental circumstances. The behavior can be viewed as the solution of a problem involving simultaneous multiple constraint satisfaction. (For an interesting discussion in the context of designing adaptive computer algorithms, see Ackley, Hinton, & Sejnowski, 1985.) Normal physiological capacity confers a large number of redundant degrees of freedom for the solution of such problems, but this number may be drastically reduced by brain damage.

Successful performance also depends upon the ability to construct an action-oriented internal representation of the body and the environment, based upon previous experience (Arbib, 1981). This internal "model" can be maintained in memory and used to generate predictions about action requirements, which guide the action from

TABLE 9-1 Functional Independence Measure (FIM): Description of General Levels of Function

In-dependent: Another person is not required for the activity *(no helper).*

    Level 4: *Complete independence.* Activity typically performed safely without modification, assistive devices, or aids, and is completed within a reasonable amount of time.

    Level 3: *Modified independence.* Activity requires any one of the following: an assistive device, more than reasonable time, or there are safety considerations.

Dependent: Another person is required for either supervision or physical assistance in order for the activity to be performed, or it cannot be performed *(requires helper).*

    Level 2: *Modified dependence.* The subject expends more effort than the helper. The levels of assistance required are:

        a. Supervision—no more help than cueing or coaxing, without physical contact

        b. Minimal assistance—no more help than touching

        c. Moderate assistance—more help than touching, but subject expends more effort than the helper.

    Level 1: *Complete dependence.* The helper expends more effort than the subject. Maximal assistance is required.

Source: Task Force for Development of a Uniform National Data System for Medical Rehabilitation. *Guide to the Use of the Uniform National Data Set for Medical Rehabilitation* (p. 16). Buffalo, NY: Project Office, Department of Rehabilitation Medicine, Buffalo General Hospital, 100 High Street, 14203.

the present into the future. Thus acting successfully to solve a problem can be reduced to the need to anticipate accurately. It is the capacity to detect and retain contingent relationships, and to utilize such internalized "knowledge" to make accurate predictions, that forms the essential basis for learning and adaptation (Ingvar, 1985). Accurate anticipation depends, in turn, upon the construction of precise probabilistic models of the future from which predictions can be drawn (Bernstein, 1967; Goldberg, 1985a; Requin, Semjen, & Bonnet, 1984) so that successful memory-driven control of function can occur. The locus of control can also shift to a data-driven mode in which function is directly responsive to external inputs (Norman & Bcbrow, 1975). These two control modes have been referred to as *projection* and *response,* respectively (Goldberg, 1985b). Separate brain systems can be identified with each of these processing modes (Goldberg, 1985a, 1985b), and they can be viewed as applying equally to the control of action, perceptual processing, and selective attention (Norman & Bobrow, 1975; Rabbitt, 1981). This flexibility of control over processing is important for the ability to adapt to new circumstances (i.e., to learn) and to meet efficiently the demands of various tasks. Local brain damage may impair this flexibility and may have differential effects on the two fundamental processing modes. The general effect of aging is a gradual impairment of the projectional system (Rabbitt, 1981; Rabbitt & Vyas, 1980). The older person comes to rely more heavily upon the data-driven responsive processing mode. As Rabbitt states,

> It seems that as people grow old they can still benefit from appropriate data-driven control but become increasingly unable to exercise active memory-driven control. Thus they cannot respond as flexibly to task demands as the young, because they have fewer options of locus of control and they may be unable to rapidly switch between even their remaining options. [1981, p. 569]

Thus the elderly stroke patient begins with relative impairment of the projectional, memory-dependent control mode, which appears to be a concomitant of the aging process. The effects of a stroke, which may have an impact on either or both control modes, are superimposed upon this background. This suggests that careful structuring of external circumstances and environmental regularity become more important with increasing age, and that the elderly stroke victim whose stroke significantly impairs brain systems dealing with responsive control (i.e., produces major impairment of sensory input processing systems) may not be able to utilize data-driven processing to compensate for the age-dependent deterioration of memory-driven control. This hypothesis, which needs more careful experimental verification, suggests the correlation of impaired sensory function with limitations of outcome in hemiplegia (Kusoffsky, Wadell, & Nilsson, 1982; Van Buskirk & Webster, 1955).

The capacity to achieve a particular goal is the result of an interaction between the subject and her or his environment, with constraining factors being contributed from both sources (i.e., extrinsic and intrinsic). It is thus critically important to know as much as possible about the environment to which a patient will be returning when planning a rehabilitation program and to recognize that important advances in patient function may be achieved through judicious alterations in the environment and/or by providing specialized equipment, aids, or orthoses.

Thus, "function" emerges through a mutually interdependent interaction between the individual and the environment, through either feedback (reactive) or feed-forward (anticipatory) mechanisms

(Goldberg, 1985a, 1985b). In daily life, an individual will employ a wide variety of different functional skills that can be characterized as complex, goal-directed behaviors. The term *disability* refers to the reduced capacity of the individual to perform essential routines of daily living that are expected, in accordance with social norms. The World Health Organization (1980) has defined six major dimensions of daily experience in which competence is generally required for the fulfillment of expected social roles: orientation, physical independence, mobility, occupation, social integration, and economic self-sufficiency. Stroke is clearly quite capable of producing significant disability in each of these realms. The major goal of a program of rehabilitation is the amelioration of this multidimensional disability. As noted earlier, some functional improvement can occur through specific modifications of the environment which may offer new "affordances" (Gibson, 1982) for the accomplishment of a particular goal. When this concept is combined with the idea that entirely different (i.e., previously unutilized) strategies can be taught to the patient, a comprehensive program directed toward facilitating adaptation and minimizing the functional deficit can be designed. Rehabilitation thus focuses on the operational consequences of disease, and its therapeutic model is based upon dynamic principles of interaction and education.

THREE ELEMENTS OF THE REHABILITATION PROGRAM

Prevention

The prevention of complications and recurrent strokes that would lead to further deterioration of function is the first major element of the program. To this extent, medical rehabilitation of the stroke patient should include careful consideration of measures for secondary stroke prevention (see Gent et al., 1985; Leonberg & Elliott, 1981). At present, there are no clinically proven specific therapies other than careful management of the recognized risk factors. Medical complications related to diseases frequently associated with stroke such as diabetes mellitus, coronary artery disease, and venous thrombosis must also be carefully managed and require early recognition and institution of appropriate medical therapy in order to minimize the "down time" during which patients cannot actively participate in their rehabilitation programs. These conditions have to be taken into account in the design and prescription of the program of rehabilitation therapies so that an appropriate balance, for each individual patient, between the benefits and risks of physical activity and training can be achieved.

Restitution of Function

A. R. Luria and his colleagues dealt extensively with the problem of restoration of function in patients with local brain lesions, in a review that appeared several years ago in the *Handbook of Clinical Neurology* (Luria, Naydin, Tsvetkova, & Vinarskaya, 1969). While much has occurred in the time since this book appeared, the issues identified by these investigators remain central to the rehabilitation of stroke patients. They begin their chapter as follows:

> Destroyed nerve cells do not regenerate, and it would seem therefore that functions lost as a result of damage to these cells cannot be restored. However, it is equally well known that during recovery from a disease, the functions disturbed as a result of a local brain lesion are gradually restored, and in some cases—perhaps after several years—considerable recovery may take place.
>
> How can we explain this paradoxical phenomenon, so important in clinical neurology? To consider another aspect of the problem, on the basis of our knowledge of the pathophysiological mechanisms of disturbance and restoration of functions damaged after local brain lesions, how can we organize rational rehabilitative treatment, designed to bring about the most complete recovery of the disturbed functions as quickly as possible? [Luria et al., 1969, p. 368]

A detailed discussion of this problem and a complete review of recent research in neuroplasticity and adaptation is well beyond the scope of this chapter; however, a limited survey will be attempted in a later section. Interested readers are referred to additional sources (Abelson, Butz, & Snyder, 1985; Bach-y-Rita, 1980, 1981; Cotman, 1985; Finger, 1978; Stein, Rosen, & Butters, 1974; van Hof & Mohn, 1981).

Luria et al. (1969) recognized two basic forms of functional disturbance due to local brain lesions: (1) those due to induced remote physiological inactivity (RPI) or the "diaschisis" of von Monakow (1914) and (2) those due to irreversible destruction of nerve cells. The former condition has been documented in the cerebellum with positron emission tomography in patients with stroke affecting the cerebral hemispheres (Baron, Bousser, Comar, & Castaigne, 1981; Frackowiak 1985; Lenzi, Frackowiak, & Jones, 1982; Martin & Raichle, 1983). Thus, one major goal in the understanding of recovery of function will be to determine the basis for remote physiological inactivity, and to develop the means for "de-inhibiting" (Luria et al.,

1969) those brain regions affected by this process. Pharmacological therapy may eventually be of particular value. Diaschisis might occur because of reduced release of neuromodulating biogenic amines in the cerebral as well as cerebellar cortex (Boyeson & Feeney, 1984; Moore, 1982; Morrison, Molliver, & Grzanna, 1979; Robinson, Shoemaker, Schlumpf, Valk, & Bloom, 1975); hence, pharmacological manipulation of these neuromodulators may modify the diaschitic state. Methods such as positron emission tomography (see Chapter 5) will likely provide additional important insights into the nature and frequency of this process in stroke. Alternative and somewhat more accessible though less precise physiological techniques such as electroencephalography, sensory evoked potentials, or topographic mapping and spatial analysis of scalp electric fields (e.g., Lehmann & Skrandies, 1984) may also prove useful in this application.

The development of methods for restoring functions previously subserved by neurons that have been destroyed poses a greater challenge and will be forthcoming only with a more thorough understanding of the neurobiological basis of learning, adaptation, and the capacity for dynamic restructuring of functional representations in the CNS (more on this later). In this case, restorative retraining of lost functions is important and may be viewed in some instances as the training of substitutive functional strategies, this being the third major conceptual pillar of stroke rehabilitation.

Restorative Retraining of Substitutive Functional Strategies

When an area in which a particular function is represented is irreversibly damaged, it is unlikely that the restoration of the impaired function to its intact original form can be accomplished. In such cases, Luria et al. (1969) suggest that

> The only way left is to reconstruct the disturbed function, to include intact nerve cells in its restoration, to transfer it to another intact neural apparatus, and sometimes to modify its psychophysiological composition radically, so that the original task is performed by new methods and by means of a completely new neural organization. . . . *The decisive role here is played by the methods of restorative retraining.* [p. 369, emphasis added]

Luria et al. (1969, pp. 380–381) then proceed to argue that restoration of function occurs through a "fundamental reorganization of the functional system." When the term *function* is used to refer to the "complex adaptive activity of a subject," it can be recognized that the performance of such a functional task can be accomplished within various contexts and the goal of the task often can be achieved by using several different strategies. The performance occurs in association with the activation of widely distributed processing networks within the CNS which cooperate as a "working constellation" or functional network of "collaborating zones," each of which makes its own contribution to the overall operation of the system and may correspond to an important feature of the elaborated behavior. Focal brain damage weakens or removes a link of the functional system, requiring that the whole system performing a particular function become reorganized (Luria et al., 1969, p. 381). Guiding principles for rational rehabilitation and the development of a program of restorative retraining can then be developed in the context of this understanding of brain function. Four basic principles are as follows:

1. Create a precise characterization of the functional defect.
2. Develop substitutive strategies that utilize preserved function.
3. Retrain extended functional subroutines of daily living.
4. Provide the patient with accurate feedback.

Precise Characterization of the Functional Defect. An operational analysis of the nature of the breakdown of function is performed so that the defect can be adequately characterized and a differential approach to the problem can be developed. The treatment approach should be anchored in an indepth understanding of the operational nature of the breakdown in a particular function and the corresponding disruption in the associated brain system. Prescription of restorative training must proceed from a careful functional evaluation of the patient.

Substitutive Strategies Utilizing Preserved Function. Preserved operational elements must be recognized and methods for incorporating them into alternative strategies for achieving useful function must be devised and taught to the patient. Luria et al. (1969) refer to this as the principle of "taking advantage of the intact link," recognizing that, with a bit of imagination, creativity, and common sense, means for accomplishing important daily functions can be devised utilizing operational functions that the patient retains. Many examples can be given. The use of tactile substitution for visual loss and auditory impairment is well recognized and forms the basis for new prosthetic techniques (e.g., Bach-y-Rita, Collins, Saunders, White, & Scadden, 1969). Training of one-handed activities in patients with poor motor return in a hemiparetic arm is another commonly employed tactic. Providing external cues or signals that the patient is able to process in order to reintegrate defective motor programs can be done in a number of different contexts, with the slow withdrawal of dependence upon the external inputs as the patient's performance improves with practice on a task. Alternatively, teaching the patient techniques for self-cueing in a particular context can also facilitate performance, as long as the patient is able to recall and utilize the strategy. A growing body of basic neuroscientific literature supports the idea that the process of learning new strategies through experience and practice may be associated with significant changes in synaptic organization within the CNS (e.g., Farley & Alkon, 1985; Kandel, 1985b).

Retraining of Extended Functional Subroutines of Daily Living. Breaking an activity down into component behavioral units, training performance on individual units, and then "chaining" units together into an ordered behavioral structure is another means of developing a restorative program. This method can be viewed as effectively "reprogramming" a complex behavior. Lesions, particularly of the frontal lobes, can lead to a situation in which a particular overlearned activity can no longer be performed relatively effortlessly as a unified whole, but disintegrates into a disordered sequence of isolated components each of which requires an independent effort and an inordinate concentration on the task (Roy, 1981; Stuss & Benson, 1986). Training attempts to make the activity automatic once again. This is done by first training on each task component using external auxiliary means to support the performance. Sequential ordering of the components is then taught, again using external cueing, in an attempt to reestablish an internalized regulation of the sequence which can then, with practice, be slowly condensed and made independent of external cueing (Mayer et al., 1986).

In this context, one can identify component behavioral units of a complete daily activity routine that could be referred to as basic motor skills. A training program would begin with the goal of restoring competency in the performance of individual motor skills. The next step would be to assemble these skills into linked sequences that become effective goal-directed subroutines (which may be referred to as "routines of daily living") that have then to be associated with the appropriate context in daily life (see Mayer, 1984; Mayer et al., 1986). Once the ordering of the sequence of skills has been established, *extended* performance of the routine is possible, perhaps with some external cueing from the therapist to facilitate transition from one component skill to the next. (Such performance requires a great deal of conscious effort on the part of the patient; for a personal account, see Brodal, 1973). Training then concentrates on reestablishing a smooth flow of performance that is *internally programmed* and requires less conscious effort. This process probably involves a gradual transition in the way different brain systems participate in each performance of the routine and may be viewed as entailing a change in the locus of control from a data-driven to a memory-driven control mode, or from "responsive" action to "projectional" action (Goldberg, 1985b). Studies of physiological correlates of motor skills performance in humans (Lang, Lang, Kornhuber, Deecke, & Kornhuber, 1984; Taylor, 1978) and instrumental motor learning in nonhuman primates (Sasaki & Gemba, 1982) are beginning to shed light on how this occurs.

Accurate "Knowledge of Results." Giving the patient appropriate feedback regarding the accuracy of each performance attempt can facilitate the relearning of a lost function. The ability to evaluate outcome of self-initiated acts and to modify a central representation of the task accordingly is crucial to successful learning (Mackay, 1984). The therapist becomes a substitute for defective internal feedback mechanisms that normally would permit self-regulation of performance. This information, and the ability to use it in a corrective fashion, are crucial elements in the process of adaptation (Granit, 1977).

Special measures can be taken to augment and enhance the ongoing feedback of salient physiological signals the patient is receiving about performance. These measures are globally referred to as *biofeedback techniques* (Basmajian, 1979). Such techniques would include the use of a mirror during the retraining of standing and balance, to allow visual input to be used to enhance awareness of body position, or the use of a tape recorder or more elaborate means of playing back and presenting verbal output during retraining of speech. Various forms of biofeedback equipment have been devised which can translate important task-relevant information—such as the loading of a limb, the position of a joint, or surface electromyographic activity of a muscle that is to be activated or relaxed—into sensory information presented in a form that the patient can more readily assimilate and interpret in the context of the task (Basmajian, 1979; Wolf, 1979). As noted earlier, these techniques can be viewed as facilitating the data-driven mode of processing control and aiding in the transfer of locus of control from the data-driven mode to the memory-driven mode. With practice, performance becomes independent of the biofeedback.

These are general principles guiding the design of a program of restorative retraining. Clearly, such programs must be carefully tailored to each individual. More specific concepts that may apply would depend upon the nature of the functions to be restored. The reader is referred to Luria et al. (1969) for a detailed discussion, as a comprehensive discussion of such specifics is beyond the scope of this chapter.

THE REHABILITATION PROGRAM

Rehabilitation Goals for the Elderly Stroke Patient

The rehabilitation process is comprised of two major complementary programs: preventive rehabilitation and comprehensive medical rehabilitation. Preventive rehabilitation is designed to minimize the complications of inactivity associated with any chronic disabling process in which the recovery process is protracted (Vallbona, 1982). The elderly, because of age-associated decreases in physiological reserve, are particularly susceptible to the consequences of inactivity. Comprehensive medical rehabilitation focuses on the restoration of specific functions through the application of individualized training programs designed and carried out by a multidisciplinary team employing the general principles outlined in the previous section.

The overall goals of a program of rehabilitation for the elderly stroke victim would include the following:

1. Preventing complications of prolonged inactivity, including deterioration in intellectual function and slowing of psychomotor processing; depression; decreased muscle strength and disuse atrophy; contracture formation; decreased cardiopulmonary reserve; orthostatic hypotension; deep venous thrombosis; constipation; hypercalciuria and renal lithiasis; impaired immunity; skin atrophy and pressure sores; and osteoporosis.

2. Preventing recurrent stroke and other vascular events that occur with greater frequency in the patient with stroke.

3. Identifying and characterizing the patient's functional deficits as well as those functions that remain relatively intact.

4. Improving overall physical performance through conditioning exercises that increase the functional capacity of organ systems less directly affected by the stroke.

5. Improving functional ability through training in specific daily living tasks that fall into the following general areas (Perry, 1983): mobility and locomotion, goal-directed handling of objects with the hands, self-care, cognitive functions, and communication.

6. Assessing the need for specialized equipment for mobility and daily living and providing individualized prescriptions for specific aids or orthoses; making recommendations regarding modifications of the home environment that may improve patient function in the home.

7. Assessing and providing needed support to the patient and his or her family in the difficult process of social adjustment to a long-term change in the patient's overall state of health.

8. Identifying and treating affective disorders and providing counseling and support to the patient as well as pharmacological therapy where appropriate (see Chapter 12).

9. Preventing complications through careful evaluation and treatment of all associated medical conditions, such as hypertension, coronary artery disease and diabetes mellitus; particularly important problems include

   a. Early recognition of urinary sepsis and careful monitoring of bowel and bladder function to minimize the possibility of persisting incontinence.

   b. Nutritional evaluation and management, often overlooked in the recovering elderly stroke patient, and about which very little is known, with the result that unrecognized malnutrition is not an infrequent occurrence in hospitalized debilitated patients with brain damage (Newmark, Sublett, Black, & Geller, 1981); particularly important in patients with dysphagia.

10. Identifying and, where possible, facilitating recreational activities in which the patient can become actively engaged, including, leisure activities and hobbies in which the patient participated premorbidly, and driving an automobile, once the patient has been evaluated by a specially trained instructor.

11. Ideally, returning the patient to a state of complete self-support, including gainful employment.

Economic versus Quality-of-Life Justification of Rehabilitation

Comprehensive medical rehabilitation by a multidisciplinary team in an inpatient setting is expensive and does not remain unchallenged, particularly in the current climate of fiscal constraint.

Studies have shown that the costs of comprehensive team-based rehabilitation in stroke are recovered when one recognizes the expenditure required for the alternative of long-term chronic care (Kottke, Lehmann, & Stillwell, 1982; Lehmann et al., 1975). Thus the costs of *not* rehabilitating can be greater than the costs of early, intensive inpatient rehabilitative care. For each stroke patient who is enabled by rehabilitation to live at home rather than becoming dependent upon custodial care, the savings to society can be as high as 10 times the initial rehabilitative care investment, depending on how long the patient survives following the stroke.

The more persuasive argument of returning a disabled individual to full employment, as, for example, can be made for the young spinal-cord-injured patient, is obviously less relevant to the rehabilitation efforts for the elderly stroke patient. This raises some very difficult questions concerning who should receive comprehensive rehabilitation in an age of diminishing resources; purely economic considerations would tend to place a higher priority on the rehabilitation of the potentially reemployable disabled individual than on that of the retired person. There is no doubt that, with increasing economic constraint, there will have to be greater accountability for rehabilitative care. If outcome is to be measured purely in economic terms, then it will become increasingly difficult to justify efforts to rehabilitate elderly stroke patients. If, however, the measurement of outcome is to be made in terms of quality of life (see Table 9–2), and if we are sensitive to the profound moral and ethical considerations that must enter into decisions regarding the provision of optimal health care to the elderly, then a strong argument can be made for such efforts.

In the assessment of the stroke patient, it is important not to overlook the importance of quality of life (Ahlsio, Britton, Murray, & Theorell, 1984). Quality of life is difficult to evaluate accurately and objectively, so evaluations will always entail some subjectivity. While physical functioning and level of independence in activities of daily living are important determinants of self-perceived quality of life, depression and anxiety related to stroke are just as important and imply careful attention to the psychological care of the stroke patient (Ahlsio et al., & Theorell, 1984; Feibel & Springer, 1982; Robinson, Bolduc, Kubos, Starr, & Price, 1985).

A recent study of the outcome of stroke as a function of age is particularly relevant to this issue (Andrews, Brocklehurst, Richards, & Laycock, 1984). These investigators found that age, in and of itself, is not a significant barrier to physical recovery and that stroke survivors can be expected to recover similarly regardless of age. However, the frequency of institutional placement was significantly greater for patients over the age of 75. Thus, for the very old, it appears that, despite physical improvement and adequate management of stroke-related disability, a good social (and economic) outcome, in terms of the ability to return home, is not so readily achieved. This finding suggests that other factors, most likely stemming from psychosocial circumstances, play an important role in determining whether or not the older stroke survivor becomes institutionalized. It will be important to determine what these factors might be and to what extent they may be modified (Andrews et al., 1984).

TABLE 9-2 Quality-of-Life Issues for Stroke Patients

1. Accommodation to the disability associated with the disease
2. Adjustment to new limits of physical ability
3. Alteration in lifestyle with focus on wellness
4. Achieving mastery over disruption and loss of control produced by the disease
5. Reintegration and establishment of a positive self-image
6. Reestablishment and adjustment of relationship with spouse/closest other
7. Adjustment of relationships within the family unit; maintaining closeness and solidarity of the family structure
8. Achieving new ways to fulfill family roles and responsibilities
9. Reestablishing a productive life, either through return to work or through the development of alternative plans to established vocation
10. Avoiding social isolation through regular participation with friends and relatives in formal and informal social gatherings
11. Reestablishing independent mobility in the community
12. Resuming religious practices and beliefs
13. Making appropriate adjustments in economic situation in order to insure economic security and stability
14. Obtaining access to and appropriately using community resources
15. Developing ability to cope with and solve problems in everyday life
16. Developing avocational interests and recreational opportunities
17. Adjusting and reestablishing course toward achieving realistic life goals
18. Reestablishing an enjoyable, meaningful life in which the stroke and its consequences are no longer the major focus

Source: Adapted from Cobble, N. D., & Burks, J. S. (1985). The team approach to management of multiple sclerosis. In F. P. Maloney, J. S. Burks, & S. P. Ringel (Eds.), *Interdisciplinary rehabilitation of multiple sclerosis and neuromuscular disorders* (pp. 11–31). Philadelphia: J. B. Lippincott.

Multidisciplinary Team Care

A rehabilitation program is most effectively designed and implemented by a multidisciplinary team of professionals. It is because of the multidimensional nature of the clinical consequences of stroke that multidisciplinary team care becomes the only way of mounting a complete approach; the training of one particular type of specialist is not sufficient to encompass comprehensively the range of problems that may be encountered. Table 9–3 shows how responsibility for various clinical problems encountered in the management of the stroke patient might be distributed.

The team is composed of the physiatrist,[1] the rehabilitation nurse, physical therapist, occupational therapist, speech pathologist, medical social worker, neuropsychologist, orthotist, dietician, and recreational therapist, as well as other rehabilitation professionals whose expertise may be required under special circumstances. These would include the rehabilitation engineer, vocational counselor, driving instructor, prosthetist, and others. Cooperation in the design, implementation, and monitoring of the treatment program is crucial to the success of the team and depends upon frequent, open communication among team members, a recognition of the extent and limitations of the expertise of each team member, and mutual respect for the unique talents and competencies that each member contributes to the overall effectiveness of the team (Halstead, 1976).

There are many different clinical problems that may arise in the rehabilitation management of the stroke patient. A complete discussion of the details of management of each of these clinical problems is not possible here. However, in Table 9–3, the reader is provided with a brief outline of some of these problems and how they may be dealt with by interacting groups within the multidisciplinary team.

---

[1]A physiatrist is a physician with specialty training in physical medicine and rehabilitation who has spent several years of postgraduate education focused on the rehabilitation management of disability. This specialist has acquired skills, knowledge, and a basic philosophical orientation specific to the functional model of disease as complementary to the standard medical model. A physician thus trained has the unique capability to understand the nature and sources of disability through an integration of the medical and functional approaches to disease. In addition, the physiatrist is uniquely prepared for the tasks of prescribing and guiding specific methods of management implemented by associated rehabilitation professionals. This person may be additionally involved in selecting and, with appropriate training, performing specific physiological investigations such as electromyographic kinesiology of either gait or goal-directed arm movements, and electromyography or sensory-evoked potentials that delineate the physiological basis of disability in a particular patient. Furthermore, the training of the physiatrist confers skills needed in acting as an overseeing "case manager" who, with a contextually based, holistic view of the patient in mind, coordinates the rehabilitation effort.

Table 9–3 Multidisciplinary Team Interaction in Stroke Management

Problem	Goals	Team[a]	Plan
Weakness	1. Strengthen disuse component 2. Improve fitness	MD/N/OT/PT	Strengthening exercises Endurance exercises Standing tolerance Protective splinting
Disordered motor control (spasticity)	1. Reduce tone without loss of functional strength 2. Reestablish functional movement patterns	MD/N/OT/PT	Medication Stretching Cold application Positioning Motor control lab evaluation Nerve and/or motor point blocks Progressive casting (fixed contractures) Stroke orthopedic conference

Problem	Goal	Team	Intervention
Incoordination/poor balance	1. Improve balance control	MD/OT/PT	Coordination/balance exercise Limb-load feedback Standing tolerance Mat exercises Standing in front of mirror Trunk-control exercise Gait training
Impaired somatic sensation	1. Enhance sensory awareness 2. Evaluate physiology 3. Teach precautions	MD/N/OT/PT	Education Teach visual compensation Evoked potentials Tapping Brushing Range of motion exercise
Ambulation/transfers	1. Safe, independent mobility	N/OT/PT Gait Lab	Decrease tone Active range of motion Balance exercises Improve trunk control Weight-shifting Transfer training Progressive gait training Assess for orthosis/shoes Assess for walking aids Gait lab evaluation Practice on ward Stroke orthopedic clinic Wheelchair management training Home environment assessment Training on curbs and elevations Family training

Table 9-3 *(Continued)*

Problem	Goals	Team[a]	Plan
Activities of daily living/community skills	1. Safe, independent self-care 2. Access to community	Driver ed. Npsych/N/OT/PT/RT	Transfer training Standing balance exercise Bed mobility exercises Training in daily skills Teach new strategies Adaptive equipment Tub/toilet transfers Energy conservation ed. Supervised recreational activity Avocational activity Train dressing techniques Train grooming techniques Evaluate vision/perception Cognitive retraining
Bowel dysfunction	1. Regularity without constipation, diarrhea, or incontinence	D/MD/N/OT/PT	Diet Medication Regular toileting Bathroom transfers
Bladder dysfunction	1. Freedom from incontinence or infection	MD/N/OT/PT/Urologist/Urodynamics Lab	Evaluate (urodynamics lab) Urinalysis and culture Renal function Medication Timed voiding Controlled fluid intake Rx infection Intermittent cath.

Problem	Goals	Team	Interventions
Sexual dysfunction	1. Minimize dysfunction 2. Adjustment	MD/N/OT/Psych/PT/Urologist	Evaluation Education Mat mobility Bowel/bladder management Counseling
Aphasia	1. Restore vocal control 2. Teach compensation 3. Maintain functional communication	MD/N/OT/PT/ST	Evaluation Specific retraining Language therapy Stimulation Programmed language Compensatory techniques
Dysphagia	1. Nutrition 2. Safety 3. Retrain swallowing	D/MD/N/OT/ST	Diet adjustment Patient/family training Alternate routes if required Evaluation—flouroscopy Retraining
Nutrition	1. Optimize nutritional intake	D/MD/N/OT/PT	Evaluate nutritional status Establish eating routines Hand-arm coordination Sitting balance and posture Body position Establish correct diet Proper food consistency Identify and Rx depression
Mood disorder	1. Facilitate adjustment 2. Prevent social isolation 3. Relieve organic depression 4. Stress management	MD/N/OT/Psych/PT/RT/SW/ST	Supportive counseling Family involvement Evaluation Positive reinforcement Positive social/recreational activities

Table 9-3 *(Continued)*

Problem	Goals	Team[a]	Plan
Mood disorder *(continued)*	4. Stress management *(continued)*		Antidepressant medication Antianxiety medication Relaxation therapy Emphasize progress made Encourage involvement with other patients Stroke support group involvement
Painful shoulder and/or hand	1. Evaluate and establish dx 2. Reduce pain 3. Reduce inflammation 4. Maintain function 5. Prevent loss of range of motion	MD/N/OT/PT	Evaluate to establish reason for pain Reduce subluxation when standing with hemi-sling or subaxillary cushion Control increased tone in shoulder girdle muscles with medication, motor point blocks, stretching exercise (see Disordered motor control, above) Manage pain and inflammation with an-algesic and anti-inflammatory medication Mobilize the shoulder and hand joints with passive/active ROM exercises Apply physical modalities (heat and/or cold) to reduce pain and inflammation Arm through or overhead sling to support shoulder joint with patient seated in W/C

[a]Team members listed in alphabetical order; MD = physician; OT = occupational therapist; PT = physical therapist; D = dietician; RT = recreational therapist; ST = speech therapist; SW = social worker; Npsych = neuropsychologist; N = nurse; Psych = psychologist/counselor; ROM = range of motion; W/C = wheelchair
Source: Cobble & Burks, 1985

124

THEORY AND EXPERIMENTAL BASIS FOR REHABILITATION OF THE STROKE PATIENT

Neuroplasticity and Mechanisms of Dynamic Adaptive Change in the CNS

Biological evolution guides the process of adaptation to a variety of different environmental conditions. The evolution of mammals, and the mammalian central nervous system particularly, has produced species with progressively more complex abilities to adapt to widely different external circumstances. Self-regulating adaptive organisms are purpose-driven (Granit, 1977; Pickenhain, 1984b) and are organized with respect to the achievement of certain ends through cyclical interaction with the immediate environment. It is no accident that Darwin was fascinated by the actively adaptive and apparently "intelligent," goal-directed abilities of even relatively primitive creatures (Reed, 1982). *The same mechanisms that allow adaptation to environmental change can be applied to help the organism adjust to changes in the functioning of internal systems.* The organism that survives an intrinsic insult is able to reconstruct itself into a "new" self-regulating system, although it may not have all the levels of complexity it had in its intact state. It nonetheless does reacquire its ability to act in teleonomic fashion (Pittendrigh, 1958) to achieve goals (modified in some ways as compared to those possible before) through interaction with its environment (Pickenhain, 1984a). What makes this purposive reorganization possible and how it occurs are basic questions that relate directly to the nature of biological adaptation (i.e., purpose-directed biological change) and are of fundamental relevance to the development of a theoretical basis for rehabilitation.

These considerations suggest the existence of an extensive capability for adaptive reorganization in the human brain. Traditionally, the human nervous system has been viewed as a static organ which, if damaged, loses function irreversibly because of the inability of central neurons in the mature mammalian nervous system to divide. However, this idea is slowly being eroded in favor of new conceptualizations that recognize the dynamic capability for CNS adaptation, even in the older individual (Bach-y-Rita, 1980, 1981).

It is interesting to consider the response to partial denervation of muscle as a paradigm for adaptive recovery following damage in the nervous system. The well-recognized phenomenon of "sprouting" of nerves allows strength to be recovered, sacrificing some precision in force control. Thus, polio patients can retain remarkable levels of function despite major losses of motor neurons. The mechanisms through which motor nerve sprouting is stimulated and sustained are not well understood but appear to occur through a "recapitulation" of the ontogenetic mechanisms that established the neuromuscular system during development (Brown, 1984). It is not wholly unlikely that this may be a general principle of adaptive recovery throughout the nervous system. Thus those processes that guide the development of the nervous system through ontogeny may be reenacted in the damaged mature nervous system.

Edelman (1978; Edelman & Finkel, 1984) has proposed a neuronal selection theory of brain function which postulates that cortical function is dynamically modifiable by the experience of the individual, within certain limits. The idea depends on activity-dependent selection of active neuronal groups during behavior and would allow for the possibility of restructuring of functional representations in the central nervous system (e.g., Jenkins, Merzenich, Zook, Fowler, & Stryker, 1982; Jenkins & Merzenich, 1986). Neuronal group selection, operating through competitive interaction, would allow the definition of a dynamically modifiable "secondary repertoire" of functional specificity superimposed on the less mutable but highly redundant "primary repertoire" of structural specificity determined by genetically guided patterns of basic connectivity.

Bach-y-Rita in 1981 discussed the concept of plasticity in the brain and the capability for dynamic change in the organization of brain systems, as they relate to the problem of developing innovative procedures for the rehabilitation of patients with stroke:

> Traditionally neurology has emphasized the correlation between the localization of the lesion and the deficit of function. While certainly essential to an understanding of neurological symptoms and syndromes, this approach has frequently been accompanied by therapeutic nihilism. Greater emphasis on the plasticity of the brain (specifically, on its capacity to mediate recovery of function) should lead to increased efforts to obtain the maximum recovery and reorganization that the damaged nervous system is capable of sustaining. [p. 73]

Anatomical and physiological considerations indicate that some functional brain systems are not particularly well localized but rather entail elements that are widely and bilaterally distributed throughout the CNS (Moore, 1980), a fact that suggests the presence of redundant neural circuitry. With regard to this observation in the motor system, Kornhuber (1984) has recently stated, "The distributed system theory of voluntary movement . . . is stressed . . . in order to encourage psychologists, physicians, and teachers to believe in the possibility of finding roundabout ways by learning and to prevent them from giving up too early in the training of patients with lesions of the central nervous system" (p. 170).

Recent work has shown that the redundant connections of somatosensory inputs to the primary motor cortex, for example, may be involved in supporting recovery of motor function (Asanuma & Arissian, 1984), perhaps through a process of unmasking (Wall, 1980) or revealing the presence of previously inactive synaptic sites. It has also recently been observed that the function of one area, the primary somatosensory cortex, in controlling wrist movement can be dynamically modified when the primary motor cortex is temporarily incapacitated by local cooling (Sasaki & Gemba, 1984). The observed performance of the wrist movement has a degraded quality but is not abolished. There appear to be a number of methods by which compensation can occur within brain networks. Immediate reorganization may take place, due to unmasking of previously inactive synapses (Wall, 1980) or to a compensatory rerouting of impulse traffic as a result of a rapidly acting feedback mechanism (Sasaki & Gemba, 1984). The slower reorganization may be explained by axonal sprouting in which axons that remain connected to a partially denervated structure branch and establish new contacts within the structure (for a description of this process in the mammalian red nucleus, see Tsukahara, 1985). Even the doctrine that neurons in the adult vertebrate brain cannot undergo reproductive division has recently been seriously challenged (Paton & Nottebohm, 1984; Rakic, 1985).

Rehabilitation medicine uses a model of care that draws heavily on educational psychology and learning theory in its understanding of how change in performance can come about as a result of specific training and/or environmental manipulation. Changes in neural form and function that occur during normal development, experientially dependent changes that occur in synaptic function and structure as a result of learning, and physiological changes and reorganization of brain systems that accompany recovery of function following local brain damage are conceptually interrelated by the theme of *dynamic change in neural specificity* in the central nervous system and its relationship to functional adaptation as manifested in behavior. These areas are currently receiving a great deal of attention in basic science laboratories, and this concentration of effort has begun to yield important insights that may eventually be translated into new clinical approaches to rehabilitating patients with focal brain damage. A comprehensive examination of the current literature is not possible, but a few recent findings will be highlighted here.[2]

Experiments performed on the invertebrate marine snail, *Aplysia californica,* have shown that classical conditioning of the gill-withdrawal reflex becomes internally represented through activity-dependent change in synaptic transmission at key synapses mediating the reflex (Byrne, 1985; Carew, Hawkins, & Kandel, 1983; Kandel, 1985b), and that long-term learning can induce morphological changes in the relevant synapse (Bailey & Chen, 1983). Classical conditioning can be viewed as a means through which the organism is able to discriminate and internalize biologically relevant cause-and-effect relationships in its environment. This then allows the organism to make reliable predictions about its immediate future which may be directly relevant to its survival. This ability appears to be a highly conserved feature in phylogenesis, with basic survival value. The elaboration of the neural mechanisms supporting this function in evolution was probably one of the basic driving forces in the evolution of the human central nervous system.

Thus, experientially induced, activity-dependent alteration in synaptic function underlying forms of associative and nonassociative learning can be documented and studied at the cellular level in invertebrates. Associative forms of learning depend critically upon the temporally ordered convergence of inputs from conditioned and unconditioned stimuli to key synaptic sites involved in the mediation of the reflex (Kandel, 1985b). The organism thus learns that the conditioned stimulus predicts the subsequent arrival of the biologically relevant noxious unconditioned stimulus and internalizes this "knowledge" into the structure and function of its nervous system. The more frequently the temporally ordered coincidence of conditioned with unconditioned stimulus is encountered, the more enduring its internal representation is likely to become. The detection of this particular form of coincidence produces the long-term modification of synaptic function occurring through heightened presynaptic facilitation, which is associated with the acquisition of the

---

[2]The interested reader is further referred to recent reviews and monographs that have examined cellular mechanisms in learning (Alkon & Woody, 1986; Farley & Alkon, 1985; Kandel, 1985b; Thompson, Berger, & Madden, 1983), as well as mechanisms of synaptic plasticity (Cotman, 1985; Cotman & Nieto-Sampedro, 1985; Tsukahara, 1981).

learned behavior (Byrne, 1985; Hawkins, Abrams, Carew, & Kandel, 1983).

Analogous studies of learning-impaired fruitfly mutants suggest that the basic mechanisms involved in learning and memory are genetically encoded and involve modulation of calcium-dependent control of the metabolism of cyclic adenosine monophosphate (AMP) in this species as well as in *Aplysia* (see Dudai, 1985). It is possible that this particular mechanism involving specific interactions among membrane-active neurotransmitters/neuromodulators, intracellular calcium, and cyclic nucleotide systems, which function together to control neurotransmitter release from the presynaptic terminal, may be a highly conserved and widely utilized means by which dynamic changes in neural function related to learning occur (Byrne, 1985).

Recent studies of the classical conditioning of the nictitating-membrane response in the rabbit indicate that a similar process may be occurring in the mammalian cerebellar cortex (Gellman & Miles, 1985; McCormick & Thompson, 1984; Thompson, 1983; Yeo, Hardiman, & Glickstein, 1985a, 1985b, 1985c). The cerebellum may play a particularly important role in detecting the coincidence of conditioning stimuli and modulating motor outflow based upon such detection. The cerebellum may thus function as a storehouse of motor-relevant cause-and-effect relationships that enable prediction required for well-tuned motor programs.

The cerebellum also plays an important role in the process of learning operantly conditioned visually initiated hand movements in monkeys (Sasaki & Gemba, 1983, 1984). While the earlier stages of learning, during which the animal recognizes the association between performance and reward, remain intact following cerebellar hemispherectomy, the final stages in the learning process, during which the temporal focusing of activation in the primary motor cortex occurs, are impaired. Thus, the lesioned animal is able to make temporally unstable hand movements, with long and variable reaction times, indicating that "recognition" learning has occurred. However, the animal is unable to refine the performance further without the participation of the cerebellum. While a separate system, possibly involving the basal ganglia reentrant circuit (see Goldberg, 1985b), can recognize action-relevant associations and reward contingencies, the cerebellum is required for the temporally refined use of learned cause-and-effect relationships that are needed in the predictive refinement of motor skill performance (see also Hore & Vilis, 1984).

These findings suggest that the cerebellum is an important site of plastic change related to motor learning. Its role in the induced modification of gain of the vestibulo-ocular reflex has been intensively studied (e.g., Ito, 1984; Melvill-Jones & Mandl, 1983). It may be in part through cerebellar-based changes that recovery of motor functions occurs following local cerebral lesions. The early, cerebellar-independent "recognition" learning may involve a bihemispheric system including associational cortices in parietal and prefrontal regions together with basal ganglia, culminating with activation of the premotor regions. This system is associated with the assembly of sequences of component skills in an extended version of the task, as discussed earlier. Subsequent training then enables skilled performance, which recruits cerebellar participation in the refinement of the sequential program performance and enables a condensation of the motor program (see Goldberg, 1985b; 1986b).

Adaptive changes in the cerebellum may involve the norepinephrine projections, which, since the initial proposals of Crow (1968) and Kety (1970), have been shown to participate in various ways in the plasticity associated with motor learning (Freedman, Hoffer, Puro, & Woodward, 1977; Watson & McElligott, 1984), memory (Arnsten & Goldman-Rakic, 1985), development (Kasamatsu, Pettigrew, & Ary, 1981), and recovery of function following brain damage (Boyeson & Feeney, 1984). This would suggest that manipulation of central catecholamine activity, and norepinephrine levels in particular, may have beneficial effects in patients recovering from a stroke. Much more basic work needs to be done on the neuropharmacology of plasticity and recovery of function, but these recent findings support an optimistic outlook. Additional related research areas include (1) the use of various trophic agents, such as nerve-growth factor and gangliosides, to enhance the rate of formation of central synapses and to facilitate sprouting in partially denervated structures and (2) the recent work on the functional consequences of transplants of fetal brain tissue into adult brain (for a recent review, see Bjorklund & Stenevi, 1984).

I would like to turn finally to a remarkable series of recent experiments performed by Merzenich, Kaas, Jenkins, and their colleagues on the plasticity of central representations of the upper limb in the primary somatosensory cortex (SI) of the monkey. These investigators have found that the structure of the somatotopic maps of the hand in SI changes in a systematic fashion in association with major changes in input from the periphery, produced by severing the median nerve at the wrist or by amputating a finger (see Figure 9–1).

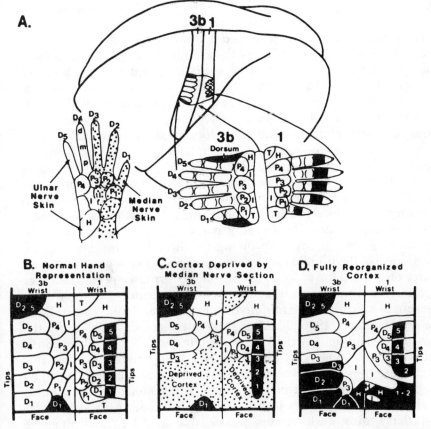

FIGURE 9-1. Functional reorganization of the somatotopic representation of the hand in primate somatosensory cortex following a complete lesion of the median nerve at the wrist. **A:** Regions of the hand represented in area 3b and 1 of primary somatosensory cortex and area of skin made insensate by median nerve lesion. Digits and palmar pads are numbered in order; insular (I), hypothenar (H), and thenar (T) pads, and distal (d), middle (m), and proximal (p) phalanges are indicated. Dorsal skin is represented in black, and ventral skin is represented in white. **B:** Closeup view of the somatotopic maps in area 3b and 1 prior to nerve section. **C:** Regions of cortex effectively deafferented by the median nerve section are marked in dots (deprived cortex). This is the situation obtained immediately after median nerve section. **D:** Structure of the reorganized somatotopic maps of the hand following median nerve section. Much of the deprived cortex is now activated by stimulating the dorsal hand and digital surfaces. The palmar pads innervated by the ulnar nerve have increased their cortical representation. This map is obtained several weeks following median nerve section.

Reproduced, with permission, from J. H. Kaas, M. M. Merzenich, & H. P. Killackey (1983). The reorganization of somatosensory cortex following peripheral nerve damage in adult and developing mammals. *Annual Review of Neuroscience, 6,* 325–356, Figure 1, © 1983 by Annual Reviews, Inc.

Cortical regions that had responded to input conveyed by the median nerve or from the skin surface of the amputated digit began to show responses with stimulation of adjacent skin regions that had not previously been able to drive these regions (Kaas, Merzenich, & Killackey, 1983; Merzenich & Kaas, 1982; Merzenich et al., 1983; Merzenich et al., 1984). After several weeks, the "de-afferented" regions had been almost completely reoccupied by inputs from adjacent skin. Further studies show that similar reorganizational changes can occur following a restricted lesion placed within SI (Jenkins et al., 1982). Finally, these investigators trained monkeys to press the tips of their middle fingers down onto a grooved rotary disk placed on a turntable for a food reward, without placing any of the other fingers onto the disk. When the monkey placed pressure down onto the turntable, a contact began revolving the turntable, thus stimulating the surface of the middle fingers continuously. After several thousand active presses on the grooved surface of the turntable performed over a period of several weeks, the area of cortex responding to input from the skin of the tips of the middle fingers had greatly increased (Jenkins & Merzenich, 1986; Jenkins, Merzenich, & Ochs, 1984) and the number of sampled cortical neurons found to have small receptive fields on these fingertips also increased. It is interesting that this modification in the central representation may also be influenced by the active voluntary set of the animal. If the monkey is trained to apply the middle fingers to a nonrotating, smooth turntable under less demanding task circumstances that require less intensive monitoring of the action for successful performance and reward, the changes observed in the SI somatotopic map are far less dramatic (personal communication, W. M. Jenkins). This is observed under other circumstances (Gemba & Sasaki, 1984) and suggests a general principle of biological adaptation; active engagement of the organism in a task (i.e., the orientation of voluntary "set") is a prerequisite condition for the biological changes associated with learning and adaptation. This principle has important implications for rehabilitation of stroke patients.

These findings suggest that central functional representations in the brain may be dynamically modifiable, within the bounds imposed by genetically determined anatomical constraints and by other poorly understood limits on plasticity in the adult CNS. Regions that are functionally vacated are "taken over" by inputs from adjacent skin regions that achieve a finer-grained representation of the skin surface by expansion of their cortical territory. The ongoing competition for cortical territory indicates a highly interactive and dynamic relationship between the periphery and its brain representation (Edelman, 1978). The basis of the competition is a use-dependent principle: Those peripheral components that do not activate their central representation will lose it; those peripheral components that drive their central representation through active use in excess of adjacent regions may expand the territory of their representation. There is no reason to think that these principles apply only to the representations in the somatosensory cortex. It is more likely that the potential for dynamic reorganization of central representations is a principle with generalized application throughout the brain. The details and verification of this hypothesis await further research.

The findings at the molecular and cellular synaptic level in very simple animals such as *Aplysia* and *Drosophila* mesh remarkably well with studies in plasticity performed in the mammalian brain. This applies, for example, in studies of the effects of monocular deprivation in kittens (Blakemore & Cooper, 1970; Hubel & Wiesel, 1963; Kasamatsu et al., 1981; reviewed by Movshon & Van Sluyters, 1981) as well as the work on cerebellar cortex of the rabbit and the somatosensory cortex of the monkey mentioned earlier. These findings may be explained by the properties of modifiable synaptic connections proposed by Hebb (1949; see also Phillips, Zeki, & Barlow, 1984; Sahley, 1985). Hebb (1949) proposed a form of synapse in which synaptic strength would be dynamically modifiable as a function of its rate of use. The invertebrate work, however, suggests that the picture may be somewhat more complicated. In these simple animals, transmission in a reflex pathway can be modified as a result of detected temporally ordered coincidence (associative learning of cause-and-effect relationships) as well as in response to stimulus irregularity (habituation-sensitization).

Neurobiodynamics: Understanding the Biological Basis and Limitations of Adaptation in the CNS

The ideas discussed below provide a biological basis for the theory of restorative training examined earlier in this chapter. There clearly appears to be some capability for dynamic reorganization of functional systems in the brain which can be produced through a specific program of training. These basic investigations emphasize the dynamic nature of the representation of function in the nervous system, as development and adaptation to environmental change occur. The study of dynamic adaptation and plasticity within the nervous system, whether in relation to learning and memory, development, or recovery of function in the damaged nervous system, indicates a widespread capacity for active change in effectiveness of central connections. Everyday experience can have profound biological influences on the nervous system (Kandel, 1985b). The process of behavioral adaptation through CNS modification may not only depend upon experience but also require that the organism actively orient to that experience as a result of the context in which the experience is occurring. There must be biological meaning and relevance for adaptation and learning to occur.

There are, however, various constraints that control the manner in which adaptation can occur; rampant, inappropriate, and undirected "adaptation" would clearly lead an organism into chaos, while excessive rigidity would lead to an inability to accommodate to significant change. (For a discussion of self-regulation of this "stability-plasticity dilemma," see Grossberg, 1984.) I would propose the introduction of a new term—*neurobiodynamics*—to refer to the biological study of dynamic alteration in the organization of CNS function and structure (i.e., plasticity) under circumstances of adaptation to both external and internal factors, resulting in learning and development. This area of study would also delineate mechanisms that control and constrain the range of adaptive dynamic change possible within different contexts. I would then argue that it is through such study that the processes associated with recovery of function in the nervous system are being and will be further elucidated, and that the clinical application of this knowledge will result in a solid theoretical basis for restorative retraining, new and innovative rehabilitation treatment methodologies developed in response to basic insights obtained, and improved functional outcomes in the rehabilitative treatment of stroke patients (Bach-y-Rita, 1981).

Neuroplasticity and Aging in the CNS

It should not be assumed that the capacity for neuroplasticity and behavioral adaptation necessarily diminishes with age. The effects of age on the brain per se must be differentiated from the effects of concomitant disease processes (Creasey & Rapoport, 1985). Examination of the complexity of dendritic trees in brains from older individuals indicates that the same factors that are at play during early development continue to function (Coleman & Buell, 1985). Neuron loss may actually be associated with a compensatory net *proliferation* of dendritic processes under some situations in the brains of healthy older individuals. Also, the dendritic trees are clearly capable of exhibiting significant growth in response to controlling factors in the local environment of the cell (neuronal fallout and afferent activity), although the rate of growth may be slowed somewhat compared to that during development. Dendritic growth in the presence of senile dementia, by contrast, is grossly impaired (Buell & Coleman, 1981). This would imply that the capacity for neuroplasticity is severely limited in the presence of Alzheimer's disease, for example. Thus, cortical neurons in the brain of an older person not affected by a progressive dementing illness are capable of responding with plastic change through dendritic proliferation, and the complexity of the dendritic tree can be sustained and advanced through afferent activity directed to the cortex.

CONCLUSION

Some of the current issues in the rehabilitation of the elderly stroke patient have been examined. Stroke is a major disabling disease of the older person. Despite significant decreases in the overall incidence of stroke (see Chapter 2), stroke in the elderly has become a health problem of growing concern.

Ideally, the problem can be reduced in magnitude through a basic understanding of its etiology and through development of methods of primary prevention. However, this does not appear to be a likely prospect in the near future. What might be achieved in the short run is a decrease in incidence through better identification and management of risk factors, and perhaps an improvement in the acute management of the stroke patient, resulting in greater short-term survival. Achieving these goals will require an intensive program of public education and an emphasis on preventive medical practice as well as continuing medical research.

Rehabilitation of the elderly stroke patient and its goals of actively minimizing functional disability and improving quality of life will become increasingly more important as the number of disabled elderly stroke survivors increases. Rehabilitation of the elderly stroke patient rests on three main conceptual bases:

1. Prevention of complications or recurrence
2. Restitution of function
3. Substitution of alternative strategies

The concept and methods of comprehensive medical rehabilitation of the stroke patient have been discussed, and the goals of such a program have been outlined. The process of active rehabilitation carried out by a multidisciplinary team of health care professionals in a therapeutic milieu is distinguished from passive convalescence (Rusk, 1959). A theory of restorative retraining in patients with focal brain lesions has also been reviewed, together with emerging information from recent basic work which may provide a foundation for the evolution of such a theory.

It is proposed that the study of dynamic neuro-psychobiological changes in the nervous system associated with learning and adaptation to environmental or organismic change (i.e., *neurobiodynamics*) will produce insights that will profoundly influence the practice of rehabilitation of patients with brain damage, and will yield new and innovative treatment methods. This study is currently receiving a great deal of attention in basic neuroscience (e.g., Cotman, 1985). These new views of dynamic CNS function and the adaptability of the brain are revolutionizing our understanding of brain-behavior correlation and our general understanding of how the brain works. The challenge presented to the clinical rehabilitationist will be to evaluate and integrate this newly emerging flood of basic science information on mechanisms of dynamic change in neural specificity, and to utilize this new knowledge in the context of clinical rehabilitation of patients with focal brain lesions.

With specific regard to the rehabilitation of the elderly stroke patient, we must recognize the additional considerations of age-related factors and the complicating and interacting effects of concomitant disabling illness. Disease entities, such as those producing a progressive dementia, may significantly retard the capacity for dynamic reorganization and plasticity in the brain, which correlates with behavioral recovery. It appears also that, even when physical disability is adequately treated with rehabilitation, psychosocial factors specific to the elderly, and particularly to the very old, may restrict the social outcome (Andrews et al., 1984). Advances in the rehabilitation of the elderly stroke survivor will depend not only on an improved understanding of the neurobiological basis for behavioral recovery but also on an understanding of the psychosocial and cultural factors that affect the social reintegration of the elderly stroke patient.

REFERENCES

Abelson, P. H., Butz, E., & Snyder, S. H. (Eds.). (1985). *Neuroscience: Vol. I. Neuroplasticity.* Washington, DC: American Association for the Advancement of Science.

Ackley, D. H., Hinton, G. E., & Sejnowski, T. J. (1985). A learning algorithm for Boltzmann machines. *Cognitive Science, 9,* 147–169.

Ahlsio, B., Britton, M., Murray, V., & Theorell, T. (1984). Disablement and quality of life after stroke. *Stroke, 15,* 886–890.

Alkon, D. L., & Woody, C. D. (Eds.). (1986). *Neural mechanisms of conditioning.* New York: Plenum Press.

Andrews, K., Brocklehurst, J. C., Richards, B., & Laycock, P. J. (1984). The influence of age on the clinical presentation and outcome of stroke. *International Rehabilitation Medicine, 6,* 49–53.

Arbib, M. A. (1981). Perceptual structures and distributed motor control. In V. B. Brooks (Ed.), *Handbook of physiology: The nervous system, Vol. 2. Motor control.* Washington, DC: The American Physiologic Society.

Arnsten, A. F. T., & Goldman-Rakic, P. S. (1985). α-adrenergic mechanisms in prefrontal cortex associated with cognitive decline in aged nonhuman primates. *Science, 230,* 1273–1276.

Asanuma, H., & Arissian, K. (1984). Experiments on functional role of peripheral input to motor cortex during voluntary movements in the monkey. *Journal of Neurophysiology, 52,* 212–227.

Bach-y-Rita, P. (Ed.). (1980). *Recovery of function: Theoretical considerations for brain injury rehabilitation.* Baltimore: University Park Press.

Bach-y-Rita, P. (1981). Brain plasticity as a basis of the development of rehabilitation procedures for hemiplegia. *Scandinavian Journal of Rehabilitation Medicine, 13,* 73–83.

Bach-y-Rita, P., Collins, G. C., Saunders, F., White, B., & Scadden, L. (1969). Vision substitution by tactile image projection. *Nature, 221,* 963–964.

Bailey, C. H., & Chen, M. (1983). Morphological basis of long-term habituation and sensitization in *Aplysia. Science, 220,* 91–93.

Baron, J. C., Bousser, M. G., Comar, D., & Castaigne, P. (1981). Crossed cerebellar diaschisis in human supratentorial brain infarction. *Transactions of the American Neurological Association, 105,* 459–461.

Basmajian, J. V. (Ed.). (1979). *Biofeedback: Principles and practice for clinicians.* Baltimore: Williams and Wilkins.

Bernstein, N. A. (1967). *The Co-ordination and regulation of movements.* Oxford, England: Pergamon Press.

Bernstein, N. A. (1984). Biodynamics of locomotion. In H. T. A. Whiting, (Ed.), *Human motor actions: Bernstein reassessed* (pp. 171–222). Amsterdam: North-Holland.

Bjorklund, A., & Stenevi, U. (1984). Intracerebral neural implants: Neuronal replacement and reconstruction of damaged circuitries. *Annual Review of Neuroscience, 7,* 279–308.

Blakemore, C., & Cooper, G. F. (1970). Development of the brain depends on the visual environment. *Nature* (London), *228,* 477–478.

Boyeson, M. G., & Feeney, D. M. (1984). Role of norepinephrine in recovery from brain injury. *Society for Neurosciences Abstracts, 10,* 68.

Brodal, A. (1973). Self observations and neuranatomical considerations after a stroke. *Brain, 97,* 675–694.

Brown, M. C. (1984). Sprouting of motor nerves in adult muscles: A recapitulation of ontogeny. *Trends in Neurosciences, 7,* 10–14.

Buell, S. J., & Coleman, P. D. (1981). Quantitative evidence for selective dendritic growth in normal human aging but not in senile dementia. *Brain Research, 214,* 23–41.

Byrne, J. H. (1985). Neural and molecular mechanisms underlying information storage in *Aplysia:* Implications for learning and memory. *Trends in
Neurosciences, 8,* 478–482.

Carew, T. J., Hawkins, R. D., & Kandel, E. R. (1983). Differential classical
conditioning of a defensive withdrawal reflex in *Aplysia californica. Science, 219,* 397–400.

Cobble, N. D., & Burks, J. S. (1985). The team approach to the management of
multiple sclerosis. In F. P. Maloney, J. S. Burks & S. P. Ringel (Eds.),
*Interdisciplinary rehabilitation of multiple sclerosis and neuromuscular
disorders* (pp. 11–31). Philadelphia: J. B. Lippincott.

Coleman, P. D., & Buell, S. J. (1985). Regulation of dendritic extent in
developing and aging brain. In C. W. Cotman, (Ed.), *Synaptic plasticity*
(pp. 311–333). New York: Guilford Press.

Cotman, C. W. (Ed.). (1985). *Synaptic plasticity.* New York: Guilford Press.

Cotman, C. W., & Nieto-Sampedro, M. (1985). Cell biology of synaptic plasticity. In P. H. Abelson, E. Butz, & S. H. Snyder (Eds.), *Neuroscience* (pp.
74–88). Washington, DC: American Association for the Advancement of
Science.

Creasey, H., & Rapoport, S. I. (1985). The aging human brain. *Annals of
Neurology, 17,* 2–10.

Crow, T. J. (1968). Cortical synapses and reinforcement: A hypothesis. *Nature*
(London), *219,* 736–737.

Dudai, Y. (1985). Genes, enzymes and learning in *Drosophila. Trends in
Neurosciences, 8,* 18–21.

Edelman, G. M. (1978). Group selection and phasic reentrant signaling: A
theory of higher brain function. In G. M. Edelman & V. B. Mountcastle,
*The mindful brain: Cortical organization and the group-selective theory of
higher brain function* (pp. 51–100). Cambridge, MA: MIT Press.

Edelman, G. M., & Finkel, L. H. (1984). Neuronal group selection in the
cerebral cortex. In G. M. Edelman, W. E. Gall, & W. M. Cowan (Eds.),
Dynamic aspects of neocortical function (pp. 653–695). New York: John
Wiley.

Farley, J., & Alkon, D. L. (1985). Cellular mechanisms of learning, memory
and information storage. *Annual Review of Psychology, 36,* 419–494.

Feibel, J. H., & Springer, C. J. (1982). Depression and failure to resume social
activities after stroke. *Archives of Physical Medicine and Rehabilitation,
63,* 276.

Finger, S. (Ed.). (1978). *Recovery from brain damage.* New York: Plenum Press.

Frackowiak, R. S. J. (1985). Pathophysiology of human cerebral ischemia:
Studies with positron tomography and (15)-oxygen. In L. Sokoloff (Ed.),
Brain imaging and brain function (pp. 139–161). New York: Raven Press.

Freedman, R., Hoffer, B. J., Puro, D., & Woodward, D. J. (1977). A functional
role of adrenergic input to the cerebellar cortex: Interaction of norepinephrine with activity evoked by mossy and climbing fibers. *Experimental Neurology, 55,* 269–288.

Gellman, R. S., & Miles, F. A. (1985). A new role for the cerebellum in
conditioning? *Trends in Neuroscience, 8,* 181–182.

Gemba, H., & Sasaki, K. (1984). Studies on cortical field potentials recorded
during learning processes of visually initiated hand movements in monkeys. *Experimental Brain Research, 55,* 26–32.

Gent, M., Blakely, J. A., Hachinski, V., Roberts, R. S., Barnett, H. J. M. & Bayer, N. H. (1985). A secondary prevention, randomized trial of sulocti-dil in patients with a recent history of thromboembolic stroke. *Stroke 16*, 416–424.

Gibson, J. J. (1982). Notes on affordances. In E. Reed & R. Jones (Eds.), *Reasons for realism: Selected essays of James J. Gibson* (pp. 401–418). Hillsdale, NJ: Lawrence Erlbaum Associates.

Goldberg, G. (1985a). Response and projection: A reinterpretation of the premotor concept. In E. A. Roy (Ed.), *Neuropsychology of apraxia and related disorders* (pp. 251–266). Amsterdam: Elsevier/North-Holland.

Goldberg, G. (1985b). Supplementary motor area structure and function: Review and hypotheses. *Behavioral and Brain Sciences, 8*, 567–615.

Goldberg, G. (1986a) Current practice issues in stroke rehabilitation. (in preparation).

Goldberg, G. (1986b). A two-loop model of motor preparation and learning. (in preparation).

Granger, C. V. (1982). Health accounting—Functional assessment of the long-term patient. In F. J. Kottke, G. K. Stillwell, & J. F. Lehmann (Eds.), *Krusen's handbook of physical medicine and rehabilitation* (3rd ed., pp. 253–274). Philadelphia: W. B. Saunders.

Granit, R. (1977). *The purposive brain*. Cambridge, MA: MIT Press.

Gresham, G. E., FitzPatrick, T. E., Wolf, P. A., McNamara, P. M., Kannel, W. B., & Dawber, T. R. (1975). Residual disability in survivors of stroke: The Framingham study. *New England Journal of Medicine, 293*, 954–956.

Grossberg, S. (1984). Some psychophysiological and pharmacological corre-lates of a developmental, cognitive and motivational theory. In R. Kar-rer, J. Cohen, & P. Tueting (Eds.), *Brain and information: Event-related potentials* (pp. 58–151). New York: New York Academy of Sciences.

Halstead, L. S. (1976). Team care in chronic illness: A critical review of the literature of the past 25 years. *Archives of Physical Medicine and Rehabilitation, 57*, 507–511.

Hawkins, R. D., Abrams, T., Carew, T. J., & Kandel, E. R. (1983). A cellular mechanism of classical conditioning in *Aplysia:* Activity-dependent amplification of presynaptic facilitation. *Science, 219*, 400–405.

Hebb, D. O. (1949). *The organization of behavior*. New York: John Wiley.

Hore, J., & Vilis, T. (1984). Loss of set in muscle responses to limb per-turbations during cerebellar dysfunction. *Journal of Neurophysiology, 51*, 1137–1148.

Hubel, D. H., & Wiesel, T. N. (1963). Receptive fields of cells in striate cortex of very young, visually inexperienced kittens. *Journal of Neurophysiology, 26*, 994–1002.

Ingvar, D. H. (1985). "Memory of the future": An essay on the temporal organization of conscious awareness. *Human Neurobiology, 4*, 127–136.

Ito, M. (1984). *The cerebellum and neural control*. New York: Raven Press.

Jenkins, W. M., & Merzenich, M. M. (in press). Reorganization of neocortical representations after brain injury; a neurophysiological model of the bases of recovery from stroke. *Progress in Brain Research*.

Jenkins, W. M., Merzenich, M. M., & Ochs, M. T. (1984). Behaviorally con-trolled differential use of restricted hand surfaces induces changes in the cortical representation of the hand in area 3b of adult owl monkeys. *Society for Neuroscience Abstracts, 10,* 665.

Jenkins, W. M., Merzenich, M. M., Zook, J. M., Fowler, B. C., & Stryker, M. P. (1982). The area 3b representation of the hand in owl monkeys reorganizes after induction of restricted cortical lesions. *Society for Neuroscience Abstracts, 8,* 141.

Kaas, J. H., Merzenich, M. M., & Killackey, H. P. (1983). The reorganization of somatosensory cortex following peripheral nerve damage in adult and developing animals. *Annual Review of Neuroscience, 6,* 325–356.

Kandel, E. R. (1985a). Brain and behavior. In E. R. Kandel & J. H. Schwartz (Eds.), *Principles of neural science.* New York: Elsevier.

Kandel, E. R. (1985b). Cellular mechanisms of learning and the biological basis of individuality. In E. R. Kandel & J. H. Schwartz (Eds.), *Principles of neural science* (pp. 816–833). New York: Elsevier.

Kaplan, P. E., & Cerullo, L. J. (1986). *Stroke Rehabilitation.* Boston: Butterworths.

Kasamatsu, T., Pettigrew, J. D., & Ary, M. (1981). Cortical recovery from effects of monocular deprivation: Acceleration with norepinephrine and suppression with 6-hydroxydopamine. *Journal of Neurophysiology, 45,* 254–266.

Kety, S. S. (1970). Biogenic amines in the CNS: Their possible roles in arousal, emotion and learning. In F. O. Schmitt (Ed.), *The Neurosciences: Second Study Program* (pp. 324–336). New York: Rockefeller University Press.

Kornhuber, H. H. (1984). Mechanisms of voluntary movement. In W. Prinz & A. F. Sanders (Eds.), *Cognition and motor processes* (pp. 163–173). Berlin: Springer-Verlag.

Kottke, F. J., Lehmann, J. F., & Stillwell, G. K. (1982). Preface. In F. J. Kottke, G. K. Stillwell, & J. F. Lehmann (Eds.), *Krusen's handbook of physical medicine and rehabilitation* (3rd ed., pp. vi–ix). Philadelphia: W. B. Saunders.

Kusoffsky, A., Wadell, I., & Nilsson, B. Y. (1982). The relationship between sensory impairment and motor recovery in patients with hemiplegia. *Scandinavian Journal of Rehabilitation Medicine, 14,* 27–32.

Lang, W., Lang, M., Kornhuber, A., Deecke, L., & Kornhuber, H. H. (1984). Human cerebral potentials and visuomotor learning. *Pflugers Archives European Journal of Physiology, 399,* 342–344.

Lehmann, D., & Skrandies, W. (1984). Spatial analysis of evoked potentials in man—A review. *Progress in Neurobiology, 23,* 227–250.

Lehmann, J. F., DeLateur, B. J., Fowler, R. S. Jr., Warren, C., Arnhold, R., Schertzer, G., Hurka, R., Whitmore, J. J., Masock, A. J., & Chambers, K. H. (1975). Stroke: Does rehabilitation affect outcome. *Archives of Physical Medicine and Rehabilitation, 56,* 375–382.

Lenzi, G. L., Frackowiak, R. S. J., & Jones, T. (1982). Cerebral oxygen metabolism and blood flow in human cerebral ischemic infarction. *Journal of Cerebral Blood Flow and Metabolism, 2,* 321–335.

Leonberg, S. C., & Elliott, F. A. (1981). Prevention of recurrent stroke. *Stroke, 12,* 731–735.

Luria, A. R., Naydin, V. L., Tsvetkova, L. S., & Vinarskaya, E. N. (1969). Restoration of higher cortical function following local brain damage. In R. J. Vinken & G. W. Bruyn (Eds.), *Handbook of clinical neurology* (Vol. 3, pp. 368–433). Amsterdam: North-Holland.

Mackay, D. M. (1984). Evaluation: The missing link between cognition and action. In W. Prinz & A. F. Sanders (Eds.), *Cognition and motor processes* (pp. 175–184). Berlin: Springer-Verlag.

Martin, W. R. W., & Raichle, M. E. (1983). Cerebellar blood flow and metabolism in cerebral hemisphere infarction. *Annals of Neurology, 14,* 168–176.

Mayer, N. H. (1984). Concepts in head injury rehabilitation. In P. E. Kaplan (Ed.), *The practice of physical medicine* (pp. 373–412). Springfield, IL: Charles C Thomas.

Mayer, N. H., Keating, D. J., & Rapp, D. (1986). Skills, routines and activity patterns of daily living: A functional nested approach. In B. Uzzell & Y. Gross (Eds.), *Neuropsychology of intervention*. Boston: Kluwer-Nijhoff.

McCormick, D. A., & Thompson, R. F. (1984). Cerebellum: essential involvement in the classically conditioned eyelid response. *Science, 223,* 296–299.

Melvill Jones, G., & Mandl, G. (1983). Neurobionomics of adaptive plasticity: Integrating sensorimotor function with environmental demands. In J. E. Desmedt (Ed.), *Motor control mechanisms in health and disease* (pp. 1047–1071). New York: Raven Press.

Merzenich, M. M., & Kaas, J. H. (1982). Reorganization of mammalian somatosensory cortex following peripheral nerve injury. *Trends in Neurosciences, 5,* 434–436.

Merzenich, M. M., Kaas, J. H., Wall, J. T., Sur, M., Nelson, R. J., & Fellerman, D. J. (1983). Progression of change following median nerve section in the cortical representation of the hand in areas 3b and 1 in adult owl and squirrel monkeys. *Neuroscience, 10,* 639–665.

Merzenich, M. M., Nelson, R. J., Stryker, M. P., Cynader, M., Schoppmann, A., & Zook, J. M. (1984). Somatosensory cortical map changes following digit amputation in adult monkeys. *Journal of Comparative Neurology, 224,* 591–604.

Moore, J. (1980). Neuroanatomical considerations relating to recovery of function following brain injury. In P. Bach-y-Rita (Ed.), *Recovery of function: Theoretical considerations for brain injury rehabilitation* (pp. 9–90). Baltimore: University Park Press.

Moore, R. Y. (1982). Catecholamine neuron systems in the brain. *Annals of Neurology, 12,* 321–327.

Morrison, J. H., Molliver, G. E., & Grzanna, R. (1979). Noradrenergic innervation of cerebral cortex: Widespread effects of local cortical lesions. *Science, 205,* 313–316.

Newmark, S. R., Sublett, D., Black, J., & Geller, R. (1981). Nutritional assessment in a rehabilitation unit. *Archives of Physical Medicine and Rehabilitation, 62,* 279–282.

Norman, D. A., & Bobrow, D. G. (1975). On data limited and resource limited processes. *Cognitive Psychology, 7,* 44–64.

Paton, J. A., & Nottebohm, F. N. (1984). Neurons generated in the adult brain are recruited into functional circuits. *Science, 225,* 1046–1048.

Perry, J. (1983). Rehabilitation of the neurologically disabled patient: Principles, practice and scientific basis. *Journal of Neurosurgery, 58,* 799–816.

Phillips, C. G., Zeki, S., & Barlow, H. B. (1984). Localization of function in the cerebral cortex. Past, present and future. *Brain, 107,* 327–361.

Pickenhain, L. (1984a). Goal-directed behavior and self-regulation in the organism. In T. Elbert, B. Rockstroh, W. Lutzenberger, & N. Birbaumer (Eds.), *Self-regulation of the brain and behavior* (pp. 273–276). Berlin: Springer-Verlag.

Pickenhain, L. (1984b). Toward a holistic conception of movement control. In H. T. A. Whiting (Ed.), *Human motor actions: Bernstein reassessed* (pp. 505–528). Amsterdam: Elsevier/North-Holland.

Pittendrigh, C. S. (1958). Adaptation, natural selection and behavior. In A. Roe & G. G. Simpson (Eds.), *Behavior and evolution.* New Haven: Yale University Press.

Popper, K., & Eccles, J. C. (1977). *The self and its brain.* Berlin: Springer Verlag.

Rabbitt, P. M. A. (1981). Cognitive psychology needs models for changes in performance with old age. In J. Long & A. Baddeley (Eds.), *Attention and performance* (Vol. 9, pp. 555–573). Hillsdale, NJ: Lawrence Erlbaum Associates.

Rabbitt, P. M. A., & Vyas, S. M. (1980). Selective anticipation for events in old age. *Journal of Gerontology, 35,* 913–919.

Rakic, P. (1985). Limits of neurogenesis in primates. *Science, 227* (4690), 1054–1056.

Reed, E. S. (1982). Darwin's earthworms: A case study in evolutionary psychology. *Behaviorism, 10,* 165–185.

Requin, J., Semjen, J.-C., & Bonnet, M. (1984). Bernstein's purposeful brain. In H. T. A. Whiting (Ed.), *Human motor actions: Bernstein reassessed.* Amsterdam: Elsevier/North-Holland.

Robinson, R. G., Bolduc, P. L., Kubos, K. L., Starr, L. B., & Price, T. R. (1985). Social functioning assessment in stroke patients. *Archives of Physical Medicine and Rehabilitation, 66,* 496–500.

Robinson, R. G., Shoemaker, W. J., Schlumpf, M., Valk, T., & Bloom, F. E. (1975). Effect of experimental cerebral infarction in rat brain on catecholamines and behavior. *Nature* (London), *255,* 332–334.

Roy, E. A. (1981). Action sequencing and lateralized cerebral damage: Evidence for asymmetries in control. In J. Long & A. Baddeley (Eds.), *Attention and performance* (Vol. 9, pp. 487–500). Hillsdale, NJ: Lawrence Erlbaum Associates.

Rusk, H. A. (1959). Advances in rehabilitation. *Practitioner, 183,* 505–512.

Sacco, R. L., Wolf, P. A., Kannel, W. B., & McNamara, P. M. (1982). Survival and recurrence following stroke. The Framingham study. *Stroke, 13,* 290–295.

Sahley, C. L. (1985). Co-activation, cell assemblies and learning. *Trends in Neuroscience, 8,* 423–424.

Sasaki, K., & Gemba, H. (1982). Development and change of cortical field potentials during learning processes of visually initiated hand movements in the monkey. *Experimental Brain Research, 48,* 429–437.

Sasaki, K., & Gemba, H. (1983). Learning of fast and stable hand movements and cerebro-cerebellar interactions in the monkey. *Brain Research, 277,* 41–46.

Sasaki, K., & Gemba, H. (1984). Compensatory motor function of the somatosensory cortex for the motor cortex temporarily impaired by cooling in the monkey. *Experimental Brain Research, 55,* 60–68.

Stein, D. G., Rosen, J. J., & Butters, N. (Eds.). (1974). *Plasticity and recovery of function in the central nervous system.* New York: Academic Press.

Stuss, D. T., & Benson, D. F. (1986). *The frontal lobes.* New York: Raven Press.

Taylor, M. J. (1978). Bereitschafts potential during the acquisition of a skilled motor task. *Electroencephalography and Clinical Neurophysiology, 45,* 568–576.

Thompson, R. F. (1983). Neuronal substrates of simple associative learning: Classical conditioning. *Trends in Neurosciences 6,* 270–275.

Thompson, R. F., Berger, T. W., & Madden, J. IV. (1983). Cellular processes of learning and memory in the mammalian CNS. *Annual Review of Neuroscience, 6,* 447–491.

Tsukahara, N. (1981). Synaptic plasticity in the mammalian central nervous system. *Annual Review of Neuroscience, 4,* 351–379.

Tsukahara, N. (1985). Synaptic plasticity in the red nucleus and its possible behavioral correlates. In C. W. Cotman, (Ed.), *Synaptic plasticity* (pp. 201–229). New York: Guilford Press.

Vallbona, C. (1982). Bodily responses to immobilization. In F. J. Kottke, G. K. Stillwell & J. F. Lehmann, (Eds.), *Krusen's Handbook of Physical Medicine and Rehabilitation* (3rd ed., pp. 963–976). Philadelphia: W. B. Saunders.

Van Buskirk, C., & Webster, D. (1955). Prognostic value of sensory defect in rehabilitation of hemiplegics. *Neurology* (Minneapolis), *6,* 407–411.

Van Hof, M. W., & Mohn, G. (Eds.). (1981). *Functional recovery from brain damage.* Amsterdam: Elsevier/North-Holland Biomedical Press.

von Monakow, C. (1914). *Die Lokalisation im Grosshirnrinde und der Abbau der Funktion durch korticale Herde.* Wiesbaden: J. F. Bergmann.

Wall, P. D. (1980). Mechanisms of plasticity of connection following damage in adult mammalian nervous systems. In P. Bach-y-Rita (Ed.), *Recovery of function: Theoretical considerations for brain injury rehabilitation* (pp. 91–105). Baltimore: University Park Press.

Watson, M., & McElligott, J. G. (1984). Cerebellar norepinephrine depletion and impaired acquisition of specific locomotor tasks in rats. *Brain Research, 296,* 129–138.

Wolf, S. L. (1979). EMG biofeedback applications in physical rehabilitation: An overview. *Physiotherapy Canada, 31,* 65–72.

Wood, P. H. N., & Badley, E. M. (1978). Setting disablement in perspective. *International Rehabilitation Medicine, 1,* 32–37.

World Health Organization. (1980). *International Classification of Impairments, Disabilities and Handicaps.* Geneva: World Health Organization.

Yeo, C. H., Hardiman, M. J., & Glickstein, M. (1985a). Classical conditioning of the nictitating membrane response of the rabbit. Part 1. Lesions of the cerebellar nuclei. *Experimental Brain Research, 60,* 87–98.

Yeo, C. H., Hardiman, M. J., & Glickstein, M. (1985b). Classical conditioning of the nictitating membrane response of the rabbit. Part 2 Lessions of the cerebellar cortex. *Experimental Brain Research, 60,* 99–113.

10

The Efficacy of Language Therapy for Aphasia

Robert T. Wertz, Ph.D.

Kurtzke (1982), writing in *Neuroepidemiology*, observes that neurologists have two axioms. The first is "Find where the lesion is," and the second is "Be paranoid." Speech-language pathologists who treat aphasic patients have one axiom: "Be paranoid."

The source of the speech-language pathologist's paranoia has been a paucity of acceptable scientific evidence to support the efficacy of language therapy for aphasia. Until recently, research has failed to provide a consistent and unassailable answer. Does language treatment for aphasia do any good? Opinion has varied and so has the quality of the evidence generated by studies designed to provide an answer. The purpose of this chapter is to take stock of what we know about the efficacy of language treatment for aphasia.

This report was supported by the Veterans Administration Cooperative Studies Program, Medical Research Service. I am indebted to the VA Cooperative Study Group (James L. Aten, Robert H. Brookshire, Luis Garcia-Bunuel, Audrey L. Holland, John F. Kurtzke, Leonard L. LaPointe, David G. Weiss, Franklin J. Milianti, Richard Brannegan, Howard Greenbaum, Robert C. Marshall, Deanie Vogel, John Carter, Norman S. Barnes, and Roy Goodman); research associates (Kurt Kitselman, Leslie Deal, Ellen Furbacher, and Linda Burger); treatment therapists (Ellen Minick, Amy Clark, Karen Lambrecht, Janet Brown, and Nancy Debner); Operations Committee (Frederick L. Darley, Thomas Friden, and Allen Rubens); C. James Klett and the staff of the VA Cooperative Studies Program Coordinating Center, Perry Point, Maryland; and Zelda Ballantine and Luci Varian for secretarial support.

DATA: PRO AND CON

Little agreement exists in the literature on whether language therapy for aphasia works. Over 15 years ago, a *Medical World News* article ("Struggling with Aphasia," 1969) quoted a prominent neurologist who observed, "The classic aphasic patient comes in on a stretcher and isn't talking. When he leaves, he is walking but not talking" (p. 40). This was not a glowing testimonial for the efforts of speech-language pathologists who spent their days treating aphasic patients. Three years later, Darley (1972) concluded his review of the literature, which was composed of less than a dozen aphasia treatment studies, by summarizing, "More data are needed applying to clearly specified samples of the aphasic population subjected to clearly specified regimens of therapy by clinicians, for clearly specified periods" (p. 8). Since Darley's review, approximately 10 additional aphasia treatment trials have been conducted. The results of some of these are summarized here.

Hagen (1973) compared treated patients with a self-selected group of untreated patients. He concluded that, "while both groups exhibited spontaneous improvement during the first three months of the program, only the treatment group continued to progress beyond the point of spontaneous recovery to attain functional communication ability" (p. 454). However, a *Lancet* editorial on prognosis in aphasia (Editors, 1977) soon told us that "assessment of the value of therapy is virtually impossible" (p. 24).

Basso, Capitani, and Vignolo (1979) must have missed the *Lancet* conclusion, because the results of their comparison of treated patients with a self-selected no-treatment group led them to observe, "Rehabilitation had a significant positive effect on improvement in all language skills" (p. 190). Benson (1979) appeared convinced, because he ended his editorial that preceded the Basso et al. (1979) report with, "In summary, language therapy has a demonstrated effectiveness in the treatment of aphasia and, as such, occupies a place in the therapeutic armamentarium of the neurologist" (p. 189).

The first Veterans Administration Cooperative Study (Wertz et al., 1981), designed to compare individual with group treatment for aphasia, did not employ a no-treatment group; therefore, the authors could only speculate on the efficacy of their efforts: "If the belief that significant spontaneous recovery is complete by six months postonset is correct, continued significant improvement in our patients treated beyond this point implies that both individual and group treatment are efficacious means for managing aphasia" (p. 593).

An apparent trend toward positive results was checked by Lincoln et al. (1984), who reported the first comparison of randomly assigned treated and untreated patients. They concluded, "Patients in both groups improved and there were no significant differences between the 104 patients allocated to the treatment group and the 87 allocated to the no-treatment group" (p. 1197). But the results of a Canadian effort by Shewan and Kertesz (1984) that compared three types of treatment with a self-selected group receiving no treatment observed, "Comparisons of treated aphasic subjects . . . with untreated aphasic subjects revealed that treatment was a significant factor in the greater recovery observed in the former group" (p. 290).

The most current results on the efficacy of language treatment for aphasia are from the second Veterans Administration Cooperative Study (Wertz et al., 1986), in which aphasic patients were randomly assigned to clinic, home, and deferred treatment. The authors' exit line was, "Treated patients make significantly more improvement than untreated patients" (p. 9).

Does language treatment for aphasia do any good? The answer appears to depend on who you read and when.

COMPLICATIONS IN TREATMENT TRIALS

Three complications thwart aphasia treatment trials. First, spontaneous improvement of language during the early period postonset, believed to result from physiological restitution, must be measured and compared with improvement resulting from the treatment administered. To do so requires random assignment of patients to treatment and no-treatment groups. The second complication, the difficulty in defining an acceptable no-treatment group, usually prevents use of a randomized design, due to ethical considerations about the withholding of treatment. Because treatment exists, the general feeling is that it must be offered. Use of a "self-selected" no-treatment group is not scientifically acceptable, because there are numerous reasons why a patient may refuse treatment, and each may bias results. The third complication is inability to control biographical, medical, and behavioral variables that may influence response to treatment. Age, etiology, severity, type of aphasia, and time postonset are only a few factors that may affect improvement. Few treatment studies have dealt adequately with these three confounding factors.

COMPARISON OF LINCOLN ET AL. (1984) AND WERTZ ET AL. (1986)

The recent efforts by Lincoln et al. (1984) and the second Veterans Administration Cooperative Study (Wertz et al., 1986) are the only investigations that employed random assignment of aphasic patients to treated and untreated groups. Thus, both controlled for the influence of spontaneous recovery by utilizing acceptable no-treatment control groups whose progress could be compared with treated groups. Both also employed selection criteria to control some of the variables that may influence response to treatment. However, the two studies are markedly dissimilar, including their results. Lincoln et al. (1984) found no difference between treated and untreated patients. The VA Cooperative Study (Wertz et al., 1986) found treated patients obtained significantly more improvement than untreated patients. A comparison of the two investigations may indicate whether language treatment is or is not efficacious for improving aphasia.

Design

Lincoln et al. (1984) screened all acute stroke patients who were admitted to the Nottingham Hospitals in England. Those who met selection criteria were evaluated at four weeks postonset with the Porch Index of Communicative Ability (PICA) (Porch, 1967) and given a study patient number. By six weeks postonset, patients had been assigned randomly to treated and untreated groups. Reevaluations with the PICA and the Functional Communication Profile (FCP) (Sarno, 1969) were conducted with patients in both groups at 10, 22, and 34 weeks postonset. Patients in the treatment group were offered two one-hour therapy sessions each week for 24 weeks, between 10 and 34 weeks postonset. Groups were compared at 10 weeks postonset (pretreatment) and at 22 and 34 weeks, during and at the end of the treatment trial. Performance on the PICA and FCP was evaluated with *t* tests for independent data at the beginning of treatment (10 weeks postonset), after 12 weeks of treatment (22 weeks postonset), and after 24 weeks of treatment (34 weeks postonset).

The second Veterans Administration Cooperative Study (Wertz et al., 1986) screened all stroke patients in five VA medical centers. Those who met selection criteria were assigned randomly to one of three treatment groups: (1) clinic treatment by a speech pathologist, 8 to 10 hours a week for 12 weeks, followed by 12 weeks of no treatment; (2) home treatment by a trained volunteer, 8 to 10 hours a week for 12 weeks, followed by 12 weeks of no treatment; or (3) deferred treatment that involved no treatment for 12 weeks, followed by clinic treatment by a speech pathologist 8 to 10 hours a week for 12 weeks. A clinical neurological examination and a battery of behaviorial measures, including the PICA, were administered at entry and at 6, 12, 18, and 24 weeks after entry. PICA performance in each group was compared at each of these points with an analysis of covariance that employed two covariates, severity and time postonset at entry. The necessary sample size was estimated using PICA performance from the first VA Cooperative Study (Wertz et al., 1981), and significant clinical improvement was specified as a 15-percentile change in the overall PICA percentile.

Selection Criteria

Selection criteria for the two studies are listed in Table 10–1, which shows the similarities and differences. Males and females participated in the Lincoln et al. (1984) investigation, while only male veterans participated in the VA cooperative study Wertz et al. (1986). Age was "no bar" to entry for Lincoln, while patients were 75 years of age or younger in the VA study. Lincoln's patients were assessed at 4 weeks postonset, and the treatment trial began at 10 weeks postonset. VA patients varied between 2 and 24 weeks postonset at entry, and the treatment trial began at entry. Time postonset was covaried in the analysis. "Previous stroke or other disability" (p. 1197) did not exclude patients from the Lincoln sample, and localization of the lesion or lesions was not specified. VA patients suffered a single, first, thromboembolic infarct confined to the left hemisphere, and none had a history of previous neurological involvement nor any current major medical or psychological disorder. Lincoln did not specify sensory or motor selection criteria, while Wertz patients had to pass specific auditory, visual, and sensorimotor screening to insure they could hear and see the assessment and treatment stimuli and had sufficient motor and sensory ability in one upper extremity to gesture and write. Premorbid literacy was not a selection criterion for Lincoln, while Wertz required patients to be premorbidly literate in English. Similarly, the amount of language treatment prior to entering the study or beginning treatment was not specified by Lincoln,

TABLE 10-1 Selection Criteria for Study Patients

Criterion	Lincoln et al. (1984)	VA cooperative study—Wertz et al. (1986)
Sex	Male and female	Male
Age	Not specified	75 years or younger
Time postonset	4 weeks at entry	2 to 24 weeks at entry
Etiology	"Acute stroke"	First, single, thromboembolic infarct
Localization	Not specified	Confined to the left hemisphere
Neurological history	Not specified	No previous neurological involvement
Medical and psychological status	Patients unable "to cope with testing on the language assessment"	No major coexisting medical or psychological disorder
Sensory/motor		
Auditory	Not specified	Hearing no worse than a 40 dB speech reception threshold, unaided, in the better ear
Vision	Not specified	Vision no worse than 20/100, corrected, in the better eye
Sensorimotor	Not specified	Sensory and motor ability in one upper extremity sufficient to gesture and write
Literacy	Not specified	Premorbid ability to read and write English
Prior language treatment	Not specified	No more than two weeks of language treatment between onset and entry
Language severity	Patients who failed more than one item on every part of the Whurr (1974) aphasia screening test or more than two items on any part of sections A1–A4 were excluded as too severe. Patients who scored 4 or 5 on 8 of 10 sections of the Whurr aphasia screening test were excluded as too mild. Patients who were severely dysarthric on the Frenchay (Enderby, 1983) dysarthria assessment	PICA performance from the 10th through 85th overall percentile at entry
Living environment	Not specified	Living in a noninstitutionalized environment at entry
Informed consent	Not specified	Patient and patient's representative agree to participate in the study

while VA patients were excluded if they had received more than two weeks of language treatment prior to entry.

Both investigations employed selection criteria to limit the range of language severity. Lincoln et al. (1984) excluded patients who were too mild or too severe on the Whurr (1974) aphasia screening test, and they excluded severely dysarthric patients. VA patients (Wertz et al., 1986) were excluded if they performed below the 10th overall percentile on the PICA or above the eighty-fifth percentile at entry. Limiting brain damage to the left hemisphere excluded severely dysarthric patients. Only 10 patients were dysarthric, and none was rated above "3" on a 7-point scale in a motor speech evaluation (Wertz, LaPointe, & Rosenbek, 1984).

Lincoln et al.'s (1984) sample apparently included both inpatients and outpatients and some who changed their living environment during the treatment trial. All VA patients (Wertz et al., 1986) were outpatients in order to be eligible for random assignment to the home treatment group. Lincoln did not specify whether patients were required to provide informed consent, while all VA patients and each patient's representative were required to give informed consent prior to entering the study.

Lincoln et al.'s (1984) screening identified 333 patients who met selection criteria at 4 weeks postonset. At 6 weeks postonset, 4 of these patients had died and 2 had "recovered." Of the remaining patients 163 were assigned to the treatment group, and 164 were assigned to the no-treatment group. By the time treatment began at 10 weeks postonset, 59 patients in the treatment group and 77 patients in the no-treatment group had died, "recovered," were "unfit," lived too far away to receive treatment and follow-up, refused to participate, were too ill to participate, or were "excluded." Thus, Lincoln et al. began the treatment trial with 104 treatment patients and 87 no-treatment patients.

During a four-year period, 1,816 patients were screened in the five medical centers participating in the VA Cooperative Study (Wertz et al., 1986). Of these 121 met all criteria and were entered into the study. Ineligible patients separated into 904 who were rejected for failing to meet a single criterion and 791 who were rejected for failing to meet multiple criteria. Time postonset, previous neurological involvement, language severity, localization, etiology, and age were the most frequent reasons for rejection. Of the 121 patients who met selection criteria, 38 were assigned randomly to the clinic treatment group, 43 to the home treatment group, and 40 to the deferred treatment group.

Treatment

Lincoln et al.'s (1984) treatment patients were offered two one-hour therapy sessions each week for 24 weeks in the hospital for inpatients or at home after discharge. Type of treatment was not specified. Therapists "organized their own form of treatment as they would have normally done in their general clinics, and they were asked to monitor the effectiveness of their treatment where possible" (p. 1198). Even though 2 hours of treatment each week for 24 weeks were prescribed, few "treated" patients received the full 48 hours of treatment. Table 10–2 shows the amount of treatment received in the treatment group. Only 27 of the 104 patients received 37 to 48 hours of treatment. Reasons for patients not receiving the prescribed treatment sessions were that 38 refused treatment, 5 were ill, 16 "recovered," 5 were "unsuitable," 10 died, and 3 moved away.

Patients in the VA cooperative study (Wertz et al., 1986) received 8 to 10 hours of treatment each week during their 12 weeks of treatment. All patients in the clinic-treatment and deferred-treatment groups received treatment in their VA medical center speech pathology clinics. All patients in the home-treatment group received treatment in their homes. Patients who did not receive the prescribed number of treatment hours each week were dropped from the study. A treatment therapist was employed in each medical center to administer treatment to the clinic and deferred groups. Another therapist trained the home therapist volunteers and developed the treatment programs the volunteers administered to home group patients. Treatment for all patients in all groups was individual, usually stimulus-response treatment designed to improve language deficits in auditory comprehension, reading, oral-expressive language, and writing. General treatment principles were specified in the study protocol; however, specific techniques were selected to meet each

TABLE 10-2 Amount of Treatment Received by Patients in Lincoln et al.'s (1984) "Treatment" Group

Number of hours	Number of Patients ($N = 104$)	Percent of Treatment Group
0–12	39	37.5
13–24	16	15.4
25–36	22	21.2
37–48	27	25.9

patient's deficits. These ranged from traditional facilitation methods such as picture identification, verbal repetition, sentence completion, and confrontation naming, to specific programs such as Melodic Intonation Therapy (MIT) (Sparks, 1981). Treatment therapists completed a treatment log specifying the number of hours of treatment administered and a treatment summary listing the specific treatment tasks employed each week during a patient's 12 weeks of treatment. Every 2 weeks during the 12-week treatment period all therapists, speech pathologists, and home therapist volunteers were videotaped in a half-hour therapy session. These sessions were analyzed with the Clinical Interaction Analysis System (CIAS) (Brookshire, 1976) to insure treatment in the three groups was equivalent.

Subjects

Lincoln et al.'s (1984) patients were assigned randomly at 6 weeks postonset; 163 to treatment and 164 to no treatment. Table 10–3 shows the sample size at each evaluation date. By the time the treatment trial began at 10 weeks postonset, 59 patients in the treatment group and 77 patients in the no-treatment group had dropped out or were excluded. At 22 weeks postonset, an additional 18 treatment patients and 12 no-treatment patients were lost. And, at 34 weeks postonset, when the treatment trial ended, 6 more treatment and 4 no-treatment patients had dropped out. However, between 22 and 34 weeks, 7 treatment patients and 3 no-treatment patients had "returned." Thus, 176 of the 327 patients randomized, 54%, had dropped out at some time during the treatment trial. The most

TABLE 10-3 Sample Size in Lincoln et al.'s (1984) Treatment and No-treatment Groups

Evaluation	Number of subjects[a]			Dropouts			"Returned"		
	T[b]	NT	Total	T	NT	Total	T	NT	Total
6 weeks	163	164	327	—	—	—	—	—	—
10 weeks	104	87	191	59	77	136	—	—	—
22 weeks	86	75	161	18	12	30	—	—	—
34 weeks	87	74	161	6	4	10	7	3	10
Total	—	—	—	83	93	176	7	3	10

[a]Number remaining, minus dropouts, plus "returnees."
[b]T = treatment; NT = no-treatment.

common reasons for dropping out or exclusion were death ($N = 67$), "unfit" ($N = 48$), refused participation ($N = 20$), and recovered ($N = 17$). Living too far away to participate, illness, and "excluded" accounted for the other patients lost to follow-up. There was no apparent group influence on dropouts or exclusions.

At 10 weeks postonset, Lincoln et al. (1984) found no significant differences ($p < .05$) between treatment and no-treatment groups in age, distribution of sex, or language severity on the PICA. Mean age of the combined groups was 68.2 years, with a range from 38 to 92 years. Mean PICA performance was reported in a graph and would correspond to approximately the 35th overall percentile using unilateral left-hemisphere norms or the 50th overall percentile using bilateral norms. Mean years of education was not reported for either group.

The VA Cooperative Study (Wertz et al., 1986) sample size in each of the three groups studied is shown in Table 10–4. At entry, the 121 patients who met selection criteria were assigned randomly to the clinic-treatment group. Twenty-seven of the 121 randomly assigned patients (23%) dropped out. The most common reasons for dropping out or exclusion were illness that prevented receiving the required number of treatment hours ($N = 7$); voluntary withdrawal because of improvement, travel distance to receive treatment, or tiring of treatment ($N = 7$); suffering a second stroke ($N = 5$); and failing to keep treatment or evaluation appointments ($N = 2$). Two patients moved to another state, 1 died, 1 changed his living environment to a nursing home, and 1 was eliminated because he had received more than two weeks of treatment prior to entering the study. Group assign-

TABLE 10-4 Sample Size in the VA Cooperative Study's Clinic, Home, and Deferred Treatment Groups

Evaluation	Number of subjects[a]				Dropouts			
	C	H	D	Total	C	H	D	Total
Entry	38	43	40	121	—	—	—	—
6 weeks	32	39	39	110	6	4	1	11
12 weeks	31	37	35	103	1	2	4	7
18 weeks	30	36	32	98	1	1	3	5
24 weeks	29	36	29	94	1	0	3	4
Total	—	—	—	—	9	7	11	27

[a]Number remaining, minus dropouts.

ment had no influence on dropouts or exclusions. Further, there were no significant differences ($p < .05$) between patients completing the study and patients dropping out on any pretreatment biographical, medical, or behavioral variables.

Descriptive data for VA Cooperative Study patients at entry are shown in Table 10–5. There were no significant differences ($p < .05$) among groups regarding age, education, weeks postonset, or language severity on the PICA at entry. Mean age ranged from 57.2 to 60.2 years. Each group showed a mean of about 11 years of education. Weeks postonset ranged from 6.6 to 7.8. PICA overall performance ranged from about the 46th to the 50th percentile.

Results

Lincoln et al. (1984) compared performance between their treatment and no-treatment groups at 10, 22, and 34 weeks postonset with t tests for independent data. They found no significant differences between groups on the PICA or the Functional Communication Profile (FCP) (Sarno, 1969) in any comparison. Their results were presented graphically and indicated that, using left-hemisphere norms, both groups improved from approximately the 35th PICA overall percentile at 10 weeks postonset to approximately the 45th percentile at 34 weeks postonset. Using bilateral norms, the improvement was from the 50th to the 65th percentile. Because many "treated" patients did not receive the prescribed 48 hours of treatment, Lincoln et al. selected the 47 patients who received at least 24 hours of treatment and matched them with 47 no-treatment patients who were similar in age, sex, and 10-week postonset PICA performance.

TABLE 10-5 Descriptive Data for the VA Cooperative Study's Clinic, Home, and Deferred Treatment Groups at Entry

Variable	Clinic group		Home group		Deferred group	
	Mean	S.D.*	Mean	S.D.	Mean	S.D.
Age in years	59.2	6.7	60.2	6.7	57.2	6.6
Education in years	11.1	3.1	11.8	2.5	10.9	2.8
Weeks postonset	6.6	4.8	7.1	5.8	7.8	6.6
PICA overall percentile	46.59	16.05	49.97	22.77	49.18	19.46

*Standard deviation.

This comparison indicated that both groups improved from approximately the 55th PICA overall percentile at 10 weeks postonset to approximately the 65th percentile at 34 weeks postonset, using bilateral norms. When left-hemisphere norms were applied, the treated patients improved from approximately the 39th percentile to the 49th percentile, and the untreated patients improved from approximately the 37th percentile to the 45th percentile. Results of both comparisons indicated no significant differences ($p < .05$) between groups on any measure at 10, 22, or 34 weeks postonset. Lincoln et al. concluded that their treatment regimen was "ineffective for most aphasic stroke patients" (p. 1197). They did not report whether either group in either comparison displayed significant improvement between 10 and 34 weeks postonset.

The purpose in the VA Cooperative Study (Wertz et al., 1986) was threefold. First, in order to determine the efficacy of treatment, performance by clinic-treatment patients was compared with performance by deferred-treatment patients at 12 weeks after entry. Because deferred patients had not been treated during the first 12 weeks of the treatment trial, they provided a randomly assigned no-treatment group for comparison with clinic patients who were treated during the first 12 weeks. Second, in order to determine the efficacy of home treatment, performance by home patients was compared with that of clinic and deferred patients at 12 weeks after entry. Home patients were treated by trained volunteers during the first 12 weeks. Third, in order to evaluate the effects of delaying treatment, performance by deferred patients was compared with performance by clinic and home patients at 24 weeks after entry. Deferred patients were treated by speech pathologists from the 12th through 24th weeks, and clinic and home patients received no treatment during this period.

Comparisons were made on the primary outcome measure, the PICA, with an analysis of covariance in which two covariates were employed, namely, performance at entry and time postonset at entry. Multiple comparisons (Bonferroni method) were made following significant group tests and used an adjusted significance level to provide an overall probability of Type I error of .05.

Table 10–6 shows data that provide answers to the first two questions. These results are based on the 31 clinic, 37 home, and 35 deferred patients who completed 12 weeks of the treatment trial. All groups displayed significant improvement ($p < .05$) between entry and 12 weeks. Clinic patients, treated by speech pathologists, made significantly more improvement ($p < .05$) than deferred patients, not treated. Improvement in home patients, treated by trained volunteers, did not differ significantly ($p < .05$) from that in either the clinic or deferred groups. At 12 weeks after entry, treated patients (clinic and home groups) had achieved the specified 15-point, clinically significant improvement on the PICA percentile. Untreated patients (deferred group) had not improved. Thus, language therapy provided by speech pathologists was efficacious, as treated clinic patients displayed significantly more improvement than untreated deferred patients. The efficacy of home treatment by a trained volunteer is ambiguous.

Table 10–7 shows improvement in all groups at 24 weeks after entry. These results are based on the 29 clinic, 36 home, and 27 deferred patients who completed the 24-week treatment trial. After deferred patients had received treatment by a speech pathologist, between the 12th and 24th weeks, they caught up with clinic and

TABLE 10-6 VA Cooperative Study Comparisons between Clinic (C), Home (H), and Deferred (D) Treatment Groups at 12 Weeks after Entry

PICA percentile	% Improvement at 12 weeks			Difference		
	C	H	D	C–H	C–D	H–D
Overall	37	34	25	+3	+12*	+ 9
Gestural	37	29	27	+8	+10	+ 2
Verbal	32	30	23	+2	+ 9	+ 7
Graphic	29	28	18	+1	+11	+10

*Significant differences based on pairwise multiple comparisons at overall significance level of .05.

TABLE 10-7 VA Cooperative Study Comparisons between Clinic (C), Home (H), and Deferred (D) Treatment Groups at 24 Weeks after Entry

PICA percentile	% Improvement at 24 weeks			Differences		
	C	H	D	C–H	C–D	H–D
Overall	43	37	40	+6	+3	− 3
Gestural	44	36	48	+8	−4	−12
Verbal	39	35	36	+4	+3	− 1
Graphic	36	29	31	+7	+5	− 2

home patients who had received treatment earlier, between entry and 12 weeks. There were no significant differences among groups at 24 weeks. The significant improvement ($p < .05$) displayed between 12 and 24 weeks by deferred patients indicates an additional treatment effect. At 24 weeks, the deferred group had achieved the specified 15-point, clinically significant improvement on the PICA percentile. Thus, the answer to the third question is that delaying treatment for 12 weeks during the first six months postonset had no irrevocable influence on the amount of improvement obtained.

Comparison

The VA Cooperative Study (Wertz et al., 1986) results indicate language therapy for aphasia is efficacious. Lincoln et al.'s (1984) results indicate it is not. These studies were the first to employ random assignment of patients to treated and untreated groups, but, aside from that, they are markedly dissimilar.

Lincoln et al. (1984) employed minimal selection criteria. Patients who had suffered "previous stroke or other disability" were included in the sample, and no selection criteria were used to control localization, etiology beyond "stroke," sensory acuity, literacy, age, medical complications, or other variables believed to influence response to treatment. One wonders how many of Lincoln et al.'s patients suffered left-hemisphere, right-hemisphere, or bilateral infarcts. How many had cerebral hemorrhage? How many were indeed aphasic and how many displayed the language impairment seen in multi-infarct dementia? Poor performance on a test of aphasia does not assure a patient is aphasic (Wertz, 1982); in the absence of additional selection criteria, it is insufficient for including a patient in an aphasia treatment trial. The high incidence of death and "illness" in both their treated and untreated groups and the subsequent discovery of a number of "tumors" also testify to the inadequacy of the selection criteria employed for a study of "aphasic stroke patients."

Lincoln et al's. (1984) patients entered their study at 4 weeks postonset and were randomly assigned to treatment and no-treatment groups at 6 weeks postonset, but treatment was delayed until 10 weeks postonset, because, the authors state, "considerable spontaneous recovery takes place in the early weeks" (p. 1199). This is baffling. First, it is assumed that one uses a random assignment of patients to treated and untreated groups to control for the influence of spontaneous recovery. Second, if treatment is delayed until 10 weeks postonset, that should be the point of random assignment to treated and untreated groups.

Next, the amount of treatment prescribed was 2 hours a week for 24 weeks, due to the authors' claim that "this treatment regimen . . . is representative of clinical practice" (p. 1197). Contrasted with a minimum of 3 hours a week for 6 months in the Basso et al. (1979) study, 6 to 8 hours a week for 44 weeks in the first VA Cooperative Study (Wertz et al., 1981), 8 to 10 hours a week for 12 weeks in the second VA Cooperative Study (Wertz et al., 1986), and what appears to occur in most clinics in the United States, what is "typical" in Nottingham may be considered "token" elsewhere.

Finally, comparison of treated and untreated groups implies that one of the two groups received treatment. Examination of Lincoln et al's. (1984) data, however, indicates 38% of the "treated" patients received less than 13 hours of treatment, and only 25% received even close to the prescribed 2 hours of treatment each week for 24 weeks. Usually, in a controlled study, patients who violate the protocol are dropped. In this study, at least 75% of the patients in the treated group failed to receive the planned amount of treatment and should have been considered dropouts. Unfortunately, Lincoln et al. included them in the analyses.

There is only one conclusion one can draw from the Lincoln et al. (1984) aphasia treatment study; when one does not treat patients who may or may not be aphasic, those patients do not improve.

The design used in the VA Cooperative Study (Wertz et al., 1986) employed rigid selection criteria. Age, time postonset, etiology, localization, medical history and present medical status, sensory acuity, motor ability, literacy, prior treatment, language severity, and social milieu were specified. All patients were aphasic subsequent to a first, single, left-hemisphere thromboembolic infarct. Eight to 10 hours of treatment were administered each week for 12 weeks. Patients who did not receive the prescribed treatment were dropped from the study. Treatment was specified in the study protocol, it was monitored weekly by treatment logs and summaries, and it was evaluated every 2 weeks through analysis of videotaped treatment sessions. Patients were assigned randomly to groups, and the groups did not differ significantly at entry in age, education, time postonset, or language severity. All patients received neurological and language evaluations at entry and at 6, 12, 18, and 24 weeks after entry. Any patient who violated the selection criteria after entry (for example, suffered a second CVA) was dropped from the study. I take time to emphasize the rigor of the design, because how one obtains results is as important as the results obtained.

So, given the care used in collecting the data, what can they tell us? First, they provide empirical evidence that treated patients make significantly more improvement than untreated patients. Clinic patients, treated during the first 12 weeks by speech pathologists, made significantly more improvement than deferred patients, not treated during the first 12 weeks. Is language therapy for aphasia efficacious? Yes. What speech pathologists do for aphasic patients does some good. Therapy works.

Second, delaying treatment for 12 weeks during the first six months postonset had no irrevocable effect on ultimate improvement. After being treated by speech pathologists, deferred patients caught up with clinic patients who were treated earlier. This runs contrary to previous reports (Basso et al., 1979; Deal & Deal, 1978; Wertz, 1983) that indicate early intervention results in more improvement than later intervention. Comparison of the VA Cooperative Study (Wertz et al., 1986) results to these previous reports is difficult. Early intervention is advocated on the basis of studies that did not use random assignment to treatment groups or rigid selection criteria. Further, the length of the treatment trials differs markedly. The treatment period in the VA study was relatively short—12 weeks—and treatment was deferred for only 12 weeks. We do not know what would have happened if patients had been treated longer or deferred longer. We do know that, when the deferred group was treated, they improved as much as patients treated earlier.

Third, the efficacy of home treatment was enigmatic. Home patients did not differ significantly from clinic patients treated by speech pathologists, nor did they differ significantly from deferred, untreated patients. But, when considering group and time in treatment, home-treated patients improved more than untreated patients. The home-treatment group achieved the specified 15-point, clinically significant change in their overall PICA percentile, and the untreated patients did not. So, given a choice of home treatment or no treatment, one might lean toward home treatment.

More important, the results should not be interpreted to indicate nonprofessionals can replace speech pathologists. Considerable time and energy was invested in training the home therapists. They were told what to do, given the treatment programs to administer, and their performance was monitored rigorously. Perhaps these results suggest an additional role for speech pathologists. For patients who reside beyond our treatment's reach, one might consider training a family member or friend to provide what geographic limitations prevent speech pathologists from providing. This would require constant monitoring of home therapist and patient progress.

CONCLUSION

The fact that language treatment for aphasia works need not remain arcane. There is empirical evidence to support this belief. The questions that have plagued speech pathologists have been political and scientific. They have been asked for proof resulting from a design that withstands scrutiny. An answer to the scientific question should provide an answer to the political question. The VA Cooperative Study (Wertz et al., 1986) results provide the scientific answer. Treatment for aphasia is efficacious. The political answer will come from how well the results convince those in doubt.

Clinical researchers need not fear that all of the questions have been answered. Now that we know that what speech pathologists do for aphasic patients does some good, we need to ask how we can improve what is done by inquiring how much and what kind of treatment works best for which aphasic patients, under what circumstances. For example, Wertz et al. (1986) demonstrated that treatment is effective for aphasic patients who suffer a single, left-hemisphere thromboembolic infarct and who receive 8 to 10 hours of treatment each week by a speech pathologist for 12 weeks during the first 6 months postonset. Lincoln et al. (1984) demonstrated that 0 to 48 hours of treatment was not effective for patients who may or may not have been aphasic subsequent to one or more strokes. Is treatment efficacious for patients who suffer multiple CVA's when it is offered in more abundant and controlled doses? How intense and how long does the treatment period need to be? We do not know.

REFERENCES

Basso, A., Capitani, E., & Vignolo, L. A. (1979). Influence of rehabilitation on language skills in aphasic patients. A controlled study. *Archives of Neurology, 36*(4), 190–196.

Benson, D. F. (1979). Aphasia rehabilitation. (Editorial). *Archives of Neurology, 36*(4), 187–189.

Brookshire, R. H. (1976). A system for coding and recording events in patient-clinician interaction during aphasia treatment sessions. In R. H. Brookshire (Ed.), *Clinical aphasiology: Conference proceedings, 1976* (pp. 224–236). Minneapolis: BRK Publishers.

Darley, F. L. (1972). The efficacy of language rehabilitation in aphasia. *Journal of Speech and Hearing Disorders, 37,* 3–21.

Deal, J. L., & Deal, L. A. (1978). Efficacy of aphasia rehabilitation: Preliminary results. In R. H. Brookshire (Ed.), *Clinical aphasiology conference proceedings, 1978* (pp. 66–77). Minneapolis: BRK Publishers.

Editors. (1977). Prognosis in aphasia *Lancet, 2,* 24

Enderby, R. M. (1983). *Frenchay dysarthria assessment.* San Diego: College-Hill Press.

Hagen, C. (1973). Communication abilities in hemiplegia: Effect of speech therapy. *Archives of Physical Medicine and Rehabilitation, 54,* 454–463.

Kurtzke, J. F. (1982). On the role of clinicians in the use of drug trial data. *Neuroepidemiology, 1,* 124–136.

Lincoln, N. B., McGuirk, E., Mulley, G. P., Lendrem, W., Jones, A. C., & Mitchell, J. R. A. (1984). Effectiveness of speech therapy for aphasic stroke patients: A randomised controlled trial. *Lancet, 1,* 1197–1200.

Porch, B. E. (1967). *Porch Index of Communicative Ability.* Palo Alto: Consulting Psychologists Press.

Sarno, M. T. (1969). *The Functional Communication Profile manual of directions.* New York: Institute of Rehabilitation Medicine, New York University Medical Center.

Shewan, C. M., & Kertesz, A. (1984). Effects of speech and language treatment on recovery from aphasia. *Brain and Language, 23,* 272–299.

Sparks, R. W. (1981). Melodic intonation therapy. In R. Chapey (Ed.), *Language intervention strategies in adult aphasia* (pp. 265–282). Baltimore: Williams and Wilkins.

Struggling with aphasia. (1969). *Medical World News, 10,* 37–40.

Wertz, R. T. (1982). Language deficit in aphasia and dementia: The same as, different from, or both. In R. H. Brookshire & L. E. Nicholas (Eds.), *Clinical aphasiology conference proceedings, 1982,* (pp. 350–359). Minneapolis: BRK Publishers.

Wertz, R. T. (1983). Language intervention context and setting for the aphasic adult: When? In J. Miller, D. E. Yoder, & R. Schiefelbusch (Eds.), *Contemporary issues in language intervention* (pp. 196–220). (ASHA Reports No. 12). Rockville, MD: American Speech-Language-Hearing Association.

Wertz, R. T., Collins, M. J., Weiss, D., Kurtzke, J. F., Friden, T., Brookshire, R. H., Pierce, J., Holtzapple, P., Hubbard, D. J., Porch, B. E., West, J. A., Davis, L., Matovitch, V., Morley, G. K., & Resurrection, E. (1981). Veterans Administration cooperative study on aphasia: A comparison of individual and group treatment. *Journal of Speech and Hearing Research, 24,* 580–594.

Wertz, R. T., LaPointe, L. L., & Rosenbek, J. C. (1984). *Apraxia of speech in adults: The disorder and its management.* Orlando, FL: Grune & Stratton.

Wertz, R. T., Weiss, D. G., Aten, J. L., Brookshire, R. H., Garcia-Bunuel, L., Holland, A. L., Kurtzke, J. F., LaPointe, L. L., Milianti, F. J., Brannegan, R., Greenbaum, H., Marshall, R. C., Vogel, D., Carter, J., Barnes, N. S., & Goodman, R. (1986). Comparison of clinic, home, and deferred language treatment for aphasia: A Veterans Administration cooperative study. *Archives of Neurology, 43,* 653–658.

Whurr, R. (1974). *Aphasia screening test.* Unpublished manuscript. Obtainable from author at 2 Alwyne Road, London N1, 2HH, England.

11

Depression and Stroke

Thomas R. Price, M.D.

Depression after stroke is common. It can begin within the first few days following a stroke or in the ensuing months, and often persists for many months. The likelihood of its occurring depends on the part of the brain affected by the stroke and the amount of deficit. Although the depression that follows a stroke is frequently severe, it is treatable.

It has been recognized for many years that depression can occur following stroke. Post (1962) reported that many episodes of depression in elderly patients followed a stroke. However, until the last few years no systematic study of depression following stroke had been reported. In 1978, Dr. Robert Robinson, a psychiatrist from Johns Hopkins University Hospital, and I began a study of the problem. Since that time, four additional psychiatrists, three psychologists, two social workers, a psychiatric interviewer, two nurses, and a radiologist have participated in these studies, making it truly an interdisciplinary project. We have been aided by the in-depth studies of the stroke patients carried out for the NINCDS Stroke Data Bank.

Our first study (Robinson & Price, 1982) was of 103 outpatients seen in the Stroke Clinic at the University of Maryland in Baltimore. When this study was started in 1978, we had been operating a long-term follow-up clinic for stroke patients for 12 years. The clinic continues in operation today, and we have many patients who have been coming to the clinic for 10 to 15 years. This affords us a unique opportunity to study problems usually not considered in most outpatient settings.

In the study, each patient was given the General Health Question-naire (Goldberg & Hiller, 1979). The 30 patients scoring five or more on the questionnaire had in-depth interviews for depression, which subsequently confirmed the diagnosis of depression. Patients be-tween 6 months to 2 years post-stroke had the greatest likelihood of being depressed. Fifteen of 33 such patients (45%) were depressed, a statistically significant difference from the other time periods post-stroke. These patients were then followed to establish how long the depression lasted. No attempt was made to bring the patients back early or to treat them. Patients seen after 5 to 8 weeks were very likely still to be depressed, and of those seen after 6 months, about 65% were still depressed. After 9 months, most had recovered, and the five patients seen after 1 year had all recovered. This recovery time, of course, has to represent the minimal duration of depression, since the patients were not necessarily identified at the beginning of the de-pression. This study gave a cross-sectional view of depression and confirmed depression was common and tended to last many months in the untreated state.

We then studied patients prospectively just after a stroke (Robin-son, Starr, Kubos, & Price, 1983). We were able to see 128 ischemic infarct patients and 36 with intracerebral hemorrhage. Fifty-three of these patients had a decreased level of consciousness or were so severely aphasic that we did not feel they could be interviewed. One patient refused permission for the study, and seven were so mildly ill that they were discharged before the interview could be done. There were, therefore, 103 patients interviewed. This was an entirely differ-ent group; that is, none of this group of 103 patients had been in the first study (see Table 11-1). The interviews were done an average of eleven days post-stroke. Each of the 103 patients included received the Zung Depression Scale (Zung, 1965), the Hamilton Depression Scale (Hamilton, 1960), and a modified Present State Examination (Robinson, Starr, Kubos, & Price, 1983; Wing, Cooper, & Sortorius, 1974). A psychiatric diagnosis was obtained using the Present State Examination and *DSM III* (APA, 1980) criteria. An overall depression scale was made by combining the results of the three tests.

We also used the Mini-Mental State Examination (Folstein, Fol-stein, & McHugh, 1975) to evaluate cognitive processes. To look at other factors relating to the possible etiology of depression, we ad-ministered a Social Functioning Examination and a Social Ties Checklist (Starr, Robinson, & Price, 1983) especially developed for stroke patient studies. We wanted to test the hypothesis that social factors might have something to do with whether or not patients got depressed. To evaluate the patient's physical abilities, we ad-

TABLE 11-1 Patients Eligible and not Included in the Second Study

Patients with ischemic infarction	128
Patients with intracerebral hemorrhage	36
	164
Not included because of decreased level of consciousness or severe aphasia	53
Refused permission	1
Discharged before interview	7
	61
Interviewed and in the study	103

ministered the Johns Hopkins Functional Inventory and a Barthel Scale (Mahoney & Barthel, 1965) as well.

We found that 27% of the patients interviewed just after a stroke had a major depression, 20% a minor depression or dysthymia, and 53% had no psychiatric diagnosis. Nine of the patients were "unduly cheerful": unconcerned or less concerned about their stroke than one would expect. This term is not completely accurate, in that these people are not particularly jolly but are often very apathetic and may be difficult to motivate for physical therapy. Most of these "unduly cheerful" patients had right frontal lesions.

In the next phase of the study, we followed these patients. Of 60 patients reevaluated at 3 or 6 months, a total of 60% were depressed (Robinson, Starr, & Price, 1984). Thus, this study again showed that depression is common after a stroke, that it is often severe, and that it can come on months after a stroke as well as in the acute period.

A select group of these patients was studied to examine the relationship between depression and lesion location (Robinson, Kubos, Starr, Rao, & Price, 1984). Patients who were right-handed, had a single lesion of the hemisphere on CT scan, and who had not been previously depressed or who had no chemical dependence were included. We found that the incidence of depression was significantly increased in those with left-anterior brain lesions, and the severity of depression increased the closer the lesion was to the frontal pole in the left-anterior-hemisphere group. Among the 10 patients with left-anterior lesions, 6 had major depression and 1 had minor depression. One of 8 with a left-posterior lesion had major depression, and 3 had minor. In the 12 patients with single right-hemisphere lesions, only 1 had major depression and 1 minor depression, but 6 had undue cheerfulness or apathy.

In a separate study (Robinson et al., 1985), we looked at patients who were left-handed to see if this association of depression with the left hemisphere is related to the fact that the left hemisphere is usually dominant for speech. Among the 33 patients left-handed, the same correlations between anterior left-hemisphere stroke location and depression were found. In patients with bilateral strokes (Lipsey, Robinson, Pearlson, Rao, & Price, 1984), the major determinant of whether the patient was depressed was the location of the left hemisphere lesion. Even if the last stroke were on the right side, the location of the previous left-hemisphere stroke was the best predictor of depression.

Other determinants such as social functioning and cognitive and physical impairment are less important. Social functioning is difficult to study because of uncertainty about whether impaired functioning is a cause or an effect of depression. There is a similar problem with cognitive impairment. In "pseudodementia," elderly depressed patients appear demented, but, when the depression improves, the thinking improves as well. We found that patients with depression failed to show the expected improvement in Mini-Mental State scores shown in nondepressed patients over time, implying that some of the continuing deficit is due to the depression.

It seemed reasonable to begin a treatment trial at this point. Previous anecdotal reports suggested that tricyclic antidepressants, stimulant medications, and group therapy techniques might be effective in treatment. In a study reported in *Lancet* (Lipsey et al., 1984), we had 34 patients complete a double-blind controlled trial of nortriptyline, a tricyclic antidepressant. Half of the patients had major depression. During the first two weeks of treatment, both groups showed some improvement in their overall depression scores. This has occurred in other treatment trials of depression and seems to be a response to being the focus of interest and to being interviewed. However, over the remainder of this six-week trial, patients treated with a single daily oral dose of nortriptyline (from 20 to 100 mgm at hour of sleep) improved significantly compared to patients taking placebo, who failed to show further improvement. After four and six weeks of treatment, those treated with nortriptyline had serum drug levels between 50 and 140 μg/ml, the therapeutic range for functional depression. Three patients on active medication developed drowsiness, confusion, or agitation, but these symptoms cleared a few days after stopping treatment.

Because depression after stroke is common, often severe, and responds to drug treatment, it is important that patients suffering depression be identified. Many stroke patients have multiple physical problems that demand attention, and they often do not spontaneously complain of feeling depressed. Many stroke patients have concomitant diabetes, cardiac disease, arthritis, or other medical problems in addition to the neurological deficits from their strokes. It is understandable that neither physicians nor patients have recognized the magnitude of the problem, in the absence of specific studies designed to illuminate it. One method for identifying depression in stroke patients might be the Dexamethasone Suppression Test, as has been advocated for other patients with depression. We have studied this test in stroke patients (Lipsey, Robinson, Pearlson, Rao, & Price, 1985) and find that stroke patients with major depression are very likely to fail to suppress cortisol secretion following dexamethasone administration (10 of 15 did not). However, specificity of the test was only 70%, mainly because patients with large lesions had positive tests even when they were not depressed. Therefore, the test is not accurate enough for general clinical use.

Clearly, the best way to find depression is to ask the patient about it. In addition, one should ask about vegetative symptoms, such as weight loss and decreased appetite, delayed sleep onset and early morning awakening, and loss of energy and libido. Other symptoms include diurnal mood variation, anxiety, irritability, hopelessness and self-deprecation, social withdrawal, difficulty concentrating and inefficient thinking, and suicidal thoughts. Since clinicians vary in their interest in and ability to diagnose depression, it is mandatory that some form of rating scale be used to identify patients likely to be depressed.

Recently we have validated the Center for Epidemiological Studies—Depression (CES–D) scale for depression (Shinar et al., 1986) in stroke patients, which was administered by the nurse at the University of Maryland hospital and compared to the diagnosis based on the Present State Examination test. The CES–D is a 20-question scale used in population studies for identifying depressed patients. Scores of 16 or above are usually thought to be indicative of depression. Using this score as a cutoff, the test picked up 73% of the depressed patients diagnosed by the Present State test, and no patient with a score over 16 was not depressed. Because of its high interrater reliability, this test may be particularly helpful in screening patients for post-stroke depression.

Although further work needs to be done on the problem of depression after stroke, we now know that depression is common, often severe and long lasting, and treatable. We have suggested which patients are most likely to be depressed and offered ways of identifying them.

REFERENCES

American Psychiatric Association. (1980). Diagnostic and statistical manual of mental disorders (3rd ed.). Washington, DC: Author.

Folstein, M. F., Folstein, S. E., & McHugh, P. R. (1975). "Mini-mental state." A practical method for grading the cognitive state of patients for the clinician. *Journal of Psychiatry Research, 12,* 189.

Goldberg, D. P., & Hiller, V. F. (1979). A scaled version of the General Health Questionnaire. *Psychological Medicine, 9,* 139–145.

Hamilton, M. A. (1960). A rating scale for depression. *Journal of Neurology, Neurosurgery and Psychiatry, 23,* 56–62.

Lipsey, J. R., Robinson, R. G., Pearlson, G. D., Rao, K., & Price, T. R. (1984). Nortriptyline treatment of post-stroke depression: A double-blind study. *Lancet, 1,* 297–300.

Lipsey, J. R., Robinson, R. G., Pearlson, G. D., Rao, K., & Price, T. R. (1985). The dexamethasone suppression test and mood following stroke. *American Journal of Psychiatry, 142,* 318–323.

Mahoney, F. I., & Barthel, D. W. (1965). Functional evaluation: Barthel Index. *Maryland State Medical Journal, 14,* 61–65.

Post, F. (1962). *The significance of affective symptoms in old age.* (Maudsley Monograph No. 10). London: Oxford University Press.

Robinson, R. G., Kubos, K. L., Starr, L. B., Rao, K., & Price, T. R. (1984). Mood disorders in stroke patients: Importance of location of lesion. *Brain, 107,* 81–93.

Robinson, R. G., Lipsey, J. R., Bolla-Wilson, K., Bolduc, P. L., Pearlson, G. D., Rao, K., & Price, T. R. (1985). Mood disorders in left-handed stroke patients. *American Journal of Psychiatry, 142,* 1424–1429.

Robinson, R. G., & Price, T. R. (1982). Post-stroke depressive disorders: A follow-up study of 103 patients. *Stroke, 13,* 635–641.

Robinson, R. G., Starr, L. B., Kubos, K. L., & Price, T. R. (1983). A two year longitudinal study of post-stroke mood disorders: Findings during the initial evaluation. *Stroke, 14,* 736–741.

Robinson, R. G., Starr, L. B., & Price, T. R. (1984). A two-year longitudinal study of post-stroke mood disorders: Prevalence and duration at six months follow-up. *British Journal of Psychiatry, 144,* 256–262.

Robinson, R. G., & Szetela, B. (1981). Mood change following left hemispheric brain injury. *Annals of Neurology, 9,* 447–453.

Shinar, D., Gross, C. R., Price, T. R., Banko, M., Bolduc, P. L., & Robinson, R. G. (1986). Screening for depression in stroke patients: The reliability and validity of the Center for Epidemiologic Studies Depression Scale. *Stroke, 17,* 241–245.

Starr, L. B., Robinson, R. G., & Price, T. R. (1983). Reliability, validity, and clinical utility of the social functioning exam in the assessment of stroke patients. *Experimental Aging Research, 9*(2), 101–106.

Wing, J. K., Cooper, E., & Sortorius, N. (1974). *Measurement and classification of psychiatric symptoms.* Cambridge, England: Cambridge University Press.

Zung, W. W. K. (1965). A self-rating depression scale. *Archives of General Psychiatry, 12,* 63–70.

12

Issues Of Social Support: The Family And Home Care

Barbara Silverstone, D.S.W.

Amy Horowitz, D.S.W.

Two compelling issues related to social supports for the elderly stroke patient are the perspective of the family and its readiness and ability to care for the patient and the adequacy of formal rehabilitation services as an adjunct to family caregiving. This chapter will contrast the salient features of the situation of the elderly stroke patient with the more common profile of the chronically impaired elder, underscore needed areas of research, cite appropriate clinical interventions, and examine the adequacy of formal rehabilitation services.

A basic premise underlying this discussion is that family caregiving will dominate posthospital care for the elderly stroke patient, now and in the future. In most situations, family care and home care for the elderly are synonymous, with the overwhelming bulk of care in the home being given by family members. Over 80% of all home care to impaired elders is actually provided by family members, supporting the fact that the elderly generally turn first to family members for help and, for the most part, receive it (National Center for Health Statistics, 1975). In turn, posthospital care in the home for the elderly stroke victim overshadows institutional arrangements. The fact of the matter is that, with the establishment of prospective payment arrangements under Medicare, family caregiving will grow as elderly patients face increasingly shorter hospitalizations.

Home care provided by hospitals and community agencies, including rehabilitative, skilled nursing, and support services, is available for some; for a small number of elderly living alone, it may be their only source of help. For the most part, formal home care services supplement family efforts, which research has demonstrated are the key factor in preventing or postponing institutionalization (Barney, 1977; Branch & Jette, 1982; Palmore, 1976; Prohaska & McAuley, 1983; Smyer, 1980; Vicente, Wiley, & Carrington, 1979; Wan & Weissert, 1981). Beyond the issue of caregiving lies the indisputable influence of the family on the overall health of its members, including the older person. The attitudes, belief systems, and family dynamics that bear on critical decision making and interactions for the stroke patient are particularly crucial (Bengtson & Treas, 1980).

Given the family's critical role in home care and in shaping the emotional and informational context of the patient's situation, attention must be paid to the family in all phases of care for the stroke patient.

THE FAMILY PERSPECTIVE

After almost three decades of research focused on family relationships and exchanges in later life, we now have available an extensive body of knowledge on family caregiving to the disabled elderly. To a large extent, the findings from this research are applicable to the elderly stroke patient and contribute to our better understanding of the patterns of care and the predicaments faced by families. These findings are briefly reviewed in the first part of this section.

At the same time it is important to note that the family caregiving research has primarily focused on the experiences of families involved with the frail, chronically impaired elderly. As will be discussed in the second part of this section, the onset and course of care for the elderly stroke patient raise unique issues for the family that have yet to be explored in any depth. Here, we must rely on clinical findings that suggest that care of the elderly stroke patient does have characteristics that distinguish it from the care of the chronically impaired aged. Such clinical evidence suggests that our general understanding of the course and consequences of family caregiving to the impaired elderly may need to be modified in the case of the older stroke patient.

Family Caregiving to the Frail Elderly: An Overview of Research

The research literature in family caregiving to the frail elderly (Horowitz, 1985) will be reviewed briefly concerning *who* in the family provides care, the *kinds* of family care provided, and the *effects* of caregiving on the family.

Studies suggest that, in practice, there is no family caregiving *system*. Rather, one family member occupies the role of primary caregiver and is the primary provider of direct care assistance. Other family members or friends, if involved at all, play secondary roles. Shared responsibility between two or more members of the informal support system is exceptional (Cantor, 1980, 1983; Frankfather, Smith, & Caro, 1981; Horowitz, 1982c; Johnson, 1983; Johnson & Catalano, 1981; Kinnear & Graycar, 1984; Noelker & Poulshock, 1982; Sanford, 1975; Stoller & Earl, 1983; Whitfield, 1981).

There is also almost universal consensus about the identity of the primary caregiver, with selection following a hierarchical pattern. Simply, the primary caregiver will be a spouse, if there is one available and capable, and a child if there is not. In the absence of both spouse and children, other relatives (primarily siblings but also grandchildren, nieces, nephews, and cousins) will take on the responsibility of primary caregiver. Only for the minority of older people who lack any functional kin are friends and neighbors identified as primary caregivers (Arling & McAuley, 1983; Cantor, 1983; Horowitz, 1982c; Johnson, 1983; Johnson & Catalano, 1981; Keith, 1983; Kivett & Learner, 1980; Shanas, 1979a, 1979b; Stoller, 1982; Stoller & Earl, 1983; Teresi, Bennett & Wilder, 1978; Tobin & Kulys, 1981).

The relationship between the caregiver and frail older person has also been identified as a primary predictor of the pattern of care provided and the stress associated with caregiving. Spouses provide the most extensive and comprehensive care and do so for the most disabled older people, suggesting that spouses maintain the caregiving role longer and tolerate greater levels of disability than other caregivers (Cantor, 1983; Crossman, London, & Barry, 1981; Horowitz, 1982c; Johnson, 1980, 1983; Johnson & Catalano, 1981, 1983; Soldo & Myllyluoma, 1983). At the same time, several of these same studies have found that spouses report the highest level of stress, compared to other caregivers.

While adult children also tend to be extensively involved in and affected by caregiving, most research indicates that the involvement is less for children than for spouses. However, the greatest contrast is between spouse and children on one end of the continuum and other relatives, friends, and neighbors on the other. The latter are not only less likely to occupy the role, but, when they do, they provide less overall care and less intensive or intimate types of assistance, and experience far less stress in the process. They are also usually found to be caring for the least disabled older people, suggesting that they do not, or cannot, maintain the caregiving role when the demands increase (Cantor, 1979, 1983; Horowitz, 1982c; Johnson & Catalano, 1981). In general, other relatives, and especially friends and neighbors, are most willing and able to meet the older person's needs when these needs are relatively less extensive.

It is also clear that caregiving remains a gender-specific activity, with females predominating over males in each kin category as the primary caregiver (Brody, 1981; Cantor, 1983; Horowitz, 1982c; Johnson, 1983; Kinnear & Graycar, 1984; Lee, 1980; Reece, Walz, & Hageboeck, 1983; Stoller, 1982; Treas, 1979; Troll, 1971; Troll, Miller, & Atchley, 1979). Thus, given the demography of family structure and gender differences in life expectancy, the usual caregiver for an older man is his elderly wife (typically in her seventies and in fair to poor health herself); for an older woman, it is her adult middle-aged or young-old daughter, who confronts the competing demands of family and/or employment.

Most studies also find that caregiving activities vary widely among families and can range from occasional errands to round-the-clock care for the bedridden (Archold, 1980; Cantor, 1980; Danis, 1978; Gross-Andrews & Zimmer, 1978; Horowitz, 1982b; Lang & Brody, 1983; Noelker & Poulshock, 1982). Much of this variation can be explained by the older person's impairment level and living arrangements (Horowitz, 1982c; Lang & Brody, 1983; Newman, 1976; Noelker & Poulshock, 1982). Such findings further indicate that families are responsive to their elderly relatives' needs and will increase supportive activities as the elder's need for assistance increases.

The types of assistance offered fall into four primary categories: emotional support, direct-service provision, financial assistance, and medication with formal providers. The research has shown that emotional support, which includes maintaining social interaction and "cheering up" when depressed, emerges as the most universal caregiving task (Horowitz, 1982b, 1982c; Lang & Brody, 1983; Sherman, Horowitz, & Durmaskin, 1982). Furthermore, both Horowitz (1982c) and Cicirelli (1983) found that providing emotional support, regardless of the extensive support and time committed to direct services, was defined by the caregiver as the most important and often the most stressful type of assistance offered to their frail relative.

Thus, in identifying the sources of stress for the family, it is not surprising that the emotional aspects of caregiving are the most pervasive and the most difficult to deal with when compared to either the physical or financial components of care (Cantor, 1983; Cicirelli, 1980; Horowitz, 1982c). For most caregivers, these emotional strains stem from a constant concern for the older person's health and safety and the need to redefine and come to terms with the changing nature of their relationship with the aging relative. This can be especially stressful in cases of mental deterioration.

At the same time, direct-service provision remains the instrumental core of caregiving support and encompasses a broad range of activities including shopping, doing errands, providing transportation, housekeeping, meal preparation, financial management, personal care (bathing, feeding, toileting, transfer, and dressing), repairs, laundry, administering medications, and health care (e.g., changing bandages and giving injections). The latter two categories of activities, personal and health care, represent the most intensive and intimate caregiving assistance. They are most likely offered to the most impaired elders by caregivers closest in relationship and proximity. Overall, the most striking characteristic of the direct-service component is, as Cantor (1980) noted, the range of services offered. Families do not specialize or concentrate help in any one or two areas but increase services to meet needs as they arise.

It is the provision of necessary services that imposes the severe restrictions on time and freedom reported by caregivers. Caregiving activities often require extensive readjustments in previous daily schedules. Disruption of domestic routines, decreased personal time, less time for social and leisure activities, inability to take vacations, rearrangement of work schedules, and restricted mobility are all common indicators of this pervasive problem (Adams, Caston, & Danis, 1979; Archold, 1980, 1983; Arling & McAuley, 1983; Cantor, 1983; Danis, 1978; Frankfather et al., 1981; Horowitz, 1982a; Kinnear & Graycar, 1984; Noelker & Poulshock, 1982; Rabins, Mace, & Lucas, 1982; Sanford, 1975).

Thus, providing care to an impaired elderly relative inevitably has some impact on the family unit; there are both costs and benefits. Caregivers have been found to vary in the extent and type of caregiving behavior, as have their evaluation of the experience. While most investigators report that substantial proportions of their respondents are undergoing moderate to extreme stress, they concurrently note

that, given the severity of the older person's problems and the demands of the caregiving role, the overall level of burden, disruption,
or stress is less than would be expected (Cicirelli, 1981; Noelker &
Poulshock, 1982; Zarit, Reever, & Bach-Peterson, 1980). Overall,
most families have impressive adaptive capabilities in the face of this
crisis.

Differential Caregiving Issues in Relation to the Elderly Stroke Patient

The research literature on family care for the chronically impaired
elderly offers us some insights into the patterns of care that are likely
to be similar for the elderly stroke patient. We have no reason to
doubt that the primary responsibility for care of the stroke patient
will still fall to one family member and that this caregiver will most
likely be an elderly wife or a late-middle-aged or young-old daughter.
Families will continue to be the primary providers of instrumental
and emotional support and will adjust the level of their assistance to
the needs of their older relatives.

It is interesting that the areas that have yet to be explored in depth
in the case of chronically impaired elderly have special importance
for understanding the care of the elderly stroke patient. First, most
caregiving research is cross-sectional rather than longitudinal and
gives little information about the dynamic nature of the caregiving
experience. For both the chronically impaired and the stroke patient,
caregiving is a dynamic process that goes through stages and
changes. The needs of the older person change, as do the internal and
external resources available to family members. It is interesting that
one of the few longitudinal studies, conducted on a small sample of
caregivers to stroke patients, found that the role of primary caregiver
was not always a continuous one (Brocklehurst, Morris, Andrews,
Richards, & Laycock, 1981). Changes in the primary caregiver were
sometimes due to the improvement in the older person's status (as in
cases where an elderly spouse was able to take over responsibility of
care from a daughter) as well as the "burn-out" of the previous
caregiver.

Second, we have little objective data on the *quality* of care families
provide to their disabled relatives. Especially in the case of stroke,
families often find themselves in the position of providing skilled
home health care and/or technical types of assistance for which they
have received no training and have little prior experience. Often they
have little choice but to learn by trial and error. Whether they are

adequately meeting the needs of their older relatives remains largely unknown.

In addition to the issues raised by the general caregiving literature, there are special issues related to the elderly stroke patient. Our clinical knowledge does suggest that the family experience of the elderly stroke patient may vary somewhat from the profile suggested heretofore. The two primary factors that define the caregiving context of the chronically impaired elderly—the gradual onset and the usual expectation that the illness or disability will eventually increase in severity—are not the case for the elderly stroke victim. In fact, quite the opposite holds true in most situations. Furthermore, the issue of and problems associated with communication take on even greater importance with older stroke patients.

Sudden Onset. The first point of contrast concerns the onset of the disability. For the chronically impaired elderly, onset is most likely to be *gradual*, be it a physical disability such as arthritis or heart disease or a mental impairment such as Alzheimer's disease. The gradual nature of the onset has important implications for family experiences and reactions. It may provide for a limited period of denial in terms of the elder's declining capabilities; this may, in certain cases, be an important psychological phase for both the family and the older relative to pass through and resolve. The gradual increase in the elder's need for support also allows families to adapt slowly to the caregiving role and to assign responsibilities implicitly or explicitly to various family members. A primary caregiver will often emerge naturally. Decision making can also be gradual, with the older person more able to be an active participant in selecting future care options.

In sharp contrast, the effects of a stroke are usually dramatically and suddenly presented to the family. Excluding the category of stroke patients already suffering from serious chronic impairments for whom the stroke is an added insult, the family and the health care system confront individuals whose premorbid conditions have been relatively healthy and who have been previously self-sufficient. When a generally healthy elder is rendered incapacitated within a very brief period of time, the occurrence of a stroke invariably constitutes a severe family *crisis*.

There is little question from our clinical experience that the family is, in turn, dramatically mobilized in this crisis. The fact that stroke, like cancer, is an honorable disease, compared to the negative attitudes often attached to such chronic conditions as Alzheimer's disease, only adds to the heightened degree of family interest and involvement.

Mobilized family energy, interest, and involvement, however, can be tempered by a number of factors, including the great disarray any dramatic change brings, prior family beliefs and attitudes, family resources, and guarded or noncommittal medical prognoses. Confusion, fear, and ignorance are not atypical and can profoundly influence important decisions as well as who the decision makers will be.

The most extreme example of the disarray a family can be thrown into at the time of stroke is the not-unusual case when the key family member, particularly in terms of decision making, is the one stricken. The sudden incapacity of the dominant family member throws responsibility on a spouse and/or a child, who may have never shouldered such responsibility, especially in relation to the stroke patient. Members of the family who have not talked in years may be thrown together. The assumption can be safely made that prior family patterns have been disrupted by this crisis and must be realigned quickly within a new context.

In the initial assessment, therefore, family resources must be carefully measured. The presence of an energized, apparently motivated, family system responding to this crisis in no way guarantees the ongoing family support required by the stroke patient. While family energies can be more easily rallied in sudden emergencies and sustained for some time, longer-term care raises a new set of issues. The capability of the family to assume longer-term care will be influenced by the family members' other responsibilities, geographical accessibility, and health status, as well as psychological and affective aspects of prior family interactions.

Paradoxically, the same crisis that motivates the family to act on behalf of the elder may also energize families to rush into decision making prematurely. Wrong decisions may be made for the right reason, and right decisions may be made for the wrong reason. Most unfortunately, the older stroke patients themselves may be left out of the decision-making process.

Potential for Recovery. The second major point of contrast with caregiving to the chronically impaired is in regard to the prognosis that is presented to the family. Unlike chronic illness which, at best, can be expected to stabilize, stroke presents the potential for some recovery. The fact that things can sometimes get better for the stroke patient makes decision making about care plans a more complex process.

The family's beliefs and attitudes, which they bring into the situation, will be an important influence on their emotional and behavioral response to the rehabilitative potential. These attitudes and beliefs regarding aging, disability, dependency, and death can have both negative and positive implications for the elderly relative.

On the one hand, family members may strongly believe that it is not possible to teach anyone of a certain age anything new. While there may be hope that the person will recover from the stroke spontaneously or with time, there may be much pessimism about the effects of rehabilitation. On the other hand, families can maintain romantic notions about the potential for recovery of the older person and expect too much of the rehabilitation process. Most destructive, of course, are those belief systems that hold to the view that anything affecting an older person's cognitive, sensory, or communication apparati is associated with senility and that chronic mental impairment is inevitable. When such attitudes interact with and are reinforced by similar attitudes expressed by the professional team, the implications for the older stroke patient are dire.

Thus, in contrast to the caregiving profile emphasized in the research literature, our clinical observations of the elderly stroke patient suggest a family scenario involving active, hopeful participants reacting to a sudden crisis and facing complex and critical issues. The potential for recovery of the stroke patient can mobilize the family and widen the cast of characters. Yet a number of barriers to effective decision making and family action can stand in the way of optimal outcomes.

Communication and Emotional Problems. A third striking difference in the family profile of the elderly stroke patient is found in the types of stress most typically experienced. As with the chronically impaired, common negative effects are experienced by the family of the elderly stroke patient, but here the conditions peculiar to stroke suggest different stresses. Burden, worry, and disruption are certainly among them, but perhaps greatest of all are the communication and emotional problems associated with stroke. These include cognitive, perceptual, sensory, and speech difficulties as well as depression and emotional lability.

Difficulty in communication becomes a multifaceted problem for the family in relation to the stroke patient. On one level, it is often the central issue in the patient's condition and, as suggested by some rehabilitation experts, should be a primary and immediate target for rehabilitation, taking priority over motor skills. Yet, protectiveness, secretiveness, and covert communications are all normal family strategies for coping with the stress of stroke. The fear of alarming the patient, expressing negative feelings, and/or discussing unpleasant options may inhibit open discussion, at the same time creating greater anxiety for the elder as well as the family and exacerbating the elder's depression.

On another level, the patient's communication difficulty is a prime source of stress for the family members, who view one of their roles as giving emotional support (and who in the past may have received much emotional support from the patient). The fact that the family system has been thrown into disarray can profoundly affect its communication patterns, particularly if extended-family members have never collaborated before.

Adding to these communication difficulties are the emotional lability and depressive syndromes typically exhibited by the stroke patient. The scenario just described strongly suggests the need for open, informative, and supportive lines of communication with the health care team. Ineffective communications can only compound the difficulties experienced by the older person and interfere further with effective decision making. Strong countermeasures are required.

Intervention Strategies

It is almost axiomatic that the family communication patterns be an immediate professional focus, since malfunctioning here can only compound the difficulties being experienced with the older person. Strong ties to the rehabilitative team are called for. These ties may be *more* critical than the relationship with the physician, who may not be versed in communication skills or as knowledgeable about rehabilitation potential.

Dyadic communications that omit one or another family member, including the elder, are to be avoided in the professional's contacts. If a family group meeting is impossible, then the physician or social worker should make sure they have talked directly to each key family member, including of course the patient. Training programs for groups of family caregivers can be very helpful (Masciocchi, 1985).

Families must be provided with compensatory means of communicating with the stroke patient. The speech therapist is particularly important. Pencils and pads, pantomime gestures, computers, and other means used to facilitate communication must be *immediately* imparted to the family so that optimal communication patterns can be established as soon as possible.

Being careful to take enough time becomes an important strategy, particularly when the pressure for discharge from the acute-care hospital is overpowering. If prognosis for recovery from the condition is not yet known, this must be conveyed to the family and options left open. Prematurely assuming an overly protective attitude or recommending nursing home placement may set into motion a family dynamic that cannot be reversed. This strategy becomes even more compelling when we consider the difficulties experienced by the patient and the family in decision making during a crisis.

When required, the extended-care rehabilitation facility is the preferable arrangement, both to give respite to the family at a time of upset and, of course, to provide for expert care and 24-hour reinforcement. Short of this, however, convalescence will occur in the home, and suitable provisions must be made. Families need to know what to anticipate under all circumstances. The normality of fear, the inevitability of some depression, and the meaning of other behavioral syndromes must be made known to families in order to reduce the natural anxiety engendered by the dramatically changed condition of the patient. Immediate intervention, careful timing, and temporary arrangements therefore set the stage for family caregiving at home and for optimal interaction with rehabilitation experts and consultants. Community facilities for rehabilitation counseling and therapy, nursing care that stresses rehabilitation, instruction in the complexities of care, and family self-help groups imbued with the rehabilitation focus can all enhance family caregiving as well as serve the older patient. Not to be overlooked are community groups for the stroke patient (Gibson & Caplan, 1984).

An appropriate distribution of tasks between the family and rehabilitation team needs to be carefully weighed. Some stroke patients will not accept personal care or instruction from family members whose appropriate role under such circumstances should be limited to emotional support or other tasks. Such "expert" tasks are usually better carried out by trained workers who are less emotionally involved.

All of these interventions point to an important phase of care for the elderly stroke victim, a phase in which the family is an active member of the rehabilitation team (Silverstone, 1984).

REHABILITATION AND THE ELDERLY

One of the most important themes of this book is the importance of timely rehabilitative interventions with the elderly stroke patient and the rejection of the notion that those over the age of 65 cannot benefit from such efforts. There is no need for us to reiterate the merits of such an approach. Yet, we must point out what we perceive to be serious flaws in present rehabilitative care for the elderly. First, there are insufficient services and too many constrictions and restrictions in Medicare coverage, a situation that only promises to worsen (Kaufman & Becker, in press). A second flaw is the locus of this insufficiency along the continuum of care. Without in any way diminishing the need for intense rehabilitative input in the acute, postacute, and early convalescent phases of recovery from stroke, let us suggest that much more attention needs to be paid to ongoing or extended intermittent rehabilitative care. As Dr. Lester Wolcott (1983) has noted, "a period of functional polishing is required" for the elderly stroke patient, for only rarely does the patient recover completely without some neurological impairment. Consequently most rehabilitated elderly will still benefit from intermittent follow-up evaluations and reinforcement of relearned skills.

The arbitrary dichotomy between short-term rehabilitative care and long-term care belies such an approach. Our system of Medicare reimbursement illustrates this dichotomy dramatically. Medicare will pay for an elderly person's posthospital skilled nursing and rehabilitative services for a limited period and as long as it can be demonstrated that functioning can be restored. Indications of long-term disability preempt ongoing Medicare support. As we all know, placement in a long-term care facility and long-term care services in the home are not supported by Medicare reimbursement.

The unfortunate aspect of these present funding arrangements is the presumption that the long-term care patient cannot benefit from rehabilitation. Here, experience has shown that the small incremental benefits that can be gained from rehabilitative efforts can sometimes result in heightened functioning and lower levels of care (Lawton, 1968). But, perhaps more important, this sharp dichotomy throws into the long-term care pool that group of elderly stroke patients who require ongoing rehabilitation but may *not* need long-term supportive care. There are *many* elderly who require ongoing rehabilitative care after the immediate convalescence following acute hospitalization; this care may extend for many months but *not* result in long-term care. Only the rare elderly stroke patient recovers completely without any neurological impairment. Consequently, most of these rehabilitated individuals will still benefit from intermittent follow-up evaluations and revised rehabilitative plans.

This follow-up phase should include provision of information essential to the patient's continued improvement and to the well-being of the family. It also should provide for essential restorative practices to be carried on by the family or others after discharge, such as continued speech therapy and follow-up for reevaluation by physician and other appropriate staff members.

It is this extended phase of rehabilitation, however, that unfortunately is now largely left in the hands of the family, who may neglect the ongoing therapeutic needs of the stroke patient, not out of a lack of concern but out of ignorance and lack of professional supportive services.

In referring to the "rehabilitated older stroke patient," Wolcott (1983) further states that

> Later secondary complications and increased disability, when present, are almost invariably the result of neglect. Some of the more common problems are obesity, increased cardiovascular insufficiency, muscle atrophy, contractures with joint deformities, and frequently, disturbances of vision. The very real danger of drifting gradually toward the emotional state of pseudosenility cannot be over-emphasized as a preventable tragedy. It is the worst hypocrisy to save this life, restored to reasonable function, and then to allow the object of that effort to degenerate through ambient indifference. [p. 183]

This ambient indifference is not that of the family, but of the formal home care system unbuttressed with extended rehabilitative services. In partnership with the family and patient, extended rehabilitative home care can greatly contribute to sustained functioning and forestall institutionalization and/or long-term family care for the patient. Both inevitably take a heavy toll on the family as well as society.

SUMMARY

This chapter has raised two central issues: (1) the need to reappraise the family system in relation to the care of the elderly stroke patient and (2) the need to test in our research and clinical work the hypothesis that considerable energy and family resources can be harnessed at this time of dramatic family crisis and sustained over an extended period of rehabilitative home care. Longitudinal studies and objective data are needed on the quality of care provided by families caring for chronically impaired and elderly stroke patients.

Also called for are clinical strategies along the continuum of care that address the multifaceted communication problems likely to arise and that will insure the flow of accurate information among family members (including the patient) and between the family and medical and rehabilitative teams. The shared function played by the family in extended rehabilitative care calls for an ongoing partnership with the professional rehabilitation team that continues as long as needed by the stroke patient.

A rethinking of our professional rehabilitative services and reimbursement strategies, so that we may extend intermittent services beyond the time limits usually required by younger patients, is required. Let us hope that the system of prospective payments now governing Medicare reimbursement to hospitals does not result in premature discharge of elderly stroke patients, placing an inappropriate burden on both family and home care agencies and draining the resources so critically needed for successful recuperation and maintenance of functions. A health care system founded on the acute-versus-long-term care dichotomy is no longer sufficient to meet the needs of our aging population. The concept of extended rehabilitative care as distinguished from long-term supportive care must be more clearly developed and integrated into our systems of health care delivery.

REFERENCES

Adams, M., Caston, M. A., & Danis, B. G. (1979, November). A neglected dimension in home care of elderly disabled persons: Effect on responsible family members. Paper presented at the 32nd Annual Scientific Meeting of the Gerontological Society of America, Washington, DC.

Archold, P. G. (1980). The impact of caring for an ill elderly parent on the middle-aged offspring. *Journal of Gerontological Nursing, 6,* 78–85.

Archold, P. G. (1983). The impact of parent-caring on women. *Family Relations, 32,* 39–45.

Arling, G., & McAuley, W. J. (1983). The feasibility of public payments for family caregivers. *The Gerontologist, 23,* 300–306.

Barney, J. L. (1977). The prerogative of choice in long-term care. *The Gerontologist, 17,* 309–314.

Bengtson, V. L., & Treas, J. (1980). The changing family context of mental health and aging. In J. E. Birren & R. B. Sloane (Eds.), *Handbook of Mental Health and Aging* (pp. 400–428). Englewood Cliffs, NJ: Prentice-Hall.

Branch, L. G., & Jette, A. M. (1982). A prospective study of long term care institutionalization among the aged. *American Journal of Public Health*, *72*, 1373–1379.

Brocklehurst, J. C., Morris, P., Andrews, K., Richards, B., & Laycock, P. (1981). Social effects of stroke. *Social Science and Medicine*, *15*(A), 35–39.

Brody, E. M. (1981). Women in the middle and family help to older people. *The Gerontologist*, *21*, 471–480.

Cantor, M. (1979). Neighbors and friends: An overlooked resource in the informal support system. *Research on Aging*, *1*, 434–463.

Cantor, M. (1980, November). Caring for the frail elderly: Impact on family, friends, and neighbors. Paper presented at the 33rd Annual Scientific Meeting of the Gerontological Society of America, San Diego, CA.

Cantor, M. (1983). Strain among caregivers: A study of experience in the United States. *The Gerontologist*, *23*, 597–604.

Cicirelli, V. G. (1980, November). Personal strains and negative feelings in adult children's relationship with elderly parents. Paper presented at the 33rd Annual Scientific Meeting of the Gerontological Society of America, San Diego, CA.

Cicirelli, V. G. (1981). Helping elderly parents: The role of adult children. Boston: Auburn House.

Cicirelli, V. G. (1983). Adult children's attachment and helping behavior to elderly parents: A path model. *Journal of Marriage and the Family*, *45*, 815–825.

Crossman, L., London, C., & Barry, C. (1981). Older women caring for disabled spouses: A model for supportive services. *The Gerontologist*, *21*, 464–470.

Danis, B. G. (1978). Stress in individuals caring for ill elderly relatives. Paper presented at the 31st Annual Scientific Meeting of the Gerontological Society of America, Dallas, TX.

Frankfather, D., Smith, M. J., & Caro, F. G. (1981). *Family care of the elderly: Public initiatives and private obligations*. Lexington, MA: Lexington Books.

Gibson, C. J., & Caplan, B. M. (1984). Rehabilitation of the patient with stroke. In F. Williams (Ed.), *Rehabilitation in the Aging* (pp. 145–159). New York: Raven Press.

Gross-Andrews, S., & Zimmer, A. H. (1978). Incentives to families caring for disabled elderly: Research and demonstration project to strengthen the natural supports system. *Journal of Gerontological Social Work*, *1*, 119–133.

Horowitz, A. (1982a). The impact of caregiving on children of the frail elderly. Paper presented at the 59th Annual Meeting of the American Orthopsychiatric Association, San Francisco, CA.

Horowitz, A. (1982b). Predictors of caregiving involvement among adult children of the frail elderly. Paper presented at the 35th Annual Scientific Meeting of the Gerontological Society of America, Boston, MA.

Horowitz, A. (1982c). *The role of families in providing long-term care to the frail and chronically ill elderly living in the community*. Final report submitted to the Health Care Financing Administration. New York: The Brookdale Center on Aging at Hunter College.

Horowitz, A. (1985). Family caregiving to the frail elderly. In M. P. Lawton & G. Maddox (Eds.), *Annual Review of Gerontology and Geriatrics.* New York: Springer.

Johnson, C. L. (1980, November). Obligation and reciprocity in caregiving during illness: A comparison of spouses and offspring as family supports. Paper presented at the 33rd Annual Scientific Meeting of the Gerontological Society of America, San Diego, CA.

Johnson, C. L. (1983). Dyadic family relations and social support. *The Gerontologist, 23,* 377–383.

Johnson, C. L., & Catalano, D. J. (1981). Childless elderly and their family supports. *The Gerontologist, 21,* 610–618.

Johnson, C. L., & Catalano, D. J. (1983). A longitudinal study of family supports to impaired elderly. *The Gerontologist, 23,* 612–618.

Kaufman, S., & Becker, G. (in press). Stroke: Health care on the periphery. *Social Science and Medicine.*

Keith, P. M. (1983). Patterns of assistance among parents and the childless in very old age: Implications for practice. *Journal of Gerontological Social Work, 6,* 49–59.

Kinnear, D., & Graycar, A. (1984). Aging and family dependency. *Australian Journal of Social Issues, 19,* 13–25.

Kivett, V. R., & Learner, R. M. (1980). Perspectives on the childless rural elderly: A comparative analysis. *The Gerontologist, 20,* 708–716.

Lang, A. M., & Brody, E. M. (1983). Characteristics of middle-aged daughters and help to their elderly mothers. *Journal of Marriage and the Family, 45,* 193–202.

Lawton, M. P. (1968). Social rehabilitation of the aged: Some neglected aspects. *Journal of the American Geriatric Society, 16,* 1346–1363.

Lee, G. R. (1980). Kinship in the 70's: A decade review of research and theory. *Journal of Marriage and the Family, 42,* 923–936.

Masciocchi, C. (1985, spring). The challenge of caregiving: Families of older rehabilitation patients. In *Newsletter of Rehabilitation, Research and Training Center in Aging.* Philadelphia: University of Pennsylvania Medical Center.

National Center for Health Statistics. (1975). *Vital statistics of the United States, 1973 life tables.* Rockville, MD: NCHS.

Newman, S. (1976). Housing adjustments of older people: A report of findings from the second phase. Ann Arbor, MI: Institute for Social Research, University of Michigan.

Noelker, L. S., & Poulshock, S. W. (1982). *The effects on families of caring for impaired elderly in residence.* Final report submitted to the Administration on Aging. Cleveland, OH: The Margaret Blenkner Research Center for Family Studies, The Benjamin Rose Institute.

Palmore, E. (1976). Total chance of institutionalization among the aged. *The Gerontologist, 16,* 504–507.

Prohaska, T., & McAuley, W. J. (1983). The effects of family care and living arrangements in acute care discharge recommendations. *Journal of Gerontological Social Work, 5,* 67–80.

Rabins, P. V., Mace, N. L., & Lucas, M. J. (1982). The impact of dementia on the family. *Journal of the American Medical Association, 248,* 333–335.

Reece, D., Walz, T., & Hageboeck, H. (1983). Intergenerational care providers of non-institutionalized frail elderly: Characteristics and consequences. *Journal of Gerontological Social Work, 5,* 21–34.

Sanford, J. (1975). Tolerance of debility in elder dependents by supports at home: Its significance for hospital practice. *British Medical Journal, 3,* 471–473.

Shanas, E. (1979a). The family as a social support system in old age. *The Gerontologist, 19,* 169–174.

Shanas, E. (1979b). Social myth as hypothesis: The case of the family relations of old people. *The Gerontologist, 19,* 3–9.

Sherman, R., Horowitz, A., & Durmaskin, S. (1982). Role overload or role management: The relationship between work and caregiving among daughters of aged parents. Paper presented at the 35th Annual Scientific Meeting of the Gerontological Society of America, Boston, MA.

Silverstone, B. (1984). Social aspects of rehabilitation. In F. Williams (Ed.), *Rehabilitation in the aging* (pp. 59–79). New York: Raven Press.

Smyer, M. (1980). The differential usage of services by impaired elderly. *Journal of Gerontology, 35,* 249–255.

Soldo, B. J., & Myllyluoma, J. (1983). Caregivers who live with dependent elderly. *The Gerontologist, 23,* 605–611.

Stoller, E. P. (1982). Sources of support for the elderly during illness. *Health and Social Work, 7,* 111–122.

Stoller, E. P., & Earl, L. L. (1983). Help with activities of everyday life: Sources of support for the non-institutionalized elderly. *The Gerontologist, 23,* 64–70.

Teresi, J. A., Bennett, R. G., & Wilder, D. E. (1978). *Personal time dependency and family attitudes: Dependency in the Elderly of New York City.* New York: Community Council of Greater N.Y.

Tobin, S. S., & Kulys, R. (1981). The family in the institutionalization of the elderly. *Journal of Social Issues, 37,* 145–157.

Treas, J. (1979). Intergenerational families and social change. In P. Ragan (Ed.), *Aging parents* (pp. 58–65). Los Angeles: The University of Southern California Press.

Troll, L. E. (1971). The family of later life: A decade review. *Journal of Marriage and the Family, 33,* 263–290.

Troll, L. E., Miller, S. J., & Atchley, R. C. (1979). *Families in later life.* Belmont, CA: Wadsworth.

Vicente, L., Wiley, J. A., & Carrington, R. A. (1979). The risk of institutionalization before death. *The Gerontologist, 19,* 361–367.

Wan, T. H., & Weissert, W. G. (1981). Social support networks, patient status, and institutionalization. *Research on aging, 3,* 240–256.

Whitfield, S. (1981, August). *Report to the General Assembly on the family demonstration program.* Baltimore, MD: State of Maryland Office on Aging.

Wolcott, L. E. (1983). Rehabilitation and the aged. In W. Reichel (Ed.), *Clinical Aspects of Aging* (pp. 182–204). Baltimore, MD: Williams and Wilkins.

Zarit, S. H., Reever, K. E., & Bach-Peterson, J. (1980). Relatives of the impaired elderly: Correlates of feelings of burden. *The Gerontologist, 20,* 649–655.

13

Rehabilitation and the Elderly: Economic and Political Issues

Robert H. Binstock, Ph.D.

Contemporary economic and political forces, especially the incentives and disincentives generated by Medicare's Prospective Payment Systems (PPS's) for acute care in hospitals, appear to be bringing about a growth of interest in rehabilitation within the broader health care arena. This increased interest includes what may be unprecedented attention to rehabilitation of persons 65 years of age and older (Brody & Ruff, 1986), virtually all of whom are enrolled in Medicare.

At the same time that this growth of interest in rehabilitating older persons is taking place, however, very little reliable information is available about many aspects of rehabilitation and aging that potentially have important implications for social policy. With respect to rehabilitation from stroke, for instance, there is a paucity of data regarding such fundamental matters as the proportion of elderly stroke victims who receive any rehabilitation, the efficacy of stroke rehabilitation, and the costs of stroke rehabilitation in its various forms. Yet, at the same time, the financing mechanisms and costs of stroke rehabilitation are undergoing increased scrutiny and analysis by the governmental and corporate entities that pay for an over-

Gratefully acknowledged are critical comments on a draft of this chapter, thoughtfully provided by Stanley J. Brody, Hilary Siebens, and T. Franklin Williams; the author, of course, is solely responsible for the content of the chapter.

whelming proportion of American health care and seek to limit their obligations for such expenditures (Thurow, 1985). Obviously, some difficult challenges confront those of us who would be therapeutically optimistic.

THE TRADITIONAL POSITION OF REHABILITATION AND AGING

For as long as most of us can remember, rehabilitation—in general— has been a comparatively drab backwater in the overall scene of American health care. This has been the situation whether the patient has been older or younger, or afflicted by stroke or some other disease or disabling condition. Rehabilitation has been eclipsed by the prestige and glamour of medical care that has the inherent drama of dealing with acute episodes of illnesses and trauma, and the relatively frequent "high tech" and "quick fix" dimensions of diagnosis and intervention.

Rehabilitation of older persons has been particularly neglected for a variety of reasons. Perhaps the most fundamental reason has been an implicit and sometimes explicit societal attitude that it is "not worth it," economically, to rehabilitate older persons. This attitude seems to have been mirrored, for the most part, in the outlook and behavior of health care professionals.

Vocational Emphasis in Rehabilitation

The central axis of rehabilitative philosophy in this nation for more than half a century has been a vocational perspective (Baumann, Anderson, & Morrison, in press; S. J. Brody, 1986). Both public- and private-sector philosophies have emphasized heavily the restoration of an individual's capacity to regain an *economically* productive role in society. Social roles outside the labor force, in the context of the family or other societal institutions, have received very little weight. Except among physiatrists and other rehabilitative professionals, issues that focus on the quality of life for the individual who might be successfully rehabilitated have been virtually ignored, except for an occasional dramatization of a human-interest story.

In the context of vocational rehabilitation it has been understandable, if not philosophically or otherwise desirable, that older persons have received low priority. Many older persons are already out of the labor force when the events leading to a need for rehabilitation occur.

Those older persons who may have still been in the labor force at the time of a stroke or other episode from which rehabilitative efforts might follow have also been seen as relatively "poor investments" for rehabilitation. Even if rehabilitative efforts with older patients were to prove successful, resulting in their return to the labor force, these persons would have comparatively little time to continue as productive workers.

Narrow View of "Small, Undramatic" Achievements

Another, related reason for the comparative neglect of rehabilitation has been the relatively undramatic or so-called "minor" nature of many of the gains that can be achieved through it. As Williams (1984) has pointed out, when a person recovering from a stroke reacquires the ability to transfer without assistance from bed to chair, commode, or wheelchair, this gain may appear "small" when viewed in isolation. But, of course, such an ability can very well mean an enormous increase in independence, even for a person who is unable to walk and depends upon a wheelchair to get around. This "minor" gain may be viewed as small in a labor-force context, but, if viewed in the larger contexts of market economics, such a rehabilitative gain can yield enormous benefits in both the societal meaning of a life and its quality for the individual in question (see National Academy of Sciences, 1986).

The Place of Rehabilitation in the Health Care Professions

Predominant societal values regarding rehabilitation, particularly rehabilitation of the elderly, have been paralleled by a relatively low priority for rehabilitative activities in the health care arena. The comparatively low status of rehabilitation within the health field, generally, has reflected not only economic forces but values in the medical profession (Starr, 1983). It is also evident in prestige hierarchies and organizational arrangements among health care professionals.

The extent to which this has been the situation has been extraordinarily exemplified by the negligible attention that rehabilitation has received among professionals in the field of aging. Gerontologists and geriatricians have been increasingly and appropriately preoccupied throughout the last decade with issues of "long-term care," the formidable challenges of providing care and social supports for chronically ill and disabled older persons. But only a few (e.g., S. J. Brody, 1984–1985; Williams, 1984) have as yet given attention to rehabilitation as a dimension of care and treatment for the chronically disabled elderly. Not even the modest rehabilitative goal of actively working to *maintain* the existing functional capacities of elderly patients has received much attention, let alone the more ambitious goals of *restoring* previous function or *compensating* for the loss of functional capacities.

In effect, until recently (see E. M. Brody, 1986), long-term care for the elderly has been viewed by most professionals in the field in terms of the economic, institutional, service-delivery, and familial burdens of giving care—without rehabilitation—to the elderly, as their functional capacities gradually erode or precipitously decline before death. Even among gerontologists and geriatricians, rehabilitation appears to have been regarded as a domain or set of activities relevant to the *younger* disabled population, even though 40% of the disabled persons in the United States are 65 years of age or older (Henriksen, 1978).

THE CHANGING SCENE

Within the past several years this traditional picture has begun to change. Rehabilitation has begun to attract increasing attention, beyond the arena of physiatrists and other rehabilitative professionals. In some measure this change has been due to the initiatives of a handful of professional reformers, but it seems much more due to the economic incentives generated by the fevered milieu of health care cost containment efforts in this country, as spearheaded by the establishment of the Prospective Payment Systems (PPS's) for reimbursing health providers for care of patients enrolled in Medicare.

Initiatives of Professional Reformers

In late 1984 what may come to be known as "the birth of a social movement" took place. The first national conference on "Aging and Rehabilitation" was convened in Washington, D.C., under the auspices of some 20 federal agencies, led by the National Institute on Aging, the National Institute of Handicapped Research, and the National Institute of Mental Health, and coordinated by the Rehabilitation and Training Center on Aging of the University of Pennsylvania. This conference appears to have marked the start of an era in which meetings convened to deal with aging and functional disabilities would be increasingly structured to include an emphasis on *both* long-term care and rehabilitation (Binstock, 1986). Since then, there have been a great many indications that rehabilitation is finally beginning to take its place on the agenda of long-term care of older persons, and that aging is becoming more relevant to the field of rehabilitation. The worlds of aging and rehabilitation appear to be discovering each other.

Consider just two symbolic examples. On the one hand, in the summer of 1985, *Aging*—a bimonthly magazine disseminated by the U.S. Administration on Aging—devoted a special issue to rehabilitation (U.S. Department of Health and Human Services, 1985). This was the 350th issue of a magazine that is circulated nationwide under the auspices of the federal agency charged with promoting and monitoring the overall well-being of older Americans. This was the first time, however, that rehabilitation of older persons was featured as a central concern. As a symbol of recognition flowing in the other direction, the American Academy of Physical Medicine and Rehabilitation designated "Rehabilitation in an Aging America" as the theme for its 1986 annual meeting.

Economic Incentives of Health Care Cost-Containment Efforts

Far more important than such symbols and the professional reform initiatives that they may reflect, however, have been the economic incentives generated by new Prospective Payment Systems (PPSs) that are bringing more attention to the rehabilitation of the elderly. Of particular importance has been the impact of Diagnosis Related Groups (DRGs), the current mechanism through which Medicare reimburses hospitals prospectively for patient care on the basis of the primary diagnosis assigned to the patient. Medicare's reimbursement for a patient's care will be the same whether that patient occupies an acute-care bed for 5 or 15 days. Operating in the context of this payment mechanism, hospitals have a strong economic incentive to discharge Medicare patients from acute-care beds as soon as it is feasible to do so.

Under the pressures of DRGs, hospitals throughout the country have been "verticalizing" into a variety of nonacute "step-down" services by developing, establishing, buying, and arranging working partnerships with agencies that provide them (Brody & Persily, 1984). Acute-care hospitals are now establishing their own inpatient rehabilitation units if they have not had them up to now, or expanding existing units; undertaking partnerships with or acquiring free-standing rehabilitation hospitals and skilled nursing facilities that include rehabilitation services as well as convalescent care; opening up outpatient rehabilitation services; and developing their own home health services that provide many elements of supportive care, including rehabilitation, in a community setting. Such services may well be perceived and used as an opportunity to improve a patient's functional capacities and quality of life. But they also enable hospitals to accelerate the movement—or stepping down—of Medicare patients from acute-care beds in a responsible fashion, when family supports are unavailable or insufficient to provide an adequate supportive environment for a discharged patient at home.

This verticalization by hospitals into what Brody and Magel (in press) have termed "short-term/long-term care" appears to have come about largely as an economic strategy by hospitals as they have responded to the pressures of DRGs and other hospital cost-containment measures. By owning and/or operating these various step-down services, which lie outside the DRG mechanism of reimbursement, hospitals are providing themselves with opportunities for additional sources of revenue from Medicare and other health care payers, particularly if these services are appropriately authorized, staffed, and equipped for providing rehabilitation. A focus on rehabilitation for older persons is central to this economic strategy because medically authorized rehabilitation is an important and at present comparatively open-ended source of available revenue under Medicare reimbursement.

In effect, as a largely unintended consequence of hospital cost-containment policies under Medicare, rehabilitation of older persons is becoming a much more important concern in the health care arena than it has been in the past. From its inception in 1965, ironically, Medicare provided reimbursement for posthospital extended-care services. The original legislation had such coverage because of the possible contributions that rehabilitative efforts would make in reducing needs for long-term care. But, until the past few years when cost-containment pressures have mounted, relatively few hospitals have given much priority to rehabilitation.

This heightened concern for rehabilitation, driven as it seems to be by economic incentives and disincentives, raises a number of important issues regarding elderly stroke victims and their rehabilitation and the financing mechanisms, costs, and professional responsibilities and relationships in the rehabilitative process. Before considering some of these issues, however, let us consider what we know and do not know about stroke rehabilitation and older persons.

STATE OF KNOWLEDGE REGARDING STROKE REHABILITATION AND OLDER PERSONS

The state of knowledge regarding rehabilitation of older persons from stroke is very limited. Although data on the age-specific prevalence of stroke are fairly good, there is very little known about some of the fundamental rehabilitative issues that have potential implications for policy, such as the percentage of older stroke victims who undergo rehabilitation, the efficacy of rehabilitative efforts, and the costs of rehabilitating elderly persons who have suffered stroke.

Prevalence of Stroke by Age

Stroke is not a disease of old age, exclusively. As is the case with most chronic disabling diseases and conditions, strokes may occur at any time during adult life. Stroke does increase substantially in prevalence in the older age ranges. Consider, for instance, the data from the National Health Interview Survey, conducted by the National Center for Health Statistics (1981) on a nationwide probability sample of persons living outside institutions. Among persons 65 years of age and older, 6.8% reported that they had suffered at least one stroke; 60% of these persons had been hospitalized for stroke, and 93% of the cases had been medically confirmed.

When the prevalence rate in this age category is combined with the age structure of the American population, the resulting picture is that a substantial percentage of stroke victims in this country are older persons. This was made clear by the 1983 National Hospital Discharge Survey, also conducted by the National Center for Health Statistics (1984). It found that, among stroke discharges from short-stay hospitals during that year, for persons of all ages, 77.4% were persons 65 years of age or older.

Efforts to Rehabilitate Elderly Stroke Victims

What percentage of stroke victims receive some authorized form of stroke rehabilitation? Are there any data suggesting an answer to this question, even among those who have been formally hospitalized for a stroke? The answer is that no firm data bear upon these questions. One leading authority on rehabilitation for older persons, for example, states that, by conservative *estimates*, only about 30% of the elderly who are disabled from any conditions (without specific reference to stroke) and could profit from rehabilitation services actually receive them (Kemp, 1985). But even for such an estimate, specific information with respect to stroke is lacking. Similarly, the same source notes that, while older persons consitute 40 percent of the disabled population, they receive less than 10 percent of services rendered by state government departments of rehabilitation throughout the nation. But this figure is greatly skewed by the fact that state rehabilitation departments were created and operate within a milieu that places primary emphasis on *vocational* rehabilitation, an emphasis that we have noted tends to make older persons seem largely irrelevant as candidates for rehabilitation. In short, there is hardly any information about the percentage of elderly stroke victims who undergo rehabilitation, and only broad, estimated pictures of the general percentage of older persons, disabled from any causes, who undergo rehabilitation.

Efficacy of Stroke Rehabilitation among Older Persons

As noted earlier, enormous improvements in a patient's capacity for independent living can be brought about through seemingly small, undramatic achievements in stroke rehabilitation. But what are the probabilities that such achievements can be made? In what kinds of cases? Over what time periods? From examining the literature and conferring with some of the country's leading experts on these issues, one can only conclude that the answers are unclear. The data on efficacy of stroke rehabilitation among elderly patients are, at best, mixed.

Unless some solid research is conducted to provide valid and clear answers to such questions about rehabilitation efficacy, the upswing in therapeutic optimism that seems to have emerged in the past few years will likely be undercut by issues of costs, benefits, and effectiveness (see Avorn, 1984). Even as the economic incentives generated by DRGs have led hospitals to take a greater interest in rehabilitation than previously, the general economic concerns with health care costs that have focused attention on acute health care cost containment are inevitably beginning to turn to issues regarding expenditures on rehabilitation. The Health Care Financing Administration (HCFA), the agency that administers Medicare for the U.S. Department of Health and Human Services, is increasingly interested in the costs of rehabilitation. As soon as it begins to get some clear answers on costs, those answers will undoubtedly be weighed against whatever evidence exists concerning the efficacy of stroke rehabilitation as well as other types of rehabilitative efforts.

Costs of Stroke Rehabilitation among the Elderly

At present we know very little about the costs of rehabilitating elderly stroke victims. Rough estimates of aggregate costs are that from 2 to 3% of the Medicare budget—currently totaling between $1.3 and $1.9 billion—is expended on stroke rehabilitation annually, a figure that is growing. Other payment sources, of course, would add to the total.

In view of the size of such estimates and other rehabilitation expenditures through Medicare, and considering the probability that such expenditures will continue to grow, HCFA has funded a study designed to reveal more about the extent and costs of rehabilitation, with an eye to developing policy alternatives for prospective payment mechanisms for rehabilitation. This study, jointly conducted by the Rand Corporation and the Medical College of Wisconsin (1985), has yielded some interim data that help fill in the vague picture of stroke rehabilitation among the elderly. These data are from an 8-month examination of those hospitals in the nation that have been exempted from Medicare's DRG mechanism because of state legislation that controls hospital costs. The study involved 8,500 Medicare patients who underwent rehabilitation as inpatients, either in a hospital-based rehabilitation unit or in a freestanding rehabilitation hospital. It did not involve outpatient, nursing-home or other residential-setting rehabilitation.

Of the 8,500 patients who underwent rehabilitation during the 8-month period, 3,500 of them (41%) had been victims of stroke. Among the Medicare patients admitted to freestanding rehabilitation hospitals, 38% were stroke cases. (This compares with 33% of all patients admitted to those hospitals.) Of the Medicare admissions to acute-care-hospital-based rehabilitation units, nearly half (48%) were stroke cases. (Among all admissions to such hospital-based rehabilitation units, 43% were stroke cases.)

Both the expenditures and lengths of stay per case of stroke rehabilitation in this study show tremendous variation. Consequently, the investigators found it more meaningful to interpret their interim findings in terms of medians rather than averages. The median cost of a stroke rehabilitation case in this study group, for a first admission, is $11,700. It should be noted that 93% of the stroke rehabilitation admissions in this group *were* first admissions. The median length of stay was 28 days, but varied from 1 day to 50 days. This variance, of course, could be attributable to any number of factors, including multiple diseases and disabilities; psychological profiles of the patients; and the patients' varying social, environmental, and family situations (see E. M. Brody, 1986). More important, perhaps, such variance in length of stay underlines the formidable obstacles involved in developing even such *estimates* of the per-case costs of stroke rehabilitation efforts.

THE CHALLENGES OF THERAPEUTIC OPTIMISM

The skimpy data currently available regarding the percentage of elderly stroke victims who receive rehabilitation, the potential efficacy of those rehabilitative efforts that do take place, and the costs of undertaking such efforts for the wide variety of patients involved leave the recent upswing in therapeutic optimism highly vulnerable to erosion. This is because, whether one likes it or not, financial considerations will weigh much more heavily than humane considerations in shaping the extent and nature of rehabilitation among the elderly in the future.

Economic forces and political reform initiatives have recently helped to bring the status of rehabilitation of the elderly from that of a drab peripheral undertaking to an increasingly important activity. In the context of our contemporary political economy, in which "reducing the deficit" appears to be the overriding imperative, such forces will *now* subject rehabilitation efforts to greater analytical and critical scrutiny, as well as to likely changes in public policies that affect them. And because of the poor state of knowledge about the extent, nature, efficacy, and costs of stroke rehabilitation efforts among older persons, those of us who would be therapeutic optimists will have to confront some formidable challenges. At least three types of major challenges should be noted in this context, namely, research, rehabilitative "creaming," and fraud and neglect.

Research Challenges

First, as the few bits of data on the efficacy and costs of stroke rehabilitation among older persons are subjected to increasingly critical examination, the onus will be on leaders in the field of rehabilitation and aging to undertake highly sophisticated, complex research efforts. Consider just three related examples.

One involves the arduous tasks of subdividing into relatively discrete categories the many diverse types of potential candidates for rehabilitation, so that issues of efficacy and cost can be traced appropriately and in a highly differentiated fashion. This will require far greater efforts than those to date in distinguishing among stroke victims, for example, not only with respect to type and severity of stroke, but also with respect to the presence of multiple disabilities and diseases, psychological profiles, and economic, social, and familial situations.

Another challenge will be to match such relatively discrete distinctions with various kinds of rehabilitation. That is, empirical analyses of rehabilitative efficacy for each major category of stroke victim will need to be conducted with an eye to differences among various kinds of rehabilitation settings, and to any significant variations in the substantive content of professional efforts made within each type of setting.

Still another challenge, following from these, will be the need to develop a genuine conceptual merging of rehabilitation and long-term care as parts of the same set of activities, and as a unit of analysis for documenting the cost effectiveness of rehabilitation. A true picture of the economic benefits that may be achieved through an investment in successful rehabilitation of a particular type of patient cannot be established without the larger and longer-term picture of the costs saved, if any, in the subsequent long-term supportive care that might have been required in the absence of rehabilitation.

The *net savings* shown from an analysis conceptualized and implemented in such a fashion could be substantial. For example, even if a type of rehabilitative effort were successful only 10% of the time, it might render larger long-term care expenditures unnecessary for those patients. Thus, the amount of money saved on the 10% of stroke victims successfully rehabilitated could more than offset the investment in the 90% of rehabilitative efforts that failed. But we will never find out if such net savings exist until we approach the activities involved in rehabilitation and long-term care as a merged unit of analysis for such research purposes.

Guarding against Rehabilitative "Creaming" from among Elderly Stroke Victims

As Medicare rehabilitation expenditures come under increased budgetary scrutiny—and they surely will—pressures to demonstrate the efficacy, cost benefits, and cost effectiveness of rehabilitation will inevitably tempt some practitioners in the field to select from among their stroke patients the "best bets" for successful rehabilitation. This practice has been known in the field for years, particularly in vocational rehabilitation, as "creaming" the client population. Particularly difficult to resist will be the subtle temptations to "cream out" for rehabilitative efforts those elderly who are comparatively younger. More advanced age—say, the mid-eighties and older—frequently is not among the best predictors of unsuccessful rehabilitation efforts. Nonetheless, it will be a challenge for conscientious health care professionals to avoid using differences in age as prime criteria for sorting among older patients, because American society is currently generating stereotypes for multiple old-age strata within the elderly population.

In an attempt to obliterate long-standing stereotypes of the population conventionally termed "old," Neugarten (1974) published observations that challenged these fixed notions. To illustrate her points, she presented data grouped by conventional and unconventional age markers. Unfortunately, these age markers have been converted by journalists, policy analysts, scholars, and partisans of various causes into new conventions for old-age stereotyping. In the dozen years following publication of her article, persons 65 to 74 years of age have come to be conventionally referred to as the "young old" and perceived to be healthy and capable of earning income. If retired, they are seen as a rich reservoir of resources to be drawn upon for providing unpaid health and social services and for fulfilling a variety of other community roles. Persons aged 75 and older are now commonly termed the "old old" and tend to be saddled with the traditional stereotypes of the the elderly as poor, frail, and inactive.

Now the seeds of a new layer of old-age stereotyping have been planted. In the fall of 1984 the National Institute on Aging announced a new research initiative on "the oldest old," persons 85 years of age and older, which it described as "the fastest growing segment of the population" (U.S. DHHS, 1984). One can envision how this new label, "the oldest old," could easily join the "young old" and the "old old" in the conventional armamentarium of age stereotyping (Binstock, 1985) and lead to a situation in which persons aged 85 years and older are viewed as morbid, ridden by multiple diseases and disabilities, and socially dependent.

Rehabilitation professionals will need to be especially watchful in their clinical decision making and in their educational roles, to guard against and counter such stereotypes. The truth is that, even among persons 85 years of age and older, there is substantial diversity with respect to supportive physical and mental conditions (Suzman & Riley, 1985).

Vigilance against Rehabilitative Fraud and Neglect

It is possible that the federal government will soon "bundle" or combine Medicare payments for stroke rehabilitation with the DRG mechanism through which it provides prospective payments for acute care of stroke. In other words, in accordance with a patient's primary diagnosis, HCFA would guarantee to pay a fixed sum for both the acute care and rehabilitation of a stroke victim. If hospitals are guaranteed "up front" rehabilitation payments on the basis of each patient's diagnosis, how responsible will they and their partners be in the swiftly "verticalizing" health industry when it comes to carrying out genuine rehabilitation efforts on all Medicare stroke patients? As indicated earlier, we do not even know what proportion of stroke victims are referred for rehabilitation at the present time. We can *guess* with some confidence that it is far less than 100%. If prospective payment is made by Medicare for all hospitalized elderly stroke victims, will the percentage of such patients who undergo subsequent rehabilitation efforts increase from what it is now?

It is probable, unfortunately, that these questions are merely rhetorical. The answers will be obvious unless the rehabilitation professions and their allies in the health and human services fields are able to exercise extraordinarily effective vigilance.

CONCLUSION

This discussion has implied throughout that rehabilitation should be undertaken whenever there is the slightest hope of some gain through the effort. How can we take such a position when the data on the efficacy of stroke rehabilitation are mixed? We do so largely because it seems that the next few years will provide a rare and probably short-term opportunity to expand and test what we are capable of through rehabilitative efforts. Resources for rehabilitation have been traditionally very scarce. Today, at least temporarily, economic and political forces have generated a new set of incentives for health care organizations to undertake rehabilitation on a greater scale, using Medicare resources. While this opportunity exists, and it may exist for only a limited period of time, let us take advantage of it to see what we can achieve across the board. We will never know what we can accomplish through rehabilitation of older persons from stroke until we try, in a thorough and comprehensive fashion, and until we document our efforts through highly sophisticated research.

REFERENCES

Avorn, J. (1984). Benefit and cost analysis in geriatric care. *New England Journal of Medicine, 310*(20), 1294–1301.

Baumann, N. J., Anderson, J. C., & Morrison, M. H. (1986). Employment of the older disabled person: Current environment, outlook, and research needs. In S. J. Brody & G. Ruff (Eds.), *Aging and rehabilitation: Advances in the state of the art* (pp. 329–342). New York: Springer.

Binstock, R. H. (1985). The oldest old: A fresh perspective or compassionate ageism revisited? *Milbank Memorial Fund Quarterly/Health and Society, 63*(2), 420–451.

Binstock, R. H. (1986). Aging and rehabilitation: The birth of a social movement? In S. J. Brody & G. Ruff (Eds.), *Aging and rehabilitation: Advances in the state of the art* (pp. 349–356). New York: Springer.

Brody, E. M. (1986). Informal supports systems in the rehabilitation of the disabled elderly. In S. J. Brody & G. Ruff (Eds.), *Aging and rehabilitation: Advances in the state of the art* (pp. 87–103). New York: Springer.

Brody, S. J. (1984–1985). Merging rehabilitation and aging policies and programs: Past, present, and future. *Rehabilitation World, 8*(4), 6–8, 42–44.

Brody, S. J. (1986). Impact of the formal support system on rehabilitation of the elderly. In S. J. Brody & G. Ruff (Eds.), *Aging and rehabilitation: Advances in the state of the art* (pp. 62–86). New York: Springer.

Brody, S. J. & Magel, J. S. (in press). LTC: The long and short of it. In C. Eisdorfer (Ed.), *Reshaping health care for the elderly: Recommendations for national policy*. Baltimore, MD: Johns Hopkins University Press.

Brody, S. J., & Persily, N. A. (Eds.). (1984). *Hospitals and the aged: The new old market*. Rockville, MD: Aspen Systems Corporation.

Brody, S. J. & Ruff, G. (Eds.). (1986). *Aging and rehabilitation: Advances in the state of the art*. New York: Springer.

Henriksen, J. D. (1978). Problems in rehabilitation after age sixty-five. *Journal of the American Geriatrics Society, 26*, 510–512.

Kemp, B. (1985). Rehabilitation and the older adult. In J. E. Birren & K. W. Schaie (Eds.), *Handbook of the psychology of aging* (2nd ed., pp. 647–663). New York: Van Nostrand Reinhold.

National Academy of Sciences, Institute of Medicine and National Research Council, Committee on an Aging Society. (1986). *America's aging: Productive roles in an older society*. Washington, DC: National Academy Press.

National Center for Health Statistics. (1981, May 13). *Stroke survivors among the non-institutionalized population 20 years of age and over, United States, 1977. Advance data from vital and health statistics.* (DHHS Pub. No. PHS 81-1250.) Hyattsville, MD: U.S. Public Health Service.

National Center for Health Statistics. (1984, September 28). *Summary: National hospital discharge survey. Advance data from vital and health statistics.* (DHHS Pub. No. PHS 84-1250.) Hyattsville, MD: U.S. Public Health Service.

Neugarten, B. L. (1974). Age groups in American Society and the rise of the young old. *Annals of the American Academy of Political and Social Science, 415*, 187–198.

Rand Corporation and the Medical College of Wisconsin. (1985). Interim data from study of prospective payment for rehabilitation hospitals. (WD-2779-1, Contract No. 99-C98-48919-02.) Telephone communication from principal investigator, R. Kane, Oct. 23, 1985.

Starr, P. (1983). *The social transformation of American medicine.* New York: Basic Books.

Suzman, R., & Riley, M. W. (Eds.). (1985). The oldest old. *Milbank Memorial Fund Quarterly/Health and Society* (special issue), *63*(2).

Thurow, L. C. (1985). Medicine versus economics. *New England Journal of Medicine, 313,* 611–614.

U.S. Department of Health and Human Services (1984, November 9). Announcement: The oldest old. *National Institutes of Health guide for grant and contracts, 13*(12), 29–33.

U.S. Department of Health and Human Services, Administration on Aging, Office of Human Development Services. (1985). *Aging* (special issue on rehabilitation), *350.*

Williams, T. F. (Ed.). (1984). *Rehabilitation in the aging.* New York: Raven Press.

Index

Index